Of Mycelium and Men

Other books by William C. Tracy

The Dissolutionverse:

Novellas and Novelettes:
The Five Hive Plateau
Tuning the Symphony
Merchants and Maji
The Society of Two Houses
Journey to the Top of the Nether

The Dissolution Cycle:
The Seeds of Dissolution (Book I)
Facets of the Nether (Book II)
Fall of the Imperium (Book III)

Other Books:

Epic Fantasy:
Fruits of the Gods

Anthologies:
Distant Gardens
Farther Reefs
The World of Juno

Of Mycelium and Men

BOOK I OF THE BIOMASS CONFLUX

William C. Tracy

Space Wizard Science Fantasy
Raleigh, NC
www.spacewizardsciencefantasy.com

Cover art by MoorBooks
Editing by Heather Tracy
Book Layout © 2015 BookDesignTemplates.com

Of Mycelium and Men/William C. Tracy.— 1st ed.
ISBN 978-1-7350768-7-4

Author's website: www.williamctracy.com

Dedicated to a long-ago conversation
on a beach about mushrooms...

CONTENTS

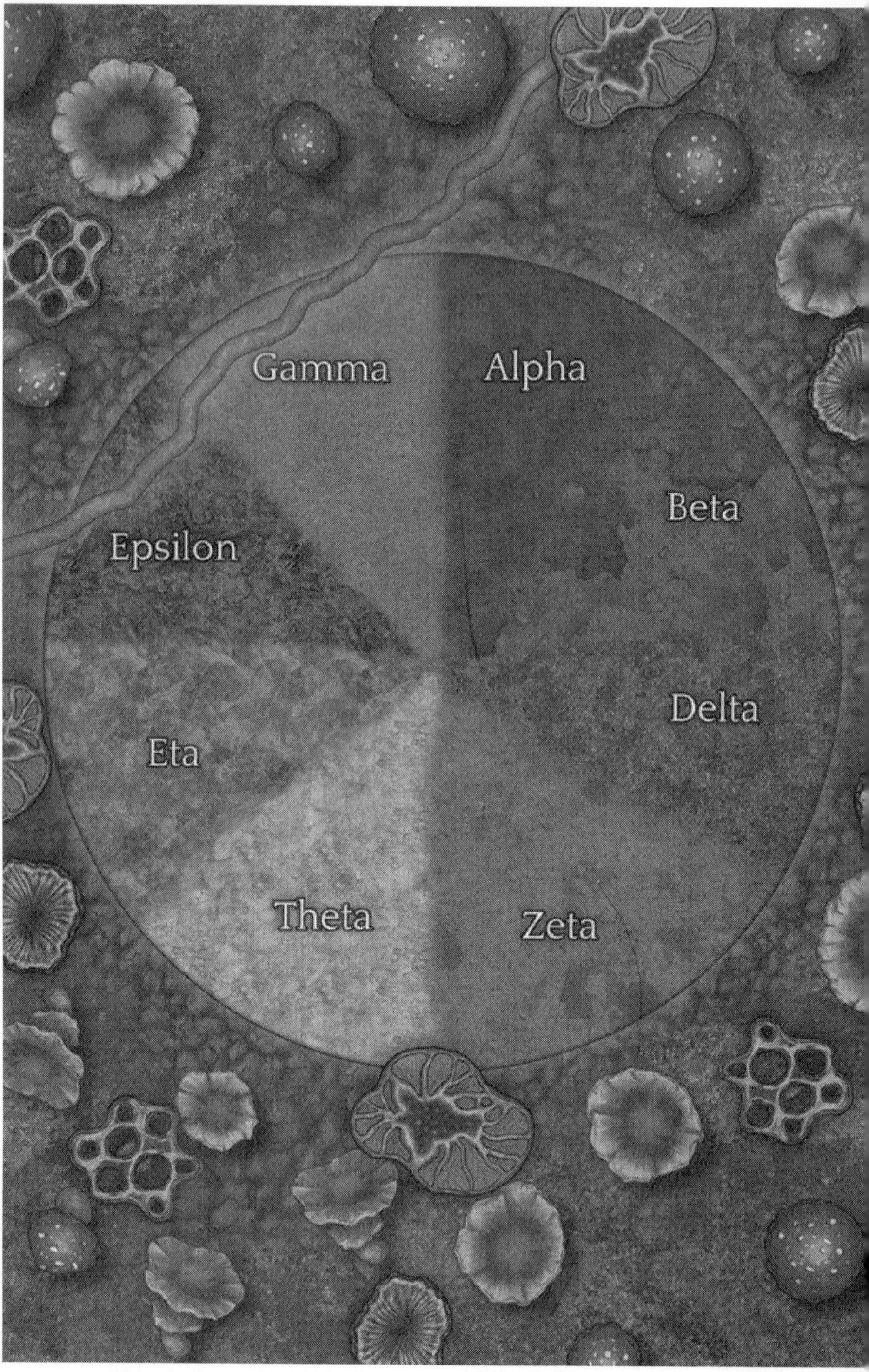

Gamma
Alpha
Beta
Epsilon
Delta
Eta
Theta
Zeta

Dramatis Personae

The Administrators:

Admin Jane Brighton of the UGS St. Christopher (she/her)

Admin Alessandro Giordano of the UGS Abeona (he/him)

Admin Dmitri Novikov of the UGS Hasamelis (he/him)

Admin Xi Wenqing of the UGS K'uei-Hsing (he/him)

Admin Ahman Ragab of the UGS Khonsu (they/them)

Admin Rajani Kumarisurajinder of the UGS Ganesha (she/her)

Admin Maria Gutiérrez Delgado of the UGS Xaman Ek (she/her)

Admin Polunu Kim of the UGS Hina (she/her)

Secretary Christiaan (they/them)

The Vagals:

General Smith (he/him)

Watch Sergeant Noce (they/them)

Corporal Hendricks (she/her)

Private Anderson (he/him)

The Generationals:

Processor Alvin (he/him)

Agetha Xenakis (she/her)

Daved Xenakis (he/him)

Frank Silver (he/him)

Jiow Pappadapilos (she/her)

Zhu Pappadapilos (he/him)

Elizabeth Harley (she/her)

Zixin Ye (he/him)

Femi Sarraf (she/her)

Ashkara Patel (she/her)

Kofus Adranafali (he/him)

Janx (they/them)

Medibe (he/him)

Sona V. Gore (he/him)

The Grounders:

Phillipe (he/him)

Choi (they/them)

Hari (he/him)

Time:

1 Hour = 3.6 kiloseconds
1 Ship Cycle = 20 hours = 72 kiloseconds
1 megasecond = 1,000 kiloseconds = 1,000,000 seconds
1 week = 0.6 megaseconds
1 month = 2.63 megaseconds
1 year = 31.54 megaseconds
20 years = 630 megaseconds
420 years = 13,245 megaseconds

PART ONE

The Eleventh System

5.77 megaseconds before landing

The UGS fleet shone in the reflected light of a new star system, the latest of many that had given heat and power to the collection of ships. There were eight spacecraft, each over a kilometer long and independently powered, but obviously from the same origin, heading to the same destination.

As the ships drew closer to this system's inner planets, waves of sublimating material flowed away from the fleet, forced away as the metal warmed in the star's heat from the cold average of interstellar space. The ships slowed, light sails unfurling to take advantage of the new light source, as they had in the ten previous systems.

It would take over five and a half megaseconds—what the passengers' ancestors would have termed just over two months—for the ships to brake using the star's light. For now, activity grew around the ships like an ant nest coming to life, bodies in suits jetting between hulls, cleaning, repairing, and setting up systems using solar power.

The fleet had come from the dead space between star systems, where power was precious, and the crews of the ships lived spartan lives. The inside of a star system was a resource rich atmosphere, and extravagant uses of system resources and food biomes were allowed.

Agetha Xenakis saw none of this from the cramped apartment she shared with her husband Daved on the United Generational Ship (UGS) Abeona.

"I've got a load of data coming in today from probes into the new system, Daved," she said. She floated near the eating hub in the tiny kitchen, spinning slowly while she put socks on. "The bacon will be fine if the edges are not as crisp as they could be. It's not like it's actually from an animal."

"I couldn't send you in with un-crisped vat-grown textured protein, could I?" Daved said, whisking the capped pan of steaming goodness from the induction element to the serving table with a *clink* as the magnets attached. Her spouse was a short man with much more melanin than her pale coloring, his compact frame easily fitting through openings Agetha had to watch her head on. A good size for their kitchen.

The overhead vent sucked in the steam, but not before Agetha caught a whiff of Daved's cooking. He was the best out of their group of friends. If his family line hadn't been tasked with animal husbandry in the original allotment, he would have made a fine chef for the Abeona.

Agetha ate quickly, trying to savor the bacon and biscuits before she floated to the analysis complex near the other end of the ship. There was quince jelly with the biscuits and honey from the ship's bees.

"Do you think this will be the one?" Daved asked as she finished up. She knew where his mind was going already.

"There's no way to say until I get to the data," Agetha said, handing her closed dish back. Daved went into work later than she did and hopefully would clean everything up. Strange man, but she loved him dearly.

"I'm sure it will be promising," he said. Daved was the most optimistic person she knew. "We've got to get it right, one of these times, don't we?" He cleaned the table with his usual chaos as she found the rest of her clothes. It was colder in the analysis complex— better insulated and a better connection to the data source. The five to six percent faster data transfer speed made all the difference with the amount of information she processed.

She was almost ready to leave when he not-so-casually dropped his next sentence. She'd been waiting for it since she got up.

"But whatever the result, they'll have to lift the ban on reproduction for all the Generationals. We can have a family, whether in space or in a gravity well. I can't wait until they reopen the decanting tubes."

Daved had yearned for children since they'd gotten married, but that was almost exactly when the decanting tube ban came through, since they were approaching a potential landing site. Natural pregnancy hadn't been used since the ships left old Earth—too high of a mortality rate. For the same reason, there were to be no small children during the chaotic transition from space to ground. It fortunately gave Agetha a long time to reflect on what she thought of children. Daved would be an excellent father, and she knew he would take as much of raising a child on himself as he could. She still wasn't sure how much part, if any, she wanted to play in that.

"I'll be sure to let you know the results as soon as I have them," was all she said as she left their apartment.

* * *

5.61 megaseconds before landing

Processor Alvin floated slowly along the outside track of the generational ship UGS St. Christopher, taking in the view of the new system. They were far enough out that their target star was still indistinct from others filling this section of space. He knew where the five planets in the system were located, even if he couldn't point them out by hand. One of the analysts on the UGS Abeona had already processed the telemetry data, however. He blinked in the HUD information overlay on the vast swath of stars out the window, zooming in. The large outline of planetary body 11e was only a few million klicks away, and the analyst had already given a cutesy name to it: "Lilly."

Alvin looked up the analyst responsible. Agetha Xenakis. She'd been responsible for other violations of standard naming principles in the past, even going so far as to name the star of Target Ten "Steve," though she must have been little more than a child then. He put in a note to report her violation, and swiped the name back to its relevant designation.

The two rocky bodies of 11b and 11c were currently on the other side of their star, Target Eleven, and so only faint dots in his vision. He tsked at the names given to these, "Libi" and "Leek," and changed them back to standard as well. 11a—or "Lia" at least until he put in a notice to the central data server to scrub the names—was a captive super planet tidally locked to Target Eleven, with a rotation of only a few hundred hours. Hardly useful even for mineral extraction, that close to the star.

Alvin's eyes paused over the last, medium planet in the middle of the field of stars. 11d had a bright green tag next to its name to show it was at least theoretically possible for humans to inhabit it, from their current scans. Their destination.

"Lida."

Saying Xenakis' name out loud, it had a nice ring to it. Maybe he could leave this one designation, even though it was in violation of protocol.

Then Alvin shivered. It would be chaos to actually land the fleet, after all this time. They might have originally been designed for atmospheric entry, but that had been long ago, and for a different planet. What would it be like to be stuck in a gravity well, unable to reach objects mere meters above his head? He had never experienced it, but he could feel the ground sickness churning in his gut and pressed a hand over his stomach. No. Things would stay the same. They would check the planet, and like the others, it would be uninhabitable. That was the only way forward. No cute or endearing names. He put in the order to change "Lida" back to its standard designation of 11d.

Processor Alvin pushed against a handhold, speeding his float, averting his eyes from the starscape. He caught another rung and banked into a side junction just in time to avoid touching the Vagal soldier floating down the corridor toward him. He didn't like the supersoldiers, but fortunately, they kept to themselves, overseeing the Generationals, and providing a buffer between Alvin's contemporaries and the almost-mythical Administrators.

The Vagal—a stocky woman with a shaved head save for a long lock of hair braided and swirled around the back of her head—gave him a stern nod, which he acknowledged with a vague wave of one hand. She had been awake for almost three megaseconds, since they'd been in deep space, but had only spoken a few words to him. What was her name? Hender? Henri? Something. He only saw each Vagal for a limited time before they went back into sus-ani. It was like they didn't *want* him to get to know them, despite his attempts. After she passed, he floated to the forward control room where the probe controls were kept. Time to find out more about Lida.

Alvin shook his head. No. 11d. *Not* Lida. It would be a lifeless husk just like the planets of Target Ten. He could keep his routine and sanity, in the comfort of space, gently dipping into rich star systems at the different stages of his life. This was the last of the nearby targets the systems analysts had identified over the past several generations. They'd run out of good opportunities in this sector of the galaxy. Once they traveled through this system, it would be nearly twenty-five hundred megaseconds until the next with a possibility of habitation. He'd be an old, old man then, if he was still alive.

Would others want to stay in the resource-rich star system indefinitely, regardless of 11d's status? The last time he had been in a star system he had been a child, though his memories of that time were happy, his mother and fathers gifting him with new toys printed from material gathered in that star system. Other Generationals had petitioned to stay in the past, always turned down by the Vagals. Only once, six generations ago, had the ones who lived their whole lives in the fleet raised their voices loud enough to get through to the Administrators, begging to stay inside a star system. It was back when Target Seven seemed like a good idea. But the Administrator the Vagals had been forced to waken—Giordano of the Abeona, so the story went—simply recounted the directive that the ship had to keep moving, to find a permanent *planetside* home, not one in space. Giordano had reduced all those who petitioned him to menial labor jobs. Luckily for Alvin, the punishment only lasted for one generation, or he would have been vacuuming mold out of vegetable tanks instead of keeping the Vagals informed of vital data as a Processor should.

Alvin floated into the main sensor processing station for the St. Christopher, where he lived most of his life. If 11d turned out to be as uninhabitable as their other targets, then the fleet's passage through the system would take twenty megaseconds or so after breaking, enough to enjoy the rich supply of minerals. Unless, of course, the probe came back with the news he feared.

He mentally cataloged each display and locker, looking for anything out of place. Maria had left the screen projection brightness up as usual, and he made the hand gesture to flip through the menu and turn it back down. He must have missed her by a few minutes due to his stargazing. The workstation was one of the only non-mobile platforms because of the shielded wire connection running to the main data repository. The only one larger was in the pure science capsule farther down the length of St. Christopher.

Alvin snapped the tethers on the workstation to the mating clips on his jumpsuit so he wouldn't float away, then methodically went through the checklist of sensor traces. Nothing out of the ordinary, and he cleared the checklist in a few minutes. He read through the blinking red message at the top of his log again, shaking his head. He hoped Watch Sergeant Noce was incorrect, and Lida wasn't a place they could land. His stomach turned sickeningly at the thought. Alvin drew in a deep breath to calm himself and flipped through the sensor processor menus. This probe wouldn't launch itself.

He began the process to wake up the drone launch bays. They hadn't been used since taking samples of Target Ten, a little over three hundred megaseconds ago.

* * *

5.09 megaseconds before landing

The encroaching lifeform was observed, high in the sky. The senses—some auditory, some ocular, a few olfactory—could detect it was made of mineral, rather than tissue. This was very unusual to the observing bodies. Nearly all other threats to this territory had been subsumed, and they had all been tissue-based. A few small mobile forms were still free, but limited freedom of future targets was advisable to produce unanticipated modification. Such evolution had occasionally proven more efficient than direct research.

Given the parallax, the lifeform moved extremely fast. Would it fall? No other forms of movement known could move so rapidly, or so high in the atmosphere. Highly specialized ocular senses were directed toward it, using multiple viewpoints to collect a multifaceted picture. There were artificial symbols on the side of the lifeform, though difficult for the collected senses to see. The symbols were memorized by several higher-functioning bodies for further contemplation.

Later.

The lifeform made exactly seven orbits of the local territory, and long-range senses identified the lifeform in other habitats. The symbols were studied for any significance.

U.G.S. STCHRIS

There was repetition, signifying one symbol might be more important than others. A smaller repeated symbol only occurred in the first half. There was speculation perhaps this symbol had a specific indicative purpose as it was smaller than the other symbols, but opinions were divided.

Much thought and many rotations were devoted in study of the memories of the lifeform and of the symbols on it. A subsumed threat, over twelve hundred planetary rotations previous, had used diagrams and symbols in a similar manner to convey information, some of which were still useful. Higher-functioning intelligences undertook a comparison.

The lifeform was not seen again. Other problems took precedence, and the lifeform was not forgotten, but moved to a lesser priority, with certain ocular organs set to observe for lifeforms of matching descriptions. In other regions, semi-autonomous systems capable of extrapolation and expansion studied memories of the flight of the lifeform. Experiments were made, most ending in failure. Several, surprisingly, were successful for a short time, but rapidly became explosive failures afterward, dropping back to the surface.

Eventually, the question of how the lifeform could travel in this manner was relegated to a lower priority level, as a small region near the equator had been incompletely subsumed and too many resources were being used to control the actions of entities there. It was probable some higher-functioning systems in the rebellious area had worked with the memory of the flight. Thereafter, that avenue of extrapolation was curtailed in all but the most agreeable systems.

* * *

4.49 megaseconds before landing

"Did you get anything back from Little Chris?"

Processor Alvin nearly let go of his datapad at the voice. He never liked the way the watch sergeants floated almost silently. At least rattle something to let others know you're coming.

"Ah...we might have, muux," Alvin answered, using the gender-neutral term of respect for the Vagal. He eyed Watch Sergeant Noce while trying not to show he was watching. The big Vagal's coordination was better than Alvin's, and they had only been awoken by the ship about a megasecond ago, during first deceleration toward Target Eleven. They could have been watch sergeant for Alvin's great-great-grandfather, or they could have been in suspended animation for the entire trip. They might have even walked on Earth.

"Well?"

"Here, muux." Alvin swiped the report from the probe over to the watch sergeant's pad. He wasn't used to being interrogated every thirty kiloseconds for a report—twice each waking cycle. He had been a Processor his whole life, as had his father, grandmother, and so on, except for his unfortunate three-times great-grandparent, who had been forced into janitorial duty by Admin Giordano. So when some newly woken bigwig constantly demanded reports from him, Alvin's nerves started to fray. They had been fraying for the last megasecond, and he wasn't sure how much more he could take.

The watch sergeant made a low rumble of interest in their throat. "This looks promising. Good atmospheric readings with no buildup of toxic chemicals. Breathable ratio mix checks out. Lots of plant life and mobile objects that could be big animals." They turned to Alvin, adjusting their position by hooking a foot under a ladder rung. "Any sign of industrialization? Sentience?"

Alvin hadn't gotten that far through the data stream yet. "I...I'm not sure, muux. Unlikely, with the amount of flora down there. It looks like rampant untended growth. There must be a lot of nutrients to sustain it."

Noce nodded once, sharply, offsetting the movement by adjusting their foot placement so they wouldn't start to spin. "This could be what we've been waiting for. I'm going to bring this to the Milli-Commander, with a recommendation to bring the ship Administrator out of suspended animation." They raised an eyebrow at Alvin's intake of breath.

The ship administrators. One per ship, eight in total. The true commanders of the fleet. The last time more than one had been woken, they had been near their original target. Alvin's janitorial predecessor had passed on the original legend from their ancestors. The rumor was, Admin had taken one look at the huge impact crater, still boiling the atmosphere, and ordered the ship to Beta Target, or as they now called it, Target Two. Alvin could have been an eleventh-generation native if they had made the decision to land. Fortunately, they hadn't. Alvin shuddered.

Now it was coming true, on his watch. The grasping fingers of the gravity well reached for him.

* * *

4.40 megaseconds before landing

Jane Brighton blinked, trying to get the mist out of her vision. Eyes didn't do well coming out of suspended animation, at least for the two times she'd been awoken. She tried to bring the two images of her handler back into one. As her sight cleared, she saw a chestnut-skinned, middle-aged woman of a blend of Asian and African descent. There seemed to be some intermixing between the original ship's fleets. This person looked familiar, though.

"Are you related to Xianming?"

The woman started, her eyes growing wide. "He was my tenth great-grandfather, Administrator." She tapped something and Jane's leg jumped. "Reflexes look good."

Jane rubbed at her left eye. That one was still fuzzy. She tried to do calculations in her head. "That's a lot of generations." This wasn't a good sign, unless the Generationals had been breeding like rabbits. Beta Target had only been twenty-five years travel time from Alpha Target, and Gamma Target was only another twelve years after that.

She looked around for Christiaan. Her secretary had been like a shadow at her side for years, and not having them around was immediately jarring. She supposed they were still in sus-ani.

"Yes, ma'am," the woman said. "Watch Sergeant Noce requested you be revived."

"Better not be another goddamned hole in this planet," Jane grumbled.

A few hours later, she floated into the room where Noce was waiting. She hated floating. Zero-G made her sick. Give her ground beneath her feet. Hopefully that would be the case, soon.

Jane rebounded off the entry hatch, cursing, as she entered the room. Noce was upside-down, and Jane resisted twisting her head to bring them right-side up. The infuriating person was probably doing it on purpose. The supersoldier Vagals were uniformly annoying.

"Watch sergeant," Jane greeted them. "How long have you been up this time?"

"A little over two weeks, Administrator," Noce said. "I was awoken at the beginning of decel. We just got the latest batch of data back from the planet. Used high-quality recording drones this time for the best assessment of the planet's atmosphere and biomass."

"There are low-quality probes?" Jane asked, then waved a hand, setting her rotating through the air. "Never mind." She flailed for a handhold of some sort, catching one near the entrance. "Why did you wake me?"

"Here's the report, ma'am," the watch sergeant said, gently tossing her a datapad. Jane caught it clumsily. "Atmosphere and surface look conducive to human life. No harmful trace elements. Radiation levels are higher than Earth, but acceptable. Very large native flora growths, and some decent-sized fauna-like things, though we didn't get any good pictures of them. We assume carbon-based, from the available elements, so they might even be compatible with our biology. Nothing tagged as self-aware or sentient, at least from observed movement patterns and lack of artifacts."

Jane tried to focus on the report, blinking eyes still adjusting to room temperature. "Good, good. Is it poisonous?"

"We don't believe so, but it's hard to tell for sure, ma'am." Noce thankfully corrected their stance to be right way up. "We couldn't take any samples, but from atmospheric readings, there's a good chance there is something we can eat down there, even if it doesn't taste very good. Should give us enough leeway to get our own crops started."

"This isn't Gamma target. What happened?"

Watch Sergeant Noce actually looked worried for a moment. That was bad. "You remember Beta target was also uninhabitable?"

"Like it was yesterday," Jane said. It had been, for her. Alpha Target had been hit by a meteor approximately four years before they arrived, and Beta Target was a cold hunk of dust, bereft of even an atmosphere, much less any native life. She waited.

"Yes, likely an error in the original data," Noce continued. "However, we found Gamma and Delta Targets were also not suitable, for a variety of reasons."

Jane cocked her head. "Then which target is this?"

"None of them, ma'am. We, ah, ran out of targets. If you map Alpha to Target One, Beta to Two, and Gamma to—"

"I can count, Noce, what number are we on? Five? Six?"

Noce cleared their throat. "This is an unsurveyed planet the analysts have labeled as Target Eleven."

"Ele—?" Jane felt a muscle jump in her jaw. She took in a deep breath. "We were supposed to reach Alpha in eighty-five years—three generations. Beta was another generation after that. How long has it been?"

"Over four hundred years, Admin. This is the first target to match our required parameters to within ninety-five percent."

Four hundred years of living in zero-G? If she'd been standing rather than floating, she would have taken a seat. Jane recalled the face of the handler who had woken her. Similar in features to a person she remembered, but taller overall, like she'd been stretched, and her eyes had been surprisingly large.

"How are the stores?" she asked. "Could we keep going?"

The watch sergeant took in a deep breath. "The ships are generational, ma'am. They're meant to be self-sufficient for an unlimited time. We could take a tour of the entire galaxy if we wanted, but we're nearing the end of an arm and to travel to another will take most of a century. The people maintaining the ships would be far different than those we left on Earth."

There had already been changes to the Generationals' genetic stock, and the drift would only get more extreme. How long until they weren't human? Could the Generationals survive on a planet's surface even now?

Jane looked out the room's window, evidently near the front of the ship. A vast starscape greeted her. It looked the same as the one from Earth's solar system, not that she knew much about astronomy. She was here to make decisions. That was why they woke her up. And she really didn't want to go into suspended animation again.

"We make landfall," Administrator Brighton said.

"Very good ma'am. I'll contact the other ships."

PART TWO

Awakening

5.20 megaseconds before landing

Agetha Xenakis waded through the streams of incoming data, vastly multiplied since they'd entered Lev's—Target Eleven's—system. There were Lagrange points, spiral approach paths, asteroid composition for those bodies nearest to their approach paths, avoidance patterns for debris, and material reports. Oh yes, and the lavatory on deck twenty-three was backing up again. For some reason the UGS Abeona particularly had been prone to toilet problems for the entire journey.

She dispatched a crew of repair drones to take care of the plumbing, just as a pile of new data crowded the displays on her station.

"What is all this?" Agetha called to Gearge in the station next to her. Her fellow analyst reclined in the zero-G, eyes twitching behind his HUD VR glasses.

"Just got sent down here from...wait. From Admin!" Gearge executed a summersault with the help of a grab handle, and floated closer, flicking information from his glasses to hers. "Look, datamarked from Giordano himself."

"Which means he's been thawed out." Agetha pulled up the report she'd compiled on Lida's composition. "Wow. They must have really liked the data I sent them from Little Chris, to wake up all of Admin."

"That's not all—check your incoming stack."

Agetha paged through data coming in to be sorted and analyzed. The computer could handle much of it, but there was no replacement for that spark of intellect needed to create new insights between seemingly unrelated information. That was what she and the rest of the analysis pool was here for.

There were biology reports, mostly successful sus-ani revives, though she noted two heart failures, one brain hemorrhage, and one kidney replacement on wakeup that looked like it would be rejected.

This was more than a shift change, or even the personnel to work with one of the Admins.

"They're waking up *everyone*," she said. "Admins and their adjuncts, all the watch sergeants, milli-commanders and all the Vagal popsicles. Gearge, I think Admin's planning to *land* on Lida."

* * *

Agetha stayed late that cycle, sorting through revivification reports and survey drones leaving to gather more information on Lida's atmosphere, weather patterns, and chemical makeup. There were more people awake now than ever before, compounding her normal workload. They had already been running out of living space, though population controls had kept the Generational numbers consistent since Target Nine. Adding ten percent more warm bodies in a few ship cycles was pushing the water, recycling, and air systems to their limits, not to mention crowding living quarters.

On top of her normal workload was the directive to dig up old disembarking procedures. She tried to match the out-of-date instructions with current protocol, got frustrated, and finally checked the timestamp. Over ten *thousand* megaseconds old. She did a quick calculation to Earth years, knowing the Admins would be stuck in the archaic system. The procedures were over three hundred thirty Earth years old. They must have been written right after the ships encountered Target One. Anything that far out of date would have to be completely rewritten. The Generationals' culture hadn't even really evolved by that point. Most systems on the ships had been reworked, re-engineered, and some even removed completely since then.

Daved pinged her again, asking when she would be back to the cabin for the third meal. Agetha checked ship time. Another kilosecond had passed while she had been distracted. She moved her display to cover one eye, marked her checked-out data silo, and began the float back along the Abeona to the cabin she shared with her spouse. She continued working as she floated.

Aside from the slightly better transfer speed, there was no reason the data analysts had to be in any particular place on the ship. Still, the systems analysts tended to congregate in the analysis complex, and it got her out of her cabin.

With Daved already sounding annoyed, she skipped her usual diversion through hydroponics, using the more efficient outside track. There was much less to look at on the track, save for the occasional tree or garden space artfully protruding from a pot set on one of the walls. Besides that, was only the vast stretch of space through the windows. They weren't actually windows, but it was an accurate representation of the starfield outside projected on the inside of the hull. No sense reducing the structural strength of the generational ship just for a transparent structure. That had been one of the first retrofits the Generationals had made. It helped with temperature regulation, risk management, and made repairs much easier.

The smell of goat cheese and pine nuts greeted her when the door to her cabin slid open. Agetha's mouth watered.

"What are you cooking, and how many food credits did you have to turn in for it?" she asked her spouse. They hadn't had real cheese in a couple megaseconds, and—was that lamb? The livestock on the ship was carefully tended for the best stock, and only rarely eaten. Most meat was vat-grown.

"Finally, you're home. Gotta use them up!" Daved answered, practically flipping out of the kitchenette with an enclosed self-heating pan of steaming heaven. The steam spout let out a whiff of cooking meat, cheese, and vegetables. "We'll be landing on 11d. The announcement just came through."

"Lida," Agetha corrected automatically. She'd been fighting the stodgy processors all day about names. She was *not* going to live on a planet that sounded like a locker designation. "And I know about the landing, but we still have to land, love. Did you use up *all* the credits today?"

Daved came in for a firm kiss, holding the pan away so the bubbles of dispersing steam didn't get in their faces. The smell was divine. "Of course you know. And no, I didn't use them all up. Just the ones I'd been banking for a special occasion. We'll be back to kale chips and vat chicken for any special meals after this."

Agetha wrinkled her nose and swiped the last of the analyses out of her vision with a save marker where she stopped for the next shift to take over. Terrey was familiar enough with her work style to pick up the breadcrumbs she'd left them. She headed for the kitchenette and began gathering the last spoons and spice jars left to float while Daved had been busy. She fastened some back in place and put the utensils in the sterilizer. Daved was an excellent cook, but tended to leave a mess until he decided it was time to clean.

While she cleaned, he doled the lamb and cheese dish into individual servers, covered, so the messy sauce wouldn't get everywhere. They floated outside the kitchenette, both savoring the smell of the dish.

"Won't have to do this on the surface of a planet," Daved said after the first bite.

Agetha took her own and moaned at the taste. "But won't it be hard to store everything where you can reach it? You'll be restricted by the gravity well, and with your stumpy legs, you won't be able to reach anything."

"I'll take it, if it means I can use a gravity stove to cook. I'll just get you with your long legs to reach things for me. Imagine, leaving pots on one surface to heat, like the artificial gravity in a long course change. It will free up my hands to experiment." He wiggled the fingers on one hand, then changed the subject, jumping around like he always did.

"Did you see the Vagals on your way home? There was a whole squad of them getting their legs outside the agricultural deck." Daved's family line had worked with almost all the livestock that had lived on the Abeona. He also oversaw some of the sus-ani animals and frozen embryos. Those wouldn't be unthawed until they had landed.

"No, I took the short way around the outer deck since you sounded grumpy in your texts," Agetha said, carefully pulling another hunk of cheese from her dish with eating sticks.

"Just making sure you were home before I burned anything," Daved answered. As if he had ever burned any dish in his life—at least over the last hundred fifty or so megaseconds they'd been together—since what would have been considered early teens on old Earth. Generationals started everything earlier than their Earth counterparts: learning, apprentice work, marriages, children. With the ship's learning tutorials, formal education had been reduced to two years, and the rest was filled in by individual family lines—each an expert in their particular area.

If the reproduction ban hadn't come through, they might have decanted their first by now and if Daved had his way, put in a request for a second, and both of them still under six hundred megaseconds. She didn't want to think about raising children yet. Much easier to think about the newly defrosted supersoldiers.

"Good thing I didn't run into the overconfident bastards," Agetha said. "It's hard enough with the revolving watch sergeants swaggering around like they own the place. I can't imagine what a whole herd of Vagals will do."

"They feel like they have something over us, just because they saw Earth," Daved agreed.

"A lot of good that will do them on Lida. We have all sorts of scans of the planet, but know nothing about being down on the surface. The Vagals are supposed to react to situations better than we do, but will that help anything if there are problems getting food to grow or livestock to live?"

"They do get their space legs pretty quick," Daved said. "Something to do with those implants they have. But it's not like they've had anything to react to on the ships. So the legends go, we were promised the most advanced military colonizing force Earth had ever seen. Why they thought we needed military force is beyond me."

"Fighting all the aliens, I assume," Agetha said, and they both laughed.

The silence between them drew out as they finished their meal— really a spectacular effort on Daved's part.

"You know," he said as they finished up, "being on the surface will open up a lot of other areas for us a well. I'm really excited about it, aren't you?"

"I...don't know if I've really processed it," Agetha said slowly.

"How can you not have processed it? You've known longer than I have." Daved was always quicker to come to decisions than she was.

"I've been doing systems analysis since Target Ten, when I was only about three hundred megaseconds old. It's all I know," she said, then mentally converted it to Earth years, like the newly awakened Admins insisted on using—she'd been ten years old. After formal education, Generationals apprenticed to the generation before them so there was no lapse in skills from accidents or early death. "What if they don't need that down on Lida?"

"Then you'll find something else you're good at, Agetha," Daved said. "We're both still young, on the early side of the generational cycle. You've been doing systems analysis half your life, but it's not so long compared to some of the older people around here. Their transition to surface life will be a lot harder. Ours will be easy, and they'll always need a vet, so we'll have enough work to support us...and others." Daved faltered just a little at the last remark.

Agetha hid a frown behind her napkin. When the reproductive ban was put into place, she thought it would give her ample time to decide if she even wanted children. The same had happened for all the other targets, and she wondered what her ancestors thought in this same situation. *If* this planet was the one, much better to conceive the next batch of children *on* the surface rather than in zero-G. She wasn't sure she wanted a small life fully dependent on her and Daved. What if she did something wrong? With the population controls on the ship, it was far more likely their request would have been denied in favor of a couple or poly with a higher priority claim. If they landed, there would be no excuse.

She cleared her throat. "You're already thinking about a family? The reports on Lida only came in last ship cycle. We have no idea what the actual conditions are down there. We don't yet know if *we'll* survive, much less a child."

"Or two," Daved added, then held his hands up in surrender. "I know it's soon, but I just...I think about starting a new life, carving out our partnership from whatever plants and animals are down there, teaching our child about the alien creatures they'll grow up with, having them teach *us* about what they learn...."

Agetha went to him, holding him close in a hug. Daved was a dreamer, where she was the practical one in the relationship. "We'll have a family, down on Lida," she promised him, but her eyes looked far into the distance, past his shoulder and out through the ship's bulkhead. Landing on a planet. A stationary gravity well. Their ancestors had lived that way, but that had been so long ago. Was she ready for such a big change? What was down on the surface?

Daved pushed back from her, likely feeling her tension. "It'll be fine. I promise. We'll have a new life together, even better than the one we have now. Come on, let's get together with Frank and Jiow in the next few days. We can see what they think over a game."

* * *

5.00 megaseconds before landing

Jiow hated toilet duty. She suspected the others in the janitorial pool of conspiring to boost her name in the rotation, while the others got cleaning duty, tightening loose bolts, and the like. Jiow was always cleaning out blocked pipes and carting crap manually to the compost. Especially the last few days, when everyone had been celebrating, eating—literally—through their food credits, her job was even worse than usual. And with another ten percent awake, their two and a half thousand had swelled closer to three thousand.

Jiow was ready for Lida. It was a chance for change. A chance to see unfamiliar faces from other ships. A chance for a new job. The apprenticing cycle on the generational ships was brutal, with little room for doing what a person wanted to do. Maybe it was just her personality. She was one of those who chose a different gender than biological sex, and if she could, she would have chosen a different job too.

But the familial job system was much more restrictive than any gender. You apprenticed to your parents, learning to do what they did, because that was how their parents learned, and theirs before them. Jiow had heard rumors the system had only been set up that way for the original target, to make sure all the required roles were filled. It was only supposed to be for three generations, not fourteen.

When she requested to change from janitorial to construction at three hundred megaseconds old, she'd not only gotten a reprimand from her fathers, she'd gotten an official mark in her record from the stingy old watch sergeant on duty at the time. It didn't stop her from studying in secret. She'd seen the same Vagal up and about in the last ship cycle, looking just the same. She'd imagined punching him in the nose, seeing if the famed Vagal implant was quick enough to stop her.

Jiow snorted behind her mask, herding the floating container down the center of the maintenance hall. It was covered at least, so the piles of feces and liquid waste didn't float out and get into the venting system. It was ugly when the shit hit the fan.

But just because things had been set up to be so restrictive in the beginning, everyone assumed that was how it had to be. Generation after generation following in the footsteps of those who had shared their genetic code, as if that was a reason to get assigned to a profession. There were people who broke out, of course, through marriage, or a fortunate opening somewhere when someone died untimely without an apprentice. But the Pappadapilos clan never had. Janitors and proud of it, all the way down to Jiow.

When the news broke last wake cycle about Lida, Jiow's heart had soared. It was her chance. She knew it. Once on the planet, there would be a need for professions no one had practiced on this ship for generations. She could be a lumberjack, or carpenter, or sculptor, or maybe even a priest—all official religions had formally been left behind on old Earth, though many families still practiced their own rites. No one was *just* a priest on the ships, though. She could start a new religion...

"Daydreaming about shit again, Jiow?"

Jiow startled, and just kept her fecal barge from plowing into a wall. She glared at her older brother, Zhu, who was smirking from one of the water reclamation rooms she had passed in the maintenance tunnel.

"Making sure the toilets are clean enough for the Admins to use," she threw back over her shoulder. Maybe Giordano himself would use one of the facilities Jiow had cleaned this wake cycle. Zhu just scoffed and waved her on.

Down on Lida, Jiow could be anything she wanted. She couldn't wait.

* * *

4.73 megaseconds before landing

Frank Silver hummed a tune as he clipped himself to a wall so he wouldn't drift away from the microscope. They'd have real samples from the planet when they entered orbit, not just probe estimations. Only about five megaseconds away. True alien life to study! His hand twitched toward the cabinet with samples from Target Six—the only other time the fleet had been able to take samples from a biome. No matter they explosively combusted in the presence of oxygen—the reason they hadn't landed—they contained tissue taken from a biome completely separated from Earth evolution. The samples had been studied by hundreds of people since, including his entire family, and everything had been wrung out of them, not that there was much. The algal-based life was simplistic at best, and Earth evolution had passed it in almost every regard millions of Earth years ago.

They knew the atmosphere and chemical balance was much more like Earth in Target Eleven than Target Six, and the probe estimations were convincing enough for the biology, geology, material science, and oceanography divisions to approve Admin's decision to land—not that he was sure what Admin would have done had anyone refused. The entire Administration staff and all but a few select Vagals had been in sus-ani since their journey started. When a planned eighty-five Earth year journey had changed to a voyage with no recognizable end, the status of the Administrators had elevated to something mythical, and it was almost genetically implanted into the Generationals to obey their commands as coming down from upon high. Well, now they'd start meeting their long-sleeping commanders face to face.

But that was something for later. On Target Eleven, which was increasingly referred to under its nickname of "Lida," the drone had sighted complex plant-like structures and even free-roaming creatures. Animals! Frank waited for the megaseconds to pass with barely constrained energy, tidying up the specimen samples requested by the horticulture and animal husbandry departments. The last living animals on the ship would soon be either turned into food, or put into sus-ani until they were safely on the surface. Plants were being transplanted into mobile pots, including the massive trees in the oxygen deck. The beehives were stored along with them, ready to be refrigerated to put the bees into artificial winter hibernation before they landed. Some plants would be left on the ships, of course, for when they were turned into the first cities, but there was much to do before then.

Frank's HUD pinged with a request from...a Vagal? High up indeed. Some of the supersoldiers were still orienting to life in zero-G, especially the ones who hadn't come out of sus-ani until now.

This was from a Corporal Hendricks, requesting permission to take the old E-Vapors out of storage? Why would anyone want those smelly things? Frank didn't know why they had been packed, taking up vital storage space on the ship. He'd deconstructed one of the vile things when he first apprenticed under his father. It seemed to be the traditional rite of passage for a new molecular biologist. The cylindrical containers had traces of addictive substances, but also a blend of potent stimulants, metabolism balancers, and vitamins. Presumably something the Vagal soldiers needed. Their name was a misnomer anyway. Their implants did much more than stimulate just the vagal nerve—though he wasn't certain what—but the name had stuck as such things did.

Frank sighed and rejected the request. No matter how high up the soldier was, there was no call to pollute the delicate air filters on the Abeona. They would still need to function after landing. The ships would become buildings, and their air systems would still need filters.

There was another ping a few seconds later and Frank frowned. The request was back, this time signed by—Frank's eyebrows shot up—Admin Giordano himself? His eye hovered over the "reject" button, and he almost blinked the confirmation out of spite, but he also knew not to cut off his own foot just because it was stuck in an airlock door. This close to such a huge change in all their lives, who knew if he'd still have this job on the surface? He *wanted* to study the life on Lida. If that meant pandering to Admin and their Vagal enforcers for a time, so be it. All his ancestors had done the same. He pursed his lips and blinked on the "accept" button.

He'd have to put in an alert to maintenance to pay extra attention to the venting system. They were less than five megaseconds from orbit, and likely not much farther from landing, but he didn't want to have a ship full of emphysemic members when they did so. This was not the last time he'd have to hold his breath and accept a fetid decision from Admin, he suspected.

* * *

4.49 megaseconds before landing

Agetha spun the container of snacks Daved had made—chocolate-coated, dried pineapple—into the center of the game room. They were still using up their food credits twice as fast as normal. "What are we playing tonight?"

"Feast of Burgundy or Settlers of SmallWorld?" Jiow asked, holding out two game boxes. It was easier to use a HUD app, but there was something about the feel of the magnetic pieces clipping to the play board that was hard to beat. Their crew had played tabletop since they were children. Now it was a tradition.

"We played Feast last time and it took almost two kiloseconds just to set up," Frank grumbled.

"Settlers it is," Jiow said.

They joked about the latest gossip on the ship while positioning the pieces and board, and Jiow told them about the last toilet malfunction. "This Vagal thought you just left it, and the toilet would take care of everything! I think she'd been frozen the whole journey."

"Everything's changing," Frank added. "I've gotten twelve more release orders, signed by Admin, for E-Vapors. One of them even stood over my shoulder watching to make sure I accepted the request. Atmospheric control is having a fit. I don't appreciate these soldiers butting into my area like they know how a starship works."

"There's a reason Admin is in command," Agetha reminded them. The ships had been too long without their leaders, and there were bound to be tensions. "We know about running these ships in space, but they were chosen specifically to start a colony. The Vagals are there to protect us as we build a permanent city."

Frank *humpfed*, but didn't disagree.

"I saw a Vagal smoking one," Daved added, opening his hands to let the others choose their color. Frank's pale hand was a contrast against his. He was even whiter than Agetha. "The smell was...not terrible, but I could tell it wasn't something that should be in the venting system."

"It is like they think we'll never need to use the ship again," Agetha allowed, picking her own piece. "I'm getting bombarded with reports on oxygen use, CO_2 levels, dwindling food rations, and crowding. I can't map a path where the ship is sustainable past another eight or nine megaseconds. It's the same on the seven others, too. The analyst pool is working all hours to keep up with the requests from Admin on, well, everything. It's like they think we're here just to satisfy their every question, not make sure the ships run smoothly."

"We *won't* use the ship again, hopefully, love," Daved said. "Not for spaceflight, anyway. We're already ten ship cycles closer to landing."

"You're like a kid," Frank laughed. "Only eight more sleeps until launch anniversary...only seven more sleeps until..."

Daved poked him companionably until Frank hushed. "Well, it's exciting. A new world! Anything could happen."

"Including starving in a micro-glacial age, if our weather predictions don't hold out over longer cycles," Frank grumbled. "Admin made the decision to land extremely quickly. We could have sat in orbit for thirty or forty megaseconds and seen how a full rotation around Lev affected Lida. Now it's too late."

"But they made it with all available data. Sometimes it's better to dive in when everyone is at their peak and ready to go. The longer we stay in orbit, the more the Generationals will get jaded," Jiow added. "You know we will. After one of Lida's years, we'd have half the fleet refusing to land, just like with Target Seven. Now, the possibilities are open. Anyone can find a new life."

"I am looking forward to investigating the plant life down there," Frank admitted. "The reports say there are some strange compounds present."

"But Frank's right. Anything could still go wrong," Agetha said. She'd been watching the others debate. Daved's eyebrows creased, but the others made motions of agreement. "We haven't gotten physical samples, like Frank wants. It's all from a noninvasive probe. Sure, everything seems good, but who knows what kind of creatures down there want to eat us."

"Well, we've got panther and bear embryos frozen in storage," Daved said. "Those would want to eat you too, once they're unthawed."

"But I *know* those want to eat me," Agetha said. "I don't know what to expect from anything on the surface. I don't even know how to *live* on the surface." She sighed. "I suppose that's what the Vagals are for. Well, we'll be hitting half a G on the final slowdown. I hope you've all started your calcium boosts and bone mods. I hate the new exercise routines, but if you ever want to walk on the surface, they're necessary too."

"We're supposed to start those already?" Jiow asked sheepishly.

"Didn't you read the notice a couple wake cycles ago?" Frank asked her.

"I was knee deep in Admin waste," Jiow shot back. "I didn't even have time to read the daily ship update. I had my own daily *shit* update."

"And none of you read the official room reassignment memo either, it seems," said a voice at the door. Agetha twisted away from the table, catching a handhold to turn her to the door. A very large person floated there, long hair back in a severe bun, arms crossed with one foot hooked under a handhold.

"I'm guessing you don't want to join us for Settlers of SmallWorld?" Frank asked.

"No. I'm Corporal Hendricks," the person said. "I'm here to clear this room out. It will be used as Conference Room Number Four from now on, for meetings including Admin and Vagal personages on the distribution of resources after landing. This was all explained in the memo."

"I haven't received any memo, and I'm in the analyst pool," Agetha said. She checked her HUD just in case something new had come through. It hadn't.

The corporal's eyes got that glassy look when someone was concentrating on the HUD rather than the real world. "Confirmed. Sent to everyone on admin.routing.all.memos."

"I've never heard of that message list," Daved said.

Agetha made a query to the main database. "Looks like that list was deprecated almost nine thousand megaseconds ago. It doesn't go to any Generationals."

"And this has been a rec room for six thousand megaseconds," Jiow added. "You need us out right now?"

Agetha did some quick math at the Vagal's confused expression. "That's about two hundred eighty, and two hundred Earth years, respectively."

Corporal Hendricks' face tightened. "The Generationals will need to rejoin that list. It's where all the important announcements from Admin are routed. For now, this room is required for Admin's use."

"We're not the only ones who use this room," Daved said, gesturing to the cabinets on the far wall. They held all sorts of diversions for the game room. Some had been traded for with other ships, and some moved back and forth between the aerobics courts and other rec rooms around the UGS Abeona.

"Then let the others know," Hendricks said. "This room will be used for intermediaries between Admin and the Vagal command structure. It is on the most efficient path between the command deck and the new Vagal barracks." Hendricks adjusted her bun, then crossed her arms again, offsetting the motion with her foot like a seasoned Generational, though Agetha knew she hadn't been out of sus-ani for more than a few days. She'd heard from the processor pool about the scarily coordinated watch sergeants who traded off every few megaseconds. They went in and out of sus-ani quickly enough the Generationals never really got to know them. The rotation was never repeated during a Generational's lifetime. There was always a new Vagal face, until the next one cycled in.

But Hendricks wasn't finished. "There will be a lot of changes in the next few weeks. We've only got about two months until we hit orbit, and we'll need everyone at peak efficiency. This ship is going to get crowded, and you Generationals can't stay to the same schedule you've kept while the whole command structure has been in sus-ani. You can be a help or a hindrance, and I know Admin will be paying attention to who helps these ships land on our new homeworld."

So stay in their good graces was the unsaid suggestion. Agetha traded a look with her husband. Daved's face was cloudy, his mouth pinched. Jiow was scowling into her playing pieces, one hand clenched, and Frank threw a handful of score markers back into the box, where they rattled around, though none floated back out.

"Well, I guess game night is cancelled," he said. "We'll have to find some space Admin isn't using."

"You say you know what's best for us, keeping up in one job, on one ship for four *hundred* of your years," Jiow said. "Now you want to change everything up?"

"We can't help that the original mission went beyond parameters," Hendricks answered stiffly. "Those rules are in place for a reason."

"And what's that?" Jiow pushed on the table, popping herself up, then changed direction with a quick tap on a stability handle. She aimed herself toward the Vagal. "No. We don't need to leave just because this person says so, whoever they are. We've had this room for—"

Agetha didn't actually see Hendricks move. One moment she had her arms crossed, staring Jiow down, the next, Jiow's face was against the wall, one hand behind her back. The Vagal hadn't shifted position at all. One foot was still hooked under a rung to keep her steady. To completely absorb someone else's momentum was not easy to do, and Hendricks made it look simple. Daved tensed beside her, but Agetha put a hand on his arm.

"He's right." Hendricks inclined her chin toward Frank. "Game nights are over, unless you can find somewhere out of the way." She released Jiow without looking at her, spun, and was out of the door with one twitch of her foot.

Jiow floated back, frowning as one hand rubbed her neck. "Well, I guess some things won't change when we get to Lida," she said. "I'll help you pack up, Frank."

PART THREE

Landing

2.63 megaseconds before landing

Jane Brighton watched the other Administrators fumble and float around the table. Several were still sideways. That they were all in one room aboard the UGS St. Christopher—*her* ship—was a minor miracle of political maneuvering, and one that had taken no small amount of wheedling and calling in old favors to make happen.

"Everyone find a seat," she called to the other Admins. She was rewarded with a chuckle from the other seven and their assistants. It felt like old times back on Earth, arguing about who would fit on the generational ships and where. She gave Christiaan, at her shoulder, a nod. Her own assistant had been thawed out soon after she had been. She didn't know what she would do without them. Christiaan had been working for her for the last fifteen years—well, four hundred and thirty-five years, if she added in the ridiculous amount of time the fleet had been floating about in space. Who would have thought a suitable chunk of rock would be so hard to find?

"It's great to see you all well and back together again," Jane began once the others had settled down to a low murmur of discomfort. She tried to steeple her fingers and lean forward, but only succeeded in a slow twist until she caught one foot under the table. She was getting better at that, but still caught a twitch of Ahman Ragab's lips. The Administrator of the UGS Khonsu didn't miss much. At least they hadn't back on Earth. Jane could only hope the sus-ani had muddled the others' brains just a little. Enough for her to stay in control of this nest of vipers.

"I hope everyone's getting a handle on all the unexpected changes," Alessandro Giordano added. "We've been cleaning Generationals out of all the conference rooms and trying to put the ship back into some semblance of order."

"It has been over four hundred years for them," said the Admin of the Ganesha, Rajani Kumarisurajinder. Her salwar kameez was pinned artfully to keep it from billowing into the assistants who floated next to her. "Surely, we can forgive some drift from the original floorplan? They've done an excellent job partitioning their living quarters, and now we're making them double with the newly re-animated to make sure everyone gets enough rest. We need to be ready when we make landfall."

"You make it sound like you're creating zombies, not waking the crew," Ahman said.

"'Re-animated' is the technical term we use," Rajani replied. "I'd tell you to take it up with the scientist who came up with the term, but they're four centuries dead."

"Much longer than that, dear Rajani," added Dmitri Novikov of the Hasamelis. "We have been traveling at an appreciable portion of lightspeed for a *subjective* four hundred years. It would have been much longer for our relatives back on Earth, if there's even anything left of them now. I thought you, as science lead, would know that." Rajani opened her mouth to reply, but Jane broke in before she could get going.

Interrupt the bickering. Always keep control. "Perhaps we should devote our resources to looking forward, not backward. There's a reason the fleet left Earth for a new home." She held out her hand, remembering this time to offset the motion with her foot, and Christiaan placed the datapad in her palm. Smooth. Commanding. Just the way she liked it. Be the focus of attention. Move the conversation away from Earth's slow decimation under the weight of unsustainable practices.

"Now, the original plan was for the ships to form the backbone of the first settlement on the planet—originally Target Alpha, but that's been blown all to hell."

"Literally," Alessandro muttered. He'd seen the desolation on Alpha, just as she had. Though the Admin of the Abeona had been consulted, several of the other Admins hadn't even been awoken before they made the decision to carry on to Beta. And only Alessandro had been awoken after that, with a possible mutiny alert near Target Seven. She'd seen the reports of his handling of the situation. She'd have been much harsher on the potential mutineers. These Generationals were only stepping-stones to full colonization of the planet. She'd make sure no one mistook his being awakened more often than her for better command potential. Jane was determined to bring her vision of a new colony to fruition. They could not fail. There was nowhere else to go, and she'd crash the ships into the planet herself if that was the only way to ensure they put all their resources into surviving.

"I've had the analyst pool running assessments on the original procedure to determine viability," she continued. "The process could still work. The only issue is a lack of open landing area."

"This is about that growth covering the surface of Lida?" asked Polunu Kim, the Admin for the Hina. Polunu was a small, chubby woman, who looked like she might flip upside down at any moment. But she also might be the smartest one among them. "I've started my own analysis of its structure and disposition."

"Right. Thanks for the original assessment you sent, Polunu. It's been invaluable," Jane said. Compliment when appropriate for positive feedback but stay in command. She threw the surface scans to project in the middle of the table. "There's a biological mat of some sort that covers nearly the entire surface of the planet. At least there's no question as to whether there's life here, though it's thankfully not sentient. We've identified three potential sites, near sources of fresh water, on relatively flat, geologically stable land, but that damnable mat covers everything, sometimes dozens of meters deep."

"So, we need to get rid of it," said Xi Wenqing, Admin of the K'uei-Hsing. "Do we have enough missiles? Can we reflect solar energy to burn it away?"

"We don't have *any* missiles," Rajani said. "These are scientific vessels."

"Of course you must be correct," Wenqing said.

Jane eyed the man. The K'uei-Hsing had been made with the most secrecy of the fleet, largely constructed in the South Asian nation states, back on Earth. She wouldn't have put it past their bureaucrats to have ignored the UN and added armaments anyway.

"Redirecting solar energy will take too long," Dmitri said, looking over a pad his assistant had given him. "Months to burn away enough growth to clear out an area the size of the city we're planning."

"The *arcopolis*," Jane corrected, and saw several nods around the table. Keep unity. Don't let the thought of assuming command emerge.

It was a combined term they had decided on early in meetings, a combination of *arcology* and *polis*, meaning the city would be self-contained, but also more spread out than one of the container cities that had been popular on Earth. It was intended to foster an atmosphere of safety and comfort to those living in it.

"We have to land engines-down anyway, don't we?" said a quiet voice—the last of the ship Admins. They all turned to look at where Maria Gutiérrez Delgado turned her hands outward, as if it were obvious. She was also the youngest of the Admins, in charge of the Xaman Ek, though they all looked younger than forty, thanks to the gene-mods they'd received before leaving Earth. If all went well, they'd all live to see their three or four hundreds, easily.

"The engines are powerful enough to move the ships at a large fraction of the speed of light," Maria said. "We'll be in orbit in a month with plenty of fuel reserves left. There should be no problem to burn through a mat of biological matter. We'll simply need to save a bit during descent, and then flare the engines right before landing. I can run the numbers through my pool of mathematicians."

Jane looked around. No one said anything. "Any disagreements?"

"Should we get samples of the area before burning everything to a crisp?" Rajani asked. The scientist sounded miffed at destroying this small area, when the entire surface was covered by that overgrown mat of chaos.

"I'll order a lander probe to get your teams more samples," Jane answered. She held Rajani's eye until the other woman nodded and looked away. "Excellent. Then we'll go with this plan unless there are any problems found. Next issue is the disposition of the Generationals against the Vagals. When we started this little journey, there were a lot less of them than there are now, even with population controls in effect." She looked around the table. "Anyone having issues with insubordination yet? Any Generationals thinking too far above their pay grade?" Just as she would keep this meeting on task, there was no room for the Generationals to think of anything but building their future home.

"We have had a few instances of removing squatters in some of the restricted rooms," Dmitri said. "They have been...dealt with."

Jane nodded, accepting the new information Christiaan sent to her pad. Ten new inhabitants of Dmitri's brig. He had the right idea. "Alessandro, you mentioned some issues as well."

The Abeona's Admin gave a sharp nod. "We have, but the Abeona will not resort to the same draconian measures as Dmitri's ship. The offending parties have been assigned to counseling. They will learn to appreciate the reinstated chain of command."

Jane shook her head. Not enough. "There's no time for counseling. We land in a month and these Generationals will be working as soon as they're on the ground. If they don't agree with our ways, assign them so much work they have no time to think."

"Jane, we can't simply—"

"Do you want to compromise all eight ships by being too lenient?" she interrupted him. Alessandro was her closest rival for the command position, but she had a plan for that. Putting him in his place now would only reinforce that.

The man's mouth worked silently, but the other Admins had joined her in staring him down. Good.

"I'll find them something suitable to do," he finally said.

"We have instituted a lottery to ensure the Vagals are adequately housed, even if they must share with Generational families," Ahman said into the silence, sporting a half-smile. "We believe it will ensure future cooperation with the command chain." They had a devious brain, and Jane jotted the idea down. It might have some merit.

"Well, keep a watch for any other issues," Jane said, eyes flicking through her agenda even though she knew exactly what was coming next. Time for the real show of power between the Admins. "As for now, we should really cover the distribution of building resources upon landing. Some of this was obviously mapped out on fleet launch, but I think it bears a new look, considering the extra time we've been on our journey, and potential wear and tear on the ships over the years." She specifically avoided Alessandro's eyes, whose ship had been point on the fleet for longer than any other. The Abeona had minor damage from micrometeorites, though nothing that would really impact the structural life of the ship. Visuals were everything.

She turned to Wenqing first, deliberately not offering the bait, not letting the others comment yet. He would be easy to handle. "I think we can all agree the K'uei-Hsing is still the best option for the military complex. Does everyone else agree?"

There was an easy round of agreement. "Ayes" from almost everyone, though Ahman said nothing, likely knowing the majority would be in favor. Their ship had been the other choice for military strength. Jane offered them an olive branch.

"And though it was originally assigned to me, I think the Khonsu has shown admirable ability in the intervening years on overall R&D." Fortunately, Christiaan had supplied her with several innovations created by the Generationals on that ship. Jane caught Ahman's head tilt. They were interested. She glanced around the others, gauging mood with both the Admins and their assistants. She'd learned that what did not show on the face of the senior administrator might well show on one who worked with them.

"I think transportation, R&D, and eventual education for first generation natives would be a challenging and rewarding assignment for the Khonsu. What does everyone say?"

Assistants furiously swiped messages to their Admins. She simply needed to keep them off balance. Ahman was well regarded, and eventually even Rajani nodded along, though her lips looked like she tasted a lemon. Jane had a plan for that as well.

Over the next hour, she wheeled and dealt with the other Admins, having Christiaan badger the other assistants with requests while she watched their workload grow. She settled the Ganesha and Rajani into the role of science advisor and medical and biological lead. Dmitri and his Hasamelis was an easy shoe-in for power generation, technology, and networking. Maria and her Xaman Ek got shunted to water and waste management, and Polunu and the Hina were the best choice for animal management and food distribution.

Now the hard work began. With all the shuffling, only crop production, and lead urban design and management were left. Jane saw glances between assistants and their Admins as the others figured out where the pieces sat. Christiaan's assessment of strengths had been spot on and she sent them a quick thank you by text. They straightened minutely beside her. She could tell the acknowledgement had hit home.

"Now, I know we had the Abeona as involved in city planning, but I really think we should take a look at this again," she said, watching

Alessandro's face darken as he understood the implications. "Mainly I wanted to say how impressed I am with the work your crew has been doing in hydroponics all these years. You've taken crop science to the next level and your biologists are top notch, even rivalling Rajani's."

Alessandro's face registered the confusion she intended as he warred with the pride over beating the resident scientific ship against her hamstringing of his leadership. She sent another text of thanks to Christiaan for digging up that particular tidbit of competition. The Ganesha and the Abeona had begun a horticulture contest some hundred and twenty years back, which had only gotten more extravagant over time.

"And do we really want the most scarred ship to be the centerpiece of our new city?" She gave the admin across from her a sympathetic smile. She'd purposefully worked him over harder this meeting than the others. "No offense, of course, Alex. That's merely a side note. I think if anyone's equipped to combat this *fascinating* biological mat we've discovered on this planet, it's the Abeona. We're eventually going to have to contend with local plant life, and I look forward to what Admin Giordano comes up with. All in agreement?"

"Sounds good to me," Wenqing said. He'd gotten what he wanted early on, and was ready to leave the meeting. Jane had used that strategy in meetings back on Earth.

"I believe this would be an admirable challenge for Alessandro," Ahman agreed. They gave her a minute nod when she locked eyes. Her gift to them had already paid benefits.

"And who will retain city planning and the lead admin position in this configuration?" Maria asked. Jane could tell she wasn't overly happy with getting assigned waste management.

"Well, the St. Christopher was assigned to recreation services in the original plan, and I can't see how we'll have much use for that while we're building," Jane rationalized. "As the Abeona has surged ahead of us on food science, I'm perfectly willing to trade for directing the city planning and construction." She flipped up the radial layout of the city. "It's already planned out, and I see no reason to change it."

"Which means you'll also handle the finances during construction," Rajani observed, but her voice held little hostility. The others knew they were beaten. It was simply a matter of mopping things up.

"As it will be the largest project by far, I think that's only fair," Jane answered. "We can certainly revisit the layout after construction is complete and I'd be most willing to cede the financial sector back to anyone with a desire for it." Though after ten years of planned construction, she'd be so thoroughly entrenched as Lead Admin, she doubted the topic would even come up.

She passed a glance around the room again, her eyes slightly wider than normal. Open. Earnest. In command. "Shall we have a show of hands?"

* * *

1.42 megaseconds before landing

More lifeforms were observed in the sky, and though these were greatly larger than the previous one, various higher-functioning nodes agreed the layout of the lifeforms was similar in several ways to the one marked U . G . S . S T C H R I S.

These newcomers did not zip and fly as the first one did, instead slowly and methodically approaching a relative position above one hemisphere, as if they were attached to that section of ground by an immensely long tendril. It was not known what function these lifeforms had, and how they reached such a large size. There were eight of them, much larger than any creature that had been subsumed recently or far in the past. It was attempted in one node to recreate a contiguous growth of a similar size, but the creation fell apart under its own weight soon after it was created.

The alert was made by local ocular nodes when the eight lifeforms began birthing children of all shapes and sizes, which descended into low atmosphere and even to the ground. Efforts were made to subsume several of them, unsuccessfully. It seemed there were no parts of similar composition to any creature on this planet. This was a sensible observation—as concluded by local knowledge apparatuses— as the lifeforms had come from outside the sphere of the planet. It was entirely likely they were not compatible at all with any native life.

Some of the children were prevented from leaving, though they did some injury to local ocular nodes in the attempt. Others were allowed to leave, to observe the method of propulsion. The equatorial region which had previously been used to experiment with flying apparatus was once again totally subsumed, and was used to observe and store information on these processes.

Soon the children ceased being birthed, and many were reabsorbed by the eight main lifeforms. It was assumed this was a method to pick only the strongest children to carry on the advantages gained, though the method for selection was not fully grasped. Some of those that had been kept had never even approached the surface and had no contact with life on the planet. Surely those had not gained as much knowledge as the ones that had made contact and returned?

Over the next rotation of the planet, the eight large lifeforms remained silent, and then their outlines began to shift, showing a smaller profile to the surface. Was this a new form of communication?

* * *

0.61 megaseconds before landing

They were going to land. Processor Alvin was a bundle of nerves. The ships were actually going to land on a planet and Alvin would be required to languish in a gravity well for the rest of his life, no matter how long that would be. He'd sent five separate requests to Admin Brighton asking for a geosynchronous survey institution to be left in space, in case of, well, anything really. What if they needed resources only available in space? Easier to have a platform already in place. What if there was a mission failure, stars forbid? They would need a platform to signal old Earth, as a last resort. Not that any help would arrive for hundreds, if not thousands of years.

But all his requests were denied. All personnel were required on the surface, he was told. Everyone would help build their new city, together. He'd spent the last few ship cycles strapping everything in his room down, including the crates he had packed.

Would the ships even make the landing? The transition from space to atmosphere was not an easy one, and yes, the ships had been designed with that change in mind, but they were also far past the original target landing date. What if something had gone wrong? He'd sent another request to the analyst pool in the previous wake cycle to check on superstructure stability, but the report hadn't come back yet.

How was that not the top priority? Surely others had the same, perfectly reasonable, concerns he did.

Alvin checked through his list of things to do once again. All three lists. He had one for technical aspects of touchdown, another for checks on ship systems and occupants, and a final, personal checklist for himself. No sense getting down to the surface, with all the accompanying anxiety, and not knowing where his things were.

The Generationals had been sent new exercise routines and repeated reminders to take their bone density supplements daily since entering the system. By now, most of the changes should have taken effect, for those that had followed the warning in a timely manner. He'd noticed a large increase in his leg muscle volume, though the new walking classes were a joke. Who could be expected to keep balanced under the effects of gravity? Still, he'd done the prescribed exercises each day, to the minute of what was requested. Lida—everyone was using that name now, despite his best attempts to keep to the correct nomenclature—didn't have the full gravity of old Earth, but it was a good portion of it. At least eighty percent.

He paged through reports probes had made of the surface. The local geography in their area had been thoroughly mapped, both for the top layer of the growth and for the ground surface underneath. Sometimes tens of meters beneath. How could anyone live on ground that was so bumpy and uneven? Things had to sit *on* other surfaces in a gravity well. The ships themselves would be landing engine-first, their entire kilometer-plus length teetering into the sky. Wouldn't the gravity well just make them fall over, especially with that uneven surface? He fired off another quick request to the analysis pool to see if anyone had checked that yet.

Alvin switched over to the "people" list from the "planet" list (the third list he had named "personal," just to continue the pleasing alliteration) and pulled up the most recent concepts for gravity well housing. They were horrific, created by Admin, naturally. Monolithic things, with most useable space confined to the lower walls and floor. Gravity precluded nearly sixty-eight percent of the storage space available in a standard cabin on the ships. Each person would have to spread out quite a bit more to have the same possessions and space claim. And where were the colored guiding lines in these designs? Every section of each ship had imbedded directional displays and efficiency suggestions for the living quarters. Without that, people would simply put things...anywhere. Alvin shivered. He hoped these ideas had been taken into account in the design for the city. No one had asked him, after all. Without the proper protocols, living in a gravity well was going to be *chaos.*

Alvin stroked the input console he'd used for the last thousand megaseconds. His setup would never work down on the surface. The entire interior structure of the ship would be gutted and refurbished after landing, if the ship even survived.

Maybe he should check the escape pods one more time to make certain all were functional. He added it to his list.

* * *

0.34 megaseconds before landing

"The samples from the surface are amazing!" Frank told Jiow. He blinked bleary eyes, trying to focus on the game pieces in Jiow's cramped quarters. Agetha and Daved were busy packing, so they'd bowed out of their last game night before landing, not that four people would have fit in the tiny compartment. Jiow and Frank were elbow to elbow, and they'd picked a game with few pieces.

"Yes, I believe this is the fourth time you've mentioned that," Jiow said. "We haven't even started playing yet."

Frank ignored her. "I wish we'd gotten more samples from the river next to the landing site as well. I haven't had time to do a full genetic breakdown, but the structures share properties with the Fungal Kingdom back on Earth. However, there are interesting crossovers with viruses on the microscopic level. The varieties in one sample are orders of magnitude larger than the diversity in Earth records. I wonder if we should even bring our own mushroom species, or just use the ones already down there."

"As long as there's solid ground—" Jiow began.

"That's a good point," Frank said. "I've been looking at the soil samples too, and the current theory among the biologists is that we're going to have to be very careful with which plants we try to grow in native soil. It's been exposed to the local culture for who knows how long. The nutrient ratio is probably far out of calibration for our plants.

We'll have soil from the ship, but the nutrients will soon be used up and mixed with the native ground down there." He pointed to his feet, though with the ships beginning their final rotation before the landing sequence, the planet's surface was more accurately somewhere behind his head.

"We'll be affecting the native soil as well," Jiow added, evidently deciding to abandon attempts to play their game. "I know that much, from cleaning out stuck plumbing. We'll be making our own soil pretty quickly, seasoned with the bacteria in our guts as well as in all the livestock." She wrinkled her nose. "I should know. I've been helping cart the remaining animals into sus-ani and cleaning up after them."

"There's nothing in the samples, however, which say the reverse is true," Frank said. "We may have trouble adapting the surface, but I doubt the life down there will have any trouble adapting to us. It seems very well suited to chimerical change, like it just adds whatever it finds to its genetic code."

"But there are animals down there too, right?" Jiow asked. "I know I've seen some of the reports labeling moving creatures."

"That's the funny thing," Frank said, the game piece still in his hand. "There *are* animals—or parts of them. We even gathered up some in the samples we took. The Animal Kingdom is a very different thing than the Fungal Kingdom, at least on Earth. But here?" He shook his head. "I'm hard pressed to tell which is which, when looking at a slide. And some cells have walls, while others don't. You know plants have cell walls, right?"

Jiow opened her mouth.

"Because animals don't. Animals move around, so their cells don't need as much protection. I'm simplifying, of course." Frank tapped the table with his game piece. Jiow's eyes followed the movement. "Fungi have cell walls too, but they're different from plants. They have chitin, like insect shells. I've seen *all three types* of cells, and more, in one sample! It's like they have different functions in one organism. That's where I'm assuming the viral aspects come in. Viruses don't have cell walls either because they're much simpler things. I think they're being harnessed here to transmit information between the different types of cells, help them communicate in some manner." He finally took in Jiow's glazed eyes.

"Anyway, no matter how fascinating and creepy all this is, we'll just have to carve out our own little place to live. Once we build a city, then we can really explore the mat that covers the entire planet."

Jiow started packing up the game.

* * *

172 kiloseconds before landing

"We can't have a child as soon as we land, Daved," Agetha said. She threw a pair of socks into their luggage. Even though the crew would accompany the ships down to the surface, they still had to pack all their belongings to be ready for the exodus from the ship.

"Well, not *right* when we land, of course," Daved answered. He was busy packing their cookware into crates. The zero-G cooking implements wouldn't be as useful in a gravity well, but there was no sense wasting them. They'd been in Daved's family since the beginning of their voyage, patched up every time something broke. "We'll have to wait for the medical center to be set up, but I imagine that will be one of the first buildings to be finished. Got to take care of all the new colonists, after all."

"Which includes making sure the colony is viable and stable, before expanding with a lot of kids. Do you know how many resources they take up? I do. I've run the numbers on daycare center costs and food consumption for children. They eat a lot while they're growing." Agetha eyed her husband from across their cabin, which wasn't far. Children were not a sure thing in the fleet. Supposedly the cabins had been three times this big when the ships first set out, but over time the Generational population of each ship had expanded—even with population control measures—and most cabins had been split into smaller sections. Not everyone could have kids anymore, and that was fine with Agetha.

"But just think!" Daved passed an open hand through the air. "The first child born on Lida. It has a historic ring to it."

"And it will probably be some Admin or Vagal child," Agetha replied. "You know they'll take top priority, just like they booted us out of the rec spaces we'd been using for thousands of megaseconds and changed all the procedures that had been working just fine since

Target Two. Anyway, we'll need to have Alpha Radian set up before anything, to give enough structure to the colony."

They had both put in for construction duty in the new colony. Neither had a lot of experience with building, but almost everybody would be learning those skills while the ships were transformed into the bulk of Alpha Radian, the first of eight pie slices that would make up the Admins' planned arcopolis.

"Imagine the UGS Abeona standing on its tail, a kilometer-high landmark. We'll be able to see all the surrounding landscape, working on the new city." Daved had let go of the covered pot he'd taken from its cabinet and it turned very slowly in a circle in front of him.

"With our new kid strapped to my hip, right, and a welding torch in the other hand?" Agetha threw the next pair of socks at her husband, which bounced off his head. Why had she mentioned children again when he'd finally gotten off the topic? "The ships will be vertical for a very short time while the main superstructure plates are removed. And there certainly won't be any people up that high. It will all be done by the automated drones. Why do you think I've been learning their control language?"

"I know, I know." Daved tossed the socks back to her. "I'm just eager to get down there and *see*. I want to experience a planet, sustained gravity, a sunrise." He came close, taking Agetha up and spiraling around the cabin. "It's going to be such an adventure, and it's happening in our lifetimes!"

* * *

72 kiloseconds before landing

The creatures above had finished their rotation and several widely placed ocular-based entities confirmed they were drawing closer. As they hit the upper limit of the atmosphere, the composition of the creature's skin began to change, glowing with a fiery red light that continued to expand across their skin. It had been theorized there was a change in friction due to air density at a high enough altitude. Now several higher-functioning bodies were busy recording these observations.

The creatures themselves were growing as well. Earlier calculations for the height of the atmosphere were quickly revised, as were calculations on distance and velocity. These creatures were larger than originally anticipated, not only larger than any creature created or encountered on this planet, but larger than some geographical features. There were mountains that were smaller than these creatures. How did they sustain their internal structure against such pressures that must be enacted by their transition through the atmosphere?

More importantly, what was the creatures' purpose? There were hurried communications as the sun traversed across the sky, various nodes pooling knowledge and making predictions based on the re-calculated velocity and distance. The place where the creatures would contact the surface was determined to a certainty, near the equator, and several different types of sensing creatures were dispatched to the area in an effort to understand what was happening. Perhaps a form of communication might be possible over time. There was an opportunity to grow, to change, to learn, and yes, to subsume. All would become clearer very shortly as contact was made.

The creatures' rapid descent suddenly slowed as their ends closest to the ground began to glow with a light even hotter than that generated by the atmosphere. Several reports were received of overwhelming heat. When a followup was requested to the first report delivered, the node making the report was found to have been removed. How had this happened? The creatures were still high in the sky, though growing in size. Their descent was agonizingly slow.

Other knowledge flooded in, faster and faster, firsthand reports of the flaring cones of heat from the bottoms of the creatures, cut off as soon as they were made. More sensory nodes were sent to the area to attempt to discover if there was any defense against the heat.

Farther ocular senses noted a wide circle forming under the combined area the new creatures inhabited. They were transitioning in horizontal patterns now, holding their vertical positions half their heights above the ground. They seemed to be deliberately scarring the land and any life on it for great distances in all directions from the calculated landing point. The ground beneath was starting to carbonize, solid ground flowing like rivers, becoming a flat, glass-like plane. Similar occurrences, though on a much smaller scale, had been observed as the aftereffects of lightning strikes near silicate deposits.

There was fire. There was death. There was confusion. Nearly all senses were directed toward this one location, even to the point of reducing control on several chaotic elements in scattered locations, letting the intelligences there roam unimpeded for significant portions of the day. There had not been this much disruption to the planetary ecosystem since very corrupted reports, far back in time, that were disputed in accuracy by many higher-functioning nodes.

What had these creatures done, and why? There were now no senses close enough to gain new insights. All mobile units sent to investigate had died in screaming fire. Several hilltops were colonized to provide a far-off view, but details were not easily discernible from the haze that rose from the area. The creatures seemed invincible, both to natural forces of the planet, and to anything biological. All contact with the area where the creatures had touched the ground was drawn back. Some pockets with sensing structures were abandoned, left to function independently for the first time in eons. More preparations were needed before attempting any form of deliberate contact.

PART FOUR

The First Days

3 days after landing

Agetha watched the scorched ground through the eyes of a drone, skimming a kilometer high in the air, still not higher than the noses of their vertical vessels. Her physical body was sitting in a mobility chair, giving her knees a rest in the unaccustomed gravity. The eight ships would become skeletons in the next few days as the automated construction bots, only used for emergency repairs until now, swarmed over what had been her home, reducing it to nanotanium plates and piles of circuitry.

Admin's new headquarters, though only a shell, was among the first buildings being constructed, as was the military complex, largely created from the plating of the UGS K'uei-Hsing. Meanwhile, the Generationals had to make do with pop-up tents and hastily-cobbled structures out of raw nanotanium plates. Daved was back at theirs now, trying to figure out how to light a fire to cook their first non-ration food for that night.

She blinked through a quick message.

How's the fire-making skills coming?

Daved's message arrived in her HUD viewscreen a few moments later.

Not used to cooking at such low air pressure. Taking longer to roast potatoes than I thought.

The low air pressure was directly related to the lower gravity of Lida than Earth. The air pressure on the Abeona had been artificial, since there was no gravity, but it had been set at that of old Earth, at sea level. More changes for them to work through.

You'll figure it out, she wrote back. *Just make sure you make the changes in your recipe book.*

The next message came a few minutes later.

Still raw. I'll have to cook these even longer. Get those ships pulled apart fast—I want my stove!

Working on it, dear, she sent back.

They had landed about five megaseconds before the longest day of the planetary year in this hemisphere. They would have plenty of planting season, and as they were near the equator, they should be able to plant nearly year-round. The first seeds had already been put into carefully prepared and processed soil, and those not on deconstruction duty were transplanting the trees and more mature plants from the ship. They were planting small samples of each species in case there were any cross contaminations from the local flora.

While the eight Admins and their assistants and lackeys bickered and strategized, the Vagal supersoldiers patrolled the outskirts of the landing site and supervised Generational workteams. Agetha's mouth twisted beneath her VR helmet. She'd thought back to the ease of her life as a systems analyst many times the past few days. Before Admin and Vagals started complicating things.

Even through the drone, Agetha could see hundreds of the supersoldiers milling around. She'd seen the sus-ani chambers on the Abeona before—everyone had—but she hadn't grasped how *many* people had been stored in the fleet, waiting to arrive on their new planet. There were somewhere around three hundred Admins, including all the hangers-on—who had the same genemods as their bosses—and somewhere over a thousand Vagals. There had only ever been two or three watch sergeants awake on each ship at once. To see them all in one place was intimidating. Why did they need such a large military presence? Did they think they were going to be fighting off aliens on whatever planet they landed on?

The Generationals outnumbered Vagals and Admins combined by ten to one, but in the original plan, the Generationals would have made up a much smaller fraction of the crew. They were only supposed to travel for three generations instead of over fourteen, looking for a world that wouldn't kill them on contact. For that matter, no one trusted the native life on this planet either. From all reports, it was incredibly fast-growing.

Agetha piloted the drone to the edge of the blast zone created by the ships landing. The vast flat plain was nearly ten kilometers across, and she could see all of it through the VR rig. She stamped a foot on the glass-like ground, then winced at the vibration through her knee. The strange fungal growths had been burnt to nothing in this area, though outside the blast radius flora undulated and shifted in the wind like a strange, gelatinous forest. Something with a lot of tendrils—or maybe legs—about the size of a mobility chair slithered across the tops of the not-trees. She couldn't tell if she was watching a vine grow, or if it was a separate creature. Nearby towers of undiscernible growth had been measured at over seventy meters deep, back when a few drones could be spared for long-range scans of Lida. Maybe they did need the Vagals after all.

Currently, all drones were engaged in aiding construction, to build up a first habitat as quickly as possible. They hadn't recorded a full year of weather systems and had to do with forecasting models from the time they'd observed so far. She'd been proud of her work on those. They were protected from strong winds by a ridge of hills forty kilometers away, covered in dense growth, and the nearest ocean—completely filled with the strange flora—was about a hundred kilometers in the other direction. According to her forecast models, they were at little risk of ocean storms or tidal waves. This area was humid, but would be temperate most of the year. She hoped she liked the weather conditions here, because they'd be focused on this little burnt away section for several rotations of the planet at least, getting their grounder legs and the city started.

Speaking of which. Agetha brought the drone down and back to its charging base, then took off her VR rig. She stood up with a creak from her mobility chair, wobbling in the still-unfamiliar gravity. After only two days on the surface, none of the Generationals were used to the intense pressure. Even with the bone growth supplements they'd all been taking, there had been dozens of broken bones and at least five deaths so far. The Vagals and Admin were fine of course. They had musculature systems built up from hundreds of megaseconds—or rather, dozens of Earth years—of living in a gravity well. It made sense now, why the watch sergeants had only been awake for limited time periods, making sure they didn't lose too much muscle tone. The sus-ani devices had a way to artificially preserve bone and muscle mass. The Generationals had been given no such consideration. Could there have been a way to bring along the technology for even a few of the genemods the Admins and Vagals had been given? Supposedly the infrastructure for any meaningful modifications took far too much space and resources to travel with. They would have to recreate the technology on Lida, if that was ever possible.

Agetha blinked her eyes against the harsh sunlight, even through her sunglasses. The light here was different than on the ships, more...diffuse, though brighter. Even though there was one source of illumination—Target Eleven, "Lev"—it felt like the light was all around her.

She took a few steps, wincing at the pain in her knees and what felt like a cow riding on her back. With a grunt, she collapsed back into the chair, her breath coming in gasps, her heart racing. It was better than the day before. At least the oxygen content on Lida was adequate. More than, in fact. It was higher than the content on the ship and on old Earth.

Coming back to the hut in a few hours, she messaged Daved. *Keep those potatoes warm for me.*

Keep? They haven't gotten warm yet. I'll keep trying, came the answer.

Daved would keep trying, as long as he possibly could. She bumped her chair along the glassed dirt toward the rest of her work crew. The two of them were together, and that was all that mattered. And if today was better than yesterday, then tomorrow would be better than today.

* * *

4 days after landing

"This day is absolutely fucked, muux," Anderson complained to his commanding officer, Lieutenant Noce. "The Generationals are moving as slow as slugs, three bots have welded themselves to the superstructure of the Xaman Ek, and the fungal mass out there already shows signs of new growth over the edges of the glassed area. If we don't get this habitat fixed up before the week is out, we're going to be living in mushrooms. Muux."

"I can't fix the first two," Noce said, "but I might be able to help you out with the last part."

Anderson perked up. Ever since he'd been thawed out like some half-forgotten turkey in the bottom of the freezer, he'd felt out of place. Add to that his Vagal implant had been acting up, making him twitchy all the time. He'd been told the cybernetic system—given to all the Vagal soldiers just before leaving Earth—would take a few months to fully acclimatize to his body. But not counting the time he'd been a human popsicle, he'd only had the implant a month and a half. He'd been one of the last to receive one before joining the fleet.

"Vagal" was a misnomer, anyway. He'd done some research on his own time. It did stimulate the vagal nerve, but also the amygdala, the hypothalamus, the adrenal and pituitary glands, and other body processes. But since the vagal nerve transversed a longer section of the body, it was used by the implant to transmit chemicals through the torso, letting those with the implant recognize and react to danger quicker than those without. The problem was what the implant reacted to as "dangerous" and what was "normal." He'd been in sus-ani for four hundred years and was now on the surface of an alien planet. Nothing was normal.

Noce turned away, leading Anderson to a supply cache in the corner of the hastily thrown-together barracks. Eventually, it would be a multi-story building hosting all the Vagals. For now, it was a bunch of nanotanium plates.

Once awoken, Anderson had bounced around the UGS Hasamelis until landing procedures started, uncertain of what to do. The implant had buzzed and fizzed in his head, triggering his nervous system at odd times and places, leaving him sleepless, or keyed up when he should have been calm. Every disruption weighed on him, and he hadn't known where to go or what to do. He told himself once the command structure was fully operational, he'd feel better. But now it was, and he didn't. He hoped Noce had direction for him. Commanding officers should be good for something.

"I think we're going to get good use out of these," Noce said as they opened a crate. Shiny tubes and packaged propellant tanks smiled back at Anderson.

"Flamethrowers?" Anderson said, hope flaring in his voice. "I thought these were restricted use?"

"Maybe back on Earth," Noce said. "But those regulations are thousands of years gone. Here, the flora grows so fast it's almost useless to chop it up or cut it back. We're going to fight fungus with fire. In full EVA suits, of course."

Anderson reverentially lifted the flamethrower from its foam bed, running his hands down the sleek structure. His implant suddenly activated all in a rush, and the room felt even smaller than it was. He tracked the bead of condensation running down the far wall, Noce's twinge of pain as they favored their left leg, and the unevenness of the ground beneath his feet. They hadn't bothered with flooring as the surface here was melted glass in all but name.

But when his eyes flicked back down to the flamethrower, his sight seemed to narrow and widen at the same time. He felt like he could see the tool, exploded into component parts, as his hands touched the outside. Tank, flow throttle, ignition, four controls for the width, height, and length of flame, protective heat shield... The list ran through his head like a shopping list.

Anderson turned to the room's entrance, raising the flamethrower to a comfortable level. Even without touching the activation switch, and with the fuel canister safely locked out, he knew, innately, how to work it. For the first time, his implant was actually helping.

"How do you feel about a trek out to the edge of the landing field, Private?" Noce asked from behind him.

"I feel like this day is turning around," Anderson replied.

* * *

7 days after landing

"Have you tried turning it off and back on?" Jane asked Christiaan, who gave her a withering glare from their hunched over position. They were beneath the desk Jane had gotten moved from her office on the UGS St. Christopher. Her assistant was the only one she let look at her like that. "Yes, yes, stupid question." She waved a hand. "And IT hasn't sent anything back yet?"

"Can't tell, ma'am," Christiaan said in their clipped, nasal voice. "It would have come over the network—"

"Which is currently down, yes." Jane bit at a lacquered thumbnail, then made herself stop. The Galaxy Gloss polish resisted chipping, but it was still a bad habit. She'd picked Void Stars for today, and the dots of white zoomed around where her teeth had met nail, a sharp contrast against the glossy black.

Her other hand flashed gestures at the interface floating in front of her eyes. She could at least use the local siloed copies of information while the network flipped off and on like it was possessed by a poltergeist with a fear of commitment. She was trying to arrange fourteen different one-hour meetings in the next ten hours, while the Admin building was literally being constructed around her. She winced as an ear-splitting screech and then a deep thumping sounded through the structure. She glared through the half-finished office to see a lanky Generational pull a riveter half their height away from what used to be a ship bulkhead. They raised a visor, revealing overlarge eyes, checking their work. They were still in a mobility chair, braked on the floor to keep it from sliding away under the pressure of the riveter. At least the Admin building would be solidly built.

It had been seven days since landing, and she assumed they'd keep the week-schedule used on Earth, so one week in. Jane wondered why the bone growth supplements weren't working as well as anticipated. Maybe because they'd been living in zero-G for far longer than anticipated. The physicians assured her most Generationals would soon be out of the mobility chairs, and walking and climbing around the radian. The construction drones from the ships handled the altitude work, so it wasn't that detrimental if much of their workforce was confined to the ground. However, there would be fine detail coming soon which would go a lot faster without eighty percent of the population sitting down.

The network flipped off again, right as Jane blinked an email to send.

"Goddammit," she swore, and pulled the rig off. "I can't get anything done without network."

Christiaan looked up from a phone connected to a blocky wireless hub box. "IT says give them fifteen minutes and they should have it back up."

"Fine, fine." Jane waved a hand and walked to where windows would be installed between her office and a twelfth-story balcony, pushing through the hanging plastic serving as a covering at the moment. She wrinkled her nose at the scent of sawdust and oxidized metal. For now, they dealt with natural ventilation. The air over the landing area was fairly clear of any native biologicals. Everything native had been seared away by the exhaust from the ships—over two thousand degrees Celsius. She couldn't wait until the HVAC was up and running. Fortunately, the landing area was temperate, and would be for most of the year.

Outside, she took in a deep breath of Lida's air, and grimaced. Even cleared of biological contaminants, the planet smelled strange. It wasn't horrible—in fact it was quite a nice, fruity smell. Like roasting apples, but mixed with layers of rotten leaves and detritus from the forest floor. It reminded her of the woods outside her parent's house in upstate New York, before the hardwoods started to die off. It reminded her of home, and it shouldn't do that. This was an alien planet.

There were no trees here, however. No grass underfoot, no woody bushes of any kind. She peered through the hulks of the generational ships into the jungle-like mass of flora—blue and green and orange— off in the distance. It moved, though there wasn't any wind. Something with rudimentary wings shot out of the canopy mass, but quickly dove back in. There were no distinct shapes in the mass. Just tendrils and extensions and growths piled on one another, dozens of meters high. Close-up reports said creatures seemingly made of fungal and plant elements crawled through the mass, from ones that were a millimeter long to ones bigger than a person. She watched the mass for a time, her eyes catching motion here and there. It was oppressively dense, threatening, but not immediately so. They would have time to build.

She shivered and looked over the glassy landing area instead. Alpha Radian was laid out like a pizza slice, one eighth of the total circular diameter, with the landed ships as the pepperoni. Kilometer-high pepperoni. The entire burn zone was much larger than this radian, and in fact the tip of Alpha's pizza slice only went to the midpoint of the circle created by the ships. Everything they had was contained in a triangle, five kilometers long and little over three and a half kilometers on the short side. The rest of the pizza would consist of radians Beta through Theta, eight in all. They would build Beta on one side of Alpha, and Gamma on the other side, then repeat the process with the next two, until Theta was the final slice, directly across from Alpha, completed some ten years from now. If all went well. The first generation of the native inhabitants would likely help build the last radian.

Jane rested her hands on the rails, seeing not scorched rock and massive ships, but a completed city, shining against the roiling mass of the flora that engulfed this planet. And then paths cut through the fungal towers, pushing it back, containing it, as they connected this city to others, around Lida.

"Ma'am? Network's back up," called Christiaan. Jane shook herself and went back in. That was a long time from now.

"What is it?" she asked as Christiaan tensed, eyes scanning something in their HUD.

"Reports from animal husbandry," Christiaan said. "They're saying sixty percent of the cattle are showing a strange infection, possibly viral in nature, though they're also showing signs of fungal growth."

"Of course it's also fungal," Jane shot back. "What else is there on this shitty planet? The viruses probably have fungal infections and passed it on."

She closed her eyes for a moment—reaching for calm—then opened them and found her rig, placing the headset on. She waded through the four...*hundred* emails she'd gotten since the network went down to find the offending report. She scanned through the words, but couldn't make much of the technical jargon.

"Do they have any solutions yet?"

Christiaan shook their head. "It's not responding to standard anti-virals or fungals. Might need a new combination." They paused, eyebrows drawn as they read more. "In fact, it looks like the report's being updated with the first three livestock deaths."

"Dammit." Jane pounded the table with a fist, then shook her hand out. "We knew there would be losses. The Generationals are smart. They'll find a solution soon. Just let them work while I get the administration section moving faster than a crawl. Things will get better soon."

Jane realized she was biting her thumbnail again, teeth white against the black gloss.

* * *

13 days after landing

Jiow wiped sweat off her brow, but felt dirt smear across her forehead from her work glove. She grimaced and tried to shake the dirt off, blinking away sleep. Even controlling drones was a lot of work, if you'd been at it for over five hundred kiloseconds straight. At least she was out of the mobility chair. She'd been one of the first, for whatever reason, almost a megasecond after they'd landed—or what Admin was calling a week and a half. She was having trouble getting used to the archaic terms. Evidently seven days was a good number for a week, as opposed to the five off/five on work cycle they'd used on the ships. And why twenty-four hours in a day? They'd had to add five leap minutes every two days to keep the calendar correct. Wouldn't it have been easier to adjust the length of an hour?

But that was Admin, still steeped in Earth culture, though the planet might not even exist anymore. They'd traveled at relativistic speeds for over twelve thousand six hundred megaseconds, or what they called four hundred years, and who knew how long, objectively, it had been since the ship departed?

Jiow was daydreaming again. She shook herself and looked up in time to see one of the drone herd she was controlling sag under the weight of a nanotanium sheet, halfway up the structure of the Khonsu. A spike of panic flashed through her, and she scrambled for the correct interface. Controlling fine movements for one drone was harder than controlling a crowd, and she'd been at it for too long. Just before it crashed into the superstructure, she found the correct view in her HUD and commanded the drone into a controlled descent, away from the side of the ship.

The construction drone was running low on charge, which she would have caught sooner if she hadn't been nearly asleep. Admin was running them ragged. She popped another stim pill, waiting for the jolt. Her heart raced and she swallowed a queasy feeling, waiting for her body to calm past the initial rush.

How much was five hundred kiloseconds? Five days? Six? She was going to be converting timescales her whole life at this rate.

Drones. Jiow looked back up, barely catching another of her herd before it drifted into the hull. She'd have to bring this bunch down to the charging station and raise another herd. They were getting low on power. Should have caught that before. Had she already thought that?

While she had the thought captured, she controlled the whole lot of her drones back to the storage depot, next to two of the eight immense ship's batteries they scavenged from the hulks. In space, they'd been kept at full charge by the ships' ramscoops indefinitely. Here, the colonists had to come up with other methods of energy generation. The batteries were responsible for powering all of the construction and keeping the drones running. Until they got a viable, renewable source of power up and running, they would depend on the batteries' last full charge from space to power their colony. They'd run one down to nothing already, and were halfway through these two. Basic solar panels were up and taking the load off, but until they had enough to both run the colony and charge the batteries to keep things powered when the sun was hidden, they'd have to rely on the remaining power.

Ah yes. That was the reason Admin had them running six days without sleep. It didn't make her feel better. Agetha and Daved were in one of these teams as well, but Frank was probably enjoying himself, studying fungus slices and not running on stim pills.

"No, not there, *here*."

"But the plate isn't the required thickness. It's bad. Needs to be recycled."

The voices broke into the fog of Jiow's brain, one growling and gruff, the other higher.

"Do you *see* a recycling plant around here? Maybe a brand new nanotanium printer? Now put the plate in the pile, soldier, we need the barracks completed before we all die of exposure."

"Not a soldier, you ass. I'm a trained metallurgist and engineer, and I'm saying this plate is *bad*."

"Doesn't matter. You're under my watch and in my command structure."

Jiow remembered to set her new herd to continue the plate removal the other drones had started, then looked around.

A Vagal soldier was growling and pointing at a Generational Jiow vaguely knew—was it Gareth? Or maybe Phil?—one of those horrible E-Vapors hanging from her mouth. All the Vagals seemed to have the habit. Growing up in an enclosed environment with limited oxygen had quelled any sort of smoking or vapor-producing habit among the Generationals.

Tensions were high with the lack of sleep, but Jiow was used to mediating between her family members while working on the ship's plumbing. She lurched to intervene before Phil (or Gareth) decided to deck the Vagal. Jiow had felt their power and reflexes up close.

"You want your bedroom wall to crumble, thirty or forty megaseconds after we finish building? It will just waste time in the future," Gareth—definitely Gareth—said in his tenor.

"Yes, we'll take care of it then, Generational," the Vagal said. She reached for Gareth's HUD, as if she would control his drones herself. "Nothing goes to waste."

Gareth danced back. "I'm not wasting anything. If you'd lived on the ship instead of taking a twelve *thousand* megasecond nap, you'd know that." The man threw out a projection of the plate, still halfway up Khonsu's height, and pointed to a scratch halfway along the length. "That's an impact crater, likely gathered from the descent to Lida. This sheet needs to be used for something less structural."

"*Everything* is structural," the Vagal growled down at Gareth. "We're building the fucking skeleton of the colony."

Jiow puffed up between the two, reaching a hand out to either side. "Just hold on a minute folks, we're all tired. Let's figure this out reasonably."

"With your degree in toilet maintenance?" Gareth shot back, and even the Vagal snorted a laugh. Jiow narrowed her eyes at the other Generational. She was trying to help.

"Here, let me see your log," she said, pushing down her desire to punch the scrawny man. "I've got some lower priority piles on my queue." She sent a query request to trade drone objectives with Gareth, but the man swiped a negative to the request.

"I've been denied on every blemish I've found so far. The colony is going to be riddled with fault lines. I'm not going to let another defect fall into the cracks."

"The colony doesn't need to resist meteor impact, just rain. Let it go, Generational." The Vagal leaned in and cupped her fingers around Gareth's HUD eyepiece, likely throwing random commands to the drone herd.

"Hey!" Jiow and Gareth shouted at the same time. Touching another person's HUD was a major misfire. Gareth danced back, accidentally tearing the rig from his head, and Jiow tried to push the Vagal's arm out of the way, but it was like moving a tree limb. The Vagal, in response, shoved Jiow down before grabbing Gareth with the other hand. She fell into a heap on the cold ground, banging her knee. She wished the Vagals had never been woken up.

"Give it back!" Gareth called, trying to claw the giant Vagal's hand away. Jiow wiped smeared dust and dirt from her face, struggling to her feet. She still wasn't that steady. What was a Vagal thinking, pushing a person who was still getting used to the gravity of this pla—

They all froze at the grinding, tearing sound above. Jiow's stomach dropped like she was in a full-burn course correction, and a cry went up. Other Generationals pointed up, or flashed projections from their HUDs.

Jiow scrambled through menus on her own HUD, heart racing, trying to get a picture from her herd. When she finally got the right angle, her eyes went wide. There was a twenty-meter-long slice of nanotanium hull metal grinding a gash through the side of the Khonsu, getting bigger by the second.

"Get control!" Jiow screamed to Gareth. The Vagal had released his HUD and was frantically swiping through her own.

"I'm trying, but the drone's caught between the sheet and the hull," Gareth screamed back. "The sheet's turning! I need to get the drone to... No. Oh no. It's going to drop...Oh shit. Run!" He put actions to words and took off, stumbling toward the next nearest ship, the K'uei-Hsing.

The Vagal cursed under her breath, a steady stream of invective. No help. The supersoldiers had no deep-space reflexes, not like Generationals who spent their entire existence one nanotanium plate away from the void of space.

"Get the other herds out of the way!" Jiow screamed. "The sheet's coming down. Uncontrolled descent!" She ran too.

People scattered, and Jiow spared only one look back and up before heading after Gareth. The picture was frozen in her mind, the plate in freefall, half a kilometer up in the air. It was from near the nose, and must have been close to twenty meters long, and likely more than three centimeters thick. Her back tingled as she ran, every moment expecting the impact. She didn't want to see what size crater it would make.

She rounded the side of the barracks structure as she was knocked to her knees. Her ears rung and a vibration passed through her like a hammer to the chest. She'd been a small child when the fleet had encountered a residual shock wave from a dying star. Everyone had buckled into their cabins and the resulting vibrations felt much the same.

Then the real shock hit. This was not something she was prepared for.

The ground jumped around her, pebbles and glass shards skipping up and falling back, only to be met by another ripple of the ground. She twisted on the ground, hands to her ears at the rumbling vibrato, and gasped as shards bit into her ankles. They were like tiny needles, stabbing and bruising. She couldn't have stood if she tried. She could see the sheet itself, imbedded in the glassified ground. The tip was still visible and the nanotanium sheet *wobbled*, something metal that thick shouldn't be able to do. The vibration was not something heard so much as felt, but it made her brain hurt. The skeletons of ships groaned around her in concert, swaying on half-deconstructed girders.

She pulled herself to hands and knees as the vibration died, leaving a silence like Jiow would never hear again. She gasped at the gashes in her legs. She didn't think any bones were broken, but her pants were shredded, blood running down her legs. She struggled to her feet. Fortunately, the area directly below the Khonsu was kept clear, for just such an emergency. Some had not gotten far enough from the falling plate in time, and Jiow could make out cries for help, some with blood running from their nostrils and ears from the intense sonic attack. Others began emerging from hiding places, slowly creeping toward the plate and injured colonists, waving away clouds of dust. Jiow limped up to Gareth as they both approached the nanotanium wreckage.

"I guess that one will go to the defect pile after all," Jiow said, and Gareth shook his head.

"If only that Vagal hadn't been such an ass about—"

CREEEEEAAAAAAAK

The sound tore the air, and as one, heads tilted upward. Then the screaming began.

Jiow's perception slowed. The UGS Khonsu, already missing most of its plates and some of its support structure, listed away from the gouge the plate had made. It was off balance. It was going to fall. The memory of the plate's impact shuddered through her. This would be a thousand times worse.

"Move!" Jiow shouted, but it was lost in the chatter and screams from everyone else. Gareth was already gone, and Jiow cast one look back at the length of the ship before running the other way. She had to get behind another ship. It was the only structure that might stop the force of wind and hail of debris that would come from this impact.

She was thirty meters into her sprint toward the K'uei-Hsing when she heard the resonating *POP POW BING*, like a high-tension wire snapping against its mooring. Jiow stopped running despite herself, to see the top third of the Khonsu bending, nanotanium girders twisting apart like taffy. The ship hadn't been designed for forces like these, in a gravity well, with half its structure missing, and vibrating like a gong. As she watched, a tear began along the nanotanium plates, from the original impact site across the hull, as if the Khonsu had decided to grow a gaping mouth, filled with sharp nanotanium teeth.

One plate had buried itself ten meters into the slagged, rocky landing site. The top third of the Khonsu was far larger.

Jiow ran toward the K'uei-Hsing, counting seconds in her head.

When she got to "six," the earth picked her up bodily and threw her, arms pinwheeling.

* * *

14 days after landing

"Tell me when you get close—but not too close," Agetha told Daved over the network. He'd volunteered to inspect the damage visually.

"I'll be careful." His voice crackled. Communications were not at their best right now. "I'll check back in when I'm nearer. Got some rough terrain."

Eighty-one people dead. Twenty-three Vagal supersoldiers and fifty-eight Generationals. Agetha clenched and unclenched her hands, reading through the list of losses. She'd known five of the Generationals. Jiow had miraculously survived, though she was in critical condition in the field hospital, with hairline fractures in both legs, a broken arm, a pierced lung, and multiple bruises and lacerations. Others were worse off. The crash had been unusually fatal—many of those injured had died immediately. All personnel with medical training had been called in to help, pulling them off the construction teams. They had a good supply of nanomedical devices left from the ships, which was supposed to last them for several years, until they got some manufacturing facilities up and running. The casualties from the crash would use many of them. Broken bones and even ruptured organs could be healed quickly. The trauma to the colony would take longer.

Agetha had been pulled back to her analyst position for the moment, along with a third of the pool, to sort through the damages. Fewer people in construction right now hardly mattered, but these losses weighed in her gut. Admin had put everything the fleet had into the gamble of building this colony. They should have stayed in space.

The drone charging station was gone. The only construction herds left were the ones that had been out when the top of the Khonsu broke off, a fifth of the original number. Their construction capabilities were crippled, animal pens were wrecked with the livestock crushed, irreplaceable nanotanium plates bent, EVA suits ripped, and canisters of chemicals vented to air. She'd worked her whole life in risk assessment. The add-on consequences kept spiraling through her brain. She couldn't guess how many months this would set them back.

From the first data scrapes after the dust cloud had blown away, she'd determined too many lower plates had been removed too early from the Khonsu, causing instability in the tall, thin structure. Two ship batteries had exploded when the massive section fell on them, tearing through the Khonsu's superstructure. What remained of the nanotanium hull had actually shielded the larger area from the capacitor release, as the batteries had been under the bulk of the ship. In a stroke of perverse chaos, the force of the impact plus the explosion re-directed much of the energy back up into the atmosphere. Otherwise, more ships might have toppled, and the entire newborn military complex would have been destroyed. As it was, the K'uei-Hsing was listing, and four of the deceased Vagals had been crushed under the collapsing front entrance to the complex, where crates of general supplies had been stored. Admin had directed power rationing until the solar plant was fully operational, but that rationing would delay construction even longer.

"Can you see anything?" Agetha asked Daved over the network. He'd been silent too long. Her leave from running drones was only long enough to do a full analysis on the wreckage, and she was parked in the back half of the new barracks—the half that was still standing.

There was a second of silence, and Agetha gripped the table in front of her, knuckles going white. Then: "Hard to tell." Daved's normally cheery voice had been muted in the last few days on Lida. "The ground is still too hot to get close. I can see the rupture in the top of Khonsu's hull." There were sounds of footsteps and cursing as Daved maneuvered around something. "The fall opened up some sort of natural cavern, beneath the radian, as far as I can tell. The crack goes all the way to...oh no."

"What?" Agetha asked, her heart seizing, but there was only the sound of running. It wasn't Daved that was in danger. It couldn't be.

"I found where it intersected the animal pens," Daved said, breathless, and something in Agetha loosened. It wasn't him. "There's a giant hole here, and it's hard to see, but I think some of the livestock fell in. I'm trying to look in, but—" More rustling, and then a curse. Agetha's hands tightened, but the network didn't have bandwidth for video yet. There was scuffling, and rapid movement, and something that sounded like a body falling.

"Daved? Are you there?" Agetha leaned forward, though the VR set was on her head. She couldn't get any closer.

"Ow. Damn." Daved's voice was faint, as if his rig was out of place. "One of my shoes started melting and I fell over getting it free. Need to draw back for now."

"Copy." Agetha tried to keep the worry from her voice as her husband clicked off. She had to do something to keep from fretting over him. She opened another spreadsheet to tally animal deaths, along with human ones. They'd only been on Lida fourteen days, and already crew were dead. Eighty-one colonists out of just over twenty thousand total. It sounded like such a small number, put like that.

She checked her texts. Nothing from Daved yet. He must be getting to safety. Not running toward danger, like he always did.

Instead, she scrolled through the list of fifty cows that had so far succumbed to an infection, with no cure in sight. Some of the chickens were starting to develop respiratory infections too, though the pigs were thriving. The other challenges on Lida wouldn't pause for them to recover from the Khonsu's fall. Anything to keep her mind off her husband.

They were struggling with situating their animals on this planet, just like the humans. The fleet had brought many animal embryos with them, but the actual livestock on the ship consisted of cows, goats, pigs, sheep, alpacas, chickens, ducks, and bees. There was also a smattering of sparrows and rats which had stowed aboard, and efforts to exterminate them had completely failed. The bees and chickens adapted best to zero-G, the ducks always seemed confused, and those with four legs were perpetually grumpy about paddling through the air to reach their food. Horses had never been taken out of sus-ani, after the first disastrous trial on board—soon after Target One—so the legends went.

Now they were in a gravity well, the livestock were slowly learning to walk again. The rats and sparrows had promptly disappeared into the towers of fungal matter, and aside from a few suspicious squawks, hadn't been seen again. Seems the fungus had solved the problem the humans couldn't.

"I'm back," Daved said as he reconnected, and Agetha jumped. She'd been reabsorbed into her work. "I'm sending a video. Take a look."

"Will do. You alright? No more melted shoes?" She switched to the video that had popped up in her inbox. Realtime video feed over network was too costly except for extreme cases, so they had to make do with workarounds.

"I'm good, but it's like being near the ship's engines out here. Go ahead and watch."

The shaky video—jumping as Daved walked quickly toward the crash site—showed a gash in the ground dozens of meters deep. The top of the Khonsu rose far above the view of the video, except for one moment when Daved looked up. Seeing the ships from the outside was a shock, after living on the inside all her life. They looked both far too large, and not big enough to have held all they did and so many generations.

The tip of the nose had dug a trench deep in the ground. Daved followed the crack leading from the foremost jagged nanotanium plate to a section of sunken dirt and rock, opening into a massive, crumbling opening. One side held a dangling fence, wire strung out and fence posts jittering back and forth in the air. A chicken sat on one of them, flapping its wings, though even from here, Agetha could also see the corpse of a sheep, crushed where a massive boulder had split and sheared.

The video panned down into the blackness of the hole and she heard a pained blatting of a goat, plus grunts from what might have been a pig. It was too dark to see the extent of the cave. Daved's hand came into the field of view, holding a rock, which he tossed forward. There was one, two, three seconds of pause before she barely heard the *clink* of it landing over the pained cries of animals.

The video moved forward, and Agetha caught the spark of a power conduit that still somehow conducted electricity. It swung in the darkness, and she glimpsed smoothed rock walls, and a clump of mushrooms. She flipped back over to Daved's channel.

"Saw it," she said. "Did you catch the fungus underground? We need to show this to Admin, fast."

"Yeah, I was hoping you would tell me I was seeing things," Daved's tired voice said over the connection. "I think there's a natural cavern here. We wouldn't have found it until we started digging foundations. Can you handle the alert? I need to round up the other vets and see how many animals we can save."

"I'm on it," Agetha said. "Be careful. Don't climb down into that pit until others know where you are and you have the right harnesses. This isn't zero-G, you know. I can't have just anyone cook me dinner."

Daved gave a weak chuckle, but she could hear the breathlessness in his voice. "I'm quickly learning about gravity. I've been out of the chair for two days, and I still feel like I'm carrying a ship on my back. I'll request the Vagals to retrieve the animals, for meat if for nothing else. Those supersoldiers seem to have no trouble adapting to the gravity."

"Stay safe. Love you," she said.

"You too," he said, and cut the line.

Agetha shook her head and turned back to her spreadsheets. This was going to be one shitstorm of a report.

* * *

14 days after landing

Anderson hefted his new flamethrower and turned on his headlamp, gazing down into the trench torn through the landing area. His team of eight other Vagals, all of them under Noce's command, stood nearby, getting their gear ready.

The Vagal who'd been involved in the original dispute was dead, or she would have faced extreme punishment from the higher-ups. There was plenty of blame and pointing fingers going around in the top Vagal command and Admin ranks. Not for the first time, his low rank had saved him from a lot of bother.

"Check those ropes," he pointed out to Brown, whose harness looked loose.

"Yes, sir," she said. The others double-checked without him asking.

"EVA suits secure?" He checked his own visor, still open for now. Over half the team was forced to wear compromised and repaired suits. Many had been damaged in the crash and they were still digging most of them out of the wreckage.

There was a chorus of agreement. The suits were a formality for any unknown environment, and they'd been on the planet for two weeks already. He didn't anticipate any issues.

The remains of the Khonsu loomed above them, casting the hole into shadow. It reminded him of war-torn cities back on Earth, something he'd traveled trillions of kilometers and hundreds of years to get away from, but at least investigating this creepy cavern gave him some action. During the last eight days, he'd gone out to the edge of the landing blast zone twice to burn down reaching filaments and vines crawling their way into what would be Alpha Radian. The new growth could add as much as ten meters of length a day—musky, shiny wet-looking tendrils more like roots than the fine fungal filaments he now knew were called hyphae—but it was make-work duty. They'd burn the vegetation out permanently when they started construction. It wasn't like the growth could create a new meters-high jungle to replace the one that had been burned away here—not before they started building in earnest.

Anderson puffed on his E-Vapor through his open visor. It was his seventh today, what with the chaos going on. His implant had started triggering whenever he got close to the fungal growth, noting how much attention he paid to it. Other Vagals said that their implants were doing the same, reacting to danger that wasn't there. The device had a tiny risk/reward-based intelligence and training them seemed to be an individual matter.

A gaggle of Generationals, some still in their chairs, made noise around the entrance. The one who'd found this, a short—for a Generational—man with mahogany skin and a nice smile, told them where the injured animals were and what he had seen. Still had those strange large eyes, though.

Anderson didn't hear any bleats or grunts, though it had only taken an hour to assemble this team. At least they'd have real meat tonight. The vat-grown stuff was chewy, but Generationals didn't seem to notice the difference.

"Lines secure?" Noce asked from their connection back at the barracks, and this time there was a round of affirmatives. "Then get in there. Find out how deep this thing is."

Anderson rappelled down into the cavern with his team, his headlamp cutting a swath of brightness down one wall. Most had their visors up still, taking a last smoke while they could. The lights of E-Vapors around him were like a bunch of angry red eyes, staring into the cave. Almost all of the Vagals used them, though they'd been warned that they would have to ration them soon. Smoking whatever concoction was in the things kept the tremors down, unfortunate byproducts of the increased metabolism of the supersoldiers. Over the last few days, Anderson had gone through over a dozen a day, and he had colleagues who had smoked more. They'd need to find an alternative soon, or the Vagals would start to get twitchy, and that was never good when you were the group carrying guns.

His feet hit the ground with a *thump* and Anderson panned around the cavern, splashing his headlamp's light over the walls. The others were doing the same, making a hypnotic, twisting shape. His heartrate increased as his implant pumped something through his system, and he tried to slow his heavy breathing. It was just a cave. He stopped moving, focusing on one section of wall, a pattern coming clear. It looked...wet. It reminded him of the new growth out by the edge.

"Over here," he said, and half the squad followed him. The other half set up a protective perimeter, scanning for the animals, or anything else down here. Sidorov lit another E-Vapor as he watched.

Closer to the wall, he saw a clear line between dry rock and glistening stone. There was what looked like a short, metallic shag carpet, clinging to the wall. That was what gave the shine, what his implant had latched on to. Above that line were a few tendrils of growth, clinging to the rock. The heat barrier from the landing ships' engines must have sterilized down to this line.

"It's not wet," said Niles, running a gloved hand down the wall, disrupting the shine. "It's the reflection of minerals, caught in this web. I think the fungus is pulling them out of the rock."

"What's a mushroom need with minerals?" Anderson grumbled, but phoned the discovery into Noce, who said they would convey it to Admin. Anderson raised a finger to the web of roots, not quite touching it, noting how they sparkled under the headlamp. His E-Vapor was reflected as a single red blur on the surface.

"We found them!" a Vagal said from across the cave, and Anderson ran to the other half of his team. He stopped next to Brown, who was standing in front of a large mound, covered in all sorts of shapes from innocent button mushrooms to growths like red clutching fingers, others like clumps of coral, and still others like mats of moss, crinkled brain-like clusters, and graceful honeycombs of material. Why were they all growing out of a rock on the floor...?

Anderson slowed. That wasn't a rock. That was a cow. His implant pumped some chemical through his system and his hands tightened on his 'thrower. The animals had only been down here a day at most, some surely less than that. It was obviously dead, half its chest rotted away, turned into a fungal breeding ground. Inside, dark, almost-black caps shone wetly against lighter red ones in the light—the colors of venous and arterial blood.

"The rest?" Anderson asked. He spit out his E-Vapor and closed his visor. He didn't want to breathe in whatever had done that. Or maybe the cow had eaten mushrooms and they had somehow grown in its stomach?

"They're around us, all the same. What does Noce say?" Brown asked. She panned her headlamp and Anderson followed her, seeing crumpled bodies of cows, goats, and chickens, all sporting clusters of growths in more shapes than he'd ever seen. Clingy webbing spread between open wounds, while fleshy wet discs like ears grew from exposed bone, and clusters of bright red domes poked from eye sockets.

"Contacting Admin," Anderson said, watching another Vagal, Jones, lean into the first cow with a sampling kit, trying to get data for the analysts. The attempts were rewarded with a puff of some sort of dust from the mushroom.

"Close your visors!" he called, and lights jumped as Vagals dropped their E-Vapors. A round of *hiss-clicks* said the visors were shut.

He twitched as his implant pumped juices around his body, his head swiveling. Was it reacting only to the mushrooms? Was there something else it identified as a threat? The higher-ups said the implants didn't create anything new, just augmented what the body naturally made. But sweat popped out on his brow, and his pinky finger tapped on the side of the flamethrower. He stilled it with an effort.

Anderson jerked as Noce's voice sounded in his ear. "Admin says clean out the fungus and rescue any animals." He swallowed, trying to overcome the need to pull in more air than the filter in his suit allowed. His vision picked out more mushrooms on the walls, the floor, veins of minerals, root mats. He couldn't tell what the target was when nothing moved but his teammates, but his implant insisted there was one. *What was the threat?*

"Yes, muux," Anderson replied, and his voice sounded too high in his ears. "We won't need to take any animals out, unless you want more samples. They're all—"

He was interrupted by a scream and his flamethrower was up in a flash. His light panned along the ground to reveal Jones bent over the cow, holding his helmet in his hands and screaming, though the sound was going all ragged. Anderson ran, each stride feeling more powerful than it should be. What was his implant doing? That he had the time to think these thoughts in the five strides to reach his teammate...

Anderson caught Jones just before he hit the ground, but when he spun the man around, he cried out and dropped the corpse. Inside his visor, his face from his nose to his throat was gone, a steaming mass of gelatinous liquid. Jones's body lay crumpled on the ground, whatever was on him eating the rest of the way through his head.

Spores? Acid particulate? Skin contact? His mind raced through the ways Jones could have been compromised. Had Anderson put his visor down in time? Not enough data.

There was another scream, across the cavern, and he spun, swallowing bile. Niles was spitting blood, a spear of wet-looking fibrous material through his midsection. He was the one who had touched the wall.

"Two down!" he screamed, and the team sprang to action, 'throwers flaring white and blue at their tips. They formed a protective circle as Anderson ran to Niles. His breath fogged his visor. Too fast. Too hot. What was in his lungs?

His implant tried to find patterns, directing his attention left and right seemingly at random. He stopped next to Niles, his right hand reaching to pull him away from the wall. He was still breathing and Anderson reached behind him. Could he break the shaft? Get him free? Another mushroom opened its mouth—mouth!?—and grabbed his hand with needle-sharp teeth.

"Gaaah!" Anderson tore his hand away, shreds of his glove coming apart along with the mushroom. Half the mouth was caught on the fabric and he pulled it free, threw it away with a shiver. He slapped a patch on his glove.

The cries and whooshing of flamethrowers behind him said he wasn't the only one attacked.

"Right, you bastards." He reached again, with a speed only a Vagal could match, and pulled Niles free, though he was certain the man was already dead. All twitching gone, Anderson fired up his 'thrower and doused the wall. The mushrooms writhed, their twisting desiccation almost like shrieks.

"You're clear to use weapons on the fungus," Noce said belatedly in his ear.

"Bit late for that, muux," Anderson growled back. All three attacks had happened within seconds of each other. There was coordination here, whether the mushrooms were interconnected or there was some other method of communication. His implant had been pumping concoctions into his bloodstream because it made the connections before he did. He would trust it after this.

He ran to the other six Vagals, who were back-to-back in the middle of the cavern, painting the walls with fire. They made a space for him.

"I need evac for the casualties," he called, as four Vagals dragged Jones and Niles toward the exit ropes. Anderson flexed his hand. The patch on his glove was holding, but with what the implant was pumping through him, he couldn't feel if there was any pain. He hoped his boosted metabolism would guard him from the brief time his suit had been open.

He made eye contact with the remaining two Vagals and hefted his 'thrower.

"Clear it all out!" he yelled, and was rewarded with a blaze of light. Gouts of flame incinerated the mats of silvery roots cascading down the walls. High-pitched keening accompanied the destruction.

Anderson held out a hand when Sidorov's flame got too close to the animal corpses. There hadn't been any more attacks. Had they cleared the danger?

"Let me call it in." He looked to his HUD to acknowledge the connection with Noce, who had been listening. "You want us to save the animal remains?"

"Good question. Hold," Noce said, their voice slightly lagged, even at this close distance. Was there signal interference? Anderson tapped a toe impatiently, eyeing the burning walls. A moment later they were back. "Save one of each species," Noce commanded. "The rest should be destroyed."

"Yes, muux." Anderson relayed the information to the team and marked one cow, goat, and chicken to save. "We'll be out of here in a few moments."

But when the fire hit the second goat corpse, it erupted in a cloud of tiny, winged things that shot toward him. His implant was already forcing blood to his muscles, and he ducked before he knew what he was doing. The winged creatures plastered the visor of the Vagal behind him, Wilson, as Anderson rolled away from the cloud. Wilson coughed once, then collapsed, her visor melted away and nose already frothing blood.

"Back!" Anderson yelled as he crabbed toward the exit. Another cloud of acid gnats erupted from the cow at head height. Anderson threw himself forward, the buzzing of tiny wings passing just above his helmet. They plastered Sidorov's front and his EVA warped and burned away. He could see the Vagal's skin sagging underneath.

Anderson ran for the rope.

PART FIVE

Creeping

15 days after landing

The next day, Anderson stood on the cavern floor, sunlight filtering down through the broken surface of the ground above him. A different, and living, Vagal team of nine was assembled, Anderson second-in-command under a Vagal named Corporal Hendricks. Sergeant Noce had delegated this incursion to a higher authority than Anderson, for which he was grateful. Admin insisted the cavern had to be fully cleared and sterilized even though Vagal command argued the hole could be sealed over with less potential loss of life. The Generationals would need to dig foundations in this place and Admin wanted to use the opening for extra storage. What Admin wanted, Admin got.

"Armor on?" Anderson asked his team. A few rays of the morning sunlight reflected off shiny teal plastic, covering the team from head to toe. They looked like ambulatory popsicles. There was a chorus of agreement. Since the EVA suits hadn't kept out the attacks from the local flora, Noce had sent a request to dig out the full combat armor from storage. The suits were made of high-density polymers which were supposed to keep out air contaminants, heat, cold, biological weapons, and blunt impacts. It had taken approval all the way from Admin Xi Wenqing to reactivate the armored powersuits. They had still been covered with clingwrap from Earth. The suits had been packed only for special contingencies, and there weren't enough suits for all the Vagals. Evidently that decision had been made by Earth bureaucrats hundreds of years ago to save on cargo space.

Anderson's hand itched where the mushroom had bitten him, and he rubbed his armored glove against the suit's thigh. It didn't help. He'd flushed the area with antifungals and antibiotics as soon as he'd returned to the barracks. The medical team assured him the treatments would kill anything that wasn't supposed to be in his system. Yet his hand still itched inside the skin. It must be the medicine killing off any contaminants.

He'd burned through two dozen E-Vapors over the last day, and the four uninjured on his original team weren't much better. His implant had been making him jumpy for no reason, and he needed to do something. Thus, he'd volunteered to go back into this hellhole. If there was an identified threat right in front of him, his implant might calm down. Hopefully the mushrooms didn't have any tricks that could get past the powersuits.

The walls of the cave around them glistened once more, new root mats climbing the stone, extracting minerals, as if the team yesterday had done nothing. The remains of the livestock—now little more than lumps of matted bones held together with fibrous tendrils—were the starting point of the new growth, coils of fungal matter reaching out from the corpses. They'd secured the original sample Niles took before he was killed, but had collected no others the day before. It would have to do, because Anderson wasn't getting close enough to those things to touch them. This mission had a different objective.

"Light 'em up!" Hendricks called and there was a burst of fire from fifteen flamethrowers. He knew Corporal Hendricks slightly, from before the ships left Earth, but she had done several rotations on watch duty with the processors on the UGS Abeona, and was more familiar with the Generationals.

Flame reflected off teal suits. They'd have to start fuel manufacture as well as E-Vapors sooner than expected if they continued to go through propellant canisters this fast. Anderson winced as the tortured sound of rock being rapidly heated came through his suit's audio.

No. That wasn't the rock heating. That was the fungus. He looked to the Vagals next to him, saw their wide eyes staring back from behind their transparent visors. It wasn't just in his head.

"Trick of the cavern, soldiers," Hendricks called. "Or some biological doohickey. Maybe there are air chambers in the fungus. Remember: the fungus is *not* screaming."

Puffs of the tiny, winged creatures exploded out from corpses of the animals and Anderson gritted his teeth as the cloud filtered past him, some brushing his arm. Would they melt his powersuit? The teal finished dulled at the acidic creature's touch, but held. He aimed his 'thrower high and turned the cloud into a sparkling explosion of sparks.

A Vagal stepped too close to the cavern wall, and flashbacks to Niles' fate went through his mind. The suits would resist impact, but he didn't want to test whether that covered spikes of fungal material as thick as his wrist. He opened audio to the whole group.

"Stay in the center of the chamber. Some of the mushrooms around the edge launched spears yesterday."

"Something here," a voice said over the comm. "Looks like a puddle of fluid leaking from the corpse."

"Burn it," Hendricks ordered.

"Hold," Noce said, from their command post back in the barracks. "Admin wants a sample of anything you find."

Hendricks waved the Vagal away who was pointing their weapon at the pool. "Fine. Sample, quickly. I want to get of here as soon as possible, with no causalities this time."

A teal-suited Vagal bent at the corpse, dipping a glass vial into the goo. "Viscous stuff," they commented. It was hard to tell who was who in the suits.

"Now, burn it," Hendricks said, and three Vagals stepped forward to reduce the animal's remains to ash. The pool of liquid flared up as the flame hit it, like it was an accelerant, and one of the Vagals stumbled back, batting flames from the front of their suit. The polymer held.

"The powersuits seem to be holding up," Hendricks told Noce over the network.

Anderson turned at a commotion from the other side of the cavern, where another teal figure gestured wildly as they stepped back and stamped their boots. As he watched, polycarbonate mesh and armor overlay footwear sizzled and dissolved. The person flailed in a circle until another began pulling their boots off, attempting not to touch the acid.

"Well, spoke too soon," Hendricks reported to Noce. "We'll need to watch the durability of the boots if these suits are used for extensive contact with the local flora."

Anderson's implant jolted him into movement, and he checked the throttle on his 'thrower by reflex. Otherwise, he would have missed the tendrils creeping across his boots.

"Damn fungus!" he tried to pull his foot free, but wet, glistening ropes crawled over his boot and ankle, holding it in place.

"A little help!" he called over the network.

Hendricks stomped over to him as Anderson beat at the mass of material with his 'thrower.

"Check your weapon, Private," Hendricks said. "We're going to test the heat-resistance of these suits."

Before Anderson could object, Hendricks delivered a blast of superheated flame at his boot, reducing enough of the growth to ash for him to stumble back. He gritted his teeth, curling his toes inside the boots to keep them from full contact with the inside of the armor. His boot surface was scorched and black. The material stopped most of the heat, but not all of it.

"Could have warned me a bit more, ma'am," he said.

"Would it have helped?" Hendricks asked. She was grinning inside her visor.

Anderson was about to give her a snappy answer, but his implant sent his heart racing and he jigged sideways as more root-like hyphae broke the ground around his feet. This stuff, whatever it was, spread faster than anything natural on Earth. There had been a firefight on Earth at the Euro-Sinai border a few years before the implant, when the insurgents had let loose a nano-goop bomb they had stolen. The results were similar.

"It's coming from the animals," Anderson said, tracing the reaching vines to the lumps on the cavern floor.

"Watch the floor," Hendricks said over the network. "Burn back to corpses. They're the likely origin. The extra calories must be spurring this growth." She seemed unconcerned, but Anderson's implant was keeping him on edge.

He formed up with the rest of the team and followed the net of roots across the floor, methodically burning their way back to the source.

Why the administrator of the St. Christopher got to decide they would land here was beyond him. Now she was the administrator of the whole colony. Bloody Americans. She'd somehow got the other ship administrators to agree that this place was safe, even after reading the reports on the planet-covering wildlife. Sure, it wasn't sentient, but that didn't mean it wouldn't kill you. Any soldier could tell you that.

There was a snap and a scream across the cavern.

Eight lights came to focus on a teal suit plastered to the cavern wall, vines crawling down the torso.

"Get them out!" Hendricks commanded, and eight flamethrowers blasted the wall around the trapped Vagal.

A scream tore through the network, the voice young. Jocelwitz—a tiny fierce woman—was the one bound to the wall.

"Don't hit the torso or head," Anderson called. "The suit doesn't fully protect against these temperatures!"

"You have another suggestion, Private?" Hendricks called. She kept up a steady stream of fire, crisping tendrils as they grew out of the wall.

"Can we cut her out?"

"No time. If we leave to get cutting tools, she'll be crushed," Hendricks said.

One of Jocelwitz's arms bent at an unnatural angle as her screams pierced Anderson's ears. The vines crushed the teal polymer on her forearm with an audible *crack*.

"We have to chance it," Hendricks said, "Direct fire on the suit."

Eight streams of liquid fire crossed over the teal strapped to the wall, blackening its surface. Jocelwitz's screams grew hoarse as the vines crisped and withered.

"Back off and concentrate on the rest of the fungus," Hendricks commanded as she and Anderson approached Jocelwitz.

One teal arm moved feebly.

"She's still alive," he said, reaching for the suit to help her out of the cavern.

Anderson's implant forced chemicals through his system, and he jumped back just as wet hyphae burst from inside the suit's arm, growing outward like a knot of tree roots in fast motion.

"Shit!" Anderson blasted the area with flame, then peered at the suits visor.

"Jocelwitz? Still with us?"

The inside of the visor was crawling with roots. The faceplate cracked as the head of a mushroom burst through. Anderson backed farther away, trying not to vomit in his helmet.

"Back to the group, Private," Hendricks said. Her voice was low. "Nothing we can do."

She opened communications to the team and to Noce. "One casualty to fungal growth. Powersuits are effective in the field, but not impervious to sustained attack from heat or blunt trauma. Sending suit biometrics for further study."

"Received," Noce's voice was crackly from interference from the cavern. "How are the other objectives proceeding?"

"Slight delays," Hendricks answered. "We should have the cavern cleaned by the end of the day."

Anderson rubbed his hand against his suit's thigh again. It still itched. He hated this planet.

* * *

2 weeks 3 days after landing

Processor Alvin, in full containment suit, walked nervously to the edge of where Gamma and Epsilon Radians would eventually be built, several hundred megaseconds in the future. There was a deep and wide river, which had been partially sterilized by the ships landing, and it was intended to be the water source for the city, assuming it could be satisfactorily purified. Alvin flexed his hands inside the suit. He'd only been out of the mobility chair for a few days, but his knees were killing him. Everything on this planet was killing him. He spent most of his time in the EVA suit, only leaving it to clean the thing when it got too rank. But rather than recognize his aversion to living in this stars-forsaken gravity well, what did Admin do? Sent him to test a water source where it was more likely he'd become breakfast than succeed.

Processors were the ones who made sure everything on the ships ran smoothly, directing the most efficient workflows. Now all of Admin was awake, they said the processors were "redundant." It wasn't as if his skills disappeared. They just didn't want Generationals, even ones of high standing like himself, running the colony. So, they sent him on survey duty. It was a good thing he was busy, or he'd be sending even more strongly worded messages to Admin about the disproportionate work the Generationals were undertaking.

Alvin looked both ways as he approached the swiftly flowing river, early morning sun slanting overhead, hoping there were no mobile fungal animals around. He'd read the reports of the swarms of acidic creatures released in the cavern, and the Vagals had encountered two larger ones at the edge of the forest-like mass. They'd been as large as small cows, but the videos showed low, creeping things with many legs and no heads. They moved in zig-zag patterns, tending to the taller fungal towers, even though the creatures were also made of fungal and plant matter, rather than flesh.

The Vagals had killed both after the things attacked. Alvin shivered at the memory of the twisted vines serving as legs coiling, then springing the creatures forward like jumping spiders. And now Alvin was out here near the edge of the colony by himself. One of the Vagals was in the medical ward with a burned arm from the animals' exothermic blood. Fluid. Whatever lubricated the fungal bodies. If they'd been wearing those teal armored suits, they might not have gotten injured. There weren't enough to go around. Alvin knew because he'd requested one of the powersuits for himself, but he'd been denied, with a note from General Smith himself, commander of the Vagals, that Generationals were not cleared to use the suits.

So, he was out here, with only the meager protection from his EVA suit.

"Hello?" he called, quietly along the bank of the river, the suit's speakers amplifying his voice automatically. The land on this side was clear, glassed from the ships' exhaust, but on the other fog-obscured bank of the mighty river, pillars like rubbery trees with no branches or leaves poked out like broken fingers. His voice echoed back to him, and Alvin tensed as the pillars bent side to side with ominous creaks. Had he caused that?

Best to do his job and get away from here before he became lunch to a fungus. He only had to collect samples, for now.

Fungus floated along the surface like hateful lily pads, tethered with ropes of hyphae to the opposite shore. This river should have been clear after the ships burned everything away, but if the number of mushrooms in the cavern under the arcopolis was any indication, the biological matter on this planet could grow with terrific bursts of speed. He could barely see the river's surface more than a few meters from this bank. Thankfully the new growth hadn't reached this side yet.

It was obvious this water source would never do in its current state. Clean water had been brought down with the ships, which the Generationals had been using and recycling the whole journey, supplemented when they crossed a solar system. But it was only barely enough to sustain them, not the Admins and Vagals, too. Even the Vagals woken on watch were notoriously wasteful, and they'd experienced the ships the longest. No, they would be out of clean water in a very short time on 11d. The planet was a wide-open expanse. There was no control here. No safe walls containing everything. No way to conserve what water they used.

If they were to use this river, there would need to be a wall keeping the pillar trees and new growth out of the river, with gates and a filtration system for the water. Alvin fired off another memo to Admin—only his third today—to investigate bulking up the water treatment plant. Had there been any plans for sterilizing native water? There must have been, though who could have foreseen *this* much contamination? Could they bring the temperature of the water up to boiling before it entered the city to get rid of pathogens? It would take more energy than they had available, at the moment, and they'd need to remove the hyphal mass by hand.

Alvin paced down the river, marking the site of the planned water treatment plant. He jumped at every noise, head twitching enough to give him neck strain.

The fog on the other side of the bank cleared as the sun rose, revealing a tangled mass of vines around the bases of the pillars. Things *moved* among them, and dozens of glowing orange dots shone out along the river. It was only when several blinked that Alvin realized they were eyes. He swallowed and almost dropped his sample vials. The moment one of those things entered the river, he'd be a blur, running back to the colony.

Keeping a close eye on the opposite bank, he investigated the closer bank of the river, carefully keeping the toes of his EVA boots away from the water. It would be a chore to clean this out, now they'd gotten an idea of how resistant the fungal mat was. The Vagals were still clearing out the last remnants in the cavern opened up by the sloppy ship crash. If Admin had read his reports on proper deconstruction, they would have known Processor Bhamin's landing of the Khonsu had been notably ill-thought-out. Now they were down resources, some of which could have been used to scout this river, instead of him offering himself as a sacrifice to hungry local flora.

Alvin shivered and knelt next to the river to take a sample, making sure the knees of his suit didn't hit any sharp stones. It he'd wanted to, he could have leaned out to touch the nearest floating masses, as close as they'd grown in the past megasecond since landing. The fungus here looked as if it was crossed with some sort of large flat leaf, hyphal tendrils knotting below to hold them in place, and bulbous blue and green domes emerging in the center of the leaves like giant frogs.

He secured his water sample and inserted the vial into the portable testing station he'd brought, slung around his back. If the Khonsu hadn't crushed so many drones, he could have requisitioned one to carry it, rather than stopping every five minutes, gasping like a dying goat. He leapt into the air when one of the floating piles of tendrils on the river's surface off-gassed something in a purple cloud. He checked his filters for the hundredth time since coming out here. Still at full integrity. He watched the cloud of spores dissipate as he waited. No telling how many of those he'd breathed already. At least the blinking orange-eyed creatures seemed content to stay on the other bank.

The testing station binged. Alvin shook his head as he checked the results. This made no sense. The water was devoid of any harmful trace minerals and elements. It would be safe to drink, except for the rate of biomatter contaminants. That was so high, he should be able to *see* them. It was practically more fungus than water. He peered down into the river, so clear he could see rocks on the bottom. Something zipped between round pebbles as he watched. A fish? He removed the waterproof imager he'd requested, attached to the end of a long pole, and plunged it into the swiftly moving water, straining to keep it still while it scanned the river.

After a moment, he pulled the recorder back in and watched what it had recorded.

The river was a flurry of activity, under the surface. Beneath the flat pads, with their bulbous domes, finger-thick growths trailed into the water, and around them swam colonies of brightly colored things, flashing multiple colors. The specks would detach from the growths, wriggling to the bottom of the river, then back up to the surface pads and the safety of the little forest of tendrils.

Alvin mused on the recording. They must be cleaning the water in some way, filtering out any minerals or chemical contaminants.

There was no way the colonists could drink water like this. Even if the little lights weren't poisonous, drinking anything from this river would be like trying to drink a thick stew, though there were absolutely no other impurities.

Alvin scooted to the edge of the river again, dunking ten more vials in quickly, as if each one might suddenly suck him under the water. The growths on the surface bobbed peacefully as he shouldered the testing station. He looked through his vials until he caught sight of one of the little glowing things. He held the glass vial close to his helmet, and as he watched, more lights blinked on and off.

Time for an experiment. If this went well, he could tell Admin he'd found the way to clear the river. Maybe they would move him to something safer for a reward.

Surely a chemical treatment could render the fungal particles inert. He squirted several drops of the all-purpose cleaner he carried with him always. It was a mixture of several high-powered disinfectants.

He watched the little glowing dots for a time, but they didn't dim or slow. If anything, they seemed brighter.

Alvin ran that vial through his testing station. He blinked at the results. Clean. Pure water. The floating particles had neutralized the cleaner he'd added. They should have been dissolved. What sort of biological thing could process industrial cleaner?

Daydreams of moving to a cushy desk job disappeared. Cleaning this river was impossible, unless they could manufacture a small enough filter screen to get rid of the floating particles. The colony was far from making those kinds of materials. They had to finish basic housing, first. What else could he—

A low grunting rumble made Alvin look around. One of the squat, orange-eyed things took a tentative step out onto the tangled mass of hyphae reaching across the river. The eyes blinked at him.

Alvin grabbed his testing equipment and sprinted away from the river, back to Alpha Radian. Nope. No more testing today. Admin could punish him if they wanted. He should have stolen an escape pod from the fleet and taken his chances in space.

* * *

Jane Brighton stared at the rumpled-looking Generational. "Say it again, one more time, and pretend I haven't spent the last ten years of my life studying mushrooms." Rajani had brought the Generational in, insisting he had something important to tell, but Jane hadn't understood any of it. Now she, Rajani, Ahman, and Polunu all stared the nervous man down. Christiaan furiously took notes behind her.

"I have samples from the cave, ones a Vagal took from the edge of the arcopolis, and ones the processor brought me from the river. So, I compared them to each other." The Generational paced in front of her desk. At least the balcony was closed in now. The interior of Jane's office still opened up into the larger Admin building, which made it extremely hard for the Vagals running security to keep random colonists—and other Admins—from barging into her office. Especially since many of them were occupied with burning mushrooms out of her new accidental cellar.

"This is when you decided the samples were the same?" Ahman asked, one of their delicate eyebrows lifted.

"Not the same." The Generational—Christiaan texted his name was Frank Silver—looked frustrated. "Identical. After the first comparison, I thought I'd mixed up samples. After the second and third checks, I confirmed all the samples had the same makeup, the same spore shape and size—bananas, if you're curious—septa in the same locations and all had clamp connections. The samples were gathered kilometers apart, from obviously different-looking fungal species, but they're genetically compatible." Silver stared at her as if all this meant something. "I even mixed the samples, and they showed signs of clamping. They can reproduce, though what the result would be, I don't know."

Jane waved a hand for him to speed it up. She didn't need a biology lesson.

"No, let him speak," Rajani said, and Jane glared at her. The woman thought she controlled everything to do with science and biology in the colony, which was a problem, because they were surrounded by mushrooms. If she decided to make a bid for leading the colony—

"I'm intrigued as well," Polunu said. The short and broad woman looked more comfortable, now they were on the ground. She had busied herself with animal infections over the past couple weeks, but she was an adept biologist in general. "How *do* the samples reproduce? Have you discovered the mechanism?"

Silver nodded vigorously. Jane sent Christiaan a note to keep an eye on how much the other Admins were interfacing with the Generationals. She didn't want them getting too chummy with this transitory population.

"You've seen my research on the cell walls? We saw this in the original samples taken by probes. What I would have termed animal, plant, and fungal cells on Earth are all jumbled together here. My hypothesis is the viral strains transiting between the three types of cells pass information between them rather than disease. The physical samples look like hyphae—" He looked squarely at her, and Jane barely kept from gritting her teeth. "See, what you call mushrooms are just the fruiting bodies of the mycelium, and the mycelium is made of stringy things we call hyphae. Those are the long connective strings that make up fungus. So, the samples look like hyphae at the surface level, but the larger products combine into completely unique mycelium, depending on the situation. Those animals and plants out there? They're just really weird fruiting bod...I mean mushrooms. They're really weird mushrooms."

"So, the viruses control the morphology of the growth?" Rajani asked.

"That's my suspicion," Silver said. "It's like the viruses turn on parts of the genetic code in response to environmental stimulus. They can sculpt which type of mushroom pops up in which area."

"What about on the genetic level? Are there any other oddities?" Polunu asked.

"My genetic breakdown of the samples was inconclusive," Silver said. "Basically, it's a mess. There are too many base pairs. So many I would assume these samples were barely viable, yet instead this thing covers the entire planet. Some gene combinations are eerily similar to those of terran-descended genes. I've categorized seventy-eight chromosomes, compared to the human forty-six. Fungus and mushrooms have even less. Perhaps some of them are inactive? I don't know." Silver scratched at his uncombed hair.

"You speak as if you think the growth that surround us are all the same species." Ahman said.

Silver looked back to them, and Jane noted the frenzied look in his eye. This wasn't all the information he had. There was something else important he hadn't shared yet. She sent a message to Christiaan to watch the man's work for the next few weeks.

"That's exactly my point," he said. "The mushrooms and other fruiting bodies we see have different functions, not just simple reproduction. There are defense mechanisms, nurturing and protective systems, filtering functions. I matched DNA sequences from the river, the cavern, and the edge of the colony. These places are separated by kilometers. The DNA matched exactly. Not to eighty or eighty-five percent, but one hundred percent. No drift, no changes. Even single spore growth in a Petri dish has some amount of drift."

"Surely there are random harmless mutations," Rajani said.

Silver waggled his forefinger in the air. "That's what I assumed. If there are, they are the *same* mutations in all the samples. All of them."

Rajani sat back, blinking.

Jane was getting tired of all this scientific babble. "So they're the same species. What about it?"

"No, not just the same species," Silver corrected her. Jane lifted her chin, but let him continue. "The *same*. As if you met a clone of yourself, but not even that. As if your clone had lived your same life, encountered the same stimuli, had the same scars. The weird fungal towers at the edge of the wild growth outside the city are the exact same organism as the mushrooms spitting winged things in the caverns and the floating blobby organisms on the river."

"And farther afield?" Polunu asked.

"I'll have to request more samples. Are there any drones that can be used?" Silver asked, then answered his own question. "No, probably not, until the ships have been stripped. But if I'm right, and I think I am, this whole planet is covered by *one* connected organism. It's one mass, one biological entity, one *biomass*."

"That...would explain the mutations," Rajani muttered. Jane saw the twitch of the other Admin's eyelid, the tremor at the edge of her mouth.

"You're saying the entire...biomass...covering this planet is *one* organism?" Jane said. "In the oceans? On land? The towers and the creatures, and mushrooms, and everything?"

"I suspect so," Silver answered.

Jane blinked away the message Christiaan sent. She'd had the same thought at the same moment.

"Is...is it sentient?" She kept her voice steady.

Silver tilted his head as if the concept hadn't occurred to him. "I...no, I don't think so. I mean, it can't be. There are no signs of a place to *have* intelligence. At its base nature, it's a fungus. I think. Wouldn't it have reacted more if we'd destroyed part of its body?" He gestured around, taking in all of the colony. "I can only assume this is some sort of agglomerating organism that has taken over the planet. It's alive, but I doubt it can *think*. In fact, it could be an accidental effect of a virus, long ago."

Rajani began to speak. "We could send a team out to study—"

"Nope." Jane sliced a hand through the air. "We know what it is. Now it's my turn." She squinted at the rumpled Generational. "What does all this mean to the colony? How hard will it be to kill?"

Ahman grumbled something but she ignored him. The Generational paled.

"It...would be impossible to kill, unless you sterilized the entire planet. It's all literally the same thing. It's *one* biological entity. You'd have to kill *all* of it."

"Then if we can't do anything about it, why have you used up"—she glanced at her HUD's clock—"twenty-eight minutes of four Admins' time? I'm waiting for the part where this affects us, Frank. Think like someone who is very busy and has a lot to do."

Frank blinked in silence for a moment, as if his train of thought were embarking on a journey to a previously unseen horizon. Ahman, Rajani, and Polunu all leaned forward slightly in their chairs.

"It's going to slow down construction of the arcopolis."

Jane leaned over her desk, too. By God, it was good to be in gravity again, where she could properly intimidate people. "*Now* you have my attention. How do we slow it down, get it away from the arcopolis?"

Frank shook his head again. "I don't think you can. It's the entire planet! It might *be* the planet. It's going to continue growing and creeping its way into the city for as long as we live here. We might be able to find a plant that will fight back against it, or slow it down, but for now burning or freezing is probably the best course to take it down quickly. We're doing the equivalent of cutting its hair."

"Christiaan, send out a note to start rationing the flamethrower fuel." Jane tapped a finger on her desk six times, thinking. "Ahman, can you move mushroom clearing and fuel production to higher priorities on the arcopolis schedule board?" Ahman nodded, and she looked back to Frank. "Is there any way to mass produce a freezing agent? Will it be any more effective?"

Frank shook his head, and Jane noted a grease spot on his collar. "It would be a better way to destroy individual segments—many plants and fungi use fire as a means of reproduction and spreading seeds and spores—but we'd have to build a dedicated liquid nitrogen production facility, or at least liquefied carbon dioxide, and that will take a lot more power. Exothermic reactions are much easier to produce."

Jane just looked at him.

"It's easier to heat things up than cool them down," Frank summarized. "And freezing doesn't kill fungal spores anyway. Not unless it gets really cold and even then, not always."

"He's right. We don't have the resources to produce that much coolant," Polunu said. "And we haven't seen any blooms from the parts we've flamed so far. If it sped up reproduction, we should have some confirmation of that by now."

"Done, ma'am," Christiaan confirmed. They air-typed something else. "If I may offer a suggestion as well? Our food rations are starting to dip, our plants are having trouble adjusting to native soil, and we have recently lost some of our livestock. Can we eat it?"

Four Admins and Frank stared at Jane's assistant. Christiaan shrugged one shoulder. Jane looked to Frank. "Well?"

"I'll...have to run some more tests and pose the question to some of the other scientists," Frank hedged.

"I'll get a team on it," Rajani said.

"But?" Jane raised a devastating eyebrow at him.

Frank swallowed. "But...I *think* the proteins are similar enough to ours to be digestible. Our stomach acids should break down the mycelium well enough, if you don't mind the taste."

Jane nodded. "Good enough. We're getting this arcopolis finished. I will not accept defeat. So burn it, eat it, tear it out by the roots—hyphae—whatever, we are going to clear a space for our city. We are going to *win* against this biomass."

* * *

4 weeks, 6 days after landing

Jiow rested on her shovel against the thumper—her name for the sonic mapping device—and massaged her sore arm, only two days out of its cast. Her first day back to work after the doctors grudgingly said her internal injuries were healed, and she'd done six sonic mappings already. The Khonsu crash had taxed the medical resources of the new colony, using nanoregeneration kits meant to be a backup supply until their fabrication was fully up and running. Who knew how long that would be. The hairline fractures in her legs and her broken arm had been the easiest to fix—though it took her sitting around doing nothing for a full half a megasecond while the rest of the healthy colonists sweated and toiled. The pierced lung had the doctors worried until four days ago, but once her arm was free of its immobilization, there was no way she was sitting around. History was being made around her.

She'd been lucky. If the nanoregeneration injections didn't help a colonist return to work, they didn't get them. She'd heard the doctors muttering about it—Admin interfering with their orders.

"Done yet?" Her brother Zhu called from farther into Alpha Radian. "About time. Would have thought you had two broken legs or something." She caught his grin from even this far away. "Let's head in. Admin is calling for more hands around the central building structure."

She started packing up the thumper, slower than she would have in the past, but already quicker than she'd been this morning. She'd be exhausted and her muscles would be sore tonight, but it was worth the pain to be moving around again.

Over the past three weeks since the Khonsu fell—she'd had to do a quick back calculation in her head to figure out that was a little under three megaseconds—the construction crews had finished bringing the most precarious sheets of nanotanium down from the ships. They'd also stripped the rest of the circuitry and important elements from the ships down to a few stories off the ground. The engines of the Hasamelis and the Hina were fast becoming their first power distribution center, fueled by solar cells, more of which were being printed every day. It was a shame she'd missed all that, but no more. She was out of janitorial work, and even if manual labor wasn't much better, it was doing *something* for the colony. The Admins were pushing the Vagals and Generationals, but that was good, wasn't it? They all had to work together to survive on this planet.

"Got that thumper ready?" Zhu called again, and Jiow blinked away the thought. "I want to be there to put my name on the first street laid in Alpha Radian. All the Generationals are."

"Almost done!" Jiow wiped her forehead with a sleeve, leaving the fabric damp with sweat. They hadn't warned her the weather would be so...hot. It was like working near the engine for days on end. But she was happy. This was a time to share with her eventual kids, once she got a moment to start a relationship, and when the colony had enough power to run the decanting tubes without interruption to successfully gestate children. She'd had a vasectomy with the other people with the appropriate parts when she was a young teenager—it was how the fleet controlled their birth rate. Much easier to grow a child in a decanting tube, with a controlled environment, and no danger to the parent who would have been carrying the child.

She was a part of a moment of history. Assuming there was a history to tell.

Jiow folded up the third, sticky leg of the thumper, checking her marking flags to make sure the area was ready for the Vagals tomorrow.

The original cavern opened by the Khonsu's nose section had been burned, poisoned, lightly irradiated, and frozen, and the exobiology team had finally declared it free of any biomass contamination. That was what everyone was calling the mushrooms now, since Frank had discovered they were all the same plant, or fungus. Whatever.

But once the ships were gutted, Admin had sent the manual labor crews to find other caverns they'd missed beneath Alpha Radian. They'd found five above the sterilization line from the ships' landing and another two deeper ones that were still filled with mushrooms and spores. The one she'd found today was the third.

After the losses from the first cavern, the teams had taken to drilling a hole to intersect each cavity and pour enough accelerant down there to set the place on fire for three consecutive days. Then one lucky individual would climb down the shaft to do a thorough inspection of the cavern for any biomass traces.

Jiow was going to volunteer to check this cavern, once it was cleared. She would make this colony succeed single-handedly, if she had to. With Admin's direction, or in spite of it.

"Ho! Slowpoke!" Zhu was halfway to where their bicycles were parked.

"Coming!" Jiow called, and leaned down to pick up the thumper.

History was waiting.

* * *

4 weeks, 6 days after landing

Agetha texted Daved, looking across the gathered people at the head of the new street. *I'm going to be late again.*

While she waited for his answer, she checked the drones laying the printed concrete squares around the Admin building. It would have taken much longer without automated help. Each interlocking shape—made from local limestone and other aggregate bound together on top of a nanotanium plate—would resist rain, snow, hot and cold temperatures, and hopefully, crawling mycelium nets. No one had found the resources to create new nanotanium, and they didn't have a foundry capable of those temperatures yet anyway, so it was a costly process to lock that much of their limited building material under the road. But Admin had insisted. Agetha hoped they'd find some mineral veins before they got finished with Beta Radian, because they'd be out of original ship materials by this rate. They'd planned to use the nanotanium in the ships for the structures through the entire arcopolis.

Her HUD pinged.

Again? What is Admin doing this time? I'm using the last of the string beans in deep freeze from the ship, Daved texted back. Agetha sighed. She really liked how Daved cooked string beans.

Everyone's signing the first block of concrete in the road outside Admin. We poured it specifically instead of printing it.

Agetha watched the waiting symbol in her HUD while Daved typed something else. The concrete was almost dry, but by the time everyone signed, it would be late into the evening. Maybe she could write a quick algorithm to get the drones to tidy up the area for the night? She usually didn't like to leave them unobserved, but this was going to take a while.

They focus on this monument to their own leadership when we're not even sure all our animals will survive. I was hoping we'd have horses for transportation soon.

The horses had...not done well. Only one megasecond out of sus-ani and ninety percent of them were dead of a strange intestinal illness. There were only three left, and they wouldn't last more than a few days.

There are more embryos in cold storage, she texted back. *Someday perhaps we can grow more.*

Daved's next text took a moment to come through, and Agetha could tell he was working himself up again. *We'll figure something out, if we're here that long. You didn't see the cavern, the abundance of growth here. We're venturing into a biome that is already fully populated. The niches we're trying to occupy are already filled.*

Agetha watched the lines of teal suits, with none other than General Smith, leader of the Vagals, at their head. They must have pulled out all the limited powersuits they had for this ceremony. Did that mean the Vagals still watching the edges of the radian were less protected than the ones acting as statues here?

Admin has a plan for this place, Agetha texted back, while watching the teal suits salute. *I'm sure they know what they're doing.*

Is that why they were confused when all the birds and rats from the ships ran off into the biomass? Daved texted back. *One of my friends in the agriculture division says the peach trees already have a fungal rot. Why are the Admins placing monuments when they don't even know if they'll survive here long enough to procreate?*

It always came back to children with Daved. Not that she disagreed, but that decision still had to wait probably another ten megaseconds or more. The colony was barely settled. No way they could support children yet. She understood now, the ship directives to cease reproduction so far before the approach to a planet. If they'd come down here with a small child... Agetha shivered at the thought.

Still there?

She shook herself and texted back. *Just watching them lower the final slab. I wonder if they're going to include the names of those who died in the Khonsu crash?*

Daved switched gears, likely knowing she didn't like to get ahead of things talking about children. *Maybe they'll put up a real memorial when there's time.*

Hey. The string beans are almost ready. I'll keep some warm on the stove for you. Sign for me?

Agetha smiled. Daved was one of the least concerned with his own legacy in any form, save when it came to actual children.

Of course, she answered. *I'll make sure we're both remembered.*

* * *

5 weeks after landing

Anderson rubbed his hand against his pants again, the rough texture soothing the itching for only seconds. He needed another E-Vapor, but there was no smoking inside the Vagal barracks. The back of his hand was noticeably puffy, the skin raw and oozing from scratching and rubbing it. He'd been using the antifungals the doctors recommended. It would have killed anything residual from the mushroom that bit him. So it couldn't be that. Was he just allergic to this planet? But only for one of his hands?

"Anderson, pay attention," Noce called from the briefing room, and Anderson's head snapped up.

"This is the second time. Something wrong, private?" Noce's low voice was a growl today.

"Distracted, muux," he answered. The other Vagals shifted around him, their implants likely responding to his state. He got the sense he was surrounded, though these were his teammates. His implants had been injecting various stimulants through his system, but none could take away the itching for very long.

"What's wrong with your hand?" Noce was staring at his right fist, scraping against his pant leg. Anderson jerked it away but didn't hide it behind his back. That was a toxic behavior, and he knew it. Instead, he held it up for all to see, puffy and red and weeping. The soldier next him wrinkled her nose.

"Don't know, muux," he said truthfully. "It's been itching, but the doctors prescribed me antifungals. I don't know what's wrong." Aside from the raw skin on the back of his hand and the swelling, there were no other signs.

"When did you last see the medical team?"

"Two weeks ago, muux."

"That hand looks terrible," Noce said. They pointed to the woman next to Anderson. "Gonzalees will take your place on fungus burnout today. Get back to the medical department now, and don't come back until you know what's wrong with your hand. You'll be no help to anyone until then."

"Muux." Anderson ducked his head and ran from the building.

* * *

The medical annex was, for once, not full of patients. In the past weeks since the crash, life had become more routine, tearing down the ships, constructing new buildings, getting production for food and resources up and running, and burning out any biomass they found. There were injuries, but nothing like the scale of what had happened when the Khonsu crashed. They were down a total of one hundred and three people out of twenty thousand. Less than half a percent of the population, in what many agreed was the most risky time of colonization. Despite the rows of graves, they were doing well. Anderson just hoped he wouldn't be the hundred and fourth.

He got in quickly to see a young doctor with metal bindings in tight black braids, framing a pretty Mid-Eastern or African-descended face. She'd likely been on the UGS Khonsu, back when it was in space. The Generationals had mixed and changed over the years Anderson had been in sleep, getting taller and their eyes growing noticeably larger than in the humans in sus-ani. Many of them where physically younger than him, but had spent more years training in their jobs than he had before he'd been frozen for the trip. It was a strange dynamic, talking to them.

"What's the problem, Private?" the doctor said, then saw his hand and her eyebrows rose. "Oh. I see. Did something get lodged in your hand? A sliver of rock or metal maybe?"

Anderson shook his head at the brusque tone. "Not that I know of, Doctor..."

"Harley," the Generational supplied.

"Doctor Harley. The top feels tender and swollen. I've been treating it, but it's not getting better."

"May I?" Doctor Harley reached a gloved hand for his and gently palpated the area. "What are these from?"

She pressed three tiny holes in the back of his hand, and Anderson took in a sharp breath.

"What?"

"Down in the cave," he said. "A mushroom...bit me."

That got both eyebrows raised at him. "It *bit* you?"

"It didn't hurt that much," Anderson said. "And I was more concerned about getting out of that cave with my life. Lost four Vagals that day, and Jones is still eating through a tube. The Vagal doctor prescribed antifungals, and I've been using them, but..."

Doctor Harley shook her head. "Franks had never been off Earth before he got thawed out. No offense, but I wouldn't trust him to treat anything more complicated that scrapes and bruises. The mycelium here reacts differently than Earth fungus. Let's take a look at it." She led him to a table where she prepped a small cylinder and pressed it against his wrist. His hand went numb.

"I'm going to make an incision at the bite area," Doctor Harley said. "You might want to look away."

Anderson didn't. He'd seen enough of people's insides to get used to them.

The skin parted at the scalpel's touch, oozing a stinking brown liquid, and the doctor jerked her head away. Anderson swallowed bile. Something smelling that bad was in his *hand*.

"Don't move." She hurried to a drawer and produced two filtered masks. "Put this on."

She helped him, as he only had the use of one hand. The smell was still there, but muted.

"I'm going to palpate this a little," the doctor said, gently pressing around the incision, releasing more brown goo and...strings? "Oh, this isn't good."

Anderson tensed. It was never a good sign when a doctor said that. "Do you know what it is?"

"You tell me," Doctor Harley said as she gently pulled a long white tendril from the cut in his hand. "Look familiar?"

Anderson very deliberately didn't pass out. He blinked rapidly, trusting the Vagal implant to regulate his blood flow and heart rate. "It's a mushroom root."

"Exactly." The doctor seemed almost happy as she pulled more out. "It's a clump of hyphae that's taken root in your hand. Probably injected by that biting mushroom. Now, fungus generally needs air. It can't survive in your body. It's why we can breathe spores without everyone erupting in mushrooms. Now where is—"

She looked over his hand, before lifting his fingers.

"Do you clean under your fingernails, Private?"

Anderson looked at his hand. His cuticles had been stained from days of working with the oils in the 'throwers and digging through the dirt of Lida. "I try, but the oil and dirt is hard to get out."

The doctor shook her head. "Not dirt." She put his hand down and grabbed a set of tweezers, gently picking under his numbed fingernail. What she pulled out was stringy and dense. Anderson swallowed hard to keep from vomiting.

"Is that...fungus?" He looked at the distance from the middle of his hand to the tips of his finger.

"Seems like it. It explains how the fungus is staying alive. You'll have to give me some more information about the one that bit you so we can watch out for others."

"But my hand, doctor," Anderson said.

"Yes, I'm going to irrigate the opening here and see if I can flush out more hyphae strands." Her voice dropped. "But I'm afraid it doesn't look good. We have no way of knowing how far the mycelial network is spread through your hand. Your white blood cells have been fighting it, but I fear it may be a losing battle, with the amount of matter in this wound." She was still pulling white threads out, until one seemed to catch on something and snapped. "Shit."

Anderson gulped. It was *also* not good when a doctor said that. "What is it?"

"That resistance tells me the strands are wrapped around something. Possibly bone or muscle. The hyphae are not just in a cavity but reaching out through your hand. I think we need to take an MRI. I'm calling in some help on this one. Sit tight."

Two hours later, Anderson sat with a bandage on the back of his hand slowly turning brown, looking at an image of his bones. Doctor Harley pointed out little white strands starting from a small cavity, and reaching out to the tips of his fingers, around the bones of his hand, and intertwined with the muscle. They stretched down to his wrist, reaching for his arm.

"Can you burn it all out?" he asked. "Give me stronger antifungal medication?"

Doctor Harley stared at him a moment, fingering her long braids. The soft tapping of the metal wrappings was the only noise.

"No," she said, finally.

"Then what other option is there?" Anderson asked.

"Unless you want that mycelial network taking over the rest of your body, I'm afraid we're going to have to remove your hand."

PART SIX

Growing

6 weeks after landing

It had been confirmed through several different methods that the original eight creatures had given birth, and in efficient fashion, the young had eaten the giant hulks of the parents, who had landed in what was termed "the ring of death."

Now those young expanded their claim on the ring of death where the parents had done battle as they descended to the surface. Only the smallest sensing apparatuses had gone unnoticed, buried far below the ground. Though most of the activity was observed to be in one eighth of the ring of death, the protective cast of the young roamed the other sections, burning out ocular, auditory, and haptic sensing networks. The smallest sensing apparatuses were forced to move often to evade the protective cast's burning devices.

It had been observed that one parent, during its fight with its children and in its final death throes, had damaged some of its young. This was likely an unwanted trait among the parents. It was hoped the offending trait had been pruned away in the progeny, as their actions were proving immensely educational. The battle had opened a connection with a forgotten cavern network, disconnected during the creation of the ring of death. That area had attempted to grow into the ring of death, but its purpose had been forcefully stopped by the new creatures.

Information was lacking on the creatures' progeny and their purpose. They appeared to be separated into casts or forms, each specialized to a purpose. There were aspects of the children that were more mobile, including the building and protective casts. Other aspects were confined and used for generation of organic materials for liquid and solid protein. Finally, there was cast that did not move at all, but had to be tended by the first children until they were slaughtered, with parts used for sustenance of the other casts. Other parts became structural and ornamentation materials.

This last cast of children was the most deserving of study in the current time, as it possessed the possibility for easiest interface and communication. Floating bodies stocked with messaging and communication components—destined to enlarge the overall network—were sent above the ring of death. The few that survived the protective cast's burning devices sought out the stationary children and began deciphering their means of communication.

It would take time to fully interface with any of the stationary children, but there was a pleasing amount of variety cataloged from simple observation. This many different forms had not been subsumed for hundreds of cycles of this planet around the solar body. Not since the troublesome equatorial region had there been new lifeforms generated with no direction. So many possibilities for new combinations and expansions of expression were a rich feast of knowledge.

The stationary children, used throughout the ring of death, would give better access to the more complex and mobile children. Though their communication methods were different, blending with them was an intriguing first challenge. There would be time later for intensive studies of the mobile casts when a method was determined for observing apparatuses avoiding the detrimental actions of the protective cast.

Time was in ample evidence. For now, it was better to observe and catalog, which had proven the most efficient method with every other subsumed entity on this planet.

* * *

2 months after landing

"Over here," Agetha said. "This cucumber shriveled up since yesterday."

Daved plucked the offending fruit from the vine with a gloved hand and put it in the basket with the other fruits and vegetables the biomass had affected. The affected plants and fruits seemed almost random. Some of every type of plant was infected, but certain species were harder hit, like the transplanted peach trees, and pumpkin seedlings.

"We're going to be down to potatoes and carrots for our gardens," Daved said, wrinkling his nose at the pile of infected produce. This was the third garden they'd started at their new apartment, almost five and a half megaseconds—two months—after they'd landed.

The first batch of full-grown plants had been moved directly from the ship, and fared badly in the switch from hydroponics to soil. There wasn't enough power, or water, to continue the hydroponic methods for now, and the Generationals had each started their own gardens, anyway. Agetha wasn't sure they'd ever be able to go back, once the colony was up and running. Rather than all being in a few ship bays, the plants were spread all around Alpha Radian.

A second batch of seedlings was already planted, and as soon as the Lida's ground was tilled and dirt and fertilizer from the ship added, they had started the third round of seeds. Based on the infection rate, it was good they'd started so quickly.

"I'm sure there's a way to stop this contamination," Agetha said. "We'll just keep taking samples for Frank and the other biologists. Surely, they'll come up with an effective fungicide at some point. If I knew more about it, I'd volunteer to help out. Something has to affect this lifeform."

They'd run through all the standard fungicides fairly quickly in the first month after landing. None of them had a large effect on the biomass, or at least not on all aspects of it. Frank told her it was because the biomass contained the equivalent of fungus, plant, and animal cells inside it. Herbicides had the same lack of effect. The scientists were busy developing new poisons to kill off the creeping tendrils of biomass, but with little luck. The floating filters in the river could even neutralize harsh chemicals, and Frank insisted this was all one organism, even though parts of it looked vastly different.

"We're having similar issues with some livestock," Daved told her, holding up a pale and sickly-looking squash. "Lots of the chickens are losing feathers, and all of them have respiratory issues. Some of the dead ones we've looked at have lungs half the size they're supposed to be. All but three of the cows are dead, and we may just call it and have a beef night, at this rate. No human infections, as far as we can tell, at least."

"But there are more frozen animal embryos, right?" Agetha asked, picking a tomato that seemed unblemished.

"There are, but several canisters were without power after the Khonsu crashed, and we don't know how viable they are. Same with the sheep. Several are developing a strange sort of mange, which really defeats the purpose of raising sheep in the first place."

"There's always mutton," Agetha said, "and especially if the cows aren't surviving, we need another source for meat."

"I have a feeling meat of any kind is going to be scarce for a while," Daved told her.

"For us, maybe," Agetha said. She pulled a tomato from the vine with more force than necessary, then checked it for spots of fungus. There were small growths on the main stem of the plant, but so far most of the fruit seemed to be clean. "Where is the meat going, anyway? No one I know has seen much of it. Is it for Admin and the Vagals?"

"A lot of it isn't fit to eat," Daved said.

"But not all of it. If the garden keeps going like this, I'm not sure we'll have enough to eat. The last of the nanomeds are being used to heal Vagals injured fighting the biomass, but Generationals on my construction crew who've lost limbs in accidents are left to heal as best as they can. The whole colony is in danger, and the Generationals will be the first to die."

"Well, the Vagals are protecting us from being overrun, and Admin is busy giving us the best chance to survive." Daved replied. He had that quiet tone he got when Agetha got angry, which just made her madder.

"Are they?" She hefted a squash trailing a mass of hyphal roots. She tossed it to her husband, who caught it awkwardly and put in the basket with the others slated for incineration. "A building collapsed two days ago because a mycelial net got into the corner of the concrete somehow and made it fail. But the two who were injured can't be seen until next week because there are too many Vagal injuries!"

Agetha realized she was shouting and took in a deep breath. Daved was staring at her, his brow creased, the basket of infected veggies hanging limply from one hand.

"We're all stressed. I've been hearing a few on my crew muttering that they could do a better job than Admin. But they can't. Unless we all work together at this, the whole colony will fail."

"And it's hard for all of us," Daved said. "Admin Brighton is likely having just as hard a time as we are, but for different reasons. Like you said, we *can't* fight among ourselves. We're too near to failing as it is."

"But the Vagals and Admins will live for centuries," Agetha said. "Are Vagal and Admin lives are worth more than us?" Agetha waved a vague hand, gesturing to the small apartment they'd moved into a few weeks ago.

"Absolutely not. You know that." Daved's face was stony. "Our ancestors protected the Admins while the fleet came here. Now it's their turn to lead. Give them a chance. We lived by our schedules and systems in the fleet. Anything else was death. Now we can breathe the air, drink the water, and plant our own food without depending on the ships, some idiots think they can survive on their own?" He shook his head. "They'll find out quickly that's not a good plan."

"But does Admin have to make it so apparent we Generationals are just stepping-stones to their colony?" Agetha asked. What was she angry at, really? There was no reason to take this out on Daved just because she felt insecure.

Daved left the basket on the concrete path and stepped around the vegetable boxes to hug her. "We *are* stepping-stones, but our children will be the ones inheriting this place, not theirs. There are a lot more of us than there are of the Vagals and Admins. Once the decanting tubes are set up, we can build a family here."

And there it was. She'd avoided the question of children wherever she could while married to Daved. Now that question stared back at her as her only legacy. If she didn't make a place for her children to live—if she didn't *have* children—no one would remember her. No one would even know she was here. It put things into perspective.

"Tell me we'll be alright," Agetha murmured into Daved's shoulder. "I don't know if I can keep going with these setbacks. First the biomass itself, then the Khonsu, the underground caverns, the livestock, and now the plants. Maybe we should have just stayed on the ships."

"That wasn't our decision, and it's too late now in any case. The drives that took us through the stars are powering or homes. The nanotanium plates make up out streets and our buildings." Daved looked at her until Agetha stared back. "This *is* our ship, and we've got to take as good care of it as we did of the UGS Abeona."

Agetha sighed and leaned into her husband. "I know. Just don't leave me in all this. I don't know if I can survive on my own."

"I would never leave you," Daved murmured into her hair.

* * *

2 months 3 weeks after landing

"This whole landing was a disaster," Jane told Christiaan. She sat at her desk, her face resting in her hands. Christiaan stood primly in front of her, their pressed suit immaculate as always. How they had time to keep up appearances was beyond her. She hadn't even combed her hair this morning. "Two and a half months in, and we're already five months behind. I thought this world was supposed to match Earth to ninety-five percent. This is nothing like Earth."

"Technically, ma'am—"

"Don't 'technically' me. Fine, go over it again. How is our entire ground force unable to kill a mushroom?" Jane scowled.

"It's not techni—it's not a mushroom, ma'am. Mushrooms are only the fruiting bodies. Earth had fungi on smaller scales. At most, we had small country-sized mycelial mats. Our scientists think this is like those mats that primarily lived beneath forest floors, except this isn't *under* the forest, it *is* the forest. And the grass, the flying and crawling creatures, and everything else. The growth of the biomass is unprecedented, ma'am," her aide said. "We can *literally* watch it grow. The mat here is both above and below ground, and all types of flora and even fauna are all connected to it in some way. So, when the Vagals burn out a piece of the biomass, they're not actually killing anything. It's more like cutting someone's hair. It just grows back."

Jane thought for a moment, glad she finally had a door to her office that closed. It was much easier to concentrate on the administration of the colony when she could shut out distractions, and people trying to waste her time doing unnecessary things. "Then can we get to the source? Stop cutting the hair and take out the head?"

Christiaan scrunched up their nose like they did when Jane had said something dumb, but they didn't want to tell her that. They protected her. Likely were in love with her. They didn't have a life outside of providing her information and keeping the other Admins at bay. It was not uncommon, for the Admin assistants. Her feelings in return were...complicated. But she could be herself around them.

Jane sighed.

"Alright. Spit it out. What did I say? If I'm going to be telling the other Admins this stuff, you have to tell me if I'm saying stupid things. Rajani is already on me about letting her take the whole science team on a field trip. I think it's a suicide mission."

"It likely would be, ma'am. We guess the mycelial network is highly distributed." Jane cocked an eyebrow at them, and Christiaan got to the point. "It doesn't have a head. It's just a large mat of fungus that has grown over the planet. And 'fungus' is only the nearest Earth approximation. It's much more complex, containing animal, plant, and fungal DNA. It didn't react at all to us killing off a ninety square kilometer section of it with the ships when we landed. The individual injuries sustained by the Vagals are the defense systems of each fruiting body—the mushrooms, for lack of better word. It's not like there's anything coordinated about it."

Jane spread her fingers. "Then it's uncoordinated and undirected. Which leads to the same question. Why can't we kill it?"

Christiaan shook their head. "It's too big. It's literally one life form that has taken over the entire planet, ma'am. It *is* the biosphere. We can chop at the individual pieces of it, but there's always something to grow back. We'll need to find some way to keep it out of our cities permanently."

"We're already putting nanotanium under our buildings and roads to keep it from coming through them." It was a heavy use of a precious resource—one they couldn't yet replicate. The nanotanium had been meant to build the full superstructure of the arcopolis. If they used it for armoring their structures, it would only last for a few radians.

"And any place we don't put it will be where the biomass grows through." Christiaan added. "We have limestone, but the hyphal roots grow straight through that. Only metals, and high-grade metals, seem strong enough to resist it and we have not yet found those resources locally."

"I understand the risks, Christiaan. I wouldn't waste our most precious resource if there was any other way," Jane said. That decision hadn't been taken lightly, and she'd overridden both Ahman and Polunu's objections to put it into motion. The colony had to survive. That was their primary goal here. It was larger than the Generationals, the Vagal, and even the Admins. If she had to sacrifice any of those groups or even two of them, to keep the colony from failing, she would do so. She'd wanted the position of Lead Administrator and had fought to get it, and all the responsibilities that went along with it.

"Let's shelve that for now." She switched gears. "What about the biomass makeup? I have to report our status on the city layout to the other Admins tomorrow and I want to have *something*. You said the biologists have identified many different types of fungus. They're all coexisting together. How can it all be one thing, growing from the same substance?"

"Unknown, ma'am," Christiaan told her. They looked vexed as well, and when Christiaan looked vexed, there was an entire storm of frustration going on underneath the surface. It was their most endearing quality. "Animal, plant, and fungal components seem to coexist in the biomass, and are expressed in what looks to us like different species, though they are genetically the same. We have even seen examples of territorial fighting between species in the same niche. Evolution should keep this organism static, as there are no predators, but instead, it's pitted against itself. That's why the fungi still have defensive mechanisms. Yet if *that* was the case, the organism should evolve away from itself, and split into *different* individuals. But they are an entire intact biome, with everything a part of and sustained by the mat. Perhaps it reabsorbs any divergent evolution? I'm certain this will take many years of study to fully comprehend."

"If we know what it is, we can affect it. Is there anything from the biologists? We don't really know what it is, what it's made of, how it got so big, *or* how to kill it?" Jane grasped vaguely at the air, looking for some way to slow down the fungal invasion into their little oasis. They needed a solution that would last for *decades*. "Can we just nuke it and hope for the best? Do we even have any nukes, or do we have to wait to develop those too?"

Christiaan's eyes flicked back and forth, accessing files in their HUD. "It is suspected there might be nuclear payloads within the remains of the UGS K'uei-Hsing, but Admin Xi Wenqing has personally overseen most of that ship's deconstruction. There was a strict directive against bringing any form of nuclear armament within the fleet."

"You didn't answer my question, Christiaan," Jane chided, and her aide had the grace to look chagrined. "If Wenqing is hiding nukes, I'll take them away from him. I don't care if he has the Vagals behind him."

"It wouldn't matter, ma'am," they said. "The nuclear device would only kill—maybe—that portion of the mat where it impacted, and only for a certain radius. The fleet put the energy equivalent of several nuclear weapons into the ground here to kill the biomass in this area. You see what effect that had on the larger organism. Assuming we did have the capacity and armaments, by the time we irradiated enough of the biomass to potentially affect it, we would have poisoned the entire planet for our own use as well."

"Yes, I suppose that makes sense. Wenqing can keep his secret nukes, then." She squinted at Christiaan's last word choice. "What *about* poison? Regular fungicides don't work against it. How is development of other methods coming?"

"Not well, ma'am," Christiaan said. "The biomass adapts quickly to any new stimulus. This may be another reason it keeps various defensive measures. The biomass adapts through defenses and evolutionary strife, constantly becoming better at what it does. Even if we were to introduce an agent to kill the biomass, it would likely develop a method to neutralize it before the method got far enough to do any lasting damage."

Jane rubbed the bridge of her nose with both forefingers. "We don't have resources to keep it out, and we can't kill it. What *can* we do against it? What can I tell the other Admins?" This should have been Rajani's problem, except the biomass affected every aspect of their life here. All the Admins had a stake in keeping it at bay, and none of them had come up with any good ideas yet.

"We can have the Vagals continue what they are doing now, ma'am," Christiaan answered. "Remove the sections of the biomass immediately threatening us, either with fire on the new growth, or mechanically, if needed. If we cannot remove it, the highest priority must be to clear enough space, add nanotanium-backed protective measures, and complete Alpha Radian in time for the first batch of native inhabitants to be born."

"That's a war by attrition, and the biomass will win, eventually," Jane said. "We're running low on medical supplies already. We can't keep up a continual offensive by our Vagals on something that won't die. I need another option for the Admins."

Christiaan opened their mouth, then closed it again, their eyes flicking between unseen items on their HUD. The last time Christiaan looked like that was when they'd had the idea for Jane to take over the Lead Admin position. She pounced.

"Give me that idea, Christiaan. Don't bury it. Don't look up all the risk factors. You had something and I want to know what it is, no matter how crazy."

Christiaan still hesitated, until Jane made a grabbing motion with one hand. Jane wouldn't have heard their sigh if she hadn't been listening for it.

"We...*could*...build a wall, ma'am."

"Out of nanotanium." It was the only thing that keep the biomass out.

Christiaan nodded. "It would take most"—their eyes flicked between screens—"almost all of our available stock, but we could enclose all of Alpha Radian to a height of, say, thirty meters above ground and twenty below. With the foundations paved in nanotanium, we would be almost entirely enclosed. We would have enough material to start building construction in Beta, and maybe some part of a wall for that radian too, depending on priorities."

Jane jumped in when they started to run out of steam. "How much would it put us behind?"

"Months. Maybe a year," Christiaan said.

"But once complete, we could work in peace," Jane mused, more ideas coming. "We'd have bandwidth to search for larger deposits of minerals beneath the surface, something to replace the nanotanium. Alpha and maybe some of Beta would be protected. That would serve us the first five or so years of construction—enough to get us a foothold here." She looked back to her assistant. "Start working on it. I want to bring it to the other Admins tomorrow."

Christiaan nodded once, sharply. "I'll draw up the proposal and changes to scheduling."

"What would I do without you, Christiaan?" Jane let herself smile at her assistant. Her friend.

Christiaan's barest hint of a smile was enough. They didn't let much through their calm exterior. "I'm certain you would get by, ma'am," they said, then left her office.

Jane closed her eyes and dropped for forehead to her desk. Now she just needed to convince seven other highly opinionated and controlling personalities, and all their assistants, to go along with a harebrained scheme to use all of the colony's resources to make a giant barrier against mushrooms. This was going to be a long meeting.

* * *

3 months 3 weeks after landing

Anderson waggled his new prosthetic right hand, trailing behind the rest of the squad. He chewed on his E-Vapor. They were running low on supplies, but the Vagals were still burning through them. It would be a hard transition if they couldn't find an alternative soon.

It was his first time out on biomass burn since he'd had the amputation. It would have been longer, without the aid of nanomeds to heal the wound and reset the nerves to accept the prosthetic commands rather than those of his flesh and blood.

"New roots over here," Corporal Hendricks called, and the other Vagals, each in a teal powersuit, hefted their 'throwers. Anderson winced as the prosthetic caught on his 'thrower's fuel line. The suit's glove didn't fit over the prosthetic, and his nerves hadn't deciphered all of the input from sensors on the metal hand yet. He spit out the spent E-Vapor and closed his helmet. He was no newcomer to implants and prosthetics. He would get used to it in time.

"Line up!" Hendricks called, and Anderson went shoulder to shoulder with his squad mates on either side. He fumbled the safety the first time, got it on the second. His implant was pushing something through his system to make him twitchy, catching on each flash of motion around him and identifying it.

"Flame!" The line moved forward, one step at a time. The suits dissipated much of the heat backblast from the flamethrowers. He watched the writhing hyphae squirm and wither under the onslaught.

All military personnel entering the fleet had been required to go through the Vagal upgrade, which promised greater focus, resistance to disease and emotional trauma, more stamina, easier muscle growth, and more. The study had been peer-reviewed—quickly—and was rushed through certification on human subjects just in time for the soldiers in the fleet to be upgraded. He'd been one of the last. Anderson wondered what effects they'd found in the years while he had been asleep on the UGS Abeona. A shame there was no way to communicate with Earth in any reasonable time and find out what had happened to the original research.

The Vagal next to him, Gonzalees, twitched, and Anderson ducked before he knew he was moving. The stream of acid went over his head, and his 'thrower bathed the tiny six-limbed spitter with fire before it could get off another shot.

"Good reflexes," Gonzalees said.

"Thanks." The last three months and some he'd been on Lida, his implant had begun to attune to him. Rather than pump him full of adrenaline at the merest whisper of danger, it had begun to subtly show him more avenues of response to an issue. He'd found if he let it direct his subconscious, it reacted faster than he could make a decision.

He'd have been even faster if his index finger was working properly. It wasn't closing as smoothly as the other fingers. He'd had it adjusted twice since he'd gotten the prosthetic, but it wouldn't stay in tune. He'd have to get it checked again. He knew it wasn't a power issue. The hand contained a well-shielded nuclear battery in the palm. It was too large to use his body's proteins and warmth to charge as the Vagal implant did.

The line trudged forward, catching the little mobile guardians that acted as sentries for where the biomass hyphae grew. They'd learned if they took out the acid-spitters first, the biomass had a harder time covering new ground.

"How's the hand working?" Gonzalees asked.

"Itchy trigger finger," Anderson said, and Gonzalees chuckled. He almost added that his implant was getting used to the prosthetic, then closed his mouth.

The other Vagals hardly spoke about their implants, and he wondered what they had discovered. He wasn't sure if it was an unspoken agreement, or if others simply hadn't experienced the same growth as him. Subjectively it had only been a few months since he left Earth, but a few others had been out of sus-ani several times on the ships to act as watch officers.

What better time to learn than a routine flame-out?

"You, ah, ever get the feeling it's adapting to this world faster than you are?" He tapped the side of his head with his left hand, in the universal sign the Vagals used in the rare cases they referenced their implants.

Gonzalees eyed him sideways, then aimed a blast at a clump of mushrooms—the spiky kind—another Vagal was just about to step on. They wilted in the flame, though the Vagal had moved out of the way before Gonzalees pulled the trigger.

"Just feels like me in here," she said. "You feel something different?"

Anderson shook his head. "Nah. Must just be the prosthetic's reactions." He tapped a nanotanium finger on the "'thrower stock." He put his head down and kept flaming.

Maybe the others simply didn't wonder about the enhancement, but in himself, he'd noticed subtle differences, each creeping up on him.

His mind cataloged the glassified ground, the bulking wall of wild biomass ahead, the paths of the biomass roots, each cluster of spitting guardians, and the line of Vagals, Corporal Hendricks in the middle. He could keep this entire environment in his head at once. It was something he hadn't been able to do before the implant.

He continued forward with the line, occasionally replacing the 'thrower fuel canister. What was he doing here? When he'd signed up, they'd all been promised they would be the elite taskforce protecting the Admins on a new planet, and would live nearly as long as they did. They might have to protect against aliens, or division within the Generational crew, but they would ensure the colony's safety.

Here, the Vagals were glorified gardeners, and not even with any tangible reward. This section had been flamed last week and the biomass was already growing back. Was this going to be his job for the next few centuries? He was going to need a lot more E-Vapors.

He hadn't had these thoughts when he was assigned to the Euro-

Sinai border before the implant, even in the most boring assignments. Just like the biomass grew and spread across the world, the Vagal implant was expanding his mind, his ability to process information. He adapted, just as the biomass did. Maybe adapted at all costs.

Perhaps he'd name his implant.

* * *

4 months after landing

Frank banged his hand against his desk, then immediately shook it out, grimacing at the pain. He went back to the apple samples that had been turned into the lab. Why were they more susceptible than carrots? Or broccoli? Apples stored well. The trees had been healthy for hundreds of megaseconds in the fleet before being transplanted to the surface of Lida. They were one of the most stable crops.

He turned to the samples of resistant plants. Several had been brought in with aberrant growth and strange alterations, but never enough to kill the plant. The proteins of the apples were riddled with biomass DNA. Meanwhile the carrots looked normal, even if a few of them trailed secondary roots that looked a little too much like hyphae. He threw the biological strains found in the apple up on his HUD, next to those from the broccoli and carrots. It was easy to see when the biomass took control, both on a microscopic level and—he looked to the side table where he kept samples in a sealed container—on the macroscopic level.

It had been a little over ten megaseconds since they landed. What Admin would call four months. How had a completely alien species infected their plants so quickly? It had to have something to do with the viral communication systems in the biomass that translated between the animal, plant, and fungal cells.

Frank got up from his desk and went to the specimen table, peering at the sealed container. The tree that grew it once produced apples, but this was not a red spherical shape. It was purple, for one thing, and fluoresced under UV light. The stem had changed to a spongy, stretchy material that had to be cut from the tree, not picked. As for the apple, it was...not crisp. A series of pores in the fruit were shot through with malformed seeds, and the core had changed into a spiky radial formation reaching all the way through the apple to the skin, ending in strange gray blemishes, a sharp contrast to the dark skin. Where the new radial core of the apple was almost as hard as bone, the rest of the apple had become spongy and webbed, tearing at the slightest touch, and sticking to skin and clothing. It looked like a polka-dotted caltrop of bone with purple webbing between the struts.

Frank shuddered and turned away from the not-apple. Every fruit on the tree had grown the same way. It was a viral change to the genetic code of the plant. They had burned the tree out, down to a depth of two meters, as well as the rest of the orchard, which all bore the same characteristics. Fortunately, the majority of changes hadn't been that dramatic, allowing them to save some of the plant harvests.

Further, he and his fellow scientists had completely failed to recognize any pattern to the viral infections. They simply had to grow the plants and see what worked and what didn't. In fact, the plants should have been harder to infect than animals and people, due to their cell walls. Yet the biomass tried to infect all plants, and it was a crapshoot as to what resisted. He'd advised the horticulture division to tread carefully with anything more susceptible to infection, like peaches and grapes. It was already too late for the coffee beans. They'd planted their entire stock from the ships, as the Generationals were working around the clock to get the radian functional. At least in this case, the hybridization wasn't as extreme as in the apples. The coffee beans were still useable, and the roasting process got rid of any potential infectious material from the biomass, but the flavor was...well, it was bad. The coffee still worked like it was supposed to and contained caffeine, but actually drinking the stuff was torture.

Some of the livestock was worse off. The cows were almost all dead, and the pigs were developing strange coats of fibrous hair. But no humans had died of infections. Plenty had died to the biomass, however. What was stopping the biomass from contaminating humans as well as livestock and plants?

He swiped away the biological results displayed on his HUD. He needed another set of eyes on this, but everyone was working on their own problems. Eventually they would be ground down by attrition. They needed to take the fight to the biomass, clear out the radian, and create a safe base of operations to continue building the arcopolis.

Frank just wished he knew how.

* * *

5 months 2 days after landing

Jiow stabbed at her tiny piece of steak. She should be happy she even got any—this was the last of the cows that would be raised on the surface of Lida, at least in her lifetime. The whole colony had been eating beef byproducts in order not to waste the salvageable parts of the animals, which had died off at a prodigious rate.

"But we only got two dinners out of it," she said to Frank, who was munching contentedly. She had continued her train of thought, but Frank seemed to understand. He usually understood Jiow. "Do I even want to know how much steak Admin and the Vagals got? Probably a whole cow each."

"But we *did* get some," Frank said, emphasizing the point with his fork.

"And is that it? Are you just accepting the status quo?" Jiow asked.

Frank shrugged. "It works."

"It works because you're doing what you like. You're studying the biomass, making new discoveries, and making a name for yourself. They took me off surveying because we've done the whole Alpha Radian. Now all my injuries from the Khonsu are completely healed, I'm back to cleaning the colony's sewage system, and this one's not even finished yet."

"And you've found some great samples while you did so," Frank said.

Jiow glared back. "Some of us want to actually be known in the colony. Some of us want to make something of ourselves. The decanting tubes are being set up. There will be opportunities for children soon. Don't you want that? To raise the next generation?"

Frank screwed up his lip, as if his steak had gone rancid. "Never was one for kids, really. Didn't even find a match on the ship, like Agetha and Daved."

"But you *could*," Jiow said. "You have the social standing to attract a decent mate. Loners are the last ones to get children from the decanters. They prioritize couples and trios, because two or more people have more bandwidth to raise kids, while still working. We had the group centers on the ships, but the Admins want individual families here, for some reason. Something about it being like back on Earth."

"It's inefficient, but it worked for hundreds of Earth years," Frank shrugged. "You want mine? All that diaper changing, and baby talk, and dealing with an incompetent person for ten or fifteen years until they mature enough."

"Ugh. I *would* even ask you to pair up with me, if I thought it would give me a better chance at a kid," Jiow said. She didn't have any thoughts of intimacy with Frank. Frank wasn't that sort of person. "But you'd just be in the lab all the time, and I'd be cleaning the sewers *and* changing all the diapers."

"So, you want kids...why?" Frank popped another tiny piece of steak in his mouth and chewed thoughtfully. He was making it last as long as possible. Jiow cut her last piece in two and ate half of it. If she was never going to taste real steak again, there was no point lingering on this piece. The taste would be gone minutes from now. It was about as much lingering as when she had decided to go from *they* to *she* when she reached puberty. No looking back.

"Because, they're a part of you that lives on," she answered Frank. "Quite besides being necessary for the colony to survive. Your genetic code is mixed and something new comes out. A new creation, one that grows and changes and surprises you."

"You've just described fungus," Frank said, "save for having your genetic code, though I suppose that could be arranged." He held up a hand. "No, I see what you're saying. But wouldn't it be more efficient to sample everyone's genetic code, create the best matches, and spit out a whole crop of kids to be raised as a group? Less people need to take their time to raise them, and you get all the qualities you want."

"Such a romantic," Jiow deadpanned.

"Never claimed to be," Frank said. "But Admin seems to think the same way you do, anyway. They want parents to raise their own children, *while* we're trying to build the colony. At least the ships let you put your kids in a community center early on if you wanted."

"Thus, our kids will see how much pride we take in the arcopolis, and in them, and will surpass us in time to make an even better colony." Jiow had always planned to keep her kids close, back in the fleet. A lot of families did, though some preferred to simply give genetic code and forget about them, as Frank described. The Abeona had a phenomenal child village in the center of the ship, though it had been down to a few adolescents as they approached Lida, because of the decanting tube ban.

"I guess," Frank said. "Well, if you really want to find a partner, Charlay at the lab has been talking about how a bunch of Generationals have been getting together at night where the new water purification plant is being built. No Admins or Vagals allowed."

Jiow stared up at the ceiling of her disappointing house. Nothing on the walls above two meters from the floor. No path lines on the floor. No decorations on the top walls. "How did *you* find out about this before I did? This is just what I've been talking about. Back in the same dead-end job, while you have chances to hobnob with all the most attractive people, but choose to stay in your stuffy lab all the time."

"Which is what I like," Frank said. "But you obviously don't. So, stop whining and go catch a partner so you can have a bunch of smelly, whiny kids."

"I think I will," Jiow said, and ate the last bite of steak in the colony.

* * *

5 months 3 days after landing

Jiow stood awkwardly near the edge of the new water filtration building. It was a nanotanium shell straddling the river. The biomass on the far side had been firebombed back to a safe distance, but the only entrance to the building was on the near side of the river.

There were probably fifty people inside the building, empty but for chairs, three tables, a big pot and cooking station in the middle, and an access hatch leading to the river, bolted shut for now. The site was on hold until the colony figured out how to filter the biomass out of the river. She recognized a few the Generationals here, but not many. She didn't get out much. She should try to do that.

She took a deep breath and walked into the group of people sitting around the cooking station, where a large woman tended a warm pot of something alcoholic. She could smell it from here. Someone had set up a HUD link to play an album that had been popular on the Hasamelis a few megaseconds ago. It was too loud, but she expected that was common for places like these.

She took an open seat next to an attractive man about her age.

"How did you find out about this place?"

The man looked around, as if surprised to find her there. He had pale, very smooth, skin, and a handsome nose and cheekbones. "I thought everyone knew about this place. We've been coming here since the shell was built over the river. Admin though they could kill off the contaminants with fungicide, but we all saw how well that worked." His eyes took in Jiow's dull black hair, and she resisted the urge to comb it with her fingers. It never sat right, and she always had a cowlick. "You new here? What area of the radian are you working on?"

"Um. I'm the local controller for liquid passage maintenance." Jiow said, hoping the title was obscure enough.

The man's handsome face fell. "Oh, sewerage. I'm on one of the construction crews for the new residential sections."

Jiow grabbed the only opening she could think of. "I was on the survey crew until recently," she said. "Is yours the one under Agetha Xenakis?"

The man's face fell further. "Yeah, a real pushy bitch. Seems like all she cares about is finishing on schedule. As bad as Admin."

Jiow opened her mouth and then closed it. She didn't want to tell this cute guy she was friends with Agetha, nor did she appreciate his assessment of her either.

"Oh," she said.

"Yeah, well, be sure to sample the brew here," the man said, and turned to the woman next to him, laughing as she said something funny.

Jiow sighed, got up, and approached the large woman stirring the pot. She was likely from the Hina, sharing the rich walnut skin and wide face common among those Generationals.

"Want a glass? It's sure to bake a few synapses," she asked as Jiow got closer.

"What's in it?" She drank on occasion but liked to know what she was imbibing.

"Secret recipe," the woman said proudly. "The pads the biomass rests on in the river boils down real good. Ferments quickly too."

Jiow took an involuntary step back. "You're...you're drinking fungus alcohol?"

"Yeah. Are you not?" The woman was starting to look annoyed. "I thought everyone had heard about this by now. Well, all the Generationals, anyway." She lifted a ladle and something viscous slopped over the side and into the pot. "Tastes like shit, but sure does get you drunk. Are you in or not?"

"I'm...I think I'll take a quick turn around and see if...my friends are here," Jiow said, and stepped back from the pot, and the woman. She was definitely handsome, but anyone who was drinking mushroom juice was not any sort of prospect in her book.

She made hasty steps back out of the crowd and swallowed hard. How did anyone do this for more than one night? Well, that was two Generationals who would never want to talk to her again. There had to be a match for her somewhere on Lida. Someone who wouldn't mind that she worked in the sewers, and who wanted kids, and who liked things she did.

She turned and saw another person leaning against the wall, skin the color of burnished copper, looking as if they were waiting. Most everyone else was near the center of the room except her and this person. Were they just as put off by all the noise and people as she was?

"Loud in here, isn't it?" she asked.

"What?" the person said.

"It's loud!" Jiow raised her voice.

The person grimaced back and pointed to their ear. "It's really loud. Not a great place for conversation."

"Yeah, you're right."

"What?"

"You're right!"

"Oh." They looked away, then back. "Hey, I'm waiting for my friends. You have a question or something?"

"No...just...just leaving." Jiow brushed past the person and headed for the door. Maybe Frank had the right idea. She could simply work in the sewers forever and never have a chance at having a kid of her own.

"Hey, wait up," the person called, and Jiow skidded to a halt.

"Yes?" A strange hope rose in her.

The person came closer. "I'm Janx. You want to step outside for a minute? I can meet my friends there too. Didn't think it would be so loud in here."

"I'd like that." She pushed the heavy door open and sighed as the loud music faded behind her. She stared up at the stars. They weren't nearly as bright down here as they had been on the ship.

"I used to spend kiloseconds staring at them, back on the Ganesha," Janx said. "Sometimes seems like a mistake to even come down here."

"It's an interesting challenge, to say the least, but you can't say there aren't new opportunities down here," Jiow replied.

"Lots of opportunities," Janx said, their mouth turned up in an odd smile. "Especially if you don't pay much attention to Admin being busybodies and forcing everyone to do things their way."

Jiow thought back to her conversation with Frank the day before. "Like telling us how our families are supposed to work down here, rather than what we used to do on the ships?"

Janx raised their eyebrows. "Good example. Some of us think we can convince Admin to do things a better way." They gestured around, taking in the river, the biomass, and the colony. "They can't do much worse."

"What, like taking a petition to Admin?" Jiow asked. This conversation had taken a strange turn.

"At first, at first," Janx said. "But they won't listen, will they? Brighton's a control freak. Won't even see a Generational without a megasecond or two waiting period." They stepped closer to Jiow, and she lifted her chin. Janx was taller than her. "But we're looking for people who can think of different approaches to the problems in front of them. That's what we need here to get Admin's attention. Different approaches."

"Yes, that...could work." Jiow said. She thought Janx might have been interested in her as a date, and then as a new friend, and now, a...business associate?

"Hey, there's my friends," Janx said, pointing to a group of three who were approaching the filtration building. "Come on, let's find a better spot than this, and I'll tell you all about what I'm planning."

Jiow thought only for a moment. If she headed back now, she could finish her plans for rearranging the furniture, adding some new pictures to the top walls of her apartment, and painting directional lines. Or she could quit moping and meet some new people, like Frank had suggested.

"I'm looking forward to meeting them," Jiow said, and smiled.

PART SEVEN

Digging

5 months 1 week after landing

Agetha's HUD pinged with the message from Gearge, her analyst teammate from the Abeona. Her heart skipped a beat.

Come quick to construction. Daved hurt.

She was out of the apartment in moments, the pot with vegetables removed from the stove so it wouldn't set the building on fire. Agetha's mind sped through alternative situations where Daved hadn't been pulled away from the trade he was trained in. She should have been there. What happened? It had been her turn to cook because Daved was tapped this week for one of the construction crews. Even the specialists spent time on the crews, though with the cows gone and the chickens suffering from their strange feather rot, there was not as much tending to livestock as had been expected. Daved could be spared from his animal husbandry duties, and so he'd been placed in rotation. Except he should have been home cooking and she should have been there instead.

She pedaled her bicycle down the street toward the center of Alpha Radian. Gearge hadn't sent anything else except *come quickly* to her repeated questions, so she'd stopped asking and focused on pedaling. The bare bones of the Ganesha and the Xaman Ek were still visible, but everything else had been broken down, new buildings rising from their corpses. What if she had taken his place this week? She was better at handling the construction crews—it was an ability to see where things fit together and how people could work together. An unintended side effect of her systems analyst job. Then she would be cycling home, not waiting to find out if he was dead or injured, or...

She threw the bicycle to the ground as she approached Main Street, which now stretched from the Admin building, past the Vagal barracks and the first apartments constructed. There was already a crowd forming.

"What is it? What happened?" She pushed through the crowd, barely pausing to even consider the answers. There was another damn hole in the ground, LED lights already pointed down into the darkness.

Someone grabbed her shoulder and Agetha nearly screamed. It was Gearge. "He was working here, and the ground just opened up under him," her former colleague said. "We heard him calling, so he's alive, but he's hurt—don't go too near the edge."

Gearge kept her from physically climbing over the edge of a jagged hole larger in diameter than a person.

"Is...is anyone else down there?" Agetha asked, straining to see into the depths. The hole was too dark to distinguish anything, though there were a couple Vagals putting on their teal powersuits to go spelunking, noxious E-Vapors dangling from their lips.

"We don't think so," Gearge said. "Daved was the unlucky one. He actually pushed me out of the way, or I'd be down there with him."

Agetha firmly refused the thought of Gearge falling as well. At least then Daved would have someone with him.

"How deep is it?" she asked the nearest Vagal. He was a big one, with a roman nose and a prosthetic hand that didn't fit in the powersuit.

"A quick scan says it's deep. Might be caused by water flow or erosion from the structures we've built." The Vagal had an Earth accent she'd learned was from a place called the United Kingdom. He ran his prosthetic hand around the lip of the hole, crouch-walking in a circle. "We think it eroded up through the limestone from below and finally gave way."

"Have you sent a drone down yet?" Agetha asked. "I program them. I could help out."

"We would, but all the surviving drones are on construction tasks and can't be reprogrammed faster than us rappelling down. This is the quickest way to get to him, I promise." The Vagal looked up at her, and Agetha was struck by how young he looked. Not that she was much older. But he'd seen Earth, while she had spent her whole life until now on the Abeona. He'd trained for this sort of thing, in a gravity well. He'd save Daved. He had to.

He seemed to come to some decision. "You can send a drone down tomorrow, if this turns out to be bigger than we think." He nodded to the other Vagal and they slipped into the hole, holding on to a rope someone had tied to a nearby nanotanium pole.

Agetha paced, as the crowd slowly dissipated. Gearge stayed with her, as well as some others she knew from the crews. She wished Jiow was here, but her friend had been at home sick the last few days, blaming some new alcoholic drink she'd tried.

It was several hours later when Agetha—cold, hungry, and tired— watched the two Vagals emerge from the hole with her husband in tow. Daved's left arm and right leg had been wrapped in heavy cloth, though the wraps were soaked through with blood. She ran to him.

"Careful," the Vagal with the prosthetic said. His visor was covered in mud and dust.

Daved stared blearily at her, his eyes unfocused. "Agetha, I'm so glad you're here. There's so much underneath here." He waved his good hand toward the hole. "I wish you could see it. It's beautiful. The complexity…"

"He's delirious," the Vagal said. "But he's not wrong. We saw at least three iron deposits down there while we climbed. Lots of luminescent biomass growth as well, but it was all tiny—on the scale of moss, with little things crawling around in it. Probably more minerals too. I'm sure Admin will authorize a drone to explore the passage down there. Wow, do I need an E-Vapor."

They arranged Daved on a sled to take him to the medical ward.

"Thank you…" Agetha prompted.

"Anderson," the Vagal said. Just the last name, like all of them. As if they had left any other names back on Earth.

"Thank you, Anderson. I hope the doctors can fix him."

"They did a good job on me," Anderson said, flexing his prosthetic.

"We had a lot more nanomeds then," Agetha countered.

"He has some serious breaks, but he won't need anything like this," the Vagal said. "Plus, I think they'll make an exception for him, based on what he's found."

* * *

5 months 8 days after landing

"Ma'am, we've found a source of metals," Christiaan said. Jane's head popped up from reading an update on the construction of the wall around Alpha Radian. Delayed, along with everything else.

The nanotanium was going fast, and she could use a hint of good news.

"Where? How much?" They had planned to mine for metals on whatever planet they landed on, or at least for some building material. Here, there was an abundance of limestone, and not much else. The biomass had already demonstrated it could tunnel straight through the rock, which made it nearly useless as a building material. They'd already partitioned out the structural elements from cannibalizing the fleet, but eight ships simply didn't have enough mass to build an entire city, spread out on the ground.

"Almost below our feet," Christiaan said. They swiped a package to her HUD.

As usual, the good news was mixed with bad. "This pit is right in the middle of the radian?" Jane asked, though she could read the information as well as Christiaan. "How deep is it, and why didn't we spot it from orbit?"

"We were lucky to get *any* ground geometry, ma'am," Christiaan said. "Some of the biomass forests in the area are completely impenetrable to any of our surveys. Here, there's iron over twenty meters down, as well as some copper and perhaps nickel as well. We'd have never seen it from orbit."

It wasn't minerals with titanium, but it would do. They had rare earth metals enough to last for a while, but they needed structural metals. Even aluminum would do, but they'd found nothing. Until now.

"And how much will it delay things?" Jane wasn't sure she wanted to hear the answer.

"Unsure as yet." Christiaan did a few calculations on their HUD. Jane watched with a small smile. She could always tell when they did that, because their fingers moved by their side, as if counting. "We've already got thirty-five percent of construction resources dedicated to the border wall, along with Vagal patrols to knock down any infestations. Digging a mine would take another twenty percent for several more weeks, plus processing time and energy resources. Even if a mine can be created and stabilized, we will also need to reroute construction around it and provide power. Eventually, we will progress faster with the addition of new materials, but for now..."

"Tell me, Christiaan," Jane grumbled. "You know I hate it when you drag things out."

"Another five months of delays, conservatively, but we'll be able to work faster after that." They met her eyes for a second, then went unfocused again to sort through the charts and graphs that always cluttered their HUD.

"It'll have to do. What about adding these new materials to the wall around Alpha Radian instead of using nanotanium?"

"Already asked," Christiaan said, and Jane pushed down a wave of frustration. Their *job* was to anticipate what she would ask. Except for the first year they worked for her, she'd never been able to surprise them with a request, at least not visibly. It had turned into a challenge she set for herself.

"The metallurgical engineers suggest building the wall only out of nanotanium. We know the source is pure, as it's from Earth. Native metals will need to go through a purification process, and we don't know how the biomass has adapted to them. Better to keep a solid outside line of defense we know works and take our time perfecting building materials inside the wall."

"Makes sense." Jane nodded her approval of the plan and Christiaan tapped fingers in response, sending emails out to building crews, she suspected. "We're already operating six to nine months behind plan. If this adds another five months, we're heading toward a year and a half out from original estimates. If nothing else goes wrong." Jane paused as another thought hit her. There had been other caverns under the radian. Ones they didn't know about when they had landed. "Anything...else in this pit?"

Christiaan's brow furrowed just slightly. "Yes, ma'am. We found traces of biomass all through the cavern, at ten meters below the ground and deeper. We think it's grown toward the surface from where the ground was sterilized in the landing."

Jane shook her head. There was too much of this damn stuff, everywhere on the planet. It was in the ground, the seas, the air. Some of the colonists were already eating it, and it was only a matter of time until it grew back into the city. The vegetables infected with biomass DNA she'd been shown were...gruesome. She *wouldn't* let the biomass win.

"Burn it out," she said.

"Yes ma'am." Christiaan sent more instructions on their HUD.

"And Christiaan..."

"Yes ma'am?"

"If the engineers suggest nanotanium is the best way to keep the biomass out, start figuring out how much of it scheduled for construction we can divert to the city perimeter, using this new deposit. If we can line the edges of the arcopolis so the mushrooms don't get in, we have a chance to build the core of the city. I want Alpha Radian encased in a damn *nanotanium bubble* if that's what it takes. Make us safe from the biomass."

"Very good, ma'am," Christiaan said, their expression staying neutral through her tirade. They'd expected something like this too. "Shall I alert the other ship Admins as to the new plan?"

"Not yet. Figure out the resource load, and how much it will take away from our building resources now to add to them later. Bring that to me and *then* we'll let the other Admins know. I want to go into my next meeting with them with a full plan in place."

Christiaan nodded once and left Jane's office.

* * *

7 months 5 days after landing

Jiow pressed her face against the decanting room, trying to see through the darkened glass. They kept the lights dim in there, though the main waiting room was well lit.

"There's nothing to see, you know," Frank said, slumping against a wall. She'd dragged him to the reproduction wing of the medical center—built from the remains of the UGS Ganesha—despite his protests. "The first embryos were started days ago. They're just tiny clusters of cells at this point."

Jiow pushed away from the window and thumped Frank on his arm. "Just because you hate kids, doesn't mean I can't take an interest in their growth. Aren't you fascinated by how they work? You're a scientist after all. What about the media links and recorded audio from the parents? Immune boosters, physical response tracking, gene therapy, and all sorts of stimuli." Frank only rolled his eyes. "Well, come on, I want to get my name on the list."

She'd tried to be more assertive lately. Janx had suggested it. Generationals who automatically deferred to what the Admins wanted were being left in the dust. Some of Janx's other goals were...troubling, but nothing had come of them yet. For now, she was willing to use their philosophy to get what *she* wanted. In this case, a child. She'd even bowed out of Janx's latest escapade to come here. They and their band of malcontents were planning to "borrow" paint and supplies from the water decontamination plant. Admin hadn't planned for Generational housing preferences and seemed in no hurry to make amends.

"I don't *hate* kids," Frank grumbled, dragging her back to the present. "I only think they should be raised carefully out of sight, letting their parents continue with their work."

She rolled her eyes. She still wasn't completely sure how much of Frank's curmudgeon act was real and how much was simply because he enjoyed complaining. However, Admin focused on family units, not community child-rearing, like the K'uei-Hsing and Hina practiced. Because Brighton was lead administrator, she took the practices from the St. Christopher and applied them to the entire colony. Just because Jiow *wanted* to raise her children, didn't mean there shouldn't be a choice.

"You'll have to see kids at some point," she said. "They'll overrun the colony at some point, maybe in another ten years."

Agetha and Daved talked about their eventual kids all the time, and Frank had mostly stayed out of those conversations, only rarely putting in a word. But he'd never tried to stop them talking about kids, or even tried to change the subject.

Of course, she hadn't seen much of the couple recently. It had taken weeks for Daved to be discharged from medical observation, and he was only now able to move around, two months later. The doctors had found cracks in three vertebrae, as well as the broken arm, leg, and skull fractures. Fortunately, there was an abundance of mobility chairs, now that most of the Generationals weren't using them any longer. It reminded her of her own injuries after the Khonsu crash. At least then they still had a full suite of nanomedical supplies from the ships to speed her recovery. Daved wasn't so lucky, though he had been granted use of several types of nanomeds, as a reward for "finding" metals. Another case of Admin only doling out what they thought was worthwhile for Generationals to have.

But that just meant they couldn't be here today, on the first day the decanting room was officially open to the whole colony.

"Come on, best to start now, when they're just clumps of cells. You like cells." Jiow pushed the door open and pulled Frank along to the room with the List.

The few embryos already started were those of the highest of the Admins, and a few high-ranking Vagals. They'd inherit the genemods both had, and while they wouldn't live as long as their parents, they'd still live a couple hundred years past her. It didn't bother her too much, knowing she was a stepping-stone to the real colony. The Generationals had always been a transitory people, intermediaries between the Admins and Vagals who had seen Earth, and their descendants who would inherit the planet under the Admins' supervision. She simply wanted the best life for her eventual children.

"It's in here," Jiow said, tugging Frank farther into the room with the official List. It wasn't networked anywhere else, to prevent external changes to the birthing list. They'd figured out that trick in the second generation, back on the ships. The colony had kept the same tradition, which meant couples, trios, polys, and singles all had to come here to list their birth preferences and give DNA samples. Between vasectomies and other birth control, very few in the fleet were actively fertile, to keep tight control of the population. That was needed, on a generational starship. She wondered if that would change, now they were on Lida. Probably not in the first generation, at least. Not that she would ever have been able to carry a child to term herself, so it was a moot point for her, as well as other women like her.

There were a few happy couples, and a trio with at least one nonbinary member waiting in line. No singles. Jiow grimaced. Anyone could *read* a copy of the List, just not access the original. She knew how often singles were given priority. It had taken weeks of preparation for her to even come here, after prowling through every party, rave, secret orgy, public orgy, potluck, and reconstructionist service she could find for some sort of match. She made the connection with Janx and their crew, but none of them were interested in children. They were more interested in how the colony was being run. Turns out, working in the sewers left a stink of shit so strong *no one* wanted to even chance a relationship.

"Well, go on," Frank said, gesturing to the line.

"Come with me," Jiow said. "At least give me moral support for being at the bottom of the reproductive bell curve."

"It's not that bad. They'll get to everyone on the list eventually," Frank said.

Jiow linked his arm in hers and walked to the end of the line. The ones at the front were busy selecting the gene cleanings and screenings to apply to their baby. There was a small selection of variables that could be tweaked, if desired.

"No, they won't," she said. At Frank's confused expression, she sighed. "You really have never looked into this have you?" At Frank's one-shouldered shrug, she continued. "Singles have the lowest priority. You'd think the names would creep up the list eventually, but if a couple or trio with a successful child want another, then it's *zip*"—Jiow sketched a parabolic curve in the air—"right back above the singles. I could wait *decades* for my turn."

"And you really couldn't find anyone else who would go in with you?" For once, Frank's gruff manner dissolved. He straightened out of his perpetual slump, looking her in the eye.

"Not anyone who I'd want to mix my genetics with." Jiow scrunched her nose at the memory of several people she'd met who she could tell after five minutes were not ones who would care for a child the way she wanted to. One of Janx's cronies came to mind, a slouching, bitter woman.

"And you're still willing to come here and put your name on the List, when you might never receive a child?" Frank's voice was small.

"At some point, you have to do what's best," Jiow said. "I'd rather work on getting out of the sanitation industry altogether, and I can't focus on that and searching for some mythical partner at the same time. So, I'm going to put my name on the List, and hope for the best." She held her head high. Frank was a good friend, and she shouldn't have dragged him down here. Her brother would have just laughed at her, and Agetha and Daved had their own problems. Frank didn't understand what she was doing, but she'd known him long enough to know he'd support her, even if he grumbled about it.

Frank was silent for a long time. The couple in front finished their modifications and selections, finalized their child with the registrar, and left, holding hands. The next couple stepped up.

"Um."

Jiow raised an eyebrow. "What?"

"How bad do you want this? Like, is raising a child one of the things you want to do with your life? Do you know how much time it would take, especially as a single parent?"

Jiow gestured around. "I'm here, aren't I? I just told you I made my decision."

"That's what I thought." Frank took in a huge breath, then let it out slowly. "Alright. But you can't tell anyone. I don't want any say in anything, don't want them to even know about this. I don't do this sort of thing."

Jiow stared. He'd finally flipped his over-analytical mind. "In what? Want *who* to know?"

"The child, of course," Frank answered.

Jiow continued to stare at him.

"I'll sign with you. For the child. Donate genetic material, if I don't have any weird genetic errors. If this is that important to you, I want you to do what you want with your life."

"You'll—" Jiow couldn't understand what her friend had said. Hadn't even considered him, after he'd made his thoughts about child-raising clear. "Really?"

"Really."

"I...I don't know what to say, Frank," Jiow breathed. "You'll do that for me?"

Frank raised a thick finger. "But no one knows, agreed? And...I get to pick some of the kid's characteristics. Don't want another sewer-cleaner on our hands, after all." He grinned.

Jiow smiled back and straightened up, waiting for her place on the List.

* * *

7 months 2 weeks after landing

Processor Alvin—now just regular Alvin, as his lack of any sort of input into the colony structure had been made *abundantly* clear when Admin Delgado herself called him into her office to tell him to stop sending in recommendations—stared at the inside of his apartment.

It was boring, non-functional, and inefficient. The dwelling plans given to the Generationals had been designed by some advanced algorithm back on Earth to be pleasing to people, but it evidently hadn't considered thirteen thousand megaseconds of living in space. Changing the designs hadn't been high on anyone's list while landing, which meant the Generationals who'd been stuffed into the terrible things when they were first built now had time to appreciate the true horrific nature of their designs.

He turned to the pile of paint cans, brushes, tape, sticks, and other odds and ends he'd collected over the past couple months. He'd stored away a few things while overseeing the construction of the water filtration site, but never quite enough to do what he wanted with his home. However, in the last few days a crew of Generationals had come around to offer free paint to anyone who wanted to redecorate. They also had a few surprise extras. They said it was a new service to increase Generational morale, though Alvin was suspicious. When he'd asked if the program was approved by the Admins, they evaded the question. Alvin got several colors anyway. It was too good to pass up. There was a lot of raw material from the ships that hadn't filtered out of storage yet.

The first step would be to paint the routing lines. Any good apartment should have the standard set of routes painted at the wall starting from the entrance: black for emergency exit, blue for kitchen, green for sleeping quarters, yellow for entertainment. He got to work.

The other materials he'd been able to salvage and trade for, while working at the water filtration building. During the months it was being built, they'd tried stars alone knew how many experiments to kill off the fungal life in the river. The biomass became resistant to fungicides, herbicides, and pesticides far quicker than anyone imagined. At one point the entire mycological department had stayed up for three days straight to attempt a full sterilization. It hadn't worked. The next morning, there had been new hyphae creeping into the river, forming into floating pads with colonies of organisms sheltering beneath.

There had been so many tests on the biomass they'd built up a sizeable pile of resources, some of which had jumped into his pockets. Alvin removed one of the pre-installed shelves lining his entrance hall, intending to convert the shelf into another hanging unit. Who wanted all their art situated so low down on the walls? Plus, they blocked the routing lines. His new hanging fixtures connected by cables to the ceiling, and while they weren't exactly the same as working on all six sides of a room, they gave a good approximation of how space had been used in the fleet. He could display his artwork and plants the way they'd been intended.

He stared at the prybar he'd used to remove the shelf. He'd removed it from where it had been abandoned in a corner of the filtration building the day one scientist got so mad, they threw *all* the floating mushroom samples back through the access hatch into the river. That's when they had found their answer. Clog the water source with the strange black and brown growths that floated on top of the river. It turned out they contained high concentrations of melanin, which crowded out any *other* biomass species from growing in the water. With enough of them, they were dense enough to keep most other biomass fragments from getting through. It was a surprisingly smart answer. Alvin had promptly written several reports on other ways they might make the fungus fight itself.

He worked his way across the apartment, following the grid lines he'd already laid out on the walls to make the flow of the colors stand out on the white walls. No one had ever gotten lost on one of the fleet ships, as long as they knew the color scheme.

The kitchen was the easiest endpoint, and he finished the blue line first. After that was the black for the emergency exits, one in the kitchen and another upstairs. The green and yellow lines would be a bit more fragmented, as they crossed over the other lines.

It was nice to see the house becoming more of a home. It was a place to relax, instead of being terrified. He'd been around the biomass so long now he'd even stopped wearing his EVA suit. It had been five months after landing when it started developing irreparable cracks, and no one would lend him a new one. Said they were all slated for "higher priority" uses. He'd had to continue his work at the filtration building, but after testing the water himself—twice—to find only the barest traces of biomass, he'd finally been satisfied. People were even drinking the stuff, and the mycologists had finally responded to his fifth request, saying the spores couldn't survive to create a hyphal network inside a body.

Still, he hoped people didn't find him in his apartment, turned into a mushroom in another thirty or forty megaseconds.

Painting the rest of the lines and removing obstacles in their way took the rest of the day. The next morning, Alvin started installing the hanging plant holders and curio display boxes on the ceilings of all the rooms. At last, a little more color. He used the new bolt they were making to secure the hanging lines to the ceiling. Those had been harder to find discarded, and it was only the "free paint" Generationals that had been able to supply new bolts.

The metallurgists had come up with what they called "steelcrete" a month and a half ago, using metals dug from their new mine. It had sped the water filtration building to completion with new wiring, nuts and bolts, and structural elements, enabling the colony to stop hoarding water quite so much. They could tap into the planet's water supplies with much less hesitation than before.

The steelcrete went into houses too, at least when Generationals could get it voluntarily. The earliest homes not made with nanotanium had been reinforced with the new steelcrete metals, and Alpha Radian had bloomed in a construction frenzy, buildings rising as the thirty-meter nanotanium wall rose around them. Scaffolds were more common now than finished buildings. But still bolts were restricted for general use.

Alvin finished the plant cages in the entrance hallway by the midday meal. His apartment was starting to look like a place where people would actually live. He'd position his plants to the best viewing effectiveness after he ate. He sat down to his meal eyeing his handiwork. With the biomass tamed for their water source, and steelcrete forming the main body of Alpha Radian, it was the first time Alvin thought he might actually live comfortably on the surface of 11d.

* * *

8 months 5 days after landing

"Almost there. There's a bench inside to rest on," Agetha told Daved. He'd insisted on using his canes to get to the reproduction wing, and not rely on the mobility chair. He'd tried so hard over the past few months to get up and walk on his own again, but the cracks in his spinal vertebrae were causing no end of sleeping problems and pain while he walked. Agetha tried not to get angry at him for pushing himself, but sometimes it was so *hard*.

"Heh. I'll be learning how to walk unaided with our child at this point," Daved puffed. He leaned on both canes, his mouth twisting to one side like it did when his back hurt. Agetha held her tongue. Saying something would only make him tell her he wanted to do this despite the pain. And she couldn't argue with him. Again.

"You'll be up and about sooner than that," she said instead. "You'll be swinging the kid around by their toes a couple months after they're born." Her right hand clenched but she hid it behind her back. The colony needed kids. Daved wanted kids. She was the odd one out for hesitating. She'd told herself she would make no complaints today. This was Daved's day.

He chuckled at the weak joke, but sighed as he lowered himself to the bench in the room with the List. There were five other couples in front of them, a single, and a poly group, discussing child options loudly at the back of the line and ignoring annoyed looks from the registrar.

"I'll hold our place in line," Agetha told him, and turned to stand behind the poly group, but Daved caught her hand, his fingers callused in new places from the crutches.

"Stay with me. I just need a few breaths, and I'll stand in line with you. No—" He cut her off before she could argue. "I want to do this. It's important."

"You're..." She made herself stop. Didn't point out the obvious that his back hurt, or he would be in agony the next day. He knew all that better than she did. She would have to deal with his winces and gasps, trying to hide his true pain. "Alright. Just tell me when you're ready."

"The pigs are doing well, despite those growths on their backs," Daved said, evidently to get their minds off his injuries. He couldn't work in construction anymore, so Admin had assigned him back to the animal husbandry team, where he could work from a mobility chair most of the day. "We're even experimenting with a few of them to see if they can keep the biomass from encroaching on the animal pens. They don't seem to have any reaction to what they eat. We can't remove the new growths on their skin—they just grow back—but at least none of them is further affected by the biomass. In fact, their digestive systems seem to break down the new growth easily, before it has time to develop the defenses we've seen in the caverns and outside the arcopolis." He got that faraway look in his eye again. The one that said he was remembering one of his dreams.

Agetha hastily asked a question—anything to keep him from bringing it up. He'd just drift sometimes and talk about the little bits of moss and creatures he'd lain in while he waited for help. "What about the sheep? Any chance of seeing fuzzy ones again?"

Daved looked at her and blinked, as if he didn't remember what they were talking about. Then he smiled sadly. "Afraid not. They've all got that strange mange. Unless you want a lion-cut sheep, they're practically useless. We've even tracked the new lambs' growth. They show the same wool pattern as their parents. Frank says the biomass is changing their DNA, like it did with the veggies, and the cows."

"But not fatally, this time."

"Right." Daved nodded, sighed, and pushed to his feet with a grunt of pain he tried to disguise. He hobbled to the line and Agetha followed. "We think the alpacas might have a good run though. They seem much more resistant to the changes."

Agetha was about to ask another question to keep him talking, but it was too late.

"The biomass acts in such harmony," he said, almost hypnotically. "I had the dream again last night; saw the patch of moss I landed in at the bottom of the shaft. This time I could see everything, even those creatures I could never have made out in the darkness. The bioluminescence was the same, but it was like my eyes were stronger. I could see all the tiny biomass creatures as they tended the moss. They were fixing the parts I'd crushed when I landed. They were flying, or hopping, or crawling all around. It was a beautiful symphony."

"Well, what should our child look like?" Agetha said and tried not to wince. It was a desperate attempt to get him off the subject. "Your complexion or mine, or a mix? Had any thoughts on the sex yet? Or do you still want it to be a surprise?"

Daved shook himself, and barely caught himself with a cane before he toppled over. He waved her help away. "I know you don't like me to talk about it, but if we're going to survive on this planet, someone will eventually need to venture out into the biomass. I don't know if my subconscious is just processing what I saw extremely slowly, or if there's something else involved. But it was beautiful, no matter the situation." He took a step forward as the couple in front left. "There is much more to the biomass. If we could really understand it, I think we could live in harmony with it. We should let it aid us, rather than fighting it. We would complete it."

"You of all people have seen what it does to the plants and the animals," Agetha replied. "Do we just let it change everything? We'd die."

"No, I don't think we would," Daved said, waving a hand. "But no one wants to talk about this. So, let's pick out everything for our perfect child. Maybe in a year or two, we can have a second."

Agetha let herself be directed back to their child. She honestly tried to think about what she would want in a kid, since it was a reality she'd be raising one now. They moved forward at a crawl, moving both far too fast and not fast enough.

They discussed what they'd select about their child's development and what they would leave to chance. Agetha kept herself from reaching out to steady Daved, though she knew the wait was making his back cramp. By the time they got to the front they had everything figured out. But the registrar surprised them after they put in the details.

"Follow me," he said, and Agetha traded a look with her husband, but followed.

"Admin has extended a benefit to help compensate for your injuries, in light of the bounty you've discovered for the colony," the registrar said as they walked down a back corridor. "We have your genetic information on file already, and if you'd like, we can start the process today."

Daved was huffing to keep up, but he was the most animated Agetha had seen him in months. "You mean we skip the wait? We can start our child today?"

"That's right. If you want."

"We do!" Daved said, then looked to Agetha, concern showing in the ridge between his eyebrows.

"Of course we do," Agetha told him. She kept the smile on her face, reaching her eyes, until he nodded. "Please pass on our thanks to Admin. We're delighted to be able to start a child this early."

None of their friends had been able to start yet, and Admin had firm penalties in place for anyone who stopped using sterilization treatments and tried natural pregnancy. Vasectomy reversals weren't authorized either. The colony simply didn't have enough resources yet.

Agetha gripped Daved's arm to show her solidarity with his excitement, and to ease his walking just a little.

"We're going to be parents," she told him, and watched the smile spread across his face. She mimicked his, but her jaw clenched.

* * *

1 year after landing

Jane met the other Admins' gazes, all sitting around the table in the Lead Admin building. Her building, because she was responsible for city planning and development. One year in, and no one had made a serious bid for leadership of the fledgling colony. Christiaan had been right, as usual, in their assessment of the other Admins. It helped that the biomass was so hard to contain. Everyone had their hands full maintaining the colony—whether it was Dmitri dealing with faulty and dying power cells, and putting enough solar panels around to offset them, or Alessandro demanding continual updates on which foods were surviving and which were dying, or even Maria, dealing with the waste management plant.

The other Admins were busy keeping the colony running, which was excellent. Especially since she was running the colony planning, designing city layout around the new mine, and determining what resources were the highest priority. She'd developed a system with Christiaan to weigh the use of materials from the ships now, versus saving them for future emergencies. Usually the answer was to wait, though she'd received many angry emails from Generationals wondering why they couldn't have everything they wanted right now. Typical short-term thinking.

"Well, gentlemen, ladies, and"—she dipped a tiny nod to Ahman— "others." They'd been busy directing R&D for combatting the biomass. "Shall we compare notes? It's almost the anniversary of our landing, and I know we're all eager to get to the festivities, so maybe keep it short?" The others mostly nodded in agreement, and Jane swiped a thanks to Christiaan. She could practically feel their tiny smile behind her back. She was not relishing the cleanup after the entire colony got smashed later tonight on the newest type of fungal intoxicant. She hated the waste. The colony was barely surviving, and people wanted to use up their meager resources celebrating?

Jane turned to Wenqing, who was already shuffling his notes. Rather than the usual Admin assistants, he had three of the commanding Vagals behind his chair, though the only one she knew by name was General Smith, the leader of the military organization. "Shall we start with you, Wenqing? How are the Vagals handling the biomass?"

"We continue the offensive," Wenqing said. Jane waited a beat to see if the terse man would say anything else. She turned her eye on General Smith, who somehow straightened even more from his parade rest. The general biologically looked like a very well-kept sixty-year-old—large without being a giant, thick without tending to fat. Jane had investigated his files long ago, and knew he was one of the first recipients of the Vagal implants. He was nearing his eightieth year.

"Ma'am," Smith said. "We are running low on flamethrower tanks, so manufacturing more should be top priority. My Vagals continue their patrols, but we did not anticipate this level of activity when we chose our landing target. The biomass is difficult to contain, and I am relieved there is not another vector on this planet that needs military attention. Otherwise, our colony might have been severely under-defended."

So, business as usual. Jane kept the smile off her face as she read Christiaan's text. The Vagals were very vocal about how much they were doing to contain the biomass incursions, often forgetting how much the Generationals were supporting them. At least it kept them busy. Wenqing had put in requests for a larger Vagal presence guarding essential buildings, but Jane had managed to plant enough suspicion with Dmitri and Rajani that the other two Admins had gotten the rest to quash the idea. Wenqing had been cowed in meetings since. Jane had been one to propose a much smaller military presence when planning the voyage on Earth, but she had been overruled. She hoped the other Admins saw her reasoning now, even if the supersoldiers were useful in keeping the biomass away.

She turned to Dmitri. He'd been on her side from the beginning and seemed to have no clear discernible political aspirations. He'd come from an engineering background.

"And how are the power cells coming?"

"We are down to two from the original eight, and one of those is at half-charge." Dmitri Novikov looked as if an unjust god had given life to a knife blade. Everything about him was razor sharp and thin. He'd grown even sharper, on Lida. "The hydroelectric plant is progressing slower than expected, as fungal remnants keep growing into the turbines. We are researching recharging the ship batteries from solar panels, but they weren't meant to be rechargeable. The charge dissipates too quickly to be of use."

"The climate in this zone is trending even warmer than we estimated," Ahman said in their quiet voice. "We should be able to grow crops year-round if the pattern holds. I don't believe this area will ever be in danger of freezing temperatures."

"That's a benefit with our reduced crops selection," Jane said, and looked to Alessandro. "Have you developed any new resistant varieties of fruits or vegetables?"

Alessandro shook his head. He looked young, but then, all the Admins did. His curly hair had a sprinkling of salt and pepper, but only a touch, and it would stay that way for the next hundred years or so, if the genemods had no issues. "If anything, more species are becoming infected by the biomass. For example"—he gestured to the assistant behind him, then looked down to his datapad—"with every grape varietal we've tried, the fruit has hardened to a crystalline structure on the vine, so no wine in the foreseeable future."

There was a chorus of groans from the other Admins. Jane heard Christiaan tsk behind her. They had been looking forward to trying their hand at fermenting. They often told of their family's winery in the Netherlands, though who could say if it still existed.

Alessandro ticked off names on his fingers, reading down his datapad. "Apples, peaches, asparagus, pumpkins, cabbage, and yams are all failing. However, pears and strawberries, most squash, cucumbers, tomatoes, green beans, and chickpeas retain enough of their original form to be useful. The tastes and textures have changed though. Our chickpeas are double size now, with over twice the amount of stored protein. It's been a boon for the colony." He looked up and shrugged.

"Those chickpeas may come in handy," Polunu said, then cleared her throat when she found the others looking at her. She was handling animal science and food distribution. "The chickens are growing scales and many of their eggs have shells too hard for the chicks to open on their own. Aquafaba—chickpea water—can be used as a substitute for eggs. We may want to bump up crop distribution and teach how to use it effectively in baking."

"We have missing supplies," Rajani said when Jane got to her. She frowned at the other woman. That hadn't been in the report.

"Why haven't I been informed yet?"

"Have you not noticed?" Rajani challenged, rearranging her blue and orange sari. "You are supposed to be accounting for all the colony's materials."

Jane pinged Christiaan, though she knew they were already working on it, then put her full attention on the other Admin. So, it was going to be that sort of conversation.

"We're all trying to survive here," Jane countered. "Anyone who finds a discrepancy should report it."

"My assistants had to run the reports several times to be certain," Rajani said. "I assumed you would inform us of what you found."

Inaccurate inventories identified, Christiaan's message pinged in her HUD. *There were attempts to disguise the errors, thus discrepancies were purposeful. Reports indicate items are mostly construction-related.*

What purpose? Jane sent back.

There has been a spike in Generationals redesigning their home interiors, Christiaan sent back. *Likely related.*

Typical Generationals. They ignored her directives when they thought they knew better.

"Thank you for bringing this to our attention, Rajani," Jane said, too sweetly. "I believe this is linked to out-of-scope changes to the colony layout we've identified."

Anything detrimental to colony survival?

Unlikely. There has also been a three percent increase in Generational satisfaction, covering the same period. Suggest we allow this infraction.

Jane didn't catch Rajani's answer while she messaged with Christiaan, nor did she care. "There is little threat in these thefts. How about we let the Generationals get away with their mischief this time? Promote some goodwill?"

Rajani pursed her lips, but Jane caught Dmitri and Alessandro's nods. Wenqing looked bored.

Jane glanced around the room, gathering the Admins' attentions. There were two more items which had the potential to hamstring their still-young colony.

"The wall around Alpha will be finished within three weeks," Jane said, "but it's greatly reduced our nanotanium reserves. We thought we'd have enough for the groundwork of the entire colony, but we've had to use so much keep out the biomass, we can barely encircle Alpha Radian."

"Until a Generational fell down a mineshaft," Ahman prompted, their eyes questioning.

"Yes. And now we have steelcrete, using the new minerals with the natural limestone deposits. But," Jane replied. She waited until even Wenqing looked up from his datapad. "The latest analysis from the research pool shows the mineral veins drying up faster than we expected. We'll get a fair bit of minerals from this mine, but not as much as we'd hoped."

Maria sighed. "Will we have enough to finish Beta Radian? Are there other potential dig sites?"

"Yes, and no," Jane said. "The steelcrete should hold out until the completion of Beta Radian, so for the next two to three years, if all goes well. We'll have bits and pieces for additional buildings, but nothing substantial. I've had surveyors traveling across the entire arcopolis footprint, taking soundings down to fifty meters."

The room was silent, waiting. "Save for the one source of minerals, there is no appreciable other sources of metals in the city footprint."

"Which means?" Ahman asked.

"It means, we hadn't planned on having *no* minerals. We expected to range outside our landing position to search for other sources. The biomass stops that." She turned to Wenqing again. "Has there been progress on incursions into the surrounding forest?" She said "forest" because that sounded much friendlier than "overgrown fungal mat."

"Negative," Wenqing said, and flicked a finger toward General Smith, who pushed his chest out as he read from his pad.

"We have sent three teams into the surrounding...jungle, ever deeper," he said. "The first two are being treated for burns, poisoning, and bone fractures, while only one member of the third returned. Her left leg and arm were shredded, and she used the remains of her flamethrower as a crutch to return home. We're doing an in-depth psych analysis, but so far, she only rambles about...monsters, ma'am. We've lost enough Vagals already, and I would advise against sending any more in until we have better intel." The general looked embarrassed to be delivering his news.

Christiaan had delivered her a copy of the report an hour before the meeting, but she showed her fair share of shock and outrage at the news. Thinning the herd of supersoldiers wasn't a bad plan.

"We are surrounded," she said, panning her gaze around the room. She made sure to include the assistants as she let the silence grow. They talked between themselves far more than the eight lead admins did. They would be the ones to brainstorm solutions. "Right now, this city is also a prison. If we do not want it to also be our grave, we must deal with the biomass. This is our highest-priority issue, above the lack of resources, the dying crops and livestock, above the power and water supplies. One city is not a viable civilization, friends, and that is what we undertook to build here. We have a *new world* at our disposal, but we are hemmed in by a hostile organism."

She gauged the atmosphere. Ahman, Wenqing, and Maria were nodding. Dimitri looked thoughtful, and Rajani and Alessandro had their heads together while Polunu held Jane's eyes.

"If our first year on this planet was about surviving, then we have succeeded. But our second year, and beyond, must include a way to harness the biomass. To be clear, I'm not looking at our fifth year, but our five *hundredth* year. We've made it purify our water. I want ways to turn it into power, materials, and food." She pointed out the window, where even from here, she could see the top of the canopy peeking above the nanotanium wall. "We must control this planet."

PART EIGHT

Reaching

1 year after landing

Anderson held his E-Vapor while he took another swig from the mug of vile stuff gripped in his prosthetic hand. One of the Generationals had given it to him for the year celebration. Supposedly derived from the biomass, and it tasted like it. Kicked like a mule, too.

"You can almost ignore what's outside the walls," he said to Noce, who was staring up thirty meters of solid nanotanium, a mug of the same horrible brew in their hand.

"Almost," Noce said, letting out a puff from their own E-Vapor. They'd dyed their hair purple in celebration—not within the regulations they followed before the fleet left Earth, but then no one called them on it. "I'll still feel better when it's completed, and the biomass is locked out of Alpha."

"It'll happen, muux," Anderson assured. His implant was silent for the first time in months. He was hoping it was too busy neutralizing his drink to focus his attention. The buzz was pleasantly foggy.

He gestured expansively to the buildings around them, yells and fireworks echoing off the nanotanium and steelcrete. Everyone was out, and even the Vagal higher-ups had let down their hair for the year-end party. Nothing was as tall as the ships had been when they landed, but the newest buildings soared ten or twelve stories, greenery hanging over their top edges. Lights shone from most of the windows, now the sun had set.

"Cora," he said.

"What?"

"I'm naming my implant," Anderson said. Noce just looked at him. "Do you know any other Vagals who've done that?"

"Not any who were willing to publicly mention it," Noce replied. "It's not even a thing. It's just a collection of signal-response algorithms."

"That's a terrible thing to say about your implant. Mine's saved my life multiple times already."

"Still just a program," Noce muttered into their drink.

"Ah, well. I'm sure it will catch on," Anderson said, watching the sun set. "Time to get your partying in before the lights go out, muux." The batteries weren't great at holding a charge from the solar array, so by an unspoken rule, everyone ran whatever they wanted until they went to sleep, draining the energy that would be lost anyway overnight. Tonight especially, a riot of color shone from the Admin building, a rainbow of metallic reflections coating the nearby structures. Someone ran past, holding hands with another person, cast in shadow. "You have anyone to party with?"

He just caught Noce's head shaking in the semi-darkness. His commanding officer was a terse one, never giving out an unneeded word. They had been awake for several shifts in the fleet, he knew, though they never talked about it.

"Not tonight, Anderson," Noce finally said. "Had enough Vagals to take care of for the past year, and not much time for frivolities." They took a deep swig from their mug. "Maybe ask again after I've had two or three more mugs of this shit." Anderson caught a steely gray gleam from Noce's eye as they turned their head just slightly. Had that been a proposition?

Anderson opened his mouth to answer when another couple ran by, shouting at each other. Then he staggered as his heart rate soared. He straightened, his head on a swivel. Noce had let their mug fall to the ground.

Oh. His implant had kicked in. Cora. He spit out his E-Vapor.

More people were running by, and their shouts had turned from excitement to panic. That must have been what he picked up on, and as usual, Cora processed it faster than his brain had.

"Sitrep," Noce said, their body still and their head tracking left, right, up and down.

"Unsure, sergeant," Anderson said, falling into a clipped speech pattern. "I'll check it out."

"I'll contact with updated information," Noce replied, and he saw their HUD flare to life, a film growing over their left eye, information streaming upward.

Anderson ran against the tide people flooding toward them.

Cora spiked his adrenaline levels just in time for him to swerve and duck around a falling—what was that? It crashed with a *thud* and a *splat* against the street. He jigged left, cross-stepping to get out of the way at the same time he turned to face the object. It was huge, like an oak branch in size, but bisecting and forking like a frond. Tendrils wriggled against the pavement, some leaking brown liquid.

He traced its path upward to the slab of nanotanium, where one of the immense fungal trees was leaning over the wall, spreading branches draped inward, clouds of tiny, winged things floating into the city.

It was at least twice as tall as the thirty-meter wall. The Vagals had cleared out a small perimeter outside Alpha Radian, but this giant was still close enough to fall over the wall. They hadn't thought of that, but no one had seen one of the trees fall, until now.

The top section was bent over the wall's upper reaches like an old piece of celery, bending and wrinkling in the middle, scores of branches splaying out in every direction, reaching toward the Admin building and the military complex. The tree was a microbiome of the biomass just by itself. He could spot five different types of offensive mushrooms, plus caretaker creatures, moss like he'd seen in the cavern, fronds, sap pustules, and at least one of the larger spider-like critters that tended the trees. If even one branch took root inside Alpha Radian, they'd be set back months. They were already running low on propellant for the 'throwers.

Cora sent a shock of ice through his system. Fight or flight. Time to make a snap decision. In front of him, chaos. A residence and a general store near the wall were crushed, though the wall itself seemed intact. He could see bodies—people down under other branches that had fallen from the trunk. Clouds of flitting creatures—maybe harmless caretakers, maybe living, acidic flechettes—were almost invisible in the thickening darkness, and the lights were already dimmer than they had been a few minutes ago. Not too long until a forced lights-out.

Anderson spun away from the destruction and sped to the military complex. People might die in the time it took for him to find a powersuit, but if he was compromised, no telling what the future effects would be. He'd seen fellow Vagals melt, explode, go crazy, or fall to the ground, paralyzed.

It took eleven and a half minutes for him to run to the complex, find his teal powersuit and his 'thrower, check the propellant level, confirm oxygen tank levels on the suit, and sprint back to the wall. He saw other Vagals arriving at the same time: some suited up, some in plainclothes helping the Generationals.

"Where are you, Anderson?" Noce's voice crackled in his ear.

"In a powersuit and ready to help, muux."

"Good work." Was there a hint of relief in Noce's terse voice? "We've lost three Vagals already to biomass-related complications. I need you on the wall team. Ladders are going up. Repel the invaders, Private."

"Acknowledged," Anderson said, and joined a team lugging a folded ladder from a nearby storage center. They had constructed a few ladders longer than thirty meters from nanotanium, specifically to tend the upper reaches of the wall. The steelcrete wasn't strong over that distance, and the nanotanium was lighter.

The woman next to him, also in a powersuit, slipped in a patch of fungal ooze and he barely steadied her with his prosthetic, his real hand clamped on the ladder. Fortunate he'd had the appendage serviced last night. The finger joints had been loosening over the past week.

"Thanks," the woman said—he wasn't sure of her name—as they reached the wall, levering the ladder with a clang against it. The length rested partially against the fungal tree's branches—there was no avoiding them, this close. They spanned along a stretch of wall wider than it was tall, writhing without wind, branches curling around houses or other ladders.

"Watch the limbs!" he called and unslung his 'thrower. Would the flame be hot enough to burn through the branches? Some were thicker than he was tall.

Too late. His impromptu team scattered as the ladder shook under a twisting branch and bucked away from the wall. He winced in pain at the ringing *clang* as the nanotanium made a dent in a nearby barbershop.

"Get it back—!" Someone called, but their cry was cut short as a limb swung down and smacked them into a paste on the pavement.

Anderson was already moving, leaping over a stand of parked bicycles, then taking cover behind a building. The woman he had been next to puffed after him and skidded to a stop beside him. Anderson spoke into his com.

"Muux—I think the tree is reacting to warm bodies. Can you alert the Vagals?"

"Done," Noce's voice faded even as they answered, switching to a broadcast channel. He read through the incoming high-priority message on his HUD warning all Vagals of the threat.

"Quick reflexes," the woman said. Then, "Murphy."

"Anderson," he introduced himself. "What's your take?"

"Got to get around the tentacles to stab Cthulhu in the head, er, so to speak," Murphy answered.

Anderson gave her a quick glance, then back to the tree. It did sort of look like some tentacle god, draped over the wall, its limbs curling around ladders, buildings, and the few people who weren't yet out of the way. Three Vagals were fighting the spider-caretaker near the wall. One of them screamed and went down under too many legs.

"You don't know how many mortars we have left, do you?" he asked.

Murphy shrugged and pointed up, in the universal gesture to ask the higher-ups. "Find out."

"Muux, we're going to need heavy artillery for this one. Don't think the 'throwers are going to cut it. What do we have left?"

"Down." Murphy dropped and Anderson rolled to the ground before conscious thought, Cora poking his reactions faster than he could. A cloud of green fluorescing flapping things soared overhead, dissolving a chunk of the building as they did. Anderson rolled, brought his 'thrower up, and fired. The cloud turned into a miniature fireworks display, and he squinted behind his faceplate.

"Thanks, Cora," he mumbled.

"Restricted supplies, Private," Noce said. "Everything okay?"

"Just some floaters," Anderson breathed. "Requesting restricted access under threat of containment breach and imminent casualties."

"Granted restricted access supplies." Noce went through the code phrases in a monotone, not even pausing before the next sentence. "We have thirties and forties in mortars, and ten fifties left. What ordnance?"

"I think we're going to need to bust out the fifties, sarge," Anderson said, scanning for more spore clouds. "Branches are an estimated two- to two-point-five meters in diameter. Main trunk is at least five meters across. If we're going to separate it where it's draped over the wall, we're going to need heavy firepower."

"Agreed. I have eyes on the main trunk," Noce said. They switched to the broadcast channel again, and Anderson heard their voice mirrored from Murphy's HUD. "Clear point of impact on main trunk. Heavy ordnance being deployed in ten seconds."

Anderson peeked around the building and saw Vagals scurrying out of the way, some escorting Generationals who were still too near the fungal monstrosity.

Three. Two. One.

He heard the mortar before he saw it, launched from the top of the military complex. It intersected the tree right at the crest of the wall, and his powersuit's visor dimmed at the explosion of light and fire. A wave of heat washed over him, but he stared until the smoke cleared.

Several branches were missing, and another fell with a crash as he watched, twisting on the pavement like a twenty-meter worm trying to dig back into the soil. Fronds scraped spores over the newly cleaned interior of Alpha Radian.

He grimaced, seeing cleaning duty in his future, then investigated the crater in the main trunk. It hadn't been enough to sever it, but the mortar had made an impact. Fortunately, the nanotanium wall was made of stronger stuff—the plates that used to be a ship's hull shrugged off something as measly as a fifty mortar.

"Another, Noce?" he asked his sergeant.

"Requesting approval," came their voice. "Only nine fifties left." Then, "Approval granted."

The broadcast warned everyone again, and the second mortar hit in the exact same position as the first. The *crack* of the fungal trunk was louder than the explosion had been, shearing off just beneath the highest point of the wall.

"Clear the area!" Anderson broadcasted, but Cora had done her job, and he and Murphy were jogging away from the wall.

Thirty meters of steel-strong mushroom crashed down along the stores, residences, and storage units near the wall, limbs crushing bicycles and awnings. A cloud of acidic winged protectors rose into the air like someone had blown away a whole haunted house's worth of dust.

"Powersuits with me," Anderson broadcasted, and Murphy followed him to the impact site. She'd found a 'thrower somewhere, and they raised them in unison with four other Vagals.

The cloud shimmered and popped and sparked like a factory of fireworks, glowing green, orange and blue in the fire.

"Cleanup duty," Noce told him, and Anderson looked up at the doubled audio. Noce was four meters away, hefting their own 'thrower. They nodded in greeting, teeth bared through the powersuit faceplate.

Anderson pointed his flamethrower down. It was easy to talk about these things like trees because that's what they resembled, but close up, they looked nothing like trees. Instead of bark, the flesh was mottled brown and purple, with outcroppings of fruiting bodies in whites and reds and oranges. The skin of it was like a vertical city, festooned with mushrooms of all sizes, little things climbing and oozing and flying around them. The branches were more like forking fronds, the "bark" covered in spiraling coils of dangling hyphae, in hairy, leaf-like clusters that poked out in all directions, and webs of tangling, sticky vines.

He blasted the nearest mass with flame, and it shriveled and shrieked as it curled inward. The hyphae burned away easily, but the main trunk, and even the branches, were too thick. They were going to have to cut these up and drag them out of the arcopolis. Before they took root.

"New orders from Admin," Noce said over his com. "We're to remove this debris, then travel outside the walls in groups and remove any other growths than might potentially fall on the wall. We'll work out to a depth where one of the growths horizontally won't touch the wall."

"Acknowledged," Anderson said, and sighed inwardly. Just when he thought they'd been getting a handle on the biomass. It always had another trick ready.

* * *

1 year 3 months after landing

Frank prepared the two dead honeybees, side by side, under his microscope. Ever since the fungal tower had fallen over the wall seven or eight megaseconds ago, there had been ever more biomass-related complications with their plants and livestock. The latest complaint was when someone brought in a frame from one of the beehives, the cells filled with a strange bright pink honey. With a deepening pit of apprehension in his stomach, Frank had asked for samples of their bees as well.

The Vagals said they'd cleaned up all trace of the tree's creatures and remains, but he knew that was bullshit. They'd barely managed to sterilize a few enclosed caverns, where the spores and critters *couldn't* be blown about on the breeze. The instant the tower came crashing over the wall, Alpha Radian was doomed to a spike in biomass contaminants, mobile, stationary, and unknown. They'd be flaming mushrooms out of the streets for dozens of megaseconds—if they ever got rid of them. Admin had been right, in this instance, to order clearcutting outside the wall. They should have done it before now, but there hadn't been enough resources. It was a priority now. Better late than never.

He put his eye to the scope. They'd started small—only fifty hives in Alpha Radian compared with the over eight hundred that had been on the fleet ships, pollinating the hydroponics bays. But they'd already lost fifteen of these hives due to various environmental pressures. The rest were in sus-ani, so they had room to experiment before bringing all the colonies back out. Still, the arcopolis was going to be short on sweeteners to back up the beet crops—the sugar cane had changed into something resembling bamboo five megaseconds after landing—until the bees started producing.

The bee on the left was a small worker from one of the Radian hives. The legs, wings, and head all looked the same between the two, but the native worker was fuzzier than the one he'd taken from sus-ani. There shouldn't have been that much adaptation in only a year. He increased the magnification on the scope, zooming in to the rows of tiny branching hairs on the bee's thorax. The hair was all over the creature—even on the eyes—branching strands to help the bee trap pollen. It was what made the little things so darn cute.

There were some odd colored hairs among the brown ones, tinged green and pink, but the thorax was too hairy to really discern the differences. He moved down to the—usually—less fuzzy thorax, at least in the bee from sus-ani. On the native one, there were even more of the green and pink filaments than the brown ones. The branching structure was nearly the same between the two, but...

He clicked over to a higher magnification, singling out a patch with all three colored hairs.

"Fuck."

Now he could see the difference. The green and pink filaments were because biomass had colonized the hairs—and evidently prompted the bee to grow more than normal. It was similar to something he had seen in the Earth native *Scytalidium cuboideum*, back on the ship, down to turning the affected area pink.

Where there was biomass contamination, there might be a larger mycelial body.

Frank found his tiniest scalpel. Peering through the magnification lens, the cut into the bee's thorax pared away a section of the exoskeleton. He did the same to the bee from sus-ani. He rested his arm on the table to steady it, then, in both bees, carefully pushed aside the stomach and intestines with the tip of the scalpel. The sus-ani bee looked normal, but in the native bee there was a small black knob attached to the interior of the exoskeleton.

Hyphal threads sprouted from the knob, spreading out to the bee's surface to attach to the hairs. The fungal mat went all the way through the bee's system, even reaching up into the heart and brain. But it didn't seem to have restricted any organ functions. The bee had been killed by an alcohol wash, not natural causes or disease. In fact, the organs all looked perfectly healthy. The bees from the fleet had always had a propensity toward digestive problems—something to do with the lack of gravity. The native bee's intestinal tract looked perfect. There was no evidence of any mites or other infections. The bee from sus-ani looked in far worse shape, comparatively.

There also hadn't been alerts from the beekeepers about dying bees. Yes, some colonies had died, but this bee was from one that was still thriving. They suspected the dead colonies had been from a lack of adaptation to the native magnetosphere—the bees tended to get lost and die without gathering any nectar to take back to the hive.

If the hyphae weren't harming the bees, what did they do?

Frank shoved down the vague sense of dread that had been growing in him the past few megaseconds.

"Sample. Where's that sample," he muttered to himself. Dropping the scalpel on the table, he rifled through the storage cabinet that held frozen bits of plants, animals, fungus, and...bees.

"Aha!"

He defrosted the samples of bees from the failed colonies, jiggling a leg anxiously as they thawed. He hoped he was wrong. Was the fungus simply using the bees as a carrier? A propagation model? The bees went everywhere in the arcopolis. They could contaminate every single plant with spores, viruses, biomass genetic material, and more. No wonder the plants were so affected.

Lida wasn't going to be conquered by them, despite what Admin boasted. Instead, over the years, they would adapt to the planet. And as the defining feature was the all-encompassing biomass, that meant adapting to *it*.

What would future generations look like on this planet? It was one reason he hadn't wanted kids. Except.

Except now he had one, no matter how much he had promised Jiow he'd have nothing to do with the child once it was born. He realized he was staring at the wall, looking at nothing. His right hand clenched in a fist. The baby was due to be decanted in less than fifteen megaseconds—six months in the colony's inexact measurement. Jiow went down to the decanting room every day. She kept careful track of the baby's progress. Frank's eyes flipped across his HUD, where in one corner there was a realtime thread of all the fetus' vitals. Even if he had promised to have no hand in raising the child, that didn't mean he couldn't keep a scientific eye on the process. Just for documentation's sake.

He and Jiow had started up their own weekly game nights, now Agetha was helping Daved heal up. They had attended a few times, but Daved's injuries made it difficult for him to sit still long enough to concentrate on a game. They were also busy preparing for their own child, who would be born about eight megaseconds sooner than his. Than Jiow's.

Plus, Frank liked Jiow's company. He always had, really, as much as he liked being around anyone. She'd seemed more satisfied lately. He'd thought it was the gestating child at first, but then he'd called her HUD one evening and she'd put him off—said she was going out with friends. Not that he begrudged her friends, only that he hadn't ever seen her with them.

The warmer dinged and he snatched the samples up—ten bees from the failed colonies.

He went through the same preparations he had with the other two, laid them out, and set the microscope over each one in turn, pouring over the outside of the bee, then making a few incisions to check the inside.

"Fuck," he said again. None of the bees from the failed colonies had the colored hairs, hyphae or the little black mycelium. He'd bet money against a pile of rotten cabbages that none of the failed colonies had the growths. And that the surviving colonies *did*.

Was the fungus actually *helping* the bees navigate Lida? That would mean they'd already passed the point of depending on the native biomass for their survival. Without bees, they'd have no effective pollinators. With infected bees, there would be biomass traces on nearly every crop they ate, not to mention the honey.

The honey.

He inhaled, let out a long sigh, and turned to the frame of honeycomb lying on a different specimen table. Most of the comb was what you would expect from a beehive—light yellow wax, darker honey stored in some of the cells. However, covering a corner of the rectangular frame was a batch of bright pink, showing through beneath a layer of wax capping. There had been other instances of bees getting into dye or colored flavoring on the ships, and the UGS Hina had even been known to give their bees dye on purpose every so often, to celebrate occasions with blue or green or purple honey.

This, however, was not some food coloring. He donned a filtered mask and scraped the covering from some of the cells, revealing an amber-colored liquid, with pockets of dazzlingly bright pink. It almost sparkled as the light reflected off suspended particles in the fluid.

He gathered a bit of the honey, prepared it, and investigated it under the microscope. Just as he thought. The pink particles were some sort of crystalized hyphae, like little booby traps inside the honey. He'd have to contact Admin before anyone started experimenting with the pretty-colored honey. Would they have to burn the hives? Put all the crops in enclosed areas with the bees? No, that could never work. There was already biomass all over the hives.

He was halfway through a panicked memo to Admin when he slowly swung back to the hive frame. There was honey in it that wasn't pink. Some parts of the biomass were fanciful colors, even beautiful in a way. But much of it was drab, *blending into the environment*. It was what made removing the biomass so hard.

He prepared another sample of the honey—normal colored this time—held his breath and looked through the scope.

It contained the same crystals as the pink honey. But these were amber—the same color as the honey.

They'd been eating honey from the hives for two dozen megaseconds, both from the hives that had died, and the ones that had lived. The temperate environment where they landed meant they could grow crops all year long, and the bees had been busy as, well...

Frank took a long look at the rack of tea mugs on the other side of his laboratory, the half-eaten jar of honey he'd received as a gift from a thankful Generational when he'd cured blemishes on their tomatoes.

He took a scoop of the honey he'd been eating every day, prepared a slide.

Hyphal crystals. How much had he already eaten? How much had the colony eaten? If it hadn't affected them by now...

"Fuck it."

He dipped a finger into the pink honey and brought it to his mouth. If he hadn't turned into a mushroom already, either he was safe, or it was only a matter of time.

The pink honey was quite tasty, with a spicy undertone. They'd attributed that taste to the something in the soil here. Now he knew what it was. The crystals dissolved in his mouth with tiny pops, releasing whatever fungal load they contained. They must have dissolved in his tea, which was why he hadn't experienced the sensation before.

Frank swallowed.

They would never conquer Lida. The most they could hope for was not to *be* conquered by Lida.

* * *

1 year 4 months after landing

Jiow crept after Janx and their crew. This was the third time she'd been on an "acquisition" run, and she was starting to get nervous. The paint and construction supplies were one thing. No one had been using them. Then Janx had them sneak into the food storage one night and move high-protein Vagal rations to Generational supply packages, tucked under the other rations. They hadn't been caught.

"Metals?" she whispered to Janx. "Admin is sure to notice. The colony doesn't have enough."

"Which is why we're reallocating some to Generationals in need of it for necessary repairs," Janx expounded in a whisper. They always talked as if they were another Admin who just happened to lose their invitation to the meetings with the other leaders. "There are shovels that need new heads, mallets and nails that need to be made, plows and shears for planting and trimming. Admin, in their infinite wisdom, didn't include enough in the storage crates on the ships, thinking we would use local materials once we landed. You see how well that went."

They finished their speech, and directed Maarsi and Jonthin with hand signals to creep around the side of the mining annex. It had been built over the cavern Daved fell into almost a year ago, now thoroughly explored and sanitized of biomass. Jiow could see the two Vagals stationed at the entrance from here. She'd heard they had something like a sixth sense, and sunk down lower behind the scrap bin where they were hiding.

"Don't you think the Vagals will see them?" she asked.

Janx shook their head. "They've been doing this since they were children. Didn't I tell you about what we got up to back on the Xaman Ek?"

They had told Jiow. Many times. She sighed.

"I told you, I'm not stealing anything. I have a child growing and I'm not willing to abandon them."

"You're just a distraction," Janx promised, one hand out in a placating gesture. "Just ask the Vagals for one of their E-Vapors. That's all you need to do."

Janx had refused to tell her what was going on before they started for "security reasons," and Jiow almost told them to shoot the whole thing out an airlock, then, but they had insisted. For all their flaws, Janx was a charismatic speaker.

"It's not going to work." Jiow tried one more time.

"It will. Just ask them for one and when they refuse, walk away. Maarsi and Jonthin are already on their way. You don't want them—and us by extension—to be spotted, do you?"

Jiow grumbled, but she was here already. It couldn't hurt to talk to the Vagals. She'd done that many times before.

She pushed up from her crouch before she could think better of it and walked to the two guards. That they even had guards at the metal storage depot showed Admin had some small fear of the metals being misused.

She didn't recognize either of them, but that wasn't unusual. There were over fifteen hundred Vagals in the colony, and these were likely the lowest ranked. Just like her. They were watching her approach. They were doing the equivalent of cleaning the sewers in the fleet, and Jiow's shoulders relaxed at the realization. She nodded to the nearest.

"Stuck on guard duty? Lose a bet or something?"

The Vagal on the right—a large, stern, amber-skinned woman—only glared at her, but the shorter tanned man on the left cracked a smile. He was cute, in a bulky, supersoldier sort of way.

"Guessed it in one. Lost a bet with the sarge we could clear out the Alpha Radian perimeter before another squadron."

"We would have won if you hadn't stopped to play with that spider creature," the woman hissed.

"It was trying to eat my leg. What did you expect?"

"You have any of those weird drugs on you?" Jiow asked. "You know, the E-Vapors? I've been wondering what the draw is. Thought I might try one myself."

The woman laughed in her face. "Those would kill you in six months just from the carcinogens."

"And we don't have enough for us as it is," the man said. But his partner narrowed her eyes, head starting to turn as if she sensed something.

"But you use them all the time," Jiow said. She didn't want the E-Vapor. It sounded disgusting. But she needed something else to distract the pair.

"Too strong for the Generationals," the woman sneered. "Go find some fungus to drink or something."

Out of the corner of her eye, Jiow saw Maarsi creeping back to their hiding spot.

"Yeah, I hear there's a new kind of brew coming out," Jiow said. "I guess I'll get my fix that way."

"You do that," the man said. His eyes were searching the nearby buildings. He must have sensed something too.

Jiow walked—quickly—away from the guards and down the street before doubling back behind a building. She met up with Janx and the others a few blocks away. Jonthin was cradling a large chunk of metal in his arms, back stooped.

"Got it," Janx told her.

"Good, because the Vagals were getting suspicious," Jiow said. "I'm out of this. Don't call me again."

"Sure, sure," Janx said. "Just one last job and we'll be done. No need for anymore sneaking around."

"Yeah? What's that?" Jiow was in no mood for Janx's games.

"We're going to steal one of Admin Xi Wenqing's nukes."

* * *

1 year 6 months after landing

"Come on Daved, it's the opening ceremony. You've got to make an appearance. You've been talking about decanting Phillipe for the last month." Agetha gently shook her husband's shoulder. He took a long time to get out of bed, these days. His healing was slow, even a year after the accident.

Daved groaned, squinting his eyes up at her even as he offered a weak smile. "Five more minutes, love."

"Another headache?" They'd been increasing over the past two weeks. The doctor they went to suspected it might be from the misalignment in Daved's spine. Agetha kept the gentle smile on her face. Supportive.

"Yeah, a big one. But I'll be up in a few minutes, really. I couldn't miss this day."

Agetha let him sleep, pouring her nervous energy into getting a few items packed for the day. Their child—Phillipe, they'd decided—would be decanted in a ceremony the Admins had insisted upon.

She would have preferred a private moment with their new child, but Daved had agreed, saying it would be a morale booster for those Generationals who didn't yet have a child, or had one still developing, like Jiow. Agetha had reluctantly agreed, though everyone would expect her to smile and be happy about her new child. They were some of the first to contribute to the next generation of the colony. There were no population controls like there had been on the ship. A baby boom was just what they needed. But she still wasn't certain *she* needed a baby, especially while taking care of Daved.

He appeared a few minutes later, leaning heavily on his cane. Some days he needed it more than others. He limped toward her and gave her a peck on the lips, his unshaven cheek scratching hers.

"Please tell me you're not trying to grow a beard again," she said. She looked between his pupils. Was one larger than the other? No. She was overreacting. They were both stressed about today.

Daved chuckled. "I'll shave in a minute. Just getting my eyes adjusted to the light. I had the dream. It was lovely this time. I think I've explored the whole network."

Agetha tried not to grimace, thoughts of children disappearing. There was no need to label *which* dream. It was always the one. The only one he had, or could remember. He was back in the underground cavern, filled with denizens of the biomass, though the real one was fully sterilized and mined out a hundred meters under the colony. He'd seen dozens of different growths and shapes—even sketched some of them out. They might be accurate, they might not. There was so much diversity almost anything was possible in the biomass.

She put the dream out of her mind, wondering how he would last the day out in the bright sun, when there was only one sickly LED lamp in this room and he was squinting. They were still recommended to conserve power as much as possible. Engineers had found biomass growth in the solar array and sections of it were on a rotating shut down while they cleaned it out.

It was raining, and they had to rest on several benches on the way to the birthing center. They got to the ceremony late, but not late enough to impact anything. After the catastrophe of the first-year celebration, Admin had moved their main medical complex to the middle of the Alpha Radian, farther away from the wall and potential contaminants. There had been more growths spotted inside the Radian since then, and the Vagals had been working hard to contain the fast-growing biomass offshoots from the tree. Several buildings near the wall had been completely demolished, sterilized, and rebuilt from the ground up.

At the ceremony, they sat through the interminable speeches and proclamations, placed on a stage—not the stage where the Admins sat of course, but another, secondary stage for the Generationals serving as examples of the community. Admin Brighton had been showing off "good" Generationals every chance she could, since no one had yet discovered how the block of steelcrete had been taken from the metal repository. Agetha shook her head at the memory. Division was not what they need now, not with everything else.

Despite that, she had taken a small bit of steelcrete from the tiny bits that moved, anonymously, through the Generational community. The pan Daved had dropped wouldn't fix itself.

All eight Admins gave their own speeches about how their sections of the arcopolis were going, though everyone could see the results for themselves. Agetha listened more attentively to Admin Giordano's talk about how well food production was going with the surviving crops, mainly out of some strange sense of pride, even though she'd never seen the man when he was the Admin of her ship. Admin Brighton had to give the final speech, naturally, as she was lead Admin and in charge of city planning. And because she was a ruthless bitch who would stop at nothing to keep the arcopolis construction on schedule. She drove the construction crews mercilessly, or rather her assistants and aides did.

It was only after all the boasting and self-congratulations that Agetha and Daved got to see their child. The birthing center was crowded with Admin assistants she had never met, nor wanted to, and a number of Vagals. Frank and Jiow were here somewhere, but she couldn't find them in the mass of unfamiliar faces.

Phillipe was not the first child to be decanted, not even the first from Generational parents, but Daved's fall into the shaft of minerals was touted as the most wondrous accident that had ever happened. If it hadn't, their construction would have stalled by now. Agetha was happy it had gotten them a place near the head of the line for children, and that the colony was progressing, but she sincerely doubted it was worth the pain Daved had gone through over the last year, and the frustration, anguish, and anger of dealing with him as he convalesced. The last thing she needed was *another* helpless being living with her. Her fingernails bit into her palm. What was wrong with her? She should be happy today of all days.

Daved limped with her to the front of the room. Admin Giordano himself was there, a false smile on his tanned face, his salt and pepper curls expertly styled to look as if he had put no effort into them.

"Still alright?" she whispered.

Daved reached a finger up as if he would rub his temple, then made a fist and dropped his hand. "Perfect. I can't wait to see Phillipe." His voice was strained.

"You two must be so proud of your new child," Admin Giordano said loudly, gesturing to the decanting tube. They had removed the stimuli chamber that mimicked the perfect parent's womb, and what was left was essentially a large bottle containing a bunch of liquid and a new life. Phillipe was visible inside, looking perfect in every way. Well, looking like a wet and squishy potato, if Agetha was honest with herself. She and Daved reached out as one, to pull the lever and drain the amniotic fluid.

"Very proud, sir," Agetha said. They pushed the large red button to release the catches. Fans whirred, tubes sucked, more immune boosters were administered, and a mysterious process delivered a wailing, red, lump of human into Agetha's arms, swaddled in a blanket. She didn't know whether to cry or vomit.

"Phillipe." Daved said, a true smile breaking through his pain for the first time in days, as he juggled his cane to free up his hands. He leaned over their child, resting his hip against the table the decanting tube sat on to steady himself. He gently took the bundle from her. "Welcome to Lida. We're your parents."

Agetha blinked away tears she hadn't realized were running down her face. "Welcome home," she whispered.

"Can you take Phillipe back for a moment?" Daved asked, and Agetha caught the tenseness in his voice. He'd need a free hand for his cane.

She took back their child, hugging Phillipe to her breast, a strange bond she had never known or wanted tying them together. Affection.

That's what it was.

Daved grunted, and staggered, reaching for his cane.

Agetha looked back up. "What's wrong?" She tried to keep her voice level.

"Just need to catch my balance," he said.

Agetha turned to Admin Giordano to thank him for taking the time to be there. She had to get Daved and Phillipe back home as soon as possible. But she saw the Admin's eyes widen and swiveled to her left, just in time to see Daved crumple to the floor.

* * *

1 year 6 months 1 day after landing

"They've got him stable, for the moment," Frank told Agetha as he passed her another bottle of milk. He and Jiow were both sitting with her, helping her with Phillipe as much as they could while doctors worked on Daved. At first the diagnosis was dehydration, then fatigue, then a cold, and then they hadn't heard anything else for several kiloseconds. In the meantime, she'd fed Phillipe twice already, and the child had finally settled down against her breast, breathing as quietly as a mouse.

"I can hold Phillipe if you want," Jiow offered again, but Agetha only shook her head. She needed to do this. She already felt guilty enough thinking the child was an imposition while her husband was unconscious for some unknown reason.

"Maybe I'll take a walk," Agetha said. "Let you two get back to it for a while and show Phillipe the city." She began the process of gathering all the bits and pieces of baby paraphernalia, but a nurse pushed through the swinging doors, aiming for her.

"Or not," Agetha said.

"Agetha Xenakis?" the nurse questioned, and she nodded, something like ice coursing through her chest. It was never good news.

But then the nurse looked away from her. "And you're Frank Silver, correct?" At Frank's confused nod, she continued, "We'd like your opinion as well."

"I'll take Phillipe," Jiow said. "Please. You need to focus on this."

Agetha finally assented and handed the child over. Jiow looked down and cooed. Had Agetha looked at Phillipe that way?

The doctor, a tall, spare man with blindingly white skin—probably from the UGS St. Chris or Abeona, originally—met them in front of the room that held her husband.

"We thought it was a combination of fatigue and his injuries until we did an MRI," he said after introductions.

"Well, what is it?" Agetha said. The continual evasions made her jaw clench. "Another complication? A virus? And why would you need Frank..."

She trailed off as her brain finally fought through the fatigue of the past day. There was only one reason they'd ask the colony's premiere biomedical and genetic scientist along.

"Is it viral or a larger incursion?" Frank asked. He'd gotten to the answer ahead of her, naturally.

"It's large, but unfocused," the doctor said. He seemed more comfortable looking at Frank instead of her. "We'd like you to glance over the MRI results with us. You have more experience with this sort of thing"

"Is he awake?" Agetha asked, and the thin doctor's eyes flicked back to her. As if Frank was more important. He shook his head. "We have him sedated for now. We thought it better to let him have a painless rest."

Which implied there would be more pain later.

Inside the room, Agetha went to her husband while Frank and the doctor poured over several scans, sending images back and forth between their HUDs.

Daved was resting, seemingly at peace for the first time in months. His dark skin was pale and ashen, except for purple bags under his eyes. She laid a hand gently on his tightly curled hair, noticing the white that hadn't been there before a year ago. They were barely into their six hundreds—megaseconds that was. A little over twenty years in local time for her, and another sixty megaseconds for him. Still young. Just starting a family. Like this, she could almost see the time they'd spent together on the ship, ever since they were just old enough to know they wanted to spend their lives together. She could see years of strife, hardship, challenge, and triumph ahead of them, raising Phillipe, seeing the construction of the arcopolis completed, and eventually reaching out farther into Lida.

"Agetha."

She jumped, and swiveled to Frank, who was standing at her shoulder.

"Sorry to scare you."

"No, it's...I was just thinking."

"Want to come see this?" It was a strangely tentative question, coming from Frank. He didn't usually mince words. She frowned at him, seeing his expression unchanged.

"I think so?"

He tilted his head toward the doctor and her stomach clenched. He acted as if he expected the worst from her. Why?

Once nearer, the doctor flicked an image to her HUD. "This is what I had Mr. Silver looking at." She opened the file to see ghostly, black and white images of a body. They were divided into torso, arms, legs, and head, at several depths.

"What am I looking at?" Daved's insides, she knew, but that wasn't what her question meant.

"Here and here," Frank said, highlighting areas in the upper chest on the shared images. "Look closely."

Agetha did, her breath catching as she saw the squiggly lines every colonist had learned to fear. She glanced through the other images, now she knew what she was looking for. It was everywhere—tendrils seeping into organs, into the skin, through his bones, in his brain. It was in his finger and toenails.

"Biomass. Is that what caused his collapse? Do you know how long he's had it?" Should she have noticed something wrong? Watched him more closely?

"They weren't visible on any of his previous scans," the doctor said. "The fact that it's progressed this quickly is concerning."

"That's not all of it," Frank said. At Agetha's confusion, he clarified. "I mean, what's on the scan is unusual, but it's the way the growth is presented that's weird. In fact, anyone else showing these signs should be...sorry...dead already."

Agetha waved away the words. "Daved's been living in the medical ward practically more than at our apartment. Why wasn't any of this detected before?"

"We don't think most of it was there or we would have seen it," the doctor said.

"I've been working with some specimens lately, and there are similarities with Daved," Frank continued. "Look here."

At Frank's digital pointer, Agetha squinted at the MRI of her husband's chest. "What's that black spot?"

"Something I've seen in bees, of all things, but much larger," Frank answered. "The hyphae come from this node and spread out through the body. Except in the colonies with this infection, the bees are doing *better*, adapting to Lida. The colonies without it are dead."

"So...how...what...?" Agetha looked between the doctor, Frank, and Daved.

"Maybe it's the same infection, crossing to a human. We know the biomass partially communicates through a virus. That's how it uses plant, animal, and fungal parts. Maybe it's something he picked up from the mine and took a year to navigate through his body. We can't say for certain," the doctor told her.

"But it's all over his body, and still growing," Frank said. He flicked another MRI of Daved's chest to her. "That's an image taken two kiloseconds after the others."

There were visibly more hyphae in Daved's chest region. They reached into his lungs, now. She looked to her husband, lying peacefully.

"What's going to happen?"

The doctor sighed and shook his head. "It's not good."

"Just tell me!" Agetha said. Her palms hurt where her nails dug into them. "I've lived with his broken body since he fell in that mine. It's been torture. It's been a living *hell*. And as of yesterday, I have a baby to take care of. So, I'll be very clear: tell me. All of it. What. Will. Happen."

"He's probably got a few days left," the doctor said. "This growth is unsustainable. It's going to suffocate his organs."

"Thank you," Agetha told him, the tears already welling in her eyes. She turned to Frank, whose eyes widened at something in her expression. "Why didn't it affect the bees this way? What's different?"

Her old friend looked like he was trying to fit his mouth around words that wouldn't come. Finally, "I don't know. The biomass makes little sense to us, organically or evolutionarily."

"Then find out," Agetha told him.

* * *

1 year 6 months 5 days after landing

Agetha insisted on digging Daved's grave herself, arguing with Admin until they gave her use of several construction drones for a few hours. Alpha Radian was officially finished, and construction on Beta hadn't fully ramped up. It wasn't something they did in the fleet—bodies were dissolved into the same nutrient slurry that all the other compost went to—but the tradition had sprung up after the Khonsu crash. Daved had been enamored of Lida. He would have wanted to be buried in its soil.

He hadn't ever woken up from the painless rest the sedation gave him. It was a relief in one way, and the worst, tearing, pain in another. She'd been able to tell him goodbye, had talked to him for hours as his body wilted away, smothered as the goddamn unkillable biomass ate him from the inside out. But he hadn't been able to talk to her, tell her his dreams they would never complete, what he wanted to see Phillipe grow up to be, how she should raise their child alone. It was the end of the suffering as she'd watched him struggle for the last year on Lida, and the start of an incredibly sharp, new anguish where she would never look at him again.

After the others left, Agetha wept into the grave, Phillipe nestled in a sling at her side, whimpering. A new life. A horrible burden. Daved had been the one to push for a child. She hadn't. But now Phillipe was the only part of Daved that was left. She would honor the father in the child.

His dreams over the past few months made a sick kind of sense. He had seen visions of the mat of fungus which broke his fall. Was the biomass invading his brain even then? He must have felt something from the foreign organism growing in him, like Phillipe had grown in a tube. Both nestled in a place outside of where biology intended for them to thrive.

Agetha made her way back to her cold apartment, bringing Phillipe home for the first time in a cloud of sadness, rather than the celebration the event deserved. She hadn't *been* home since Daved had first collapsed. Now she wasn't sure she ever would be again.

PART NINE

Two out of Eight

1 year 6 months 2 weeks after landing

The fascinating study of the children who had eaten their parents continued. They were expanding successfully, even to the point of damaging the older growths surrounding their place of landing—the ring of death. This was not a cause for concern. There were larger and more mature growths elsewhere, and even the eldest extrusions needed pruning from time to time for continued development and to stave off stagnation. These children responded to their environment quickly, for those who were not subsumed.

Of more interest was the addition of further types of children, from the sedentary ones, to the fully mobiles ones. Higher-functioning nodes conjectured that several sub-types of children had access to higher cognitive abilities as well, including long-term planning. This was evidenced in the children's expansion, following straight lines and boundaries with admirable control. It was a feature lacking in many nodes, much desired.

It was finally determined that many of the largest entities were not in any way alive and had instead been constructed for various shelters and stationary centers of rest. These constructions were compared to a small group of subsumed creatures in an archipelago spread across a large body of water. Before being subsumed, they built structures for themselves, though the full scope had never been understood. The subsumed descendants continued that tradition, though with less direction.

In addition, the children had completed work on a very large structure surrounding the ring of death. It was effective at keeping away many prying sensory organs, but there were always ways to slip through.

There were fascinating levels of interconnection between the various types of children, mirroring the most complex biospheres. Of new interest was a tiny, winged varietal of mobile signal carriers, who made daily trips between storage centers and the non-mobile children tended by the higher-functioning ones. A type of symbiosis had been discovered with this varietal, filling in the dearth of optical sensory organisms—the ones that had been destroyed by the children.

Communication methods in this type of entity were highly complex, with bursts of locational data encoded by physical movements. It was strangely effective, and worthy of further study. In the meantime, this symbiosis allowed a more complete analysis of the developing ecosystem, as well as the opportunity to correct several magnetic and digestive issues the tiny, winged creatures had developed. They would be a powerful force to enhance communication in small radii. A subsumed varietal had been attempted, though without success so far.

It was sadly similar to the one instance of synergy with one of the higher functioning entities. Due to the entity's close proximity to an information and analysis node, it was possible to attach a sensory vessel and mark progress over a period of time. However, several internal systems did not exist as easily within symbiosis, triggering a hyperbolic expansion of non-functional material. The results were stored for later work, and instead more focus was concentrated on the small information carriers. There was some successful symbiosis made with the non-mobile children as well, though the higher functioning entities tended to destroy this work before it was complete.

Further studies promised to be fascinating, no matter how long it took.

* * *

1 year 8 months after landing

Jiow was a bundle of nerves. She peered through the windows of the birthing center, waiting for the registrar to open the doors. Today was the day. She would finally hold her child. It had been an agony, seeing Agetha dealing with Phillipe the past few months, alone. She'd tried to help, but Agetha was still too broken, trying to tend to everything herself. At least she had accepted the three months of leave Admin had given her, before going back into her construction job. Jiow would be alone too, but that was her choice, or at least she told herself it was.

Janx updated her every week or two with how their planning was going for "the big one," and Jiow refused their pleas for her assistance every time. Admin had heightened security after the steelcrete theft, and it was nearly impossible for Generationals to get into any place where Admin didn't want them to be. Jiow still looked away whenever she saw a Vagal. The two she'd asked about E-Vapors must not have turned in her description, or they assumed she hadn't been connected with the theft. For once, being on the bottom of the hierarchy might have been a benefit.

The kiloseconds ticked by. The morning was crisp, as it was the colder part of the year, but not as cold as it would be farther from the equator. She shouldn't have come so early, but she hadn't been able to sleep the night before. Everyone would point and laugh at the sewerage maintenance person who couldn't wait to have a baby. Covered in shit at work and at home.

The thump of boots on pavement made her turn her head to see Frank slumping toward her, carrying a cotton bag sagging like it held something heavy.

"I thought you might need some more baby equipment. I've seen the inside of your apartment," he said, holding the bag out to her.

She accepted with a smile and looked inside. Towels, bottles, a canister of formula, some other unidentifiable baby things...

"What happened to not having anything to do with the child?" she said. She hadn't even known if he would show up this morning.

"I'm still not having anything to do with a baby," Frank said, then looked around as if someone might hear him, might care. No one else was here yet. The sun only barely peeking over the top of the radian wall.

"But you're here," Jiow said.

"Yeah," Frank answered. "I'm here to see...what's their name, anyway?"

"Choi." Jiow had waffled for several megaseconds, but it had been her grandparent's name, who had always been a steadying presence in her life.

Frank tilted his head to one side, then nodded. "I like it."

That little approval sparked more emotion in Jiow than it ought to, and she dabbed at an eye self-consciously.

They stood in an awkward huddle for a few moments, Frank looking everywhere but at her and Jiow alternating between staring at the front windows of the birthing center, and out into Alpha Radian. Jiow clenched her hands into fists and released them, telling herself it was the chill in the air making her hands cold.

Finally, the registrar, an elderly Generational who had headed the birthing records back on the UGS Hina, unlocked the front door and gestured them inside.

"Tea?" he asked, gesturing to a cooktop visible through a side door. "The decanting tube is finalizing the last tests, cleanup, and bacterial sprays to get them ready for the larger world. We've got three or four kiloseconds before they're ready. Yours is the only birth until later this afternoon."

Jiow gratefully accepted a pot of tea, though Frank only wrinkled his nose.

"Had my coffee already," he said. "If you can call the shit we have here coffee."

Jiow took a sip of the tea, and her eyebrows went up. "This is ship-grown," she said. It wasn't a question. She had missed the taste of authentic UGS K'uei-Hsing black tea. The crops down here tasted different, though at least they hadn't completely succumbed to the biomass.

The registrar gave a tiny nod and an even smaller smile. "I'm glad you appreciate it. Some of my last stock—no, no"—he gestured with a hand as Jiow made to protest—"I wouldn't have offered it if I didn't want to share it. Having one who can savor good tea is nearly as good as drinking it oneself. Shall we?" He led them back out into the decanting room, and over the next several few minutes had Jiow sign the last documents and birthing certificates.

They were almost done when the door creaked open, revealing Agetha, with Phillipe on one hip, looking like she hadn't slept in a week.

"I'm not too late, am I?" she asked. Even her voice was tired.

"Not at all," Jiow said. "You're earlier than my lazy brother, who couldn't be bothered to...well, speak of the star-thief."

Zhu poked his head in the door, looking around before giving her a smarmy grin.

"Never thought you'd get there before me, sis," he said. "I even made a bet with Jules that we'd pop a kid out first." He grimaced. "I owe the old wifey a home-cooked dinner now."

"Hopefully you won't set the apartment on fire this time," Jiow said. It had been on the Abeona, a hundred and fifty megaseconds before they reached the Lida system, back before she'd really figured out her gender. She'd been later than most children to choose hers. Zhu had filled the whole Pappadapilos clan's apartments with smoke and just about set off the emergency alarm for the Abeona.

"That's why Jules cooks," Zhu grumbled.

"Are you ready? I believe the decanting tube has finished final calibrations," the registrar slipped into the silence. Jiow turned back to him, her heart fluttering.

"Yes."

They surrounded the murky tube, Agetha pulling Phillipe close to her, tears on her cheeks. Jiow wanted to say something to her, but the tube was fizzing and hissing, and the registrar gestured to the large lever with "Caution" painted in red on the side. Jiow pulled it, and fluid drained from the tank—leaving her perfect child cradled inside, tiny arms beginning to move in the sudden change.

"The red button, now," Frank whispered, and Jiow realized he had taken a step forward. Jiow flicked a glance to him, and then away, but caught Agetha's narrowed eyes at the interaction.

Jiow took a deep breath and pushed the big red button.

She ignored the hissing, clanking, horrible sounds that shouldn't accompany this miracle of a birth. She, without a womb, without a partner, had a biological child that was all—nearly all—hers.

Choi was delivered to her in a blanket, crying at the injustice of being outside the warm amniotic fluid. Their mouth was already questing for food. The registrar handed her a bottle, which she put to Choi's lips, and the child drank, silencing their protest.

Jiow felt a nudge at her shoulder and Frank was there, staring down with the doofiest grin she'd even seen.

"Sort of cute, for a potato," he said.

"You want to hold them?" Jiow asked, getting ready to shift Choi, but Frank backed away, as if he suddenly realized there was an audience.

"No, no. I don't do kids. You know that."

Jiow only grinned at him. Agetha and even Zhu were watching them, calculating looks on their faces.

"You finally find yourself a partner, little sis?" Zhu asked.

"Nope. A proud single," Jiow said, not looking at Frank. She knew he would have gone red. She turned to Agetha. "We should join forces. We can care for these two together. Save some time on mixing up formula and cleaning diapers."

Jiow didn't want to add the other words, but they hung in the air, unsaid.

Since your husband is dead.

"I..." Agetha swallowed. "I've got a pattern down. I can handle it."

Jiow realized how her words must have sounded. An attack on Agetha's competence, an assumption she couldn't manage. Communal child support was still in planning stages. Not enough of the Generationals had children yet and it was still largely up to individual families to care for their offspring.

"Oh, well, maybe you could give me some tips," she said. "I'm going to be hopeless at this." Choi had already downed half the bottle. Where did it go in that tiny body?

Agetha was crying silently, but she refused to acknowledge the tears. "Sure. I can show you some things."

"Great. I know it will be good for both of them." She gestured with her chin at Choi, newborn, and Philippe, only five megaseconds older.

These children would be the ones to really colonize Lida, to branch out and discover all the amazing uniqueness of the biomass, the beautiful vistas outside the arcopolis. Despite all the setbacks so far—the Khonsu crash, Jiow's injuries, the biomass infecting their crops and livestock, Daved's death—Jiow was happy. She hugged Choi to her breast, gently rocking them.

Her child was the future. Choi and Phillipe were the reason behind this colony. She was a part of greatness.

* * *

2 years after landing

Jane leaned back in her chair, the supports taking the tension from her shoulders. It had taken two years, but the chair was finally broken in, nearly as good as the one in her office back in New York. That old thing might be a thousand years gone by now, or a lump of radioactive dust, or some fetish of a malformed tribe of meta-humans. She'd liked that chair.

She scanned the small group. Only five of the eight Admins—and their assistants—were here. Alessandro, Polunu, and Rajani were busy directing their respective divisions of crop production, animal science, and biological science. Another year in, and their biggest problem was still how the biomass was infecting Earth plants and animals. Fortunately, no other humans had been impacted, thanks to frequent medical scans based on the poor man who had died half a year ago. There were still accidents fighting the biomass—they'd lost another two Vagals last week—but only in direct confrontation. The nanotanium wall around Alpha Radian seemed to be working for now, and Jane made certain the other Admins were aware it was her gamble that paid off. Several of them had been against such a huge use of their resources. If only they had more steelcrete.

Which brought her to yet another problem they faced, and the first to be dealt with today. She scanned through the report Christiaan sent her. Shame the Generationals had picked now to get rowdy. She'd hoped to have a few more years to settle things in the colony before any attempts to reduce the Admins' control. It was inevitable, however. Planned for. She wasn't worried.

"Any update on the Generational malcontents?" she directed at Wenqing.

"Their network still evades us," Wenqing answered. "Of course, the other Generationals are protecting them, but their thefts have ceased after the two steelcrete blocks were removed. We think we may have scared them off with the addition of guards around the arcopolis." He flicked a finger at General Smith to continue.

The elderly Vagal raised his chin, smoothing his sagging neck. "However, we have barely enough Vagals to combat the biomass and guard sensitive areas, ma'am," he said. "We will either need to remove some security or reduce biomass patrols soon."

"We can't stop burning out the biomass or it will overrun the city," Ahman said. They had settled into their position in control of transportation and R&D well, acting as Jane's staunch ally.

"Agreed," Jane said. "Cut down on the guards then. Cowed Generationals are perfect for the next stage of construction. We'll enact harsher measures if they continue to create problems. For now, we can't afford to waste more time."

"Speaking of which," Dmitri said, "the solar farms are running at nearly peak efficiency for now. We are ready to support the next radian." Dmitri excelled at efficiency—in power generation, networking, and the communications network. All were still primitive, but the colony simply didn't have the resources for higher bandwidth connections and larger capacity generators.

Jane looked to the last member of the group, Maria. The cherub-faced Admin perpetually looked as if she was out of her depth, though she had done an adequate job with water management for the colony.

"How are the new foundations coming? You're the first to break ground on Beta."

"We're ready," the younger woman said. "Just tell my crews where the concentrations of people will be, and we can finalize the designs."

"Good. That brings us to the real reason for today's meeting," Jane addressed the room. "Beta Radian. We should have started on it already, but with all the setbacks, it's a wonder we're not farther behind on Alpha. The original timeline for finishing the colony was ten years, but that was when we thought we would have materials, and didn't account for the homicidal fungus outside out gates. We have to adjust our building priorities." She knitted her fingers together and set her hands on the desk in front of her. Let them know she wanted real feedback.

"I want each Radian to be unique. Even with the challenges over the last two years, capturing the soul of our colony in the first arcopolis is key. Three hundred years from now, I want this place to be standing as the capital city, in a network spread all over the planet. So, give me ideas."

"Children and culture," Ahman said. "If we want our city to survive past the next thirty years, that must be the next objective." They were already working on the education plan for the toddlers sprouting up around Alpha and Beta radians like little weeds. "If Alpha is the core of the colony, why not make Beta the heart? Show that we can build culture and time for relaxation."

"Even if the Generationals are working day and night to build the colony?" Dmitri said. "They have no time to frequent such establishments. Barely time to take care of children. Better to build structure first, dependable structure which can be used for the colony's future."

Jane privately sided with Dmitri. She didn't have any children herself, nor did most of the Admins. They had been chosen for their dedication to the colony, and that left little time for other matters. Ahman was the exception, with two kids, the second only born a week ago. Their spouse—a sturdy Generational from the Xaman Ek they'd somehow found time to meet and woo—was busy taking care of both.

"Not all Generationals are as focused as you are, dear Dmitri," Ahman replied. "And perhaps some Admins or Vagals would like to eat out once in a while. Aside from that little hole-in-the-wall Maertin started up, there are no restaurants yet. Set the foundations for a few theatres, some galleries, and plenty of restaurants in Beta, and give us all something to look forward to. Give our children culture to grow up with and parks to play in." They found Jane's eyes. Ahman hadn't just spouted this off the cuff. This was prepared. They really wanted this.

Time for relaxation will be beneficial, Christiaan texted from behind her shoulder. *Having a child yourself will show you are a leader of the people. Ma'am.* They had begun to drop little hints in their planning material—ones only she would have noticed: a greater emphasis on how many children each family was planning, reports on the safety of the decanting tubes for those with genemods, when Admin and assistant families were considering starting the next generation. They were ready, as always, to support her every need. They had made no attempt to find a partner or group. Jane tapped a fingernail on the table in thought. Six times. It was a habit she'd tried to break. Maybe children weren't a bad idea. And Christiaan...

"What about Dmitri's dependable structures?" Wenqing asked. "We need our fire stations, our power substations, our higher educational support structures."

Jane tried to imagine Wenqing with children, but only blinked at the thought. Just...no.

Dmitri had no children, of course. Any unnecessary aspects the razor-like man had ever owned, like a sense of fatherhood, had been burned away long ago. He met her eyes with his own deeply hooded ones.

"You could put higher educational structures in Gamma," Maria suggested. "The children won't be ready for apprenticing for several years, and the batteries are sufficient for powering Alpha and Beta, aren't they, Dmitri?" Jane suspected the woman would have plenty of free time to raise a family if she wanted. Jane would have to find some other obligations for her. Maybe give her part of Alessandro's failing crops.

Dmitri pursed his narrow lips, but nodded. "They are. So, we have Ahman's radian of culture, of light. Will you have enough substructure built with the sewerage system to carry away all the shit and trash this cultural oasis will generate?"

Maria only smiled. "Don't worry about the sewerage or trash collection. With the caverns beneath Beta Radian, we could handle the entire population of the fleet with food poisoning."

Ahman gave an easy laugh, and even Wenqing cracked a smile. Ahman had done their research, obviously. "You see? Nothing to worry about. Let's make a cultural center that will be the envy of the endless fungal fields of the biomass."

"Dmitri?" Jane asked.

"Fine," the thin Russian said. "We fill Beta full of restaurants and theatres. I will ensure my networking teams string extra fiber to carry high bandwidth."

"Many thanks," Ahman said.

"That's not all that's going into Beta, however," Jane said, and waited for the others to turn back to her. The Generationals' morale would only get worse as they wore themselves down building the colony. "Thinking longer term, some restructuring might also be in order. The population is growing. However, the children of Admins and Vagals will live longer than those of the Generationals, and we need to find homes for everyone."

"The arcopolis will be large," Ahman said.

"With room for everyone," Jane agreed, "which is why I want to make certain there is room for, let us say, certain *classes* of housing."

"The children of Admins and of Vagals," Dmitri said, never one to beat around the bush.

Jane could almost feel Christiaan's displeasure, and swiped a quick text to them not to worry. While she wouldn't have put it so directly, this wasn't a secret from anyone in this room. She crossed her arms, leaning forward onto the desk.

"Indeed, as Dmitri so succinctly puts it. The Generationals right now make up ninety percent of the colony, but they were always meant to be a transitory solution. We never should have been on those ships that long, and frankly, there are more of them than we anticipated—almost twice as many."

"You're suggesting a place in the Alpha and Beta radians off limits to Generationals, used only for Admins, Vagals, and their children? What about the pushback we've already seen?" Maria raised both eyebrows.

"That is only half of it," Jane told them. Even the other Admins thought too short-term. It was why she *had* to be in charge, to make the hard decisions, and keep the colony stable. She flicked a glance to Ahman. This was a touchy subject, and they had talked at length about it a few months back. Ahman twitched fingers at her as if to say, "go ahead."

"These Generationals will live for, what, ninety or a hundred years, at most?" Maria nodded, looking concerned. "And they will be virtually useless in the workforce long before that. Admins and Vagals will live for three or four hundred years, easily, and thanks to our genemods, be physically at their prime the entire time. Generationals will breed more of their kind, with the same infirmities."

"So, you want to keep us from mixing with them?" Maria hazarded, looking mortified. "Set up some sort of elite class?"

Dear, naïve Maria. This was nothing. If she had known what underhanded tricks Dmitri had pulled for his own country *before* they started on their journey, she would have wet her panties.

"Not precisely," Jane continued. "There will be mixtures, and we allow and even encourage that. It's a matter of scale. The child of two Admins, or a Vagal and an Admin, may still live for three hundred years, and their children for nearly that. The child of an Admin and a Generational will only live maybe for two hundred, and the sequence will decay faster in subsequent generations. At least so the scientists who created the genemods insisted."

Jane sat back, keeping Maria's attention. "The goal of this colony is first self-sufficiency, and then growth and expansion over the surface of Lida. Obviously, we have a few more impediments than originally expected." She paused for the forced chuckles from the others. "But eventually we hope to replicate the genemods created on Earth both for the Vagal soldiers and for the Admins of the colony. That's many years off. Until then, our goal must be integrity of information and culture."

Maria's dark eyes were squinted nearly shut. She was beginning to see, but Jane spelled it out for her. "As such, we will give higher priority to those most able to help us achieve our goal. The Generationals interfering with our supplies is only the first sign of their short-sightedness. That's why *we* are in control."

"A solid plan," Wenqing agreed, and Maria scowled at him.

"Everyone is free to make their own choices," Jane said. "But only some of the Generationals are young, and even those will live a short time on this planet. They are the backbone of this colony at the moment, the eyes and hands and brains that will build it into the monument we all hope it will be. Unfortunately, we are more resource constrained than we anticipated. In thirty or forty years, there will be a massive drop off in Generational numbers, and a rise in the new generation of children. But we will be here, observing, planning. During that time, we must ensconce those who will follow our goals near the center of power, while those who will fade away must logically be shifted to places where they can be of use as their potential allows. Do you see?"

Maria looked as if she had smelled a particularly fragrant fart. "So, we keep the longest-lived children close to the protected center of the arcopolis, in Alpha and Beta Radians, and gradually put the Generationals out to pasture in the newest and least protected radians as they're built."

"Succinctly put," Jane agreed. She broke the young Admin's gaze, finally, and turned back to the others. "Any other issues with this? I already have agreement from Alessandro, Polunu, and Rajani."

"Efficient," Dmitri said, and Ahman gave a curt nod. They understood the choices they had made, and that their children might not be as near the center of power in the future.

"Good. Then there is one more issue. How are our steelcrete reserves for construction of Beta?" she asked Ahman. Christiaan had noted a disturbing trend in the mining schedules.

The Admin frowned, and waggled a hand. "Not as great as we hoped. The vein of minerals the crash opened is deep, but we are seeing diminishing returns. As of now, we can either build the structures for Beta, Gamma, and part of Delta, or we can put the bulk of the steelcrete into a wall around Beta and as we find the last bits of minerals, use those for a few high-priority structures within Beta."

"Put it in the wall," Jane said with no hesitation. Then she sighed. At least Christiaan had prepared her. She would rather have people living in tents and doubling up than devote resources and lives to battling heavier biomass infestation. Even with the wall around Alpha, a core of Vagals patrolled the perimeter to destroy new growth that cropped up.

"We *must* find more materials. Any news on mines outside the city?" she asked Wenqing. Her finger tapped six times again, and she winced.

"None," Wenqing said, frowning. "We stopped sending drones after losing fifty of them, and a full Vagal team. Never got a clear picture of what took either down. It came from blind spots—some other infernal creation of that biomass."

"Is it worth sending another team?" Jane asked. Dmitri's lips narrowed to nonexistence as Wenqing shook his head. Maria had been silent since their talk of children, her lip curled.

"How many do you want to lose?" Wenqing said, gesturing behind him. "The general cannot guarantee safe return, and the biomass interferes with our long-range signals."

"Meaning?" Jane would throw as many Vagals at the problem as she could, if it got her another source of minerals.

"I assume we may also lose any information found, with the team's destruction," supplied Ahman, and Wenqing gave a tiny nod of affirmation. "Thus rendering the whole enterprise a waste of resources."

Jane sent a thank you to Christiaan for the idea that popped up in her HUD. She caught Maria's eye. "How about the water supply? Is there any way to farm minerals from it?"

Maria's petulant expression softened as her gaze went distant, evidently calculating something on her HUD. She turned to her assistant and had a brief and quiet conversation, while Jane directed a raised eyebrow at her back.

"We haven't found any appreciable buildup of materials," Maria finally answered. "The biomass-derived filters keep contamination out at over ninety-nine point nine percent efficiency. We have an excellent water supply, but unless you want biomass getting in with the minerals, I wouldn't change the process." She clenched her jaw, then spoke again. "You could just send Generationals out to explore if they mean so little."

"I would if I thought they would get the job done," Jane snapped. Her finger tapped six times again, and she angrily swiped away the warning about her stress levels from Christiaan. "I don't *under*value Generational lives, Maria. I'm simply practical. You'll likely live longer than the rest of us, at least by a few years. Get used to thinking that way."

Maria looked away, and Jane focused on the other Admins.

"*Alright* folks," she said, and even Dmitri tensed. Jane forced her shoulders to relax. "We are *greatly* resource constrained, but we are not going to fail. This is top priority. Ahman. Get your people working on an alternative—*any* alternative—to get the construction crews building. Wenqing, Smith, find me a way to use the Vagals." Smith snapped to attention. "Dmitri, keep the power on, and Maria, get your shit together. Literally."

Jane stared at the others. She would *not* fail. "I refuse to stop work on the arcopolis. Find. Me. Materials."

* * *

2 years 3 months after landing

"We've been working on the biomass problem for over two years, Frank." Femi Sarraf's irritated voice came over the HUD link Frank shared with Zixin Ye, an older scientist from the K'uei-Hsing, and Ashkara Patel, a researcher about Frank's age from the Khonsu. Femi, who was Ashkara's mentor, was out with a squad of Vagals, taking samples of biomass outside the walls, or she would have been here in person as well.

"Innovation takes time, Femi," Ye answered before Frank could. "We just need to keep at it."

"But Admin's breathing down our necks," Ashkara added. "If we don't find new material for the colony to use for construction, they'll blame us for slowing Beta's completion."

"Not just us," Frank said. "There are teams of material science engineers, chemists, mechanical engineers, you name it. But if we can't find another mine, there's only one place our resources can come from. It's simple deduction."

"And a complete lack of metals is looking more and more likely," Ye grumbled. "Where did that original vein even come from, if the biomass absorbs metals for structural elements? Was it such a large concentration even the biomass couldn't finish it off?"

"I'm sure there are others, somewhere," Frank said. "But lacking more data, what's the greatest resource on this planet?" he answered his own question. "Biomass. Even if we can't make a material out of it, we'll likely come up with some other useful devices. That means we'll be the ones to shoulder the brunt of the research."

How long until they had critical mass of new students and interns to help out? Four hundred megaseconds—or fifteen years, in the Admin's unruly system—at the earliest. There were a few young teenagers in the colony, but most reproduction had been halted almost a hundred and fifty megaseconds out from Lida. There was an even longer gap between the last ones born on the ships and the new ones born on the planet's surface. He thought of Jiow's new child, five megaseconds—two months—old. She was struggling to both care for Choi and help out with the maintenance jobs she was still working. He should really take some food over. Maybe some of the modified cucumbers he'd been working on. They had a greater resistance to biomass infection.

"...agree there's potential." Ashkara was speaking. Frank blinked and let his subconscious filter what had happened. Not much. "We have reports of fungal towers over a hundred and fifty meters tall farther out in the wilds. That's taller than the tallest trees that grew on Earth. If we can find out the material composition for how the structure supports itself..."

"How it supports itself is not the issue," Femi's voice interrupted. Her voice crackled and skipped. Some aspects of the biomass could block wireless signals. The Vagal team must have crossed the line of fungal old growth. "Obviously the biomass has highly efficient support systems. Yes, we believe it's sucking the minerals out of the ground, which is why we can't find any. But the main problem is the biomass' reproduction."

"Agreed," Frank said, and switched topics. "I've been working with the viral information transfer the biomass uses for reproduction, but no luck so far in turning it off."

"Same with me," Femi said. "The biomass has so many damn vectors of reproduction it's like trying to keep a bunch of horny rabbits with a thousand different genders from mating. Constantly. Spay or neuter one, and another will take its place, or the first, er, rabbit might have another set of sex organs."

Ye chuckled. "Metaphor hop away from you?"

"Bite me, Ye," Femi said. Her voice grew distant for a moment. "No. Not there. *That* fungal tower. With the red growths at eye-level." Her voice grew stronger. "Sorry. Keeping this thing from growing is just not possible without some sort of permanent watchdog on the process, and how do you do that when the material has been broken down into tiny particulates, processed, and *should* be completely inert?"

"Ashkara and I have been noodling around with blocking the reproductive process," said Ye, "but we have nothing concrete. Like Femi says, there are so many viral avenues that it's almost impossible to find them all. They should be dead in processed material, but they aren't. We're looking for prions hiding within the viruses that could continue even after the host material is dead."

"Because Admin would not appreciate us coming up with a new building material only to have our newest structures sprouting new growths and eating the inhabitants," Ashkara added. She tightened her head scarf as if it could protect her from the biomass. "We've had enough problems on that front already."

"Fortunately, the spores seem to be harmless to people, even though they're endemic," Frank said. "Some idiots are eating and drinking fungal matter straight, which, honestly, isn't a bad idea if we can get it to taste like something other than decaying mulch. But the reproduction process is so tied in with the viral strains, I can't figure out how it determines what the offspring will be. How does the biomass contain so many species? If we could control that process, just think of what we could create! But half of them act like viral cloning reproduction, and between viruses, spores, and signal receptors, I'll be damned if I can figure out how."

Ye opened his mouth to ask something, but it was drowned out in a static screech from the audio link. Frank winced in pain and reached to adjust the volume, but the sound died away, replaced with Femi's voice.

"Oh shit. Go check Singh, quick! I didn't know it could move that fast." Her voice got stronger. "I'm gonna have to go. Catch you later." The line went dead.

Frank exchanged a wide-eyed look with Ye. They both looked to Ashkara, who was lowering her hands from her ears.

"I'm sure we'll hear more about that later," she said.

"*If* they all get back," Ye mumbled. Ashkara glared at him. "What? We've lost enough supersoldiers already. If they can't handle a fungus, what chance do the rest of us have?"

Frank blew out a breath and slapped both palms on the table at which they sat. Back on the ship, it would have started his ascent to the room's exit. Here, it just made a dull *thud*. Seventy megaseconds and he was still getting used to that. "Time to get back to work, then? Let's come up with a material strong enough to build the rest of the arcopolis, or even better, a way to control the biomass. I'm getting tired of this fungus laughing at us."

* * *

2 years 4 months after landing

Frank put his hands on his hips and frowned at the latest sample. The nice, flat, brown sheet of inert, processed mush the printer had spit out yesterday was now buckled, listing over the side of the sample container. A cord of hyphae reached across the sterile counter, looking for something to grab onto. He could just see the inside of the sheet of material through a crack in the surface. It was a mass of twisted white roots.

"Well, fuck."

Frank scooped what was supposed to be a sterile sheet of building material off the table and chucked it into the incinerator chute. That had been the fifteenth attempt in the past two and a half megaseconds since Femi's ill-fated expedition. She'd returned with a bunch of material, so technically it had been a success. The two Vagals who'd been eaten by the biomass probably didn't think so, though.

He wandered across his lab, still a hastily built space even now. He'd bartered for a large sheet of clear glass from the ship early on, when he'd started his study of the bee colonies. Now there were three established hives on the other side of the glass. He liked to watch them, when he needed to think.

Bees went about their business, in and out. There were a bunch bearding from the entrance to one of the hives, living in harmony with the biomass. All of the successful hives were infested with the hyphal nodes, and the bees looked like they were wearing little green and pink fur coats.

The issue was the biomass was also using the insects like little mobile drones. He and Ashkara had detected an incredible variety of chemical signals from the hyphae on the bees, which brushed up against flowers, bushes, vegetables, and any other surface the bees touched. He had no idea what they meant, but he had observed the biomass communicated incredibly efficiently along its network. The bees were now part of that network, and there was no way to stop it without completely destroying every hive. Add to that, the hives that *hadn't* been infected had suffered crippling diseases and digestive problems. It was the most invasive aspect of the biomass they'd discovered so far. He hoped it was the most invasive.

Frank looked back to the incinerator chute. The bees were one datapoint indicating it was possible to live in harmony with the biomass. He'd broken down proteins into the smallest forms that would still hold their shapes, and even removed aspects of the biomass genetic code in an effort to halt reproduction, but the viral communication vectors kept slipping through. He suspected they were related to the chemical signals in some way. The samples all continued propagation. He already knew it wasn't possible to remove the biomass from Lida, no matter what Admin wanted. So, could he work around the problem, like the biomass had done with the bees?

He looked to the hives again, collectives of thousands of individuals, working toward a common goal. Similar to the biomass in some ways.

The two problems felt interconnected. The bees let the biomass communicate more efficiently, and even when the biomass was broken down into tiny particulates that could be printed in a desired shape, it could still receive those same viral signals—whether to plant, animal, or fungal cells—to activate and reproduce.

If he couldn't stop the biomass at its source, could he forge a symbiosis? Could he hijack the viruses and the chemical signals to alter communication between biomass cells? It might be possible to keep some information transmission, even while stopping messages that controlled reproduction.

This would not be a simple project. He'd need to reach out to other biological scientists from the fleet. Maybe Beth Hurley, for one, who he'd worked with professionally a few times. She might have names of other people more familiar with viral communication methods.

He began preparations for test sixteen.

* * *

2 years 6 months after landing

"Anderson."

"Yes, muux?" Anderson blinked in the call from Noce. He took the E-Vapor from his mouth. The higher-ups had started rationing them, and this was only his second today.

"Another situation for you to check out. On the interior edge of Alpha, close to where they're breaking ground for Beta." The coordinates popped into Anderson's HUD as Noce spoke.

Anderson sighed. Another call inside the colony, and likely more domestic disputes about food. Didn't they have enough problems already?

"I'm on it, muux," Anderson said, turning toward the new residential sections of Alpha. Some of the Generationals were already moving out toward the edges of the radian, where there was more land and larger apartments, designed for families. He crossed to a bicycle stand and picked one up from the rack, checking that it was in good condition. Until they got more solar powered vehicles up and running, which wasn't likely with the recent dearth of materials, bicycles were the best way to get around.

As he pedaled, he considered his recent assignments. He wasn't sure which was worse, the high-intensity bouts of burning out biomass incursions, where it was never certain if the fungus had a new vicious way of killing you, or the increased use of Vagals as a domestic police force, calming Generationals who were growing more stressed about adapting to life on a planet, with constrained food and metals and a deadly fungus surrounding them.

He sighed and pedaled down a side street from the main thoroughfare. At least the roads were all paved in Alpha, with a mixture of packed earth on top of nanotanium substrate. He was off mushroom burning duty for this week, which meant dealing with cranky Generationals. They greatly outnumbered the Vagals and the Admins combined, and now they were reproducing.

Two and a half years into the colony, and they'd lost five hundred of the Vagals that had been in the fleet—nearly a third. There wouldn't be any more for years. Not until they recreated the genemods used by the Admins and the neurotech used to create the Vagal implants. Even though the Vagals had long lifespans—almost as long as the Admins—they were still mortal, as demonstrated by the persistence of the fungus in killing them.

Anderson had fellow soldiers crushed, mangled, bled out, sucked dry, melted, suffocated, poisoned, cooked from the inside, turned against the others in their squad, and more. He'd had to watch many of them. They were barely keeping up with the biomass incursion.

Now the colonists were going hungry, turning against each other. The thefts against official stores had trailed off, but there was an increase in disputes between Generationals both inside Alpha radian and outside. The knuckles of his prosthetic hand clenched on the handlebars in frustration.

Then Anderson's head popped up, scanning the nearby residences. That wasn't frustration. That was Cora, pumping chemicals through his system. He hadn't told any of the Vagals except Noce about her name. He got the feeling the others didn't feel the same way about their implants.

He could just hear shouting, from the next street over. He pedaled faster and skidded to a halt in front of a strip of apartments, with two people outside.

They were within arm's reach of each other, one holding a bag of something and the other with a fist raised. It looked like the only reason they weren't brawling in the street was that each also had a crying baby perched on their hips.

Against his better judgement, he propped his bicycle against a bollard and waded between the two. Cora was going wild, his heart rate spiking. This was like getting between two bears guarding their young.

The first Generational waved the bag toward him, and something slopped inside. Anderson bent to one side, hoping nothing would slosh out on him. Both children quieted for the moment, staring at him.

"We're told to eat mushrooms. What is this shit?" the Generational said, while gesturing with the brown and viscous mess. "Is my son going to get a fungal infection?"

"What are you doing here, anyway, Vagal?" asked the other. "I bet she called you in about the vegetable patch again, didn't she?"

Anderson only got his mouth open before the first one answered.

"So, they admit they're claiming more than their share?" Now the bag wavered toward the second Generational. "It's a *common* vegetable patch. She doesn't have to eat this mess."

"Maybe we can all—" Anderson attempted.

The second person cut him off, answering the first woman. "That's because I have *two* new mouths to feed, not just one. I get that bag of mushroom goop too, but I'm also apportioned more of the garden."

"What's your name?" Anderson jumped in, trying to derail the accusations. Cora hadn't been this hyped up since a fungal sprout had almost eaten his foot.

"I'm Bekye, and that *thief* is Janx," the first woman—Bekye—said.

"Not a thief," Janx shot back. "I just got saddled with more spawn to raise." Their child sent up a wail, as if to prove the point. Bekye's child decided to join in. Anderson winced.

"Not a thief? I happen to know—"

"I got called that there was a domestic dispute, that's all." Anderson had to raise his voice over the crying children. "No one's been accused of stealing, unless you two know something about the metals and supplies that were taken." That quieted them. None of the Generationals would talk about it. "Now why don't we figure it out?"

"What we need to figure out is why I'm getting sent this bagged crap, while Janx gets to eat fresh veggies." Bekye jiggled the child on her hip, which quieted them.

"My wife and I have to eat it too," Janx said. "I just don't wave it in the street like a flag. It's printed food, the biologists say. It's safe to eat."

"It tastes like ass."

Janx shrugged. "Not my fault. Maybe if more Generationals were involved *in the community*, we could have nicer things."

Anderson looked between the Generationals. At least they weren't fighting anymore. "Wait, printed food? I knew people were eating the fungus, but this looks official." He peered at the bag Bekye held, trying to read the label. It was marked with Admin Giordano's official seal. "When did this start? I thought there was a shortage."

"Some public official you are," Bekye said, but Janx rode over her.

"Oh, it would be better if there was a shortage. No, they've made us eat that...stuff the last two weeks." Their face curled in disgust.

"Why have I not seen this?" Anderson asked the two. When they both turned to him, he almost took a step back at the look in their eyes.

"Because Admins and Vagals don't eat it," Janx told him. "You all eat stores from the ships and fresh vegetables from the gardens. You smoke those nasty E-Vapors. But they expect *us* to eat printed food, just like they expect us to keep raising children. I was a metallurgical specialist, back on the Ganesha. But now that we have no metals to work, they say I can have as many kids as I want. That's why I have the second one, and why I was *apportioned* a greater section of the common garden in return." They shot a glare back at Bekye.

"I heard it was a mistake by the biologists," Bekye offered, ignoring the jibe. "I had this friend back on the Khonsu, Ashkara, and she says they tried printing building materials and came up with this." She hefted the bag again.

"And now we have to eat it," Janx said.

Anderson took a quiet step away. Cora wasn't pinging him about danger any longer. "Our E-Vapors are running low, too," he said. "I know you all think they're just a smelly addiction, but it evens out the Vagal temperament. You should see us without them."

"Is that a threat?" Janx asked.

Anderson raised his hands. "Not a threat. I promise. The Vagals are feeling the pinch too. We may not be eating that goop yet, but I assure you we will before too long."

"You still get better medicine, better food, and better tech," Bekye said, thrusting her chin toward his prosthetic.

"And two of those are mostly gone," Anderson replied. "I'll admit we get better food, but we do keep the biomass away."

"That is true," Janx said, then turned to their neighbor. "We don't want to call any more trouble down on us from the Vagals, do we?"

"No...we don't," Bekye grumbled. Anderson squinted at the two. Cora was trying to tell him something, but he wasn't getting it. There was something else these two weren't—

"You can cut those E-Vapors, you know," Janx interrupted his thoughts. "Make them last longer."

"They're single-use," Anderson said, but Janx only laughed.

"Are you telling me none of our Vagal protectors have opened the E-Vapor casings? If they're so dear, combine a few dead ones, and I bet you'll have a new E-Vapor."

"I'll try that," Anderson said. Why *hadn't* they tried that? Because Vagals did what they were told, and the E-Vapors were single-use, from Earth. There hadn't been a shortage back then. He pointed to the bag of goop. "You know, you could do the same with that. Combine it with your veggies. Might taste better."

Bekye frowned. "I made some into a sauce last week. It might go with squash from the garden and at least be palatable."

"I hadn't thought of that." Janx peered upward, reseating their child, who was watching Anderson slowly retreat. "I've got a bunch of extra tomatoes from my side of the garden. If you give me the recipe, maybe I can add them to the sauce."

Anderson reached his bicycle and cautiously set it upright.

"I've got the Feast of Stars coming up next week," Bekye said. "Some of my friends like to keep the holiday alive from the Khonsu. What if you bring your tomato mushroom goop and I make my squash mushroom goop. Your wife and kids are welcome too, of course."

"Then we can complain about Admin making us eat fungus together," Janx laughed.

Anderson was halfway over the bicycle seat when Bekye waved the bag of printed food at him. "Don't think we've forgotten about you, Vagal," she warned. "You tell those Admins the Generationals won't stand for this printed crap you're trying to drown us in. *You* eat this for a week and let me know if you'd rather starve to death. My baby and I haven't had real or vat-grown meat in months."

Anderson ducked his head. "Will do, ma'am. I think I'm going to try that stuff out for myself and see how it is." It looked like someone had indigestion in a bag. "I'll try the E-Vapor trick too."

"Don't say we didn't warn you about the printed goop," Janx said. They actually shook a finger at him, and their child mimicked the gesture, chubby fingers waving up and down.

Anderson piloted the bicycle around until it was facing the right direction. "I'll be sure to pass your comments on to the correct authorities. In the meantime, please keep the public disturbance to a minimum, and you won't have to see any more of me."

He sped off before the two could say anything else. Goodwill or no, there was still something bothering him about those two. He was going to have to do a little digging.

* * *

2 years 11 months after landing

Jane steepled her fingers over the dull brown square on the table between her, Rajani, and Wenqing.

"You're telling me this will replace the steelcrete when it runs out?" she said. She reached out with a tentative finger and poked at the square, as long on a side as her hand. It wasn't cool to the touch like metal would be, but it wasn't warm either. It slid over the table at her prompt with a bumpy friction like plastic, but it weighed a bit more— not nearly as much as steelcrete, though.

"We're calling it 'resinplast,'" Rajani said. The Admin for the science, medical, and biological divisions had settled into her role with her usual efficiency. Rajani was very much an Admin of the people, debating personally with the scientists working under her. Almost three years into the colony, she still wore a selection of salwar kameez she had brought from Earth, but they were getting threadbare. She'd refused the cruder equivalents available so far, made with pounded bamboo, in lieu of the silk ones she'd brought.

"And this one won't erupt into mushrooms, right?" Jane had heard the horror stories in Christiaan's updates. Her assistant flicked her the certification from the scientists who had finally stabilized the material, and she sent them back a quick thanks. They'd had to completely burn out one of the labs two months ago to get rid of an aggressive infestation.

"Completely neutral," Rajani said, opening both hands, fingers spread, palms down. "My crew has even personally exposed this very sheet to a fruiting spore body. No reaction, physically observed, or with an extensive analysis. One of our scientists, Frank Silver, was able to neutralize the viral reproductive vectors in this material as it is printed. We found some evidence of prion activity as well, but blocked everything related to reproduction from communicating within the material."

Jane finally let a small sigh of relief escape as Wenqing investigated the sample. An entire year devoted to looking for more metal, another mine, anything. The only option had been to use the biomass itself. She wasn't happy about it, but she had to admit giving a similar concoction to the Generationals as a printed food source was a stroke of genius. That one had come from Alessandro. He still had some fight left in him—she'd have to keep an eye on the other Admin. She'd heard the printed goop was edible, if barely. The complaints had dried up when she invited any Generationals who were unhappy about their new food to accompany the Vagals in their expeditions outside the wall to find more resources.

Her train of thought was derailed when Christiaan, from their place behind her, sent a photo of a dumpy looking, pale, and overweight Generational in his mid-twenties. A note underneath said this was Frank Silver. He looked vaguely familiar.

"What about the structural properties?" Wenqing spoke up. He leaned forward and pushed the slab of resinplast back across the table toward Jane. "This doesn't feel as strong as nanotanium." He picked it up and knocked it against the table, which had come from the St. Christopher. It made a hollow *thunk*.

"It's not," Rajani said. "We're not going to have anything with the structural properties of nanotanium unless we find a much larger store of minerals nearby. We haven't seen any hint of metals with high yield stresses in the crust around our landing location. Even iron and copper are in short supply—only enough for supplemental items like nails, wire, switches, and a few other things."

Wenqing opened his mouth, but Rajani cut him off. "However, it *is* nearly as strong as steelcrete, and lighter. That means we can build more complex structures with it. It may even be more resilient in some compressive applications."

Jane waved away the technical specifications. "Can it be used to build our colony?"

"As long as it doesn't sprout into a murderous fungus," Wenqing muttered. "General Smith was just giving me the updated numbers. We have to cut back on the expeditions into the old growth biomass. We simply cannot lose any more Vagals. Having another internal threat would spread our forces far too thin."

"It's inert," Rajani insisted. "Fortunately, we used the last nanotanium reserves to start the wall around Beta, and we are rationing our steelcrete to finish the wall and build the core buildings for Beta, and the eventual Gamma and Delta. I wouldn't use this for a retaining wall that will constantly be under attack by the biomass, but it should be perfectly acceptable for a standard building material."

"And why can't it be used for the wall?" Wenqing asked. Jane had been just about to ask that, and frowned at the Military Admin. It sounded like he knew something she didn't.

Rajani sighed. "We've done extensive tests, but the biomass also shows an incredible propensity to mutate and grow around obstacles. The less we let it interact with resinplast, the less chance it will get to override the viral blockers in the material."

Jane leaned over the table. "You're telling me we could build seventy percent of the arcopolis with this material and *then* have it sprout into biomass?"

Wenqing was hiding a grim smile. He'd led her to ask this question, as lead Admin. She hated it when he did that, but he was completely right in this case.

Rajani's lips pursed and she twisted her left fingers with those on her right hand. "It is a *risk*, yes, but one with a lower probability of happening unless the biomass drastically changes the way it reproduces. I'm talking about when mammals changed from laying eggs to live birth, or amoebas decided having two to tango was a good idea. A *major* change. Fungus by itself might be able to do this, but my scientists think the rigidity of animal and plant DNA will make it less likely to completely adjust reproduction styles."

Jane sat back, appeased for the moment, then turned to Christiaan. "If we don't use this, how much have we got in the way of materials?"

"Approximately two months of building before we would completely run out of steelcrete, ma'am," they said, not even looking at their HUD. "With the resinplast, we would be able to build indefinitely—as long as there is biomass on Lida—and we would be able to save the remaining steelcrete for high-priority construction."

There was too much to do. The colony had to grow. The arcopolis had to be completed. She would *not* let this venture fail. Failing was for the weak.

"Sounds like resinplast is our new building material," she said. She fixed Rajani with a stare. "But I want continued testing on this material. Find more things to throw at it until it breaks. Test each batch we produce. I want to know the second we have any problems with it."

"I'll set up a permanent inspection team for production," Rajani said.

* * *

3 years after landing

Agetha sat with Jiow on a bench. They were by the playground near their neighborhood. The only reason Agetha wasn't out working on the Beta Radian foundations was that two Generationals in another crew had been killed that morning by a large, slow-moving thing, like a shuttlecraft with twelve legs that had trundled out of the biomass jungle. A squad of Vagals finally killed it, but they were still watching the area to see if any more appeared.

So, it had made sense to stay closer to home today. As she and Jiow were single mothers with one child, they hadn't been moved closer to the outskirts of Alpha, where the larger families lived. Agetha wasn't sure if she wanted to stay in the apartment she'd shared with Daved, or move away. If the steady construction and consolidation in the center of Alpha continued, she might not have a choice. There weren't a lot of living spaces left—at least for Generationals.

Phillipe and Choi sat together playing with blocks, only two months apart in age, which meant less and less as they got older. Phillipe was almost to their fiftieth megasecond—a year and a half on Lida. Choi, the quieter of the two, followed Phillipe's movements intently.

"They're getting so big," Jiow said, and Agetha nodded.

"We haven't done this in a while. It's nice," she said.

"I come to the park every day," Jiow said, but kept her eyes on the children, letting the unspoken judgement go past.

"I'll try to take more days off," Agetha answered. "It's just, with resinplast starting to be produced in volume, construction's ramped up again. They need anyone who can help and who's not busy with kids."

"But you are busy with a kid," Jiow said. She had not been asked to help with construction, but Agetha had. Poor Jiow, never quite getting to where she wanted to be.

"Yes, but I'm also being considered for foreman of my crew." She shouldn't have to defend her choices. "I've got the best qualifications for it."

"The families out near the edge of Alpha, with large families, have started a communal daycare," Jiow told her. "One place where they can all live, and learn, and play, no matter whose child they are. But there's not enough of us in the interior to do the same. I've tried to start something up."

Agetha started to ask when she had time to do something like that, but instead, said, "Maybe it is time to move out. There're only three other kids near us."

"Six, actually," Jiow said. "You just don't usually see them since you're out of the apartment so early." She continued before Agetha could object. "I *want* to raise Choi myself. But I also want to help the colony. I feel like I'm not doing that, not like you are."

Agetha let a sad smile play over her face, even though Jiow wasn't looking. If Daved was still here, he would have loved spoiling little Phillipe, and Choi. He would have gladly watched them full time so

Agetha and Jiow could both work. But it was too late for such daydreams. Phillipe would never have any memories of their father.

"We're both helping the colony," she told Jiow. "You're a great mother. Just look at the others who are trying to raise kids. We have to make the next generation strong enough to carry on the traditions we learned in the fleet. It's not the Generational way to fail at anything we do. Not for the entire length of our journey here. We never lost a ship, never let hardship wear us down. *We* were the reason we landed here, and we'll be the reason this colony survives. If we have to eat printed biomass goop now so we can raise proper crops for our children, so be it."

Jiow only shook her head. "But they're not Generationals, not anymore. They've never known zero-G, and never will. I doubt anyone will be interested in spaceflight in their lifetimes. They're born on the ground of Lida, and they'll die here, just like us. Grounders to our Generationals."

"But we'll teach them our values," Agetha told Jiow. Her HUD beeped, and she scowled. "Ugh. But right now, there's a shipment of resinplast en route to the interior of Beta, and another of those multi-legged creatures was spotted near the construction site. I've got to make sure everyone's warned to get out."

She stood up, watching Phillipe and Choi. She was letting her child down. She wasn't there for them. But if the colony didn't get built, what *would* there be for them?

"Jiow, can you..."

"Of course, I can take them both," Jiow said, not looking at her. Phillipe reached for the scrubby grass that grew here and brought it to their mouth. Jiow bent and gently pushed their little fist away. "Not that. We don't eat grass and dirt."

Agetha imagined her meal that night of printed biomass byproduct. "I...thank you. For helping out so much with—"

Jiow shooed her off and finally looked up. "Go get Beta built. I haven't been to a live show in over three years, and I want to see that theater you're working on finished. It won't build itself."

What would Daved have done in this situation? It would have been better than this. "Thanks," Agetha said weakly. She left her child in capable hands and went to build the arcopolis.

PART TEN

Surging Ahead

3 years 3 months after landing

Jiow's eyes popped open at the rustling. It wasn't the kids. Both Choi and Phillipe were sleeping here—again—but if one or both had woken up with a nightmare, there would have been screaming.

She reached for the resinplast bar she kept under the bed. It had been cut wrong on a construction site, and now it kept her safe from errant biomass...and whatever that noise was.

As she crept through her apartment, the rustling solidified into whispering.

"Slide it down gently."

"Quiet! We don't want to wake everyone, just her."

Jiow's grip on the resinplast bar relaxed. She recognized at least one of the voices, though it had been a while since she'd heard it. She thought she was done with their schemes.

She rounded the corner into her living room, where Janx guiltily looked up from crawling through her window, aided by Maarsi. The two had hooked up a year or two back.

"What the fuck, Janx?" she whispered, then pointed back across her apartment. "I have two sleeping kids who only went down an hour ago. What is this?"

Janx straightened their shirt and sat down in one of her chairs, evidently ignoring the look on Jiow's face.

"Maarsi wanted to bring you in earlier, but I said we should wait. Less chance for things to get out. We're bringing in the whole crew tonight, and you're the last one. This is it." They sat back with a smug smile, as if excepting her to drop to her knees in awe, or something.

"This is *what*, Janx? I said I'm out of it. The Admins got wise to your tricks. That's why they posted so many of the Vagals outside buildings. If you hadn't generated so much goodwill with the Generationals for handing supplies around, we would have turned you and your crew in by now. Don't go shaking things up."

"They've relaxed their guard at last," Maarsi said, and Janx nodded along. "They've lost so many Vagals fighting the biomass they don't have enough to guard all their buildings anymore."

"They've lost Vagals making sure *we* don't get overrun," Jiow said. "What are you trying to steal this time, anyway?"

"Don't you remember?" Janx sat forward. "I told you: this is the big one. We're going to steal one of Admin Xi Wenqing's nukes! That way Admin will *have* to listen to the Generationals!"

"I...Janx, that's...stupid," Jiow finally spit out. "Xi's nukes have been a star eater story since Target Five. There aren't any." That was in spite of *all* the other things wrong with that plan.

"They aren't," Janx said. Their eyes were alight with a mad obsession. "We had word from one of our members working close to the science division. Admin Kumarisurajinder let a mention of them drop one day. Seems like the other Admins think he has them too. They have to be in the barracks, and we're going to steal one tonight."

"With what army?" Jiow laughed. "Because the Vagal one lives in the barracks and you're no match for them."

"We've got a way in and out," Maarsi said. "One of your janitorial colleagues cleans the barracks and is going to sneak us in tonight. That's where you can help out."

Jiow pointed a finger at them. "You better not have gotten my brother Zhu involved in this or I will turn you in *right now*."

Janx frowned. "No. He was just as stubborn as you're being. But another on his crew was more reasonable."

She took a step back and pointed the resinplast bar at the window. "Get out. I'm not helping in this crazy plan, but I won't turn you in, either, if you leave now. If the kids wake up, I can't promise anything."

Janx rose, taking a moment to straighten their shirt again. Jiow almost threw the bar at them. "We'll go. But you're making a mistake. In the new order, you'll be just as low down as you are now. You can look forward to scrubbing toilets forever, and so can your children, and their children."

They and Maarsi slipped back out the window, and Jiow closed and firmly latched it behind them. Her hands were trembling, and she pressed them together to still them. She'd done the right thing. Choi and Phillipe came first. Even if Janx's terrible plan somehow succeeded, she'd gladly scrub toilets forever if it meant her child—her children—stayed safe.

* * *

3 years 3 months 1 week after landing

Jane banged her fist on her desk. "You're just *now* telling me Generationals broke into the barracks? What happened? Where are they?"

Wenqing raised his head, lips pursed. General Smith, standing behind his chair, had bags under his eyes, and looked older than usual. "They have been dealt with," the military Admin said. "Three of their group have—heh—'volunteered' to join the Vagals as replacements for those lost to the biomass. They will be at the forefront of the next biomass sweep. The other six, including the leader, refused to cooperate."

"Meaning what?" Ahman asked. They sat back in their chair, a slight frown on their face. "Some Generationals were speaking about a few of their number disappearing. I assumed they were taken by the biomass." Rajani, sitting next to them, nodded. She and Ahman often worked closely together, as they dealt in science and R&D, respectively.

"And what was this group's goal? Are they the ones involved in the theft of metals a few years ago?" Dmitri scowled. He had taken the theft hard, as the metals were necessary for the solar panels he'd been constructing. The delay had cost them two months.

Wenqing raised his hands. "All in good time."

Jane seethed at the other Admin's stalling. Wenqing finally had a hold over them, and he wasn't going to let it go easily.

"If this is a threat to the colony and you've been keeping it from us..." she warned.

That only made Wenqing smile. "It would have been a threat if they found what they were after, but alas, they found only my Vagals. We'd known they were coming for days."

"Tell us what they wanted, man," Dmitri growled.

"The fabled Xi Wenqing nukes." Wenqing laughed. Unexpectedly, Rajani laughed with him.

"You *did* have nukes? This whole time?" Jane tried not to let her mouth drop. Christiaan was furiously sending her reports and articles from the last three years, and even stories from the fleet about the nukes. They'd been in the Generationals' collective memories for hundreds of years.

"Of course I don't," Wenqing snapped. "Our countries made assurances to each other before the fleets left. No one was to have nuclear weapons. But I knew you all suspected."

Jane stared at Rajani, who was still laughing behind a raised hand. "What's so funny?"

"I intended that rumor as an entertaining diversion, soon after landing. Seems like it made a lasting impression! I've been careful to drop hints about 'hidden nukes' every once in a while. I'm happy it's paid off and flushed out some undesirable elements." Rajani leaned over the table. "What are you doing with the rest of them?"

Jane considered the other woman. There was a vicious streak there she hadn't seen before. She'd have to watch Rajani closer.

"They're still in holding cells," Wenqing said. "I can't just execute citizens."

Jane stared at the Admin, considering. "But no one knows where these Generationals are, correct?" She swiped the warning from Christiaan away. She wasn't stupid.

"I...well, no. No one has complained in the last week."

"I think," Jane said, "this is an opportunity to get rid of some undesirable elements and get the Generationals to fall in line, all at once." She stared at Rajani.

"But if no one knows where they are then how will...oh." Rajani stared back. "You want me to start another rumor."

"Since you seem to be so good at it." Jane smiled, showing teeth.

Dmitri leaned in, breaking their staring contest. "I assume we are not lining them up against a wall here. What did you have it mind?"

"I'm glad you asked." Jane flicked another of Christiaan's warnings away. She would talk to them later. "I'm going to invite them to take their chances out in the biomass. Since they don't seem to like the rules of our city, they can find another set out there."

* * *

3 years 4 months after landing

Agetha fumbled with the HUD on the table next to her bed at its insistent beeping, and finally got it placed on her head. She accepted the incoming call.

"Yes?" She glanced at the display. It was three o'clock in the morning.

"Accident in Gamma," said the terse voice over the call. She thought it was Kalan, from her construction crew. Video calls were still a luxury. "We need you at the new site, foreman."

"Ugh. I'll be there in twenty minutes." Agetha blinked off the call, then blinked again, rapidly, before rubbing her eyes. She pushed herself out of bed. First, she'd have to get Phillipe and...no. Jiow was taking care of both kids. Again. Because breaking ground on a new radian meant she was on call at all hours and didn't have time to take care of her own child.

The old stab of pain at Daved's empty side of the bed was growing smaller each time she woke up, and she couldn't tell if she wanted it to disappear, or to never go away.

She brushed her teeth and stuffed a printed breakfast bar in her mouth, grimacing at the musty taste. It was supposed to be oat and honey flavored, but it was all biomass products, like many of the foods she didn't grow herself. The beehives were flourishing so there might have actually been some honey in it, but it didn't disguise the rest of the flavor.

She left a note on Jiow's apartment door and pedaled through the dark across Alpha. She'd known this half a megasecond—about a week—would be tight, but she hadn't expected to be up this early. She hadn't seen Frank for a game night in over six months. She'd barely seen her own child this week and Jiow lived next door. Her crew—she'd been promoted to foreman under an older Generational, Jardan, two months ago—was complaining about the long hours as well. Many of them were in poly groups or singles without a child, to be able to pull such long hours.

Agetha skidded her bicycle to a halt outside the construction site. This would be the central hub of Gamma, eventually, but now it was just a bleak and dark landscape with the occasional trailing fleshy growth visible in the pre-dawn starlight. Several of her crew were milling around, as were a squad of Vagals, the lights of E-Vapors shining in the early morning.

"What happened?" She asked the first Generational she got to. It was Kalan.

"Foreman! Jardan isn't here yet. Stace was mapping out the site, and their foot went through some glassed crust leftover from the landing. Turns out it was only centimeters thick, and the ground beneath has been hollowed out. Looks like there are more caverns here."

Flashes of Daved's injuries whizzed through Agetha's mind. "Did they fall in? Are they alright?"

"The others pulled them out," Kalan said. "They've got a broken leg and a dislocated shoulder socket, but they're conscious and talking. We're going to take them to the medical ward in a few minutes."

Agetha followed Kalan, who was an excitable man with Ganesha and Hina ancestry, a couple hundred megaseconds older than her. She checked that Stace was taken care of and got them on a sled attached to two bicycles. A couple of her crew would get them to the doctors.

By that point, Jardan still hadn't arrived. He was nearing sixty and hadn't adjusted as well to the gravity. He still used a mobility chair most of the time, but had an encyclopedic knowledge of structural dynamics and layout planning. He was also in charge of several of the crews, though they were split between Beta and Gamma. Admin, in their infinite wisdom, had decided to break ground on Gamma before Beta was finished, since they were behind the original schedule. Agetha suspected it was also to cushion Alpha Radian, where all the Admin and Vagals lived, with a radian on either side. Let the Generationals work in Beta and Gamma and be a buffer against more biomass incursions. She would have thought to argue, except all the Generationals were working so hard there was barely time to eat. There had even been several Generationals that simply...disappeared over the last couple megaseconds. No one she knew, but the word was they'd gotten tired of all the work and walked out into the biomass. She shuddered at the thought.

The Vagal squad members, in teal powersuits, were cleaning and preparing their flamethrowers. It was led by the one with the prosthetic forearm. What was his name? Ander? Something like that. They had a rotating variety of Vagals attached to their crew, flaming out biomass incursions as they found them to clear the building sites.

They often had to follow up on the Vagal's work by manually cleaning and processing the tainted ground. They'd developed giant drums to sterilize the dirt inside. It was a time-consuming and inefficient process, but it seemed to hold incursions at bay.

"Show me the breakthrough," she said to Kalan, who led her nearby to where they were working and pointed to a buckle in the glassed ground that looked like someone had stuck their fingers in a pie. Agetha stayed a good distance from the edge, but peered at it in the dim light. It was getting toward morning, and she could just make out the shaft descending below the opening.

"Anyone do a sounding yet?" she asked. Several of the crew shook their heads, and Agetha pulled up the interface for their two construction drones. When they'd landed, she'd commanded a whole swarm at once. Now each crew only had two, and the parts were wearing out. With a lack of rare metals, or really any metals, it was getting harder to fix them. Resinplast was coming along, but it was still a new product, and could only replace so many things.

The drones shook to life as she gave them instructions, hovering out over the hole. One dipped in close to the edge to get a partial mapping. There wasn't quite enough room to fit them in the hole.

"Looks deep, and I already see signs of biomass," she called to the Vagal team. "There's—"

Something *swarmed* out of the hole and snatched the nearest drone. Agetha fell backward, desperately trying to work the drone free from the mass of legs and teeth. There were horns, too, and something like...fur?

Suddenly, the Vagal with the prosthetic was in front of her, hefting his 'thrower, which shot out a blast of flame Agetha could feel even from her place behind him. "Move! Now!" he called.

Agetha scrambled back as the creature threw the trashed drone to the ground and turned on them. It had eyes—already unusual for a biomass creature—like a goat's and...hooves? But it was low and squashed, made for running through low tunnels, trailing pink and brown masses on its sides. Ropes of mycelial tissue made up its musculature. It bleated, a wet, horrible sound, and pounced on the Vagal. Anderson. That was his name.

Agetha scampered back on feet and hands, her knees and elbows aching as she did. They hadn't been the same since landing and she didn't move fast enough.

The goat/fungus thing threw Anderson aside and pressed toward her, bleating like a toad with indigestion, sharp hooves beating holes in the glassed earth. One knocked her ankle aside and she felt her bones vibrate all the way up her leg.

Then another Vagal was there, 'thrower spewing fire, catching the tufts of fur alight that sprinkled the creature like mange. Inside their teal powersuits, the Vagals were unidentifiable, except for Anderson, with his prosthetic hand.

A hoof caught the Vagal's chest, and she could hear the *whump* of impact. The Vagal coughed like they couldn't get a breath, and then the goat thing was on them, beating holes in their armor and biting at the closed visor. They rolled, flame spitting out between them, though the biomass creature didn't seem to notice it was on fire. More streams of flame joined the first, from the other Vagals, and the creature screamed, pawing at the Vagal underneath it. Agetha could see pools of blood, seeping through cracks in the powersuit.

It turned and dove back through the hole, shadows rising along the shaft from its still-flaming hide.

Agetha crawled to the downed Vagal as soon as the 'throwers ceased belching flame, jerking the cracked chestpiece from the suit to reveal torn flesh underneath. She was about to feel for a heartbeat when the skin bubbled and buckled. It split as a muffled scream came from the helmet. Acidic bile gurgled up from multiple puncture spots and Agetha jerked her hands away. She hadn't seen it at first, but the teal armor was covered in light green spots, fizzing in the sunlight. The chemical was slowly eating through the armor where hooves had struck it.

Another Vagal flipped the mask up, revealing a young-looking face with glazed eyes, mouth frozen open in a scream. Agetha looked away.

"Acid hasn't worked on the powersuits before," they said, ignoring their dead comrade.

Anderson limped forward, his own chest piece in his hand. It sizzled from several locations. "It seems to take a while to get through. This is thin nanotanium-plated steel, but I don't think it could harm the walls. We still need to take this to Admin."

Agetha sat back, panting in the early morning light, still on the ground. That Vagal had given their life for her. She knew it happened, but had never been so close. Never had it happen to her. Was it worth the cost? Even just three years into the colony, she could see the differences growing. The younger Vagals looked as fresh-faced as they had when they landed, while even the young Generationals were starting to show gray hairs from the continued stress of building the colony. The Vagals would look the same for years to come, if they survived. Meanwhile, her crew routinely had back and foot injuries because the bones still weren't as strong as they would have been, had they been born on Lida. The Generationals were getting older, and they kept losing Vagals.

It was all to protect their future. Like Phillipe. Thankfully, her child would be different, physically. Likely not as tall, with eyes a bit smaller, relatively. They would be used to the tricks the biomass played, ready to keep building in the face of adversity. Better able to handle these horrific creatures. For any Generational with a child, it was obvious those born on the planet didn't belong to the same group of people who came here on the ships.

The hole led to a small tunnel, which the Vagals flamed out. Once it was clean, they could cover it with a single sheet of resinplast. They'd have to watch for more creatures like that—with stolen parts of their animals. She supposed it was inevitable. The biomass was nothing if not reactive and adaptive.

And now another Vagal had died, and they were down another drone, in addition to Stace's injury. Alpha Radian held a small but growing memorial yard, where the first names were of the victims of the Khonsu crash, over three Lida years ago. Now it held over a thousand markers. There were more Vagal than Generational names, but not for long. As the supersoldier numbers dwindled, the Generationals had taken up the slack in the defensive teams patrolling the arcopolis. They didn't have the same resistance as the Vagals, and twice as many were killed, on average. It could easily have been her today, if not for the Vagal's sacrifice.

Yet the construction went on.

"Let's get the new shipment of resinplast prepared," she called to the shaken construction crew, and they made their way to the pile of brown sheets. The new material wasn't like steelcrete. It wasn't a metal. It cut more like a dense plastic, melting if the temperature wasn't right. They'd wasted more sheets than Agetha wanted to admit. More slowdowns, on top of everything else.

They didn't have time to grieve their fallen. They barely had time to eat. Every day the biomass wore them down a little more, and their only hope of surviving to make a future for their children was to build as fast as they could.

Agetha rubbed sleep out of her eyes. It was going to be a long day, and it already *had* been a long day. This pace couldn't last forever.

* * *

3 years 5 months after landing

The children who had eaten their parents expanded ever outward. There was hope that those children might transition into yet another stage of evolution, but it seemed they were content, for now, to make simple copies of themselves, and increase the number of non-living storage buildings they preferred to inhabit in the ring of death. It was progressively harder for select optical sensors to gather appropriate amounts of information on the children's movements. Even the tiny winged mobile signal carriers no longer received information, and it was unknown if this was an unexpected development of the interface in their biology, or a change with intent behind it. The question could not even be asked of the signal carriers, as all attempts at communication were met with failure.

This was a setback to the observation of the children, and despite optical and auditory sensors near the peaks of the highest growths, fine details were hard to come by. Several more attempts at long-range flight as the children had displayed were attempted, but a suitable construction was not achieved. The large vertical structure surrounding the habitat was an insurmountable barrier to continued growth, for the moment. Other attempts had been made to interface directly with the children, through the use of large mobile constructs, similar in size to the children's form. Similar morphology to select children was thought to increase communication, but so far with little luck.

202 William C. Tracy

There was a further concern in the treatment of material by the children. There were now several outcroppings outside the barrier which should have been easy to communicate with, but instead were strange blank spaces. It was as if a fire had blazed through a section of old growth, but rather than new growth rising again, all that was left was uncommunicative matter.

The concern over the blank material was communicated through several groups of higher-functioning entities, past numerous sensory and calculating nodes, and subjected to intense scrutiny. Why could this space not be observed? There were two explanations agreed upon: that either an unexpected development had occurred, in which case the new form would need to be subsumed and evaluated, much as the other troublesome region near the equator had been; or the changes were deliberate. This was a much more interesting and dangerous proposition. Never had there been two rival thought processes that could not communicate with each other. Whichever the cause, this was a problem that required more data and closer consideration.

The shell the children erected around the ring of death was growing ever harder to penetrate. This new dead material was almost repellent to those entities that came in contact with it, unlike the smooth metallic structure that surrounded the first expansion. Various parties agreed that it could be time to stop observing and more actively engage with these children. The newcomers had voluntarily eschewed contact, instead severing any attempt to provide greater clarity, and this could not stand. Several overtures had been made already. Higher-functioning nodes around the surface were directed to focus on the area in which the children stayed. It was time more direct attention was devoted to this troublesome area.

* * *

3 years 7 months after landing

"Give me some good news, people," Jane said. "That damn biomass is surging through our defenses." Christiaan was at her shoulder, as always, but Wenqing, Rajani, Ahman, and Dmitri were there as well. She was starting to think of these Admins as the real leaders, whereas the other three—Alessandro, Maria, and Polunu—just didn't have the head for leadership.

Dmitri had an elbow propped on the table—head supported by his hand. The others all looked tired. Jane ignored the discomfort in her belly. She'd been taking antacids like candy.

"My Vagals are dying even faster than they have been," Wenqing said. "This surge in growth is unlike anything we've seen before."

"He's right," Ahman said. Their normally placid tone was sharp. "The hyphal roots are growing at three times the previous speed, encroaching on Beta and Gamma. They're even growing up the nanotanium wall around Alpha, though they can't get much purchase. We're running low on flammable fuel."

"We're experimenting with converting some of the construction saws to offensive weapons," Wenqing added. "General Smith has also requisitioned several of the defunct drones to salvage cutting lasers and circular saws from them."

"We're having issues with power production in some areas of Beta, as mycelium are forming over top of the solar arrays," Dmitri said. "We cut it back every morning, and it's grown back by the evening."

Jane clenched both hands. They were already behind schedule on Beta *and* Gamma, and this was slowing them down even more. Wenqing had flatly refused to send any more Vagal squads into the growth outside the city, saying they were not getting enough information to offset the potential in lost lives.

She looked to Rajani. "You're the science lead. What else can we try? Acid? Freezing? Blunt weapons? We're just over three and a half years into this colony. We've survived the yearly cycle, thank God the winters are mild, and we're building. I will *not* have us fail now. So, give me something. Anything."

"Freezing the hyphae does work the best," Rajani answered, "but we have very limited stores of liquid nitrogen and carbon dioxide left from the ships. We use it in some medical and R&D applications."

"Can we manufacture more?" Jane asked.

"Well, yes," Rajani said, "but it's a slow process and takes power we don't have to waste at the moment."

"And won't for the foreseeable future," Dmitri said, head still resting on his hand. "Not with this surge in growth."

"Then find out how much is essential for medical and research purposes, and use the rest," Jane told Rajani. "This stuff is adaptable if nothing else. Maybe if it learns we can fight harder if it grows faster, it will back off."

"I think you ascribe too much intent to these mushrooms," Dmitri muttered.

"It's just a plant," Wenqing said. "An efficient one, but just a plant."

"Technically it's not a plant," Rajani said.

"Do it," Jane growled. "Freeze the fuck out of the invading biomass and get us back on schedule. Use the parts we chop off, or burn, or freeze, and get our resinplast production up. I want Beta *finished* as soon as possible so we can devote all resources to Gamma. Beta was supposed to be finished the beginning of this year, and it's only half complete. How much steelcrete is left? Enough for the wall around Gamma?"

Ahman gave a sickly grin. "We can finish the outside edge of the circle, but not the interior wall that would go between Gamma and the eventual Epsilon Radian."

"So, our buildings are just going to be dangling out unprotected for the next ten years until Epsilon is constructed? Rajani, are you still not willing to use resinplast for a retaining wall?" Christiaan sent the breathing timer app to Jane's HUD, and she growled, but breathed in and out with the count. She hated that it helped.

"The biomass might find a way to overcome the resinplast viral blockers," Rajani answered. "Do you want a growth surge like this *with* all our resinplast buildings exploding in mushrooms?"

Jane shook her head. "I want more Generationals signing up for the construction crews. All who aren't absolutely necessary for keeping the arcopolis running. Have them train with the Vagals, too. You've got a bit of experience with that now, Wenqing." The three "volunteers" hadn't lasted a month, and the others were long gone into the biomass. Jane hadn't had to use the punishment again, but she was ready as soon as a Generational *smelled* of rebellion. "We've got to have a dedicated force to stop incursions."

"What about the children?" Ahman said. "Since we opened the slots for new children in the decanting tubes, the birth rate has skyrocketed.

In about ten years, we're going to be overrun with children, but we need that, to offset the aging Generationals."

"Schools," Jane answered. "The Generationals have been organizing haphazardly, but I want a dedicated day care—in Alpha, where they're protected—and get the minimum number of Generationals to act as caregivers. Education is your area, Ahman. Deal with it."

"That was supposed to be started in Gamma Radian, after it was complete," Ahman reminded her, leaving unsaid that construction and planning was *her* area.

"Yeah, well, we've all got to adapt to these fucking fungi," Jane shot back. "If we hadn't designed Beta to hold so many entertainment venues, maybe we'd have more room for the kiddos."

"Morale would have been abysmal if we did not have the few escapes we do," Ahman said, their shoulders back.

"I saw an excellent play about the UGS Hasamelis evading a comet last week," Dmitri added. "It was no Swan Lake, but certainly enjoyable. We need culture to raise the children who will be the first true native colonists."

"While we're fighting a losing battle against mushrooms?" Jane asked.

"Yes." Surprisingly, it was Wenqing who spoke up. "If we end up delaying the rest of the arcopolis construction, so be it. We must also raise the best minds and hearts we can. We will live long. These children's grandchildren will grow old under our direction. They will run the colony. If they are not supported, encouraged, and taught well, then what is building the arcopolis worth? We must fight with conviction, to secure the best place for our children."

Jane looked across the stony faces of the three Admins, then to their assistants, standing quietly, but with just as much resolve. Christiaan sent her a thumbs-up.

You too? She swiped back, then sighed heavily.

"Fine. I'm sure if I ask the others, they'll say the same thing. Obviously, we need moderation, from defense, to education, to research." She raised one finger. "But there's going to be a *lot* of hard work in the meantime to get basic services up and running. I want three shifts at all times on construction. I want those day cares set up. Tell everyone to buckle down. We're going to tackle the biomass and *keep* our arcopolis from being overtaken."

The three other Admins nodded.

"And Ahman?" Jane said. "Find out if this growth is some sort of cycle or what. I don't want this happening again. We've got to move to the offensive after this."

* * *

3 years 9 months 1 week after landing

Anderson strolled through the newly created Beta market. There was a fairly established one in Alpha already, selling anything from food to goods to spare parts, but he'd been through it many times. Now that more people were moving to Beta with children—even if it was unfinished—there was a need for a new place to socialize and trade.

He'd rarely been here to socialize. Most of the time he was in Beta and Gamma was to flame out fungal incursions, and occasionally deal with unruly Generationals. However, the incursions were on the outskirts of Beta, where the last sections of steelcrete wall were going up, and the Generationals were being worked too hard to fight. In this section of the radian, the biomass rarely intruded, and families were prevalent, giving those who lived here a sense of safety.

Today he was here because Noce—now technically a Staff Sergeant, as they had both been promoted—had told him in no uncertain terms that Anderson needed a hobby to satisfy Cora. Except Noce hadn't used her name. A few Vagals had started to refer to their implant in similar familiar ways, but no one really talked about it. Many were chafing under the constant pressure of battling the biomass, a dangerous, but monotonous threat. There was nothing new to analyze. Anderson's breaking point had come when he'd dived out of a second-story window while visiting a fellow Vagal's house. Turned out she had an eighteen-month-old child who liked screaming at the top of their lungs. And then Noce had ordered him here to blow off steam and find something new to obsess over. In their words, it was going to get "boring over the next several hundred years, if you don't get eaten by a mushroom."

The food market was the largest section of the market, as it was in Alpha, but Anderson only skimmed through rows of tomatoes and squash, beans, cheese, and limited meats. Pigs had adapted so well to

Lida, that Anderson was getting tired of bacon. Gardening was not his thing. He could kill a weed, back on Earth, and his thumb hadn't gotten any greener here. He was fairly handy, though, and his prosthetic lent his right hand a greater strength than usual. He routinely traded repair jobs for Generationals who could supply him with fresh vegetables.

The stalls transitioned to small carvings, jewelry, and other fabricated items. Anderson slowed to inspect them as he passed.

"Nice prosthetic," a shopkeeper said, nodding his head at Anderson's hand. He was busy filing down a burr on an elaborate timepiece, made all of scrap metal and resinplast.

Anderson looked down. He was hardly conscious of his metallic hand any longer. He'd learned the basics of maintaining it himself, rather than bringing it in to a specialist every week. It was nearly as dexterous as the hand that had been infected with fungus.

"Had it for a while," Anderson said. "Since a few weeks after landing."

The man put down his work, tipping up handmade glasses to frown down his nose at the prosthetic. "May I?" He reached out a hand. Anderson thought, shrugged, then opened his prosthetic hand in return.

He couldn't *quite* feel with it, but his nerves had adapted over the years to the tiny pressures in his wrist as the hand interacted with objects. He had a suspicion Cora had something to do with how he processed the information. He tried to keep his hand still as the man manipulated the joints and checked the lubrication ports.

"Good work, and well maintained," the man finally pronounced. "There's a tiny irregularity in the pinky mechanism, if you want me to clean it up—no charge. I'd call it a fair trade for letting me poke around your hand."

Anderson had noticed his pinky being slower to react, but hadn't had time to get it fixed, and the problem was past his knowledge of mechanics. "I think that would be an excellent trade," he answered, and unhooked his prosthetic, laying it on the table where the man tapped. "I'm Anderson, by the way."

"Medibe. It'll take a few minutes. You're welcome to watch, or you can wander around. I'll shine it up a bit while I'm at it."

"Sure—what's the insider tip for the Beta market?" he asked. "This is the first time I've been here."

Medibe cracked a smile. "You'll find some things here that aren't for sale in Alpha. There's a reason this is the entertainment section. Try through there." He pointed farther back along the stalls, past where Anderson had gone so far.

"Thanks. I'll be back in a bit," he told the man, and strolled away. He tried not to wiggle the non-existent fingers of his right hand. He didn't often go out without it, and he was very aware of the imbalance. Cora was pumping something through his system, and he tapped the fingers of his left hand, trying to burn out his nervousness.

The tents and booths here were close to each other—much tighter than in Alpha—and although there weren't a whole lot of Generationals, he still had to walk around them. He hadn't seen any other Vagals while he'd been out. There were little more than a thousand of them left, compared to the twenty thousand Generationals. He stepped aside as someone trotted past holding their child's hand, the toddler making each deliberate step with extreme concentration. The Generationals were making more of themselves.

Fewer of the Vagals had children. Too many had volunteered for the missions out in the biomass surrounding the arcopolis, and the survival rate was only about seventy percent. The excursions had cut off a few months back. Likely a good decision, as there were many years until the city was self-sufficient and well-protected. They'd need Vagals until that point, and likely after, when and if the technology to create implants was available again.

The range of items changed again as he walked farther, with jewelry and carvings becoming more sexually based before those gave out in favor of more...useful types of items. Anderson wasn't a prude by any means, but the Earth-based culture he grew up in outside of the Leicester, England was more uptight than the one the Generationals had developed over four hundred years of being in close contact with each other, where there were no avenues of escape.

All that meant he walked quicker through the stalls where semi-dressed people of all genders sat, some with customers...negotiating services. He was certain his lighter skin was turning red. If this was all the market offered back here, he'd turn around and watch the man work on his hand.

But then the sex workers tapered off, and Anderson slowed, his mouth open, at the three-meter-long painting of the fleet in motion over Lida.

"Beautiful, isn't it?" Anderson jumped at the voice. How long had it been since he was so enraptured even Cora didn't tell him when someone came up beside him?

An older Generational stood next to him, hands clasped behind their back. Wispy hairs were tied into two braids on either side of their chin. "There's a lady originally from the Xaman Ek who paints these. I was lucky enough to coerce her into selling them. Took me marrying her to do it, but it was worth it."

Anderson chuckled at the joke. "She does an amazing job."

"I'm guessing you likely don't have room to take that one home with you." At Anderson's head shake, the person pointed at other paintings around their stall, no less captivating, although much smaller. "Take a look at these, then. All using local pigments, hand mixed after we landed. The ones from the ship ran out after about thirty megaseconds—sorry, about a year."

Anderson spent longer than he anticipated at the booth, and finally came away with a claim ticket. His new painting of the view from the top of the Admin building, looking out over the biomass, would be delivered the next day. He knew the perfect spot in his living room. He even traded more time credits than the seller asked. The trade measurement was something used on the ships, and worked well here, where none of them needed currency, at least not yet. He'd never seen anything so well painted, on Earth or on the ships.

There were other stalls and booths with paintings, drawings, sculptures, and more, but none caught his eye as much as the first one. Still, he slowed once again at a little booth with piles of honest-to-goodness books. Not HUD downloads. He hadn't seen a book since Earth, though they had been rare even then.

"May I?" he asked the man tending the booth, reaching his hand out. He would have used his flesh-and-blood left one even if the prosthetic was still attached. There was something about the feel of books, and the prosthetic would never capture that.

"Please." The man watched him until he picked one up before saying, "I made them all myself."

Anderson almost dropped the book, then clutched it closer to peer at the binding, and smell the pages.

"How did you make the paper?"

"Biomass, just like everything else," the man answered. "It goes through the same process the resinplast does, so I promise it's not going to sprout and eat you."

Anderson flipped through the book with his hand, his stump supporting it, finding the pages blank. He looked back up.

"A journal," the man said. "Ready to fill with your thoughts."

Anderson stared. It was something he'd never even contemplated. He wouldn't have, before Cora. But now, when he was thinking about five different things at once and his brain was trying to process it all...

"How much?" he said.

"You interested in journals, or reading?" the man said, rather than answering his question.

Anderson had gone through all the novels he'd brought twenty times over. Cora also heightened his reading comprehension, it turned out.

"You have new books?" he asked. "Like, ones no one brought on the ships?"

The man produced a hand-covered eReader from beneath the table. "Just the ones I brought in my mind. I haven't uploaded these to the HUD network. Never liked reading on the things."

"You write books, *and* you make books?" Anderson asked.

"I do, but I'll have to warn you, they're a little...spicy, especially for how you folks from Earth tend to think."

Anderson thought back to the stalls with the sex workers. That wasn't really his cup of tea, but the thrill of reading about it... "They're romances?"

"The trashiest," the man said. "My latest is about a Generational and a Vagal who run away into the biomass, but rather than killing them, it does, well, other things to them."

"How many have you written?"

"Enough to keep even you busy for a few months, I'd guess," the man smiled. "I write as Sona V. Gore. Not my name, but it does keep people reading, it seems."

Anderson smiled back. This was turning out to be one of the best days he'd had in years. He'd have plenty to do until his prosthetic was ready.

* * *

4 years 2 months after landing

Alvin put his new succulent cactus in a place of honor in his living room. He'd installed a hanging shelf thirty megaseconds or so ago, but never found the perfect item to place there. The shelf could be seen from anywhere in the room, just like decorations back on the ships.

His living room felt complete, now. Kofus had said the cactus didn't need much water, and so as long as Alvin got up there every week or two, it would be fine. Kofus bred the last surviving ones himself. They'd met at a function in Alpha radian last week for Generationals who worked for Admin. Kofus caught his eye from across the room, and they fell to talking, about the succulents, Alvin's water sampling and scheduling for Admin, and how they both hated 11d, until they got here. Kofus implied he'd need to come by and check up on the succulent every once in a while, and Alvin thought that was one of the best ideas he'd heard yet.

This gravity well wasn't as bad as he'd been expecting. A little over one hundred twenty megaseconds—what the Admins termed four years—and he was getting the hang of it. People were building with biomass, making tools and art with it, and even eating it. Alvin thought the fungus-based food was bland, but not nearly as bad as some Generationals said.

He bustled into his kitchen to make some tea, looking over his shoulder every few minutes to catch a glance of the succulent cactus from a new angle. It was quite a handsome specimen, much like its original caretaker.

Alvin brushed a few memos from his HUD as he waited for the water to boil. They were stray files he needed to clean up for the next workweek. He'd been working as a secretarial assistant under Admin Delgado's organization, keeping track of the new waterway development in process beneath Gamma. Finally, his organizational skills were getting used, and he could keep his ears open for any other juicy gossip coming down from Admin.

The water boiled and he poured it over a new tea he'd gotten in the Alpha market the day before, on Kofus' recommendation. It was a hybrid type of rooibos the biomass had infected, but some enterprising Generational had saved the strain from destruction.

Alvin added honey, let it steep, and took a sip. It had a mellow, earthy flavor. As he cupped his hands about the handcrafted clay mug, he decided it tasted like something encountered in a secluded land, tended by old hermits. He liked it.

This wasn't the fleet, by any means, but he'd found some semblance of his old life. Alvin passed the hall mirror, looking at the new succulent cactus, then stopped, and turned his calf to the mirror. There were some things to like about a gravity well, too, like better developed legs. Kofus had been admiring Alvin's calves last night when he asked if Alvin had ever gone line dancing. There was a new class starting tomorrow night, and he said he could teach Alvin. It was out of his comfort zone, but Alvin couldn't deny the surge of excitement when he thought about it. He sipped his tea and grinned.

* * *

4 years 2 months 1 day after landing

Alvin straightened his one formal jacket for perhaps the fifth time since he'd arrived at the little square building stuck between the adult theater and the bicycle depot in Beta Radian. He'd been told the radian was safe, now the wall was almost finished, but he'd brought a cold pack, melting in his pocket, on the off chance some biomass popped up from the earth like a devilish jack-in-the-box. He'd heard the Admins discussing how cold was the most effective means against infestation, though they had limited quantities.

His shoulders relaxed as the tall and lithe form of Kofus appeared out of the shadows, his angular features a contrast to Alvin's rather pudgy ones.

"You didn't have to wait outside," Kofus said as he approached, holding out a hand for Alvin's.

"Oh, I wouldn't know anyone in there," Alvin replied, taking pleasure in the feel of Kofus' calloused hands. "And you invited me, after all. I figured we could make an entrance together."

"That's fair, isn't it?" Kofus barked a laugh, as sharp as his cheekbones. "And it gives me a chance to look you over before we go in." He accompanied the remark with a long look up and down Alvin, who straightened under the inspection, hoping the slightly too-tight pants he'd worn showed off his calves well enough. Kofus' own thin legs showed well beneath his jumpsuit. He'd mentioned he was a runner.

"Shall we?" Alvin said, and they passed into a wall of conversation, music, and laughter, making Alvin grip Kofus' hand tightly.

"I've met a few of the Vagals who started this place up," Kofus shouted in his ear above the music. "Turns out it's like something some of them had way back on Earth, and they taught a few Generationals, who liked the idea. It's not any sort of dancing like we did back on the ships."

Alvin hadn't gone to the dance parties on the Abeona. Crowded things, with people floating everywhere, as liable to bump into you as to twirl gracefully through the room. But this... He peered through the press of people at the entrance, to see four lines of people, all facing the same direction, spinning and stepping in concert, in time to the music. It was ordered, mathematical, and regular, and actually looked like a lot of fun. It was beautiful.

"I can show you a few steps before we start," Kofus said. "The next song is in about two minutes."

"Is it the same moves as those people are doing?" Alvin asked.

"I think so, why?"

"If you know it, we can jump in. I've got the rhythm." Alvin was staring fixedly at the two lines, counting under his breath.

"Heh. Of course. This should come naturally to a processor."

"No longer a processor. Just a secretary." Alvin smirked.

"Once a processor, always a processor," Kofus said, and whisked him into the crowd.

Kofus introduced Alvin to several couples and polys he knew, including an analyst from the Abeona named Gearge.

"Processor Alvin!" Gearge exclaimed. "Yes, I remember. Agetha and I used to route decision trees through you and the other processors. Still keeping an eye on things down here?" Gearge was an expressive and excitable man, shorter than the average Generational, much as Alvin was.

"Oh, keeping my hand in this and that," Alvin hedged, trying not to namedrop.

Kofus elbowed him. "Alvin is too modest. He acts as secretary to some of the Admins themselves, keeping them in line and on schedule."

Gearge gave an approving nod. "Good work if you can get it!"

"And what are you doing now?" Alvin asked, sidestepping around the fact that didn't so much keep the Admins in line, as hurry along behind them, trying to keep up.

"Oh, me and the group are on our fourth kid. Admin likes handing us child approvals, as we have a group of seven. Easy to care for multiple mouths, even with five of us working full time."

Alvin tried not to shudder. *Four* children? And they must all be three or younger. He cast a sidelong glance at Kofus, who also had his eyebrows raised.

"Quite a handful," his companion said. "Though I wouldn't mind one or two eventually myself. Singles are far down the list, I'm afraid. Better to match up with someone to get a good spot." He gripped Alvin's arm. "Or better yet, find someone cute, keep them to yourself, and see what happens..."

Gearge laughed good naturedly, and Alvin joined in, but his mind was whirling. Kofus was intoxicating and seemed to truly like him. He had to make sure not to mess this up. He wasn't at all sure about dealing with a small, messy infant in a gravity well, but that was something for a much later date. For now, he just had to prove to Kofus that he wasn't a dud.

They popped between Generationals Kofus knew, including several with babes in arms, and one old flame who greeted him with a kiss on the cheek and a wink for Alvin. She soon twirled long brunette hair around in a cloud of perfume before disappearing into the throng. She must have been growing it out since they landed. No one had long hair in the fleet, unless it was well tied down. It just got in the way.

"Shall we try this out?" Kofus asked as the music rumbled to a close. "Still have all those numbers in your head?"

Alvin thought for a moment, placing the sequence *just so* in his memory. "Ready when you are."

He held his breath as Kofus led him to the center of a rectangle of assembling people, each half a meter from each other. Kofus gave his hand one last squeeze before letting it go and facing forward.

The music started with a clash and a bang—far removed from anything Alvin had ever listened to on the St. Christopher, and he found himself sweating after only moments, mouthing the next move in a desperate attempt not to step wrong. The seconds disappeared into an unknown amount of time—Kofus beside him—as he turned, stepped, and stomped, the beat of the music flowing through him. No one in the fleet had ever danced like this. Their feet most of the time hadn't even touched the floor, except when they were making a course correction. When it ended, he let out a shaky breath and leaned toward Kofus.

"That was amazing."

"Not bad at all for a first attempt," Kofus said, taking up Alvin's hand again. "You want to sit one out, or try another?"

The prospect of *another* hadn't even crossed Alvin's mind. "Is it the same steps again?"

"Nope." Kofus peered at a chalk board someone had hung on the wall of the dance hall, "But it's not much more difficult. Just means you'll have to keep your eyes up this time and stop looking at your shoes."

"I'd...like to try it," Alvin found himself saying, though he had no idea how the words got to his mouth. His brain certainly hadn't thought them.

He found himself cheering with the others as the next song started.

Six dances and two rests later, Alvin's clothes were soaked with sweat. He'd have to take them to the lady who lived down the street. She was working on a type of dry cleaning with chemicals readily available in the colony. But looking around, almost no one was clean. Certainly not Kofus.

The taller man wiped a sheen of sweat from his brow and shook his fingers at the floor. "Woo! That was a trip, and good job you on your first time. Can I buy you a drink? This dancing is thirsty work."

Alvin nodded eagerly and they pushed through the dancers to the bar. Several fungal-based drinks later, he and Kofus laughed through each other's life stories in the fleet, him on the St. Christopher and Kofus on the Khonsu. They had a lot in common, from loving to pick out details of each job, to wanting their own things just so, to having an unspoken feud about the screen brightness with their coworkers.

"So, how's that Ovatifolia I gave you going?" Kofus finally asked.

"I've got it in a place of honor," Alvin answered. "I couldn't stand the way Admin had designed the apartments, so I added some hanging elements like the way we had things back in the fleet."

Kofus' eyes lit up. "All six walls? How did you get displays working on the ceiling? I've been stumped, and my apartment looks so bare."

"Oh, just a bit of rope and some handy leftover resinplast sheets," Alvin said. He bit his lip. "You know, I could show you what I did if...if you want to come over. I can show you the cactus too." He couldn't believe he was being so forward.

"Well, someone's got to look after that poor agave, don't they?" Kofus said, and grabbed Alvin's hand. "Lead the way."

* * *

4 years 7 months 3 weeks after landing

"I want you to behave today, Choi," Jiow told her child. "Don't let Phillipe tell you what to do." She turned to who she thought of as her adopted child. "And you, little one, I don't want to have to tell your mother you acted up at the daycare again, so do what the minders tell you."

"Yes Mommy," echoed both children. Jiow was never quite sure how much of her instruction penetrated into the minds of three-year-olds. It had been an immense relief when daycares finally opened in Alpha for the few Generationals still living there.

Janx and their crew had been gone for over a year now, and Jiow had been keeping her head low since then. She knew the stories of Generationals walking out into the biomass was bullshit, because Janx would never have done that. They'd been too committed to changing the colony. And now they were gone, effectively killed by Admin. She kept expecting someone to show up at her door and cart her away, but after a year, maybe, just maybe, she'd escaped Janx's stupid plans. She'd worked up her courage to go through training and no one accused her of trying to steal nukes. For the first time in three years, she got back to work.

Except then came reports of Choi and Phillipe acting out in class, surely because they were without a parent who was familiar to them, for the first time in their lives. Even though both had recently started speaking in more or less full sentences, there was a large communication barrier at times.

She gave both of them hugs, ushered them into the large building in Alpha, where they met Mr. Bonny, their caretaker, and got back on her bicycle, pedaling much faster now she didn't have two ever-growing children taking up the rider seats in back of hers. Even with less weight, her knees twinged as she pedaled. They shouldn't be hurting so much. She was in her mid-six hundred megaseconds, or what was equivalent to early twenties in Lida years. But she would never be as fast or resilient as the kids when they grew up, born and bred in Lida's gravity well. The separation between the Generationals and everyone else was only growing more pronounced. They were all becoming like her—an afterthought.

Jiow sighed as she crossed over to Gamma radian, the buildings falling away to a few resinplast skeletons and foundations. Construction was slow—very slow—even considering Gamma was progressing while Beta was being finished, and they were battling a nearly exponential surge in biomass growth. They'd put in only a third of the central buildings in a year and a half since first breaking ground. Agetha kept her up to date on the statistics when they had dinner together and Jiow gave Phillipe back. Neither was as often as she would have liked.

But it was work, and Jiow was working, and most especially, she wasn't working in sewerage, or pipelaying, or water management. She'd even gotten out before her brother Zhu, and he'd had a transfer application open for the last two years. Evidently quitting her job, having a child, and then re-entering the workforce was what was needed. She'd have to tell Zhu the next time she saw him.

Jiow parked her bike at the communal rack, watching a Vagal team off in the distance flaming out a new infestation. All bikes were also communal, but the addition of the two kid's seats on hers marked it as a custom job, and others left it alone. They were still a rarity, but it wasn't uncommon to see a bike with an extra passenger seat, or two or even three. Fortunately, she was the first one at this construction site, so she got her pick of spots.

She checked her HUD for the morning duties. She'd laid resinplast foundation the night before and needed to check the sealant to make sure it had set correctly. She made her way through the outlines of structures still to be started, and stopped short at the site of the building where she was supposed to be working.

It was crawling with biomass.

Literally crawling. Hyphae reached out, feeling across the smooth surface for purchase, knotting together in mycelial masses. Tiny mobile creatures the size of flies and earthworms tunneled through the growing mass, directing and caring for it. A cluster of mushrooms, already half a meter tall, grew from the very center of the resinplast.

There was a spare 'thrower in the site construction supplies nearby and Jiow grabbed it, starting it up with practiced ease after checking the tank and safeties. She threw fire at the mushroom ring, the mobile critters crisping and crackling in the heat. The resinplast was treated to take the temperatures from 'throwers for a short time, and she shut off the fuel flow as soon as the mushrooms had crisped and deflated.

"Well this is shitshow," she cursed as she got a shovel and began scraping the biomass char away. One of her crewmates ran into view—more workers were showing up—and they wordlessly got another shovel to help.

"I'll finish up if you check the resinplast," they said. Jiow nodded and squatted over the resinplast with a brush and flashlight, looking for contamination and damage.

"Fuck. We need to redo this section!" she called out. The foreman, Laeri, came over at her shout.

"Where?" he asked.

"There are pinpricks all through the resinplast sheet," Jiow told him, shining her light at the tiny holes visible in the surface. Hyphal rotos had grown through from the underside.

"Cut out all the compromised sections," the foreman directed, "and find out what's underneath."

Most of that day of construction was wasted taking out resinplast fouled by creeping biomass. By the evening, she'd removed half the sheets she'd added the day before.

Later that day, Laeri examined the scrapped plates. "I haven't seen this before. Even Vagals can't stop all growth, but this is the first time it's tunneled *through* a sheet. The biomass isn't supposed to touch the resinplast, like it's invisible or something. But this part of the biomass acts like it's trying to see what we're building, and forced its way through."

"Except the biomass isn't intelligent," Jiow said. Scientists and Admins had affirmed that message again and again. No sign of intelligent life.

"Right," Laeri said. His shoulders relaxed. "I suppose it's just responding to pressures. Probably hasn't had a bare spot this big in a long time, so it's trying to expand into an open niche no matter the location." He gave Jiow a shrug. "I used to work in ship anthropology back on the Xaman Ek before we landed."

"Sure, just pressures," she said. The thought nagged at her as she picked the kids up that night. At least they'd behaved in school today, though Mr. Bonny said Phillipe had tried to eat the writing chalk to keep it for themself. Jiow said she'd talk to them about it. She didn't even pretend she'd ask Agetha to do it. She also sent a message to Frank that she was bringing a resinplast sheet to him. She wanted his opinion on something this strange.

The next morning, she got there just as early, but in the dawn's light, she found the resinplast sheets broken and twisted, biomass tangling and growing from the interior of the sheets. The non-reactive resinplast. The material that Frank and the other scientists promised the biomass couldn't reproduce with. She stared at the worksite, covered in resinplast. At the resinplast saw, tools, even bicycle tires...

"What the hell happened?" came a voice behind her, and Jiow turned to see three Vagals.

Jiow tried to hide the waver in her voice. "Do you have anything to kill this, but not burn it? I need to get it to the scientists to study. Quick."

The largest Vagal pushed past her, unclipping a small vial from his belt. "We're only supposed to use the CryoChem as a last resort, but I think this warrants it." He sprayed a stream of mist at the twisted resinplast sheet, and Jiow could hear it screeching and cracking from the cold. When it was safe, the Vagal waved her over and she wrapped the resinplast in a containment bag. A bag also made from resinplast. She fervently hoped it would stay non-reactive until she could get it to Frank.

* * *

4 years 7 months 3 weeks 2 days after landing

"Hey there, little one," Frank said, squatting down so he could be face to face with Choi. "I've got something for you!" He pulled a box from behind his back and Choi's eyes lit up—eyes that perhaps shared something with Frank's. They loved opening presents. It was a good thing Phillipe wasn't here. They loved presents too, and were a grabby little snot. Jiow spent too much of her time on that kid. According to Jiow, Agetha had been out on the site for the last three days, and only got home this evening to take her kid back.

He'd fabricated a very thin strand of resinplast that acted a bit like aluminum foil and wrapped the box in it. He'd even been able to tint it purple, using some dyes the lab was creating from beetroot.

"Here, tear on this side, and you can see what's inside," Frank directed, pointing to the corner of the box.

"Hard," Choi grunted, as their little fingers grasped at the resinplast film.

"I can help you out." Frank reached for the box, but Choi snatched it away, setting what was inside rattling. Their eyes widened even more. Eyes that weren't quite as big as the Generationals, but not as small as those of the Admins and Vagals.

"No! I open."

Frank chuckled and let the kid figure out how to tear the pseudo wrapping paper.

"What did Uncle Frank get you for your birthday?" Jiow asked from the other room. She was wrapping up the troublesome resinplast sample she'd told him about in one of the last specimen bags he'd saved from the fleet. He'd known it would happen eventually, but did it have to be so fast? Resinplast had only been around about fifty megaseconds—a year and a half on Lida. He'd assumed he would have two or three times that long before the viral communicators mutated enough to get around the signal blockers. Long enough to create a coating for the resinplast. He'd have to start watching the bees again.

"Ungh!" Choi grunted as they finally tore the film and the box thumped to the floor. They pulled the top off and peered in. "Blocks!" they said.

"You can put them together and build things," Frank told them. He looked up to see Jiow giving him a lopsided smile. "I used to have a ball and stick set when I was a kid. I printed this out of resinplast. It's light, but should stand up to normal kid abuse." Jiow's eyes darted to the wrapped bundle on the table. "And don't worry about it sprouting. The Vagals killed those boards off good. It was likely a one-off chance that it made this batch reproduce. I'll check the inspection logs."

He directed his words down to Choi, who was busily dumping all the parts out of the box with a clatter. They immediately picked up a rod and a ball and fitted the two together. "And you can show me what you built next time. If you need more blocks or connectors, I can print you out some more. Hopefully."

"Ball fits!" Choi exclaimed, slotting another ball on the other end of the rod.

"Good job!" Frank said. "You're a natural, kid."

* * *

4 years 8 months 1 day after landing

Frank banged a fist on his resinplast tabletop the next morning. The batch had been perfect. It wasn't a problem on the production side, which meant the biomass had either gotten lucky with a mutation, which meant it could happen again, or the biomass had mutated in response to specific pressures, which meant they would need to replace all the resinplast in use in the colony. And if he was even a little unsure that it was the first option, he would need to prepare as if it was the second option.

He sighed and wished he was back watching Choi open their new toy. That had been the only time in the last two months he'd really been able to check in on Choi around their third birthday. They were a bright little kid—he was pretty sure the tyke made a benzene ring out of their new toys. Must take after him. Phillipe, on the other hand, already thought of Jiow as more of a mother than they did Agetha, and that was going to mess them up going forward. He'd seen families split in nasty divorces in the fleet, heard of kids growing up to be little hellions. Agetha was a great foreman—but she was too good. The job was going to eat her up, because Admin would take all the Generationals would give. Unfortunately, Frank was about to add to her workload.

He unwrapped the pile of resinplast planks—he was keeping them covered whenever not directly working on them—and cut off another small sample with a laser cutter. Time for the first attempt. He'd crush this piece up and see if he could reform it into new material, after going through the viral blockers again. Maybe there would be something different this time.

Frank knew the first attempt almost never worked.

* * *

4 years 10 months 2 weeks after landing

"We've tried new viral inhibitors, burning out specific cell types, and a secondary and tertiary sterilization, and nothing makes me think this version of resinplast is any more resistant to the biomass than the kind we had before," Zixin Ye complained. Frank was getting tired of the man's complaints. It was like he'd never worked in R&D before landing on Lida.

"But we can't know," Femi Sarraf echoed, sitting across the table from him and Ye. She fidgeted with her headwrap, though Frank didn't see that it needed adjusting. Femi had been restricted to the arcopolis footprint after the Vagal teams stopped going out. She was reportedly taking out her restlessness on her assistant, Ashkara. "If the biomass would just repeat whatever it did to the first sample, we could try to test our new combinations. Right now, we're in limbo."

It had been another almost six megaseconds—or a little over two months—of waiting and implementing fixes since he first got the sample Jiow collected. In that time, the biomass hadn't repeated its reproductive event, so there was no way to know which new version of the resinplast might be more resistant. They'd come up with the new viral blocking methods fairly quickly—they had some data left from the first attempt which hadn't been fully implemented, and it turned into five different new capping methods. They just needed to find out which, if any, worked.

Admin was tearing their collective hair out over the delays in construction, but there was no way they could go full steam ahead with resinplast construction if it was compromised. Nor could they stop construction altogether. After more bickering and infighting between Admin and scientists, Admin and Admin, and scientist and scientist, they had finally settled on five "weathervane" research plots set outside every new construction, where it might be overrun by biomass before the building. Then if one or more of the samples *didn't* reproduce, they could use those to go full speed with resinplast2.0 production.

"This waiting is going to kill me," Frank muttered. He was taking antacids for what was likely a stomach ulcer. "We can keep coming up with solutions for Admin, but there's no way to tell if we're even going in the right direction or if we'll need to try a completely different tactic for stopping the biomass' viral communication between cells. Plus, increasing the number of test strips means there's more variability in how the biomass interacts with them. We've tried to keep the biomass away from the resinplast completely because we knew this might happen. I don't want to voluntarily expose more measures that the biomass might evolve around."

"So, what can we do?" Ye asked.

"Sit here and rot," Femi grumbled.

"We keep making samples of the five new versions, and keep cranking out the old stuff for construction," Frank said. "We know we're going to have to replace resinplast at some point. The more we prepare for it now, the easier it will be to implement when it happens. This will be a waiting game."

* * *

4 years 10 months 3 weeks after landing

Frank accepted the HUD call from a frenzied Ashkara Patel.

"We've got an infestation in the new storage depot in Gamma, near the radian's edge." The young woman's breath came fast and sharp over the connection.

"Did you already contact Femi?" Frank asked.

"I called you first," Ashkara gasped. Was she running?

"I'll tie her and Ye in," Frank said, already looking up their contacts. He blinked the connection through while Ashkara caught her breath. "Everything alright out there?"

"This infestation was a little...explosive. Whoo." Ashkara gasped and her breathing finally slowed. Frank wished they had enough bandwidth on the planet for video, but it would be many megaseconds before they could tie up needed lines for the construction crews like that.

"What happened?" He clenched his hands, feeling his nails scrape against his palms.

"The storage depot is, er, not there anymore. There was a strange growth that resisted the Vagals' 'throwers. Two big bulbs were growing up the walls, but when the Vagals switched to cutting tools, they found out the bulbs had exothermic chemicals in them. And when the chemicals combined, there was an explosion. Lost two more Vagals, before I started running."

"But you're calling, which means you found something," Femi broke in. She had joined while Ashkara spoke.

Frank checked to see that Ye was in as well.

"Yes ma'am," Ashkara said. "Three of the weathervanes got corrupted. The bulbs grew from samples one and three, and sample four was buckled and had hyphae growing from it. I was checking them when the Vagal team arrived to clean it out."

"So, weathervanes two and five resisted?" Ye asked.

"That's right. No sign of activation, even though they'd been in direct contact with invasive biomass and the other three had been corrupted."

"Hot damn," Frank said. "Finally, we can get somewhere." Sample one was the original resinplast, so it made sense it would be corrupted. But they had two versions of resistant resinplast to develop further. "I told you the third sterilization course had merit, Ye."

"As did my cell burn cycle on the receptors," the other scientist answered. "You want to take yours and I'll take mine for further development?"

"And I'll contact Admin on switching production over," Femi said. "I advise we use both avenues at once. The biomass is adaptable enough that if we can keep ahead with two different countermeasures, we can future-proof at least some of the new buildings."

"Agreed," Frank said. "Let's get to work, people. We've got a lot of resinplast to replace, but construction is back on."

* * *

5 years after landing

Five years. Five years of building, of fighting, of love and death, scarcity and plenty. Agetha stared out over Beta Radian on the day of the opening ceremonies.

Her right hand clenched. Her left was holding Phillipe's, already three and a half years old. He had already chosen his gender, earlier than most children and with a sincerity that made Agetha accept his decision as something thought out and not any fad of childish whim. He was becoming a solemn boy, but prone to lashing out when he didn't get his way.

It had been three and a half years since Daved had died, too. Three and a half years of grueling work, fighting the biomass, and not seeing her child nearly enough.

There were other families nearby, of five, six, eight, or more members. Kids ran between their parents' legs and got in the way of others trying to set up the festivities. Their colony was surging in growth, with the oldest children nearing four years old. The new generation of Grounders—as they were already being called by the Generationals—were stronger, faster, and shorter than their parents, but they were just as inquisitive as kids had been in the fleet. The name was something to differentiate them, as it was easy to see the differences in those born down a gravity well.

Agetha had the day off, as did most construction crews. Even though they had just restarted building with the new resinplast variant, Admin wanted them all here to celebrate Beta Radian's formal opening. The original plan called for Beta to have been completed three years in, but the original plan was so far out the airlock even Admin could see they couldn't get back on schedule. The entire arcopolis was supposed to have been completed in ten years, but two of eight radians had been constructed in half the total time, and there were more challenges ahead.

226 William C. Tracy

"Come on, Phillipe," Agetha said, leading her son into the crowd ringing the central square of Beta. It was surrounded on all sides by centers of art: a museum, containing a few ship parts and diagrams, the Arcopolis Theater, the sculpture garden—where any citizen could request a spot to display their creation—and the Khonsu memorial, a plinth devoted to the one hundred and three people who had died in the worst disaster of the colony. So far. Over ten times that number had been killed in total, including biomass encounters, construction accidents, poisonings, general injuries, Generationals unable to adapt to Lida, and simple old age.

She stopped in front of the memorial and pointed out names of people she knew to her son, telling him again about what happened. Daved's name wasn't on the list. He had survived that disaster, only to be killed soon after by the biomass. Agetha took the chance to remind Phillipe of the father he'd never met, and how much he would have loved his son.

"That why you leave so much, Mommy?" Phillipe asked.

"That's right," Agetha answered, swallowing a sudden lump in her throat. "Mommy needs to help provide for the colony, since your daddy isn't here. That's why Mommy Jiow helps take care of you." She'd only aged five years since landing, but it felt like ten. She wished Daved could see what they had built—and what they'd lost.

"Mommy Jiow leaves too. Shorter," Phillipe said and Agetha tried not to sigh. It had been something he'd brought up several times lately.

"That's right. Mommy Jiow was called to help out too, once the daycares started up. You like playing with the kids in the daycare and with Choi, don't you?" He and Choi were fast friends, despite their bickering and fighting.

"Yes," Phillipe mumbled. "Like playing with Mommy too."

Agetha closed her eyes for a moment. "I like playing with you, kiddo, and I'll try to do that more often."

She led Phillipe deeper into the festivities, greeting people she knew, and showing her child off to the members of her construction crew, who cooed over how big he'd gotten. The whole time, thoughts tumbled through her head. The biomass wasn't slowing down, and even with the new resinplast, they barely kept it from overrunning Gamma. She wanted to spend more time with Phillipe, but Jardan had talked with her privately about becoming the crew leader after him. He was nearing two thousand megaseconds—sixty-five Lida years— and he hadn't handled the transition to Lida well. He wanted to get out of construction and transfer to a desk job in Alpha.

When would she have time to rest? Another forty years?

"Look! Flying balls!" Phillipe tugged her forward and Agetha snapped to the present, seeing the balloons someone had made out of thin resinplast film. They must have generated helium or hydrogen somehow—enough to fill them up. It was a nice touch for the festivities.

"Do you want to hold one?" Agetha asked, and Phillipe bobbed his head like it was on a spring. She led him over to the vendor.

She had this day with her son, this moment. She *had* to find time to spend with Phillipe. Daved would have wanted her to. Her son was growing fast.

The impossibility of completing the city before the Generationals were whittled down to nothing loomed over her.

PART ELEVEN

A New Generation

5 years 6 months after landing

Anderson's fingers tapped against his leg as he surveyed the swath of biomass where the new school was under construction. Fronds waved over two meters high, and the ground was crawling with hyphal strands and mushrooms popping up like...well, like mushrooms. There were varietals he recognized. One was acidic, breaking down barriers for the biomass to grow, and another was covered in dense spines that impaled anything that got too close. Tiny mobile creatures crawled through the mass—the vanguard of larger ones. The biomass had started spitting their livestock back at them in the last year, in twisted forms. Crawling things with goat's eyes and horns. Multi-legged climbers with boar's tusks and hooves. Feathers ringing the top of a spire of fungus. Cora went wild whenever he saw one, like she was trying to tell him something. Except it was just evolutionary mutation, wasn't it? No signs of self-awareness in the biomass, the scientist said. Just extremely fast adaptation. Then why did he feel like it was watching him?

He shook off the feeling. If the Admins and the scientists weren't worried, he shouldn't be either. He had a job to do. Two years ago, it would have been a risk to build this close to the edge of the arcopolis. Two years ago, Gamma had just been started. Now, six months after Beta officially opened, all eyes were on this new radian, with a huge forest past the edge of a river—the city's water supply. Strange things came out of that forest, the biomass never relenting in its assault on the city.

There were fewer Vagals than there had been, and all of them had to pull their weight. That was one reason this school was being built—to train the first generation of Grounders, some of whom would supplement the Vagal ranks.

Damn orders, and damn this biomass for growing so fast. He wanted to get to the next book in the Mysterious Fling series. It had taken less than six months to fly through all of Sona V. Gore's first romance series. The man had been right. They were undiluted trash, and Anderson *loved* them. Gore had the ability to condense emotion into something almost physical, and wrote like the wind, never even changing his first drafts.

"Light 'em up and burn 'em out," he told his squad, and teal powersuit armor clattered as 'throwers ignited. They started near the five slabs of weathervane research plots, which accompanied every building built. Most of the squad smoked VaporLites behind their faceplates—the trash the colony provided them rather than the old E-Vapors, which had finally given out, even after scraping and combing old cartons. They were made out of resinplast, just like everything else. He didn't want to know what chemicals were in it, but Cora kept him from feeling ill effects.

Nearly all Vagals smoked them. They provided a calming intermediary between the harsh chemical changes induced by their implants. It dulled reactions a tiny bit, but also kept surprised soldiers from flaming rocks and fellow squad mates.

"Weathervanes two and five are clear," Private Clayton announced. As usual, the crawling tendrils had torn through the other three, bursting them open with hyphae.

"Check the good ones," Anderson directed, and two Vagals searched for pinpoints of hyphae roots in the other two weathervanes. The construction crews were using this new concoction to replace the old resinplast used previously. If these last two research plots were bad in any way, it would be an indication the biomass had adapted once more to the resinplast sterilization.

"Clear," Clayton called after a moment. "The biomass grew over it, but didn't touch it."

Anderson breathed a sigh of relief. Maybe he could get a chance to read today. He'd talked to Gore when he bought the newest book about why he wrote and how. The man remained a mystery, never even revealing his real name, what he did, or what ship he'd been on in the fleet. From what Anderson could gather, he wrote because he was bored—with whatever he did—and didn't care who read it. But many people liked his work. Sona V. Gore was a name known around the arcopolis, and with only about twenty thousand people here who had been on the ships, it shouldn't have been difficult to tell who he was.

Anderson *talked* to him face to face. But no one knew who Sona V. Gore was.

He was tempted to set a few Vagals to follow the author, but somehow, that would sap the fun from their relationship, and both of them knew it. So would digging through the colony database. Worst of all, Gore might stop talking to him, or selling him books.

Anderson checked the priming valve on his 'thrower—the same tool he'd received from Noce a week after landing. It had been through upgrades, modifications, and repairs, but it worked even better now than it had when he first got it. He fired a test stream at a node of vines the size of tree roots which had popped up overnight. The flame sputtered, and he adjusted the fuel flow until the center of the fire burned blue. The root node squealed and twisted as it charred to nothing.

He'd written about that squealing in his journal. He was almost finished with the first one he'd gotten from Gore. The sound was just the mushroom structure twisting in the flame as the water was driven out, but all the Vagals agreed it sounded like the biomass was screaming. Sometimes Anderson woke in the middle of the night with the noise in his ears.

Flame leapt from eight 'thrower nozzles, roasting the growths that had popped up overnight. The delicate fronds, as tall as he was, crisped and sagged. Mounds of intersecting fungi, on their way to making a shelf of matter around the building, crumbled away. The larger mushroom growths popped in the heat, oozing acid or sap, or whatever this week's horror was. Tiny creatures buzzed and crisped.

After long minutes sweeping the area, Anderson called a halt. The mat of vines and fungus crawling through the open doorframe of the school had been turned to ash. Pools of acidic residue bubbled from where they had leaked from the growth.

The others were tending to two of his squad whose powersuits had been splashed with the stuff while they rooted it out. The biomass was adapting. The suits used to resist everything except massive blunt force, but the acid here had eaten through the armor's leggings. Flyter hissed through their teeth, eying the ragged burn hole on their greaves as they removed them. Clayton was beside them, with a resinplast patch. They were good friends, and Anderson had seen them spending the night together. He was glad his team was close. As their powersuits wore down, their team had to rely more on each other.

The biomass was gone—so why was Cora pestering him? Anderson's head swiveled from left to right, but there was nothing close. The ground was undisturbed. He lit another VaporLite. They tasted like crap, but they calmed his nerves.

He stared across the river at the wall of tree-like fungus. Some were taller than the one that had fallen over the Alpha Radian wall. The twisting growths and subtle movements in the jungle were mesmerizing. He could almost understand the Generationals who snapped and walked out into the biomass, never to be seen again. There'd been more stories over the last two years. Someone's friend, or friend of a friend, had gone missing. It was always secondhand. Always a Generational. No one ever saw them walk away.

The rest of the Generationals worked day in and out replacing the structures made with original resinplast recipe. Some buildings literally had to be torn down to the foundations and built again. Others just needed a new outer layer. Construction stayed infuriatingly slow, and he heard both Admins and Generationals grumbling about it. The Vagals were the odd ones out. Their jobs had stayed the same. There was always more biomass to destroy.

Cora pushed at him even through the VaporLite, and he tapped the fingers of his prosthetic hand together, clacking in the silence. He'd try more journaling to calm his nerves when he got back to the barracks. Along with his thoughts, feelings, and nightmares, he'd written a few short stories in his journal. Gore had insisted Anderson bring them by when he mentioned it. The author was nice enough, but Anderson could tell he thought it was bad. Anderson knew why too. He couldn't capture the characters like he wanted. Couldn't paint the broader strokes of human emotion like he read in—

There was a snap like bone breaking and one of his squad screamed. Anderson snapped out of his reverie. Cora hadn't alerted him—except that she had. He'd just ignored her.

He rushed to the squad, who were gathered around a crisscrossed framework of white calcified material, trying to free a screaming teal form barely visible between the crossing white structures. He knew that voice, distorted by screams. It was Clayton. Anderson raced around the perimeter, pulling at the white bars, trying to see how to free her. One glistening spike protruded through the back of her powersuit's thigh, bright red stark against the bone white.

"Break it!" he shouted, but his team was already fighting against the trap, pulling the individual bars that flexed, but did not break. Clayton was still screaming.

Cora pumped chemicals through Anderson's blood, and he peered close at the material. Not just bone white, but *bone* that flexed like bamboo. Another thing the biomass stole from them and flung in their faces. Another evolution, laid like a trap under new growth, as if in wait.

"Saws! Get saws!" he cried and two Vagals rushed to a shed on the jobsite, coming back with powertools. They set to work on the cage, the tools whining in protest against the saturated material. Something like fermented marrow oozed out of the cuts they made.

"Ugh," Anderson cried, and slammed his visor shut. It didn't block out all the smell. He opened a private channel to Clayton.

"Clayton—Clayton! Stop screaming! Tell me where you're pinned. We're getting you out."

The Vagal's cries ceased, replaced with rapid panting.

"Arms pinned, sir," Clayton gasped. "Something through my leg, and..and...I think through my chest." Her breathing had a wet rasp.

Anderson winced. "Hold tight. We'll be to you in a moment." He closed the connection, and opened another to the entire team. "Saw halfway through on both sides. Pry it apart," he directed, pulling a section of corrupted bone that had already been cut. It looked disturbingly like a femur. As the trap lost structure, it began to deform. A little further and they'd have her out.

Was this a deliberate response to the Vagal teams? A trap laid at the base of a new structure? But wouldn't that ascribe intelligence to the biomass? Everyone said it was simply an invasive creature, but not smart or self-aware. No. It couldn't be intelligent. If so, they had a much larger problem on their hands.

His team snapped the beams pinning Clayton and the jaws of the trap creaked open. She cried out again as dozens of thorny spikes pulled free from her arms, legs, and torso. There'd been more than any of them could see, her powersuit a mess of holes. How was she still conscious? A pool of blood formed underneath her, mixing with the ashes.

"I've got her!" Flyter ducked through the bars, catching Clayton before she fell. The rest of the team strained against the bars. If they let go, they would snap back together.

The ground rumbled beneath them, and Cora blasted adrenaline through his body.

"Let go!" he called, and his team dutifully stepped away as the trap snicked shut again. Flyter and Clayton both cried out in pain. He had to hope they'd destroyed enough of the trap's structure so it couldn't pierce the powersuits this time.

"We'll get you out. We just have to—"

The ground gave way beneath the trap, sucking Clayton and Flyter beneath the surface.

In another moment the gaping hole squeezed back together, dirt shifting as if giant hands molded it. Anderson glimpsed an instant of whipping vines and bone white stakes before Clayton and Flyter's screams cut off. He swallowed.

The ground around the school was quiet, ash sifting through the air.

"Fuck," Anderson swore. Two more Vagals killed, and they would have to dig the entire area out under the school to get rid of whatever pit the biomass had grown beneath the surface. It was a trap, made to crush Vagals. Intelligent or not, it didn't really matter. The biomass was adapting specifically to them.

This was going in his journal.

* * *

6 years after landing

Jane scanned the boardroom. They'd had to move into a new one on the fifth anniversary meeting last year, because there were so many extra stenographers, recorders, reporters, and upper managers who also insisted on attending. The older Generationals were attaching themselves to Alpha Radian, cluttering up her hierarchy. She couldn't wait until enough children of Admins were grown.

"Congratulations!" she called out, and the buzz of individual conversations muted and died. She added the message Christiaan sent her. "You've made it through six years of this shit. Give yourselves a round of applause."

There was laughter, and some of the attendees did actually applaud for themselves. Self-serving bastards.

Jane let her smile fade, glancing through the schedule on her HUD. Delays, more delays, adapting biomass, accidents, and more.

"First, we'll have the Admins update us all with what's been happening, and then we're going to talk over general strategy for the next several years..."

It took almost an hour just to get through all the introductions and Generational changes. She immediately forgot their names, but Christiaan would have them all recorded. She wouldn't need them. Several had retired or changed positions over the last year. The older the Generationals became, the less important they were for the timescales in which Jane preferred to think.

This colony only needed eight leaders, not a hundred.

Alessandro and Polunu had lost several species irrevocably to the fungus. Animals were down to pigs, goats, ducks, alpacas, and of course bees. Jane bemoaned the loss of fruits like peaches, pineapples, and grapes. She would have literally murdered someone for a real glass of wine instead of the swill decanted from a mix of pears, strawberries, and fungus.

The biomass loved Dmitri's warm solar plates and soaked up the energy if it wasn't cut away daily. Like everything in the colony, it was a constant battle. Maria's fungal wastewater sterilization was reaching the limits of the capacity of the river to contain it. Wenqing's Vagals were dying too fast. It was only a matter of time and training before they would be supplemented by Generationals. That at least was a good use for them. There were a few—troublemakers, all—who had been invited by General Smith's most loyal Vagals to take a walk into the biomass, under cover of the darkest nights. Each invitation reduced the crime rates in the arcopolis.

She swiped a message to Christiaan for greater details about the most important Generationals in the room, and got an immediate response with data on each and what ship they came from.

What would she do without Christiaan? She blinked a thanks back to them. Without them, she wouldn't have been leading this colony— stuck in Alessandro's job of dealing with their food situation mess. They'd been sleeping together for six months now, perhaps an inevitable conclusion to working so closely together. It was a way to relieve stress, but her sole focus had to be on building the arcopolis. When that was done, maybe, then she would have time for a real relationship. She had time. Centuries, if the architects of their genemods were correct.

Jane watched several of the older Generationals nod off as the meeting progressed, and pinged Christiaan to record their names. Only eight to lead.

What to do with an aging population that could no longer effectively construct the city, and didn't want to be at a desk job? They had planned for that uncomfortable period fifteen or twenty years past landing when the last of the Generationals were phasing out of their jobs, and those native to Lida did not yet have the experience needed. But they had never planned for the arcopolis to take this long to build. It was supposed to be complete in ten years, but she would be surprised if it was complete in twice that long. Other plans would need to be accelerated.

Ahman talked about the plans to develop an auto tram, upgrading to motorized vehicles, other projects that would take decades to complete. They had been popping out children with their spouse. Were they up to six now? Five of the Admins had children, in fact. They needed more. She almost swiped the question to Christiaan right then and there, but held back. Not yet. Not for her.

Rajani spoke of the new resinplast, and the measures in place to keep it from reproducing. Rajani warned that another mutation would happen, whether in six months or twenty years. But the biomass would break through at some point. It always did.

"And lastly," Rajani wrapped up, "we are nearly through the nanite-based regrowth kits left from the ships. Most have been given to Vagals for extensive injuries suffered while keeping the arcopolis safe from biomass incursions."

"This is why I want my Vagals kept out of harm's way," Wenqing interrupted. "We are running low on many resources from the ships."

"Exactly." Rajani took the reins back from Wenqing's interruption, tightening her salwar kameez. "Please urge everyone to be careful. There will be no more rapid healing. Everyone will have to go about it the old-fashioned way, without nanites."

"Perhaps we simply stick some moss on our wounds from now on," Ahman quipped, to nervous laughter.

"Aheh," Rajani laughed. "But seriously. Do *not* apply biomass to injuries. We've had plenty of that already."

"Thank you, Rajani," Jane said, and glanced over the speech she and Christiaan had spent last night perfecting, though she hardly needed to. It was seared into her brain.

"Fellow colonists," she began. "Our city is growing, and despite some setbacks"—she gestured to the other Admins—"we persevere."

She eyed the thirty or so Generationals seated around the circumference of the room. None were under fifty years old, whatever that was in megaseconds, all seasoned and experienced members of the fleet. All growing gradually useless.

"We must also speak about how the colony will grow. Older members of the fleet are retiring now we've finally found a home. You *need* to, in fact, in order to raise your families who will continue your work ethic and pride in our city." She saw a few heads raise at her last statement. Christiaan had insisted she add it, and as usual, they had been right. She kept the pleasant expression on her face, despite all these hangers-on staring back at her.

"But the arcopolis must expand *and* we must raise our children *and* we must care for those who are no longer willing or able to work full time." She paused, her eyes roving the room. "I fear we do not have enough resources to support everyone."

There were frowns at that, but she knew there would be.

"So, I turn this on you." She gestured outward, to where the Generationals sat around the perimeter of the room. "What would you do? How do you suggest keeping the colony moving, given the difficulties with which Lida challenges us?"

She waited, letting the silence grow. She wasn't going to speak again until someone else did. She could wait for *years*.

Finally, there a cough from an elderly Generational in a mobility device. Half the ones in the room used them, their bodies too used to zero-G.

"We are willing to help out," the older woman said, shaking her head, from which long white braids hung. "We are used to life in the fleet. No one was useless on the ships, and we won't be here. Put us in charge of raising the children, if you don't want us around."

Jane nodded. She'd been ready for this answer. "And how are you with teaching about life on a planet's surface?" There was audible grumbling at that. "Generationals have been marvelous at raising their children so far. We got here, didn't we?" She paused to let the few audible chuckles breathe and soften her tone. "But we are teaching children to live on the surface of a new and hostile planet. We do not have the technology we used in the fleet, nor do we have the safety and controlled environments of our ships. Who among you can teach a child to build fungus-resistant buildings? Who can teach a way to keep our strains of vegetables pure from corruption? Who knows the many variations in form the biomass shows? Who can teach a child to *walk* instead of float?"

There was silence. Jane saw embarrassment from Maria, Rajani, and Ahman. She saw stony silence from many of the Generationals.

"Then what do our opinions matter?" someone asked from their chair. Jane glanced at her HUD. Man Lau, former engineering supervisor on the K'uei-Hsing. Seventy-five. "Like it or not, we are here. Our hands have helped build this arcopolis. We know its secrets. We know how it works."

"And we thank you for that sacrifice, Lead Engineer," Wenqing said before Jane could speak.

"We've already been advised to move to the outskirts of Beta, and now to Gamma," a deep-voiced older man added. He'd been in charge of the hydroponics on St. Christopher—Jane's ship—and she felt she should recognize him. "How far are we going to be pushed away?"

More Generational voices rose. They understood their skills were appreciated, but were now more useless than not. There were more Generationals in this room than there were Admins and assistants. It would only get worse as the short-lived descendants of these people propagated, temporary lives to build their city up and restore their level of technology to something like Earth's. Only then could they truly progress on this planet. Only then would Lida become a civilization to endure.

"Then what would you have us do?" the first old woman said, when no one else spoke up. "Shall we go out into the biomass and take notes? See what we can discover before it kills us?"

Christiaan helpfully sent Jane the woman's profile and history. Jaiya Maruskel, mother of five, grandmother of twenty, lead Processor on the Hasamelis for twenty years. She was over eighty if she was a day. Jane could also guarantee the woman would never see the city completed.

"If it would help," Jane said truthfully. Maria sucked in a breath at her words, but Jaiya Maruskel only raised her chin defiantly. Others raised their voices while Jane sat back.

Yes, she would gladly feed them all to the biomass if it would mean the arcopolis would succeed.

Dmitri was waving his hands, trying to restore order, and General Smith, behind Wenqing, was lecturing a nearby Generational. Even Rajani had her mouth open, explaining though no one could hear her.

Jane sent a message to Christiaan.

Get them out.

Ten seconds later, a squad of Vagals burst into the room and silence fell. Before things could get out of control again, Jane raised her voice.

"As you see, there are many difficult decisions still to make for the good of this colony. I think for now, we shall call the public section of this meeting to a close, in order for the core leadership of the arcopolis to decide what direction to take." Only eight to lead, and her to lead them.

She waited, but no one moved.

"Please." She gestured with one hand to the door, locking eyes first with Jaiya Maruskel, then Man Lau, then to the others who had been loudest.

One of the Vagals took a step toward the old Generationals.

"I can tell when I'm not wanted," Jaiya said, and scooted her mobility device toward the door, nearly clipping a Vagal on the way out. As if that was the first piece of a crumbling dam, the others followed her, even the stenographers and other record keepers.

Soon the large room held only eight Admins, with one assistant each.

Jane took in a deep breath, then let it out.

"What was that?" Maria exploded. She was the youngest of them, the least practical, in Jane's estimation. But Polunu and even Ahman were looking grim. "Are we going to become a dictatorship if the Generationals don't like what we say?"

"If necessary," Jane answered coolly, and Maria blinked at her. "There is a vast power differential here. Surely you see it." Dmitri and Wenqing were nodding along. "The Generationals can overwhelm us in sheer numbers. They were given a task and an objective in the fleet. They knew what their purpose was. Here, they're simply leftovers."

"You would throw away the *hundreds* of years of knowledge they've gathered on the ships?" Maria pressed.

"Like knowledge about how ships engines work? Or how to navigate through an asteroid field, or repair micro-meteoroid impacts? Or how to perform a spacewalk?" Jane ticked off points on her fingers. "Yes. Throw it all away. It's useless here." She raised a hand at several Admins opening their mouths at once. "No, I take that back. We can certainly use parts of their knowledge and adapt others for different purposes. But we've been doing that for six years now. We must become more rarified as the Generationals age, and we don't. You must think in the long term. We will live for centuries, but we can be *killed*."

There was silence for a moment, as Jane let her words drill into the others.

"Then you think they would revolt against us?" Polunu asked.

"They already have," Jane replied. "They lived, worked, and died without us for over four hundred years. They think they don't need us now." She leaned forward over the table, her eyes shifting between her fellow leaders. "I've personally sent thirty-four, so far, out into the biomass. You know of the ones who tried to steal Wenqing's non-existent nukes."

"But not of the others," Wenqing warned. "You are not the sole voice of leadership here."

"That depends on who you ask, doesn't it General Smith?" Jane said.

"Absolutely, ma'am," General Smith replied from behind Wenqing, who spun around to glare at the Vagal. "The Vagals appreciate a tidy hierarchy."

Jane let the silence grow as the other Admins looked back to her.

"Now, if I've made my point clear, we have limited resources, an extremely constrained economy, and not a lot of space to live in. The

Generationals are used to doing things their own way, but they also don't know how to live on the surface of the planet. We are moving from the last of those who lived on the ships to the first of those born on this planet. I intend to do it in an orderly fashion."

"And how will this happen?" Ahman asked. "Though I fear I have an idea from your actions."

Jane knew she could count on the lithe Admin to ask the right question at the right time. She let her smile show through.

"We move the Generationals out to the edges of the arcopolis as we build it. We keep them too busy to even *think* of removing our direction for the colony. If any resist, they walk out into the biomass, under their own power or ours. We train the new natives through school and work to *expect* us to be there to guide them." She looked to Ahman. "Your schools." To Dmitri and Wenqing. "Your power to support us and Vagals to keep order." She pointed at Alessandro, Polunu, Maria, and Rajani. "Your direction to keep food and water production stable, and to keep us safe from the biomass with new innovations." She regarded them all, felt Christiaan standing straight behind her. "And finally, *my* leadership."

Jane paced again, her hands behind her back. "We will outlive the first people born on this planet, and likely their grandchildren. I don't want them to wonder how their ancestors used to live in space. There is no time for that. We must complete this arcopolis, or we will all die. The biomass will see to that. It's already adapting to our presence. Their very lifespans mean they have no concept of the long-term plans that are in place."

She turned back to the other Admins, all eyes on her. "And we *will* survive. Will I have your support in this, no matter how hard it will be?"

There was a round of agreement from the other Admins. Even Maria bowed her head in acceptance.

* * *

7 years 6 months after landing

Alvin snuggled up against Kofus on their rooftop on their first marriage anniversary. Turned out Lida years were good for something. Lida. When had he stopped thinking of it as 11d?

They lay on their backs, side by side. It was their nightly ritual, as it had been since they'd started dating, over three years ago.

Kofus took a sip from the pear brandy they'd splurged for. "Just like looking out the viewing ports on the Khonsu," he said, gesturing upward with his glass. "Do you think we'll ever get back up there?"

Alvin sighed, but shook his head, then nestled back in the crook of Kofus' arm. "As much as I would love to, not in our lifetimes. Those are getting shorter and shorter."

"Don't say that." Kofus squeezed him closer. "We have hundreds of megaseconds in front of us."

"Unless we get eaten by biomass," Alvin said. "There are new creatures poking around the city every day. I've heard the Vagals talk. It's like all our lost livestock is being thrown back at us. Like it's *laughing* at us."

"You going to put your EVA suit back on?" Kofus raised an eyebrow at him. "It's simply quick to adapt. We knew it would absorb some of our plant and animal's DNA eventually."

Alvin snorted and bumped Kofus with his hip. "You're never letting that die, are you?" His old EVA suit had crumbled apart soon after Kofus moved in. "But I'm serious. Did you hear Processor Maruskel disappeared five or six megaseconds ago? I used to trade status reports with her back on the Abeona. She was on the Hasamelis. Must have been nearing three thousand megaseconds. Didn't take any bullshit. And she just rode her chair out into the biomass, so the rumors go. It's taking everything from us."

"She wouldn't have lived much longer if we were still on the ships, would she?" Kofus asked quietly. "Almost like she was doing the colony one last service."

Alvin watched the stars before answering. "No, she wouldn't have. It's just...we're both getting older. I wonder where we'd be if we hadn't landed here. We'd be eight percent of the way to the next inhabitable star system."

"Which we'd *also* not live to see, most likely," Kofus added. "Do you really hate it down here that much?"

"I used to," Alvin said. "But with you, that's changed. I think I like it here, despite everything."

"We'd have never met on the ships," Kofus reminded him. Again. He leaned in for a kiss and Alvin met him halfway.

"And I'm grateful for that."

"But?"

Alvin shook his head. "No 'but.' I'm grateful. I can't imagine having gone my whole life and not met you."

"We certainly wouldn't have gone line dancing together," Kofus said, and Alvin laughed with him. They'd gone every week since that first time. They'd even won a competition.

They were silent for a few minutes, sipping at their pear brandy. Alvin broke the silence with, "There aren't many Generationals left in Alpha Radian, except the ones who work directly for Admin. Mostly it's Vagals, Admins, and offices here."

"We still live here," Kofus said.

"I think we're some of the only ones," Alvin answered. "Everyone is moving out into Beta and Gamma where they can have a larger residence to raise their families. Even some of the Vagals with families are moving out there."

"Do you want to move?"

"I don't think so," Alvin said. "I'm finally comfortable, with my apartment just right, and with you beside me." He smiled. "Just right."

Kofus smiled back and they shared another kiss. Alvin snuggled closer as Kofus's hand trailed down his stomach.

"So, you want to stay here, and stay all snuggly and cozy together?" Kofus' attentions were getting more insistent, which Alvin didn't mind at all. "That sounds like a good plan to me too."

Alvin leaned into his husband's caresses.

"What about the other part of it?"

He opened his eyes to see Kofus staring at him. "What other part?"

"Well, if you don't want to move, do you want to start a family?"

Alvin looked down. "I hate to break it to you, but you're not going to get the results you want that way, even if we weren't using reproductive blockers."

Kofus poked him and Alvin giggled.

"I'm serious, though," Kofus said. "I love you. As you say, we're only getting older. It's time for us Generationals to leave a legacy from the stars. The list for the decanting tubes is pretty short right now. I *may* have checked."

Alvin took his husband's head in his hands, caressing his curly hair. Kofus had recently taken to wearing a small goatee, and Alvin wasn't quite sure whether he liked it yet.

"You've thought about this a lot, haven't you?"

Kofus nodded.

For once, Alvin didn't need to process a lot of data to make his decision.

"Let's do it. Let's leave our legacy on Lida."

* * *

9 years 7 months after landing

Choi almost vibrated with excitement. Everyone they knew was coming to Mommy's house.

"What do you think we're going to get?" they asked Phillipe. It was their eighth birthdays today. Except it wasn't really. Everyone was just pretending that. Phillipe's really real birthday was a whole month ago and he'd already gotten some of his presents. Choi's really real birthday was a month away, but Mommy and Momma Agetha let them celebrate together because they did everything else together.

"Maybe Mommy Jiow will let us go on an adventure into the biomass for real!" Phillipe said. Choi felt a little afraid at that, but they didn't show it. They didn't think Phillipe listened to all the stories as carefully as they did. Sometimes they heard Mommy talking with other grown-ups and they said Vagal soldiers got killed for real out there. If the biomass could hurt big soldiers like that, it could probably hurt them too.

"I don't know if that's a good idea," Choi told their brother. "I bet Uncle Frank will get me some science stuff." That wasn't too hard a guess. Uncle Frank always got them science stuff.

"I hope it's not as boring as the present last year," Phillipe said. "I don't like chemistry."

244 William C. Tracy

Choi nodded, but they didn't really agree with Phillipe. They still played with the chemistry set Uncle Frank made them last year. It was much more interesting than the trig they were learning in school.

"Come on! They're here!" Phillipe took their hand and pulled them along the colored directional lines that ran from the entrance of the apartment to all the rooms.

Mommy and Momma Agetha were already here, of course, but Uncle Frank was at the door, along with some of Phillipe's and Choi's friends from school. Except they were really more Phillipe's friends. Choi didn't have a lot of friends.

The grown-ups all talked about a lot of things while they and Phillipe played with the other kids.

"Wanna wrestle?" Phillipe said. "I bet I'll win again!"

That wasn't a surprise either. Phillipe always won because he was bigger, and louder, and because Choi let him win most of the time because it made him stop wrestling.

"I think I hear Mommy calling," Choi said. They thought Phillipe might call them a liar, but then Mommy did call, and Phillipe frowned like Choi had cheated. Then his face cleared.

"Presents!"

They ran to the kitchen, where the table was piled with all sorts of fun things, in brightly colored resinplast paper.

"Do you want a beetsugar cookie with fresh strawberries?" Momma Agetha asked Phillipe, who shrugged.

"Did Momma Jiow make anything?" he asked.

Choi went up to Momma Agetha because her eyes looked sad. "Can I have a cookie?" they asked.

Momma Agetha smiled at them. "Of course you can, birthday kid!" She handed them one, though Choi thought her smile wasn't really real.

Mommy had made her special spicy squash kimchee, and Phillipe got some of that instead of his momma's cookies.

They all ate, but Choi didn't remember a lot of it, because they were staring at all the presents. That and because Phillipe kept poking them.

After they ate, it was time for presents. The party turned into a jumble of bright colors, and new things, and sometimes Phillipe shouting. Then it was done, with Choi and Phillipe sitting in a pile of their presents.

"Thank you, Uncle Frank!" Choi called. They flipped through the science book on different biomass species, captivated by the drawings and pictures.

"It's not out yet, kid," Uncle Frank said with a low chuckle. "You get the first one. The rest of them are going to schools next semester. Let me know what you think of it."

Choi said they would.

"Heavy thrust!" Phillipe said. "Momma Jiow, can I have some now?" He was holding up a jar with a big section of honeycomb in it, dripping with goey honey.

"Ask your mother," Mommy told him, and Phillipe rolled his eyes, but looked to Momma Agetha.

"Just a little, Phillipe," she said.

"There's something else with that," Uncle Frank added. "If you want to help me the next time I do a queen replacement in the hives, I think you're old enough now."

Phillipe bounced on his chair in excitement.

Choi got some seeds from Momma Agetha.

"They're my newest tomato hybrid," she said. "Bigger and juicer than last year."

"Mommy, I'm going to plant these in our garden!" Choi told Mommy. She smiled back and gave them permission. They had their own section of the garden.

Momma Agetha had already given Phillipe his birthday present on his real birthday, but Mommy had a surprise for both of them.

"I cleared it with my supervisor," she said. "You can both come on a field trip to the edge of Beta to watch us break ground on the new Delta Radian!"

Phillipe shook their shoulder. "Finally! We can go see the biomass!"

Choi smiled back, but they were kind of nervous at the thought.

"You're sure this is alright, Jiow?" Momma Agetha was asking.

"Come oooooon, Moooooom," Phillipe said. "We're old enough. All the other kids have gone. Jhona has gone twice!" He pointed to one of the other kids, who nodded vigorously.

Momma Agetha fixed Phillipe with one of her glares and started talking quietly to Mommy at the edge of the room. Choi tried to listen, but Uncle Frank was telling them, very loudly, about his bees again. They only caught a few snatches.

"...getting older. Need to learn..."

"Too risky to..."

"...were doing tasks just as dangerous in the fleet at three hundred megaseconds."

The grown-ups liked to talk in megaseconds if they wanted the kids not to understand, but Choi was good with numbers. Three hundred megaseconds was nine and a half Lida years, which was only a year and a half older than they and Phillipe. Had Mommy and Momma Agetha done dangerous things back when everyone was flying through the stars? They still had trouble imagining that, but all the grown-ups told stories about it, and how their ships got turned into the buildings in the colony.

"...which is when I noticed the fungal structures in the worker bees were..." Uncle Frank was saying.

"Can we go, Momma Jiow?" Phillipe broke in. "Can we?"

"Your mother and I *both* agree you and Choi can come on the field trip," Mommy said. "*If* I see good behavior at school for the next week."

"I promise," Phillipe said immediately.

"I promise too," Choi said, though they had never had any problems in school. Most of the times they got in trouble was when they tried to stop Phillipe from doing something stupid.

"You're growing up so fast," Momma Agetha told them both. "I know you'll both be a big help to the colony one day soon. I just wish your father was here to see you, Phillipe," she said. "He'd be so proud."

Phillipe only looked down at the table. He didn't like it when people talked about his father, since he'd never met him.

Choi got down and gave Momma Agetha a hug. "Thanks for letting us go," they said.

Momma Agetha smiled down at them, but her eyes were still sad.

* * *

10 years after landing

Delta Radian. The fourth of eight radians started. Agetha wiped sweat off her brow and looked across the glassed expanse, the biomass already taking portions back. Ten years into living on Lida, and they were only about a third of the way done building the arcopolis. The opening ceremony for Gamma—the third radian—was coming up in another couple months.

Admin had wanted the ceremonies now, at the nice round number of ten years, but it simply wasn't possible with the delays in replacing resinplast. Most structures nearest the biomass had been replaced already, but many in the interior of Beta and Alpha still needed to be changed out, and older tools and printed material were still around from the first resinplast iteration.

"Let's get this site started," she told her crew. Jardan had finally retired about forty megaseconds ago, leaving her as coordinator for this and several other construction teams. Kalan had taken her old spot, and Agetha had somehow found herself with even more work than she used to have. She hadn't seen Phillipe in three days.

"All the topographical scans complete?" she asked Kalan.

"Done, ma'am. No caverns detected in the immediate area, though we suspect there are some nearer the edge of the radian." He flipped a set of site overlays to her HUD. The view flickered in her view until she tapped the headset with a finger and it stabilized. Must be a loose wire. She'd have to get it looked at again. Their construction equipment was well used, and without an easy source of replacement material, it was often easier to make do with what they had.

"I want the first excavations here and here," she circled two places with an eyeblink and flicked the map back to Kalan. "The Delta Administration building can also serve as a home base while we get the other buildings started in this part of the radian." *And serve as a bunker if the biomass tries any tricks*, she left unsaid. It was standard construction practice by now.

"I'll get the crew ready," Kalan said, and ran off. For all he was almost two hundred megaseconds older than her, he acted like an excited teenager.

Her HUD blinked with an incoming call from...Daved?

Oh stars.

"Who is this?"

"Found a...mommy...in room...put on..." the line trailed off.

Phillipe. Daved's old HUD was still in their room, most of it cannibalized for spare parts for hers. It barely worked. How did he even get it to connect?

"Phillipe? Is that you? Why are you at home?" He was supposed to be at school.

"Want to talk to...school was boring...come see me?"

Her other line was pinging. Kalan had something else. She waved him off across the site.

"Phillipe, Mommy can't hear you well. Are you at home? Can you find Mommy Jiow?" No. Jiow would be out working too. Had Phillip walked all the way from the school? Where was Choi?

"Find me...want to..." The line cut off. The HUD's power was probably drained. It had been sitting in a drawer for years without being booted up.

"Phillipe?" Agetha cursed and blinked through her HUD's menus, blinked through tears, trying to find the contact for a man who'd been dead for eight and a half years.

Kalan waved again, and the line of Z15 excavators started up on his orders, trundling to where they would break ground and hopefully not break down at the same time. The machines had come to Lida with the ships, and since the construction drones were all gone, they were the front line for construction. But they were wearing out too. Everything was wearing out.

She found Daved's ID and tried to connect, but the line only buzzed with an unanswered link. It was hard to see the display through her tears.

Phillipe and Choi had been excited to ride on a Z15—under supervision—when they came out to see the official groundbreaking, as she and Jiow had promised. Agetha kept them far away from any biomass, but she'd hoped being out near the wilds would been enough for them, maybe even calm Phillipe down. Then a week later she'd lost two crewmembers to a new mycelial construction, like vines implanted with sharp spines. It had been placed exactly where they were supposed to build. The biomass was cunning. It was adapting to their presence.

So, she'd been busy again, filling out paperwork, cleaning out surface biomass to get the construction started. She'd made a promise to spend more time with Phillipe, five Lida years ago, but she'd failed him. Again. She felt him pulling away, and there was nothing she could do. Daved would have known how to make everything better. She wished she could have seen Phillipe laughing with his father.

She called Jiow.

"What is it, Agetha? We're just putting a new foundation in place."

"Phillipe just called me on Daved's old HUD."

There was silence.

"Fuck, I'm sorry, Agetha."

"Isn't he supposed to be at school?"

"What? He was home today, like you said. Didn't you see my message?"

"At home? Alone? Why? What message?"

Agetha dug through her missed messages. She'd missed several the last few days with the Delta groundbreaking. There was one from Jiow, two days back, wondering where Phillipe was.

Another that said he hadn't come back from school that day.

Another telling her he'd stayed with some friends the night before and said Agetha had let him.

Another that Jiow was dropping him at Agetha's apartment like she asked.

She realized her HUD was still connected and she was cursing under her breath.

"Jiow—what has Phillipe been doing?"

"You should know. You've evidently been giving him leave to stay with friends, stay home, and do what he wants. I assumed it was a lie, but then he had a message sent from your household ID to mine confirming everything. I asked, but you didn't answer."

Daved's HUD. It shared a household ID with hers. She'd never changed it.

"The little shit," Agetha growled. "He's been using *Daved's* HUD, somehow."

There was a sigh from Jiow's side. "He's smart, I'll give him that."

"Thanks, Jiow, and sorry. Again." Agetha blinked off the call and closed her eyes.

Kalan pinged her.

"Need your sign-off on a plan change." Agetha sighed and trudged to where he'd been waving at her for the past few minutes.

Phillipe was only a little over eight years old. How did he find so much trouble?

She signed off on the plan change—it was only to reroute foundation walls—and considered her guilty sense of relief when Jiow or school took Phillipe off her hands.

"Kalan, I'm going to have to leave the site in your hands for a few hours. Kid trouble again."

"They're trouble, aren't they? I can handle things for a while. Take care of what you need to." His eyes went far away as he blinked at something in his HUD, and off in the distance, three of the Z15s trundled forward in response. "I wanted to be a teacher, back on the Hasamelis, you know. I love seeing them learn, but take your eyes off them for a second and they'll tear you apart."

"I've started to realize that," Agetha said. She headed for her bicycle.

She watched the wall of biomass as she walked, an ever-shifting tangle of mushrooms and vines, fleshy towers and spines, with frond-like growths poking out at odd angles. Things from the size of flies to that of cows moved in its underbrush. It grew on itself, rolling out into the radian like an ever-growing tumbleweed, and then sent questing hyphae out to scout new places. Admin ignored it except to direct the squads of Vagals to burn out anything that got too close to the arcopolis. Anywhere there was a crack in their armor, it crept in. The wall around Gamma was still going up, using some of their precious remaining steelcrete. This radian, and the ones that had not yet been started, were open to recolonization by the creeping fungus that covered this planet. Just like kids, if you didn't respect it, it would eat you alive.

As she rode across Beta and back to Alpha, she wondered how they would survive. She was getting older, her crew was getting older, and the colony's first children—Grounders—were on the cusp of becoming teenagers. In the fleet, they had started apprenticeships at ten Lida years, and the schools were already gearing up to do the same here. Phillipe and Choi would have their pick of what they wanted to do. Choi would do something science-y, maybe with their Uncle Frank, but Phillipe? He was smart, but unfocused. He caused trouble. He said he wanted to train to work with the Vagals, but she'd expressly forbidden that. She wondered how long that prohibition could last. He already didn't listen to her or Jiow. And Admin wanted more bodies to supplement the Vagals.

There would be a point, ten or twenty Lida years out, when there would be a mass changeover from Generationals working, to Grounders working. What would happen to her then?

Already, the oldest of them were struggling to tend their own gardens and used mobility devices to get around. There wasn't anything in place to care for the elderly. Some, with no one to help them, had left all their belongings to walk out into the biomass in secret. None had been heard from again.

By the time construction was completed, the only Generationals left would have been less than twelve or fifteen hundred megaseconds old when the ships landed—what was forty or forty-five Lida years.

They had to care for their elders. They had to teach their children. And they had to do it all while building the place where they would live. Their future depended on it.

Agetha parked her bicycle and stared at her front door. She had to make that future a reality, starting now.

* * *

10 years 2 months after landing

The children who had eaten their parents continued to stymie communication at every turn. Although the rate of growth had been increased in the ring of death, the children increased their eviction of new growth at the same rate. They had grown smarter at finding the ways new growth might enter the place where they built their barrier and strange, dead structures. It had been necessary to outwit them. This level of strategy had not been needed for some time, and it was oddly refreshing.

There had been some effort over the past few rotations around the sun to determine the cause of the dead spaces, and as several higher-functioning nodes discovered that the hand of communication had been tied in the base substance, the children made changes to keep further communication from happening. New avenues would continue to be tried. Eventually communication would proceed unrestricted.

Yet even as the children resisted communication, they also gave it freely. Those who volunteered to exit the ring of death, where their parents had been eaten, had been welcomed. Now, more than forty of their physical shells had been gathered, though nearly all no longer responded, similar to the one where communication had been attempted in the past.

Many were attached to hard, dead structures that could move. It was suggested this was another augment, like the hollow structures they lived in. Perhaps it allowed some to reign farther from those large structures? Yet, it was quickly determined that the downside of such mobility and separation was a fragility of sentience. Even disruption of two or three internal structures often served to make the children non-responsive, and any exposure of the interior parts of the creature to outside atmosphere did the same.

The systems still appeared to be incompatible. However, adaptation with the other forms of the children—those mobile and stationary ones used for protein and organic material generation—had been successful. Attempts to reintroduce subsumed individuals into the ring of death had been met with failure, unfortunately.

One shell showed promise for communication, and had begun to make gestures with the upper two of its limbs, much as some of the higher-functioning nodes had been known to do before subsummation. This transitory phase was remarked upon, and its form was gathered close to the others in hopes their shared location might bring back communication. That area would be watched for further development even closer than the children's refuge within their shell.

There was disagreement on what the children's future might be. The barrier around the ring of death might be a new form, like the original parents, but even bigger. Further study would have to be undertaken to determine the phases of life of the children. However, if studies of the ones who had voluntarily exited were accurate, the mobile phase existed in a very limited number of revolutions of the planet around the sun.

Attention remained strong on the children's barrier and dead spaces. Though they rejected most attempts at communication, many paths had yet to be tried. There was time to know them better, and eventually, bring them into concord as so many others had been before.

PART TWELVE

Future Contact

14 years 6 months after landing

Agetha clenched her fists and stared down her son. "You're not going to that training facility. The Admins have taken enough from us already. Now they're taking our children, and you want to walk willingly into the Vagal's waiting arms? They'll kill you in a year."

"I'm thirteen, and you have no say in my future anymore," Phillipe shot back. He was still shorter than her, but not by much. He'd gotten mostly his father's coloring, but her height, fortunately. "Admin needs more people to protect the colony while you lot build it. The Vagals are a family. They look out for each other. I've basically been living on my own since I was eight. Why are you trying to stop me now, Mom?"

"Because I love you, and I don't want the biomass to eat you and spit out your bones."

"You have a funny way of showing it sometimes," Phillipe said. His tightly coiled hair nearly vibrated with his anger. It needed to be cut. "Why don't you go to your precious construction crew? They know you better than I do."

"Phillipe, now that's not fair. I've spent years providing for you, building a future for this colony." Agetha ignored the message that popped up in her HUD telling her she was late for work. Now was *not* the time to answer that.

"Who are you building that future for? Did you ever ask what I wanted?"

"I..." She hadn't. Daved had a plan for them, and she'd followed it. Then he'd died and she tried to live up to that plan for another thirteen years. It obviously wasn't working. "Well, what do you want?"

"I want to go to the Vagal training school," Phillipe said immediately.

"But *why*?" Agetha asked. Was this the first time she'd done so, rather than just telling him "no"? It couldn't be.

"Because they keep everyone safe. Like Choi, who couldn't defend themself if they tried. Like the old Generationals, out in Gamma and

Delta. Like you." Phillipe almost snarled the words, glaring up at her. They were an arm span apart.

Agetha swallowed the sudden lump in her throat. "What if I still say 'no'?"

"I'm going anyway. Are you going to watch me, every minute of every day to make sure I don't sneak out? How's that been working so far?"

He was right and he knew it. There was no way she could keep him here. Choi was working with Frank most days of the week, starting their apprenticeship. Phillipe could have worked with her, but she knew he hated construction because it took her away from him. Admin had taken her life from her, and now they were taking her son.

"It hasn't been working well, and I think we both know it," Agetha said, and was satisfied by the glimmer of surprise in her son's eyes. "I've failed you in a lot of ways. Do you think the Vagals will do better?"

This time he did hesitate. "I...think they will."

"Then I can't stop you," Agetha said. She poked a finger at her son's chest. "But so help me, you stay alive. I've already had one person taken from me here, even if you don't remember him. I won't lose another."

* * *

15 years after landing

Jiow watched the festivities for Delta's opening ceremonies with her brother Zhu, both of them munching on fried squash flowers and swinging their legs while sitting on the edge of Delta's main school building. The resinplast was not the same cool as stone or metal would be. It was instead almost the same temperature as the air, making it feel like she was sitting on nothing.

"It's not almond cakes, but still pretty tasty," Zhu said, nudging her in the side like he used to when they were kids. Jiow almost choked on her flower as she tried to swallow and flinch at the same time. She tried to glare, but her eyes watered as she coughed.

"Shame about losing the almond trees," Jiow answered after she got her coughing under control. The last one had died two Lida years back.

"Frank said it was because the peaches went first and almonds are related." She'd spent more time with her brother since he joined her construction crew. It wasn't the one Agetha led—Jiow didn't want to work under the woman whose son she had basically raised, until he went off to the Vagal training school last year. Phillipe had been a...challenging child, though he and Choi were still close.

Jiow hadn't seen Agetha in several weeks. She worked in the finishing construction, while Agetha was out breaking ground in Epsilon Radian. Delta had been a struggle to complete, over the last five years. Their pool of workers was shrinking fast. Many spoke of the fatigue that washed over all of them, prompting Generationals to walk out into the biomass. Jiow had a better idea of what caused it. She hadn't forgotten Janx and their crew, nearly twelve years gone. Surely, she wasn't the only one who noticed influential Generationals seemed to be the most susceptible. She'd kept her head low the past decade, avoiding Admin's attention, learning sometimes it was good to be stuck in the same job. The opening ceremonies today were the closest she'd gotten to their leaders in several years.

"We'll lose more plants and animals before it's all over," Zhu said, bringing her back to the moment. He took another bite and chewed contemplatively. "And more will probably mutate, like those weird ones that keep coming out of the biomass."

Jiow forced a smile for her brother. "Look at you! When did you get your degree in xenobiology? I'll have to tell Frank." Zhu rolled his eyes.

"Everyone's saying it. Not just the biomass, either. Have you seen what the pigs look like now? They have little forests on their backs, and the spines reach for you if you try to touch them."

"And why are you chasing pigs around? Mara kick you out again?" Jiow grinned at her brother's scowl. "Their bacon still tastes fine, anyway."

"Speaking of xenobiology, how is Frank doing?" Zhu asked. "I haven't seen him in months."

Jiow shook her head. "Me either. He's been furiously working on more changes to the resinplast, ever since the scare last year when another weathervane got infected. Hasn't been able to repeat the process and I think he's almost convinced it was a one-time thing." She leaned back against the railing behind her and tossed the tail end of the squash blossom out into the grass—which also looked funny, if you inspected it too closely. "Every time I call, he puts me off, but says Choi is learning a lot." Her child had been apprenticing with him for nearly two years. She wondered if Frank would ever let slip how much he'd contributed to Choi's existence.

Zhu gave her a side-eye. "And your, ah, other child?"

Jiow clicked her tongue. "Not a word in months. Last any of us heard, Phillipe insisted on going to the new Vagal training school. He and Agetha had a knock-down fight, but then reached some sort of understanding. Ever since Admin pushed most everyone out of Alpha radian, it's been almost impossible to get information about the Grounders working under the Vagals."

"So back to being single again?" Zhu had the art of needling her down after so many years. A few more, and she would have lived as long on this planet as she had on the Abeona.

"I think I'm going to stay by myself for a while." Jiow took in a big breath, then let it out. "It's nice having the kids out of the house." Easier to watch for Vagals coming to drag her away, and less people to miss her.

"Plenty of time left to find someone to share a bed with," Zhu said. "Mara has a friend who works with her in crop sciences. Says she's single too, and pretty. I can hook you up."

"You've been hooking me up for the last eight hundred megaseconds," Jiow laughed. "It hasn't worked yet."

"Not for lack of trying," Zhu said. "Come on, have dinner with us tomorrow. Mara's got lots of food around and you need someone to take care of you."

"Why do I get the feeling this is already set up and no one bothered to tell me?" Jiow asked.

Zhu had the grace at least to look guilty. "We didn't want you to turn a person down again. The last three..."

"Were a workaholic, uninterested in partners, and boring as dirt," Jiow finished for him.

"Yeah, that last guy was a real miss," Zhu muttered, rubbing his neck. "But Mara's convinced about this one."

"Do you even know her name?" Jiow asked, then laughed at Zhu's blank expression. She took pity on him. "Yes, alright, I'll come to dinner tomorrow. I've got extra in the garden anyway, since Choi's been out. I've been supplementing the next-door neighbor's pantry because they're older than the stars, but they moved out to the edge of Delta last week where their son lives." She was thinking about moving herself, if only to get farther away from the Admin buildings. The time credits for giving up a residence even on the edge of Alpha would cover a lot. Would it get her noticed as well?

"Sounds great," Zhu said. "You really should come over more often. And take a day off work now and then." He waved a hand at the celebrations. "You shouldn't only relax every five years when another radian is completed."

"I relax!" Jiow said. When was the last day she took off, anyway? It had all been a blur since Choi moved out. "If Admin wasn't riding our asses so hard to get the arcopolis complete, I'd have more time."

"I hear you," Zhu said. He hopped off the edge of the building and headed toward the crowds of people milling around the Delta administration building. The smells of roasting veggies and bacon wafted toward them as Jiow followed. "Someday it will be finished."

"Only four more radians to go," Jiow said. "Epsilon now, then Zeta, Eta, and Theta after that. One day, we'll look out over the completed city."

She could keep her head down until then.

* * *

17 years after landing

Agetha spun as the latch on the front door opened. How had someone gotten in here? The keys were biometrically locked.

She looked around her bedroom for anything to serve as a weapon, settling on a pad reader loaded with books she'd been meaning to read but hadn't gotten around to.

She could hear footsteps, down below. Whoever was here wasn't being stealthy about it. She'd been almost ready for bed, after a long day out in Epsilon. The biomass out there was coming back strong, as the area had been neglected since they landed. The last three radians would be even worse. The biomass would be as tall as the walls by the time they got to Zeta.

She creaked down the stairs in her tiny apartment, holding the pad by her head as if it would do anything. The lights in the kitchen area were on. This thief wasn't being very sneaky. Probably not very good at it—crime was almost nonexistent in the arcopolis. Everyone was either working too hard or too well-off to need to steal. Or had given up and walked out into the biomass.

She scooted through the kitchen door and found a shorter figure in front of the stove. She raised the pad.

"What do you think you're—Phillipe!"

Her son turned around, his eyes catching the pad and then coming back down to her face, unworried. "Hi Mom."

"How...what are...how did...?" She couldn't make a full sentence. But of course he had gotten in. The locks were keyed to his biometrics just as much as they were to hers. "I haven't seen you in over a hundred fifty megaseconds," she finally settled on.

"Two and a half years since I started with the Vagals, Mom," Phillipe said. "It's been seventeen since you landed here. You should be able to tell time by now."

"And you're still only fifteen and shouldn't speak to your mother that way," Agetha said, even though he would have been considered an adult back on the ships.

"Fifteen and a half, and I'm not sure you deserve that title," Phillipe shot back.

Agetha opened her mouth, then closed it, and closed her eyes too, breathing in, and out. They knew how to push each other's buttons, even if they never saw each other anymore. It had been a good idea to let him go his own way when he had.

She opened her eyes again and really took in Phillipe. He looked...good. Whatever training he was doing with the Vagals was turning him into a strong, stocky kid. He'd ended up a little taller than Daved had been, with some of her height but raised in a gravity well. His dark, frizzy hair had been buzzed into something short and inconsequential, and his warm, russet-brown skin—slightly lighter than Daved's, much darker than hers—almost shone in the weak kitchen light.

"You're right," she said. "I'm not sure I do deserve that, but it's what I still think of myself as, in relation to you."

Phillipe blinked, as if he hadn't expected her to say that. She still had some surprises for the kid, it seemed. She'd had time to think.

When he didn't say anything, she inclined her head toward the stove. "Well? Come here for a meal? A place to stay? Need anything? You didn't pop in just to say hi."

That seemed to put him back on track. "No. I don't need anything from you. That's...that's why I came, actually."

Agetha cocked her head. She realized she was still holding the pad and put it down on a counter—metallic colored, like something from the ships, though it was really resinplast. Almost everything was.

Phillipe swallowed and raised his head and shoulders like he'd come to decision. "I don't need anything, and I wanted to make it official, just so there's no misunderstanding."

"Official...that you don't need anything?" Agetha wondered if she had been this dramatic when she was a teenager. Probably.

"Yes," Phillipe said. "Ever again." He raised his chin, shoulders back, hands clasped behind him. Like a damn Vagal at parade rest. "According to the colony's new ruling on Grounders as of last month, I'm a full adult, and have total rights over my own choices."

There had been some sort of ruling that came down recently, as many Grounders were at the point of what adulthood had been on the ships. She hadn't paid much attention to it. It was obviously an attempt by Admin to get the Grounders working as hard as the Generationals. The workforce had been contracting drastically, for the first time since they landed.

"Phillipe, I haven't even seen you for two and a half years, and you've been making your own decisions since you were thirteen. Before, really. Why do you think you need to tell me this?"

"Because of exactly that!" He slashed a hand through the air, and Agetha's eyes went wide. She hadn't expected such a backlash of emotion. He was even more angry than he had been when he left. Had training with Vagals done that to him? What was he doing there?

"I'm done with this. I'm a Vagal now. I don't need you, or Mother Jiow, or Choi, or any of this. I don't want this hanging over my head."

Agetha wasn't sure what "this" was, but the kid obviously had been thinking about it a lot. Probably talking to Vagals about it too. Actual Vagals. She didn't have the heart to tell him he'd never be one, with their superhuman reactions. But he'd stayed alive until now, like she'd told him to. She hoped this wasn't an attempt to tie off loose ends before going on a mission into the biomass. The Vagals rarely did that any longer. They'd lost too many.

Agetha frowned. "You have a right to be angry," she said. "I haven't been a good mother to you. When your father and I—"

"No! You don't get to bring him into this!" Phillipe took a step toward her, and Agetha stepped back. He'd been ready to say that, eager for her to bring up Daved. There was so much she'd done wrong by him, and she thought she'd been done with regret, the last time he left.

"Don't ever bring up his name again!" Phillipe continued. His eyes were wide, and red with emotion. "I never knew him, and so you have no excuse to bring him up. You *always* brought him up to excuse what a piss-poor job you did as a mother. 'If Daved was here, I would have...' 'If your father took care of you...' No more. He doesn't matter to me, and *neither do you*. You chose the colony over me, again, and again, and now I'm choosing the colony over *you*. Mother Jiow at least made time for me, but she didn't have to. You were *supposed* to. And now I'm with the Vagals and we act as a *family* the way you never did. I can protect the colony *and* have real relationships with other people. Corporal Hendricks is *twice* the mother you ever were."

It all came out in a rush, and Agetha felt her back hit the wall even as she knew he'd practiced that speech in front of a video screen, again, and again. It had spilled out like oil from his tongue, pent up and ready for release.

She wiped a hand down her cheek, brushing away tears that had no place being there.

"I'm sorry you feel that way, but—"

"No. No more buts." Phillipe cut her off again. "You don't get the last word in this conversation. *I* do. And I'm done. Don't find me. Don't even think of me. You didn't want a son and now you don't have one."

He brushed past her, a vibrating ball of young anger. Two seconds later the front door slammed.

Agetha swallowed, tears running down her cheeks. She gulped a sob that was half a cough, and bent over to rest her head on the counter, next to her pad. She'd been done with this last time. She'd let him go. How *dare* he make her live her mistakes again!

But her tears only lasted a few minutes, and she knew they were partly from too much work, from too little sleep.

Agetha took in a deep, shuddering breath, and let it out. She rubbed hot water on her face and dried it on an alpaca-wool towel.

She sat in one of the kitchen chairs.

Her son had been right, and Agetha knew it deep within herself. She didn't have to wonder about him anymore. He had a family, and a purpose, and that was what any Generational wanted for their children.

There had always been a part of her, ever since Daved died, curled so tightly into a knot that she could never get it unknotted. That knot was loosening now, cut apart rather than untied, and the shredded strings were fading away to nothing. With this, she might have room for something else.

Agetha thought of the handful of apprentice Grounders in her construction crew, bright, and young, and full of energy where the Generationals complained of strained backs, knees, and wrists. She'd only known them a few months and already felt closer to some than she had to her son.

One, a bright, helpful boy named Hari, already helped keep track of the crew schedules. She could see him, one day, being foreman of a crew, even though he hardly knew one end of a shovel from the other right now.

She took in a deep breath, held it until she thought her lungs would burst, and then let it all out in a rush. She stood up, pushed the chair in, got her pad, and turned out the kitchen lights. She checked the front door to make sure it was locked, then went upstairs to get ready for bed. They would be breaking ground on a new building in Epsilon tomorrow and she needed her rest.

The only way this colony would be built was by Generational hands.

* * *

18 years after landing

Anderson watched the flow of people through the Beta Radian market. The amount of gray hair and wrinkles had increased remarkably over the last few years, but then, they had been on Lida for eighteen by now. Alpha and Beta Radians were starting to look lived in. The market itself was an established place where people bartered for what they needed. Money wasn't used in the arcopolis, as such, but there was a burgeoning trade in time credits, since they had so little to spare. Although they were close to subsistence levels with farming in the colony, they could produce almost any good they needed with the magic of resinplast—assuming the biomass didn't infect it for good and erupt their tables and chairs, buildings, street signs, bicycles, and even clothing into twisting masses of crawling fungus. He'd seen too much of that out at the edges of the city.

He passed through the produce section of the market and into the goods and gadgets, slowing briefly at the sex workers and pleasure booths. He'd stopped blushing when he passed through, and even visited a couple, though they weren't a big draw for him. His years of reading bodice-rippers and talking with Sona V. Gore had drastically lowered his embarrassment levels.

"Hey there, soldier," called a handsome man from one of the booths. Anderson smiled back neutrally, to show he wasn't interested. He fielded off other compliments from several more people of all genders. There were gray hairs and wrinkles here, too, though often covered by makeup. There were even apprentices waiting on their elders. A few of the Grounders were old enough to join the trade, but not many. In fact, they were the only young people at the market. Except for Anderson himself.

There were mirrors scattered around the pleasure section of the market, and he caught sight of a youthful face in them, unchanged, or nearly so, from when he'd first awoken from sus-ani. The differences in the Admins and Vagals were noticeable now. He was the youngest-looking person over twenty years old in this radian, unless other Vagals were here. He was one of the youngest of them as well. The differences would only get more pronounced as the years progressed, marking him as strange. Something other. It was no wonder the

Admins holed themselves up in Alpha and rarely emerged from the central complex.

He passed into what he thought of as "his" section of the market, the one with art, and books, and videos, and sculpture. He'd made friends here, over the years. And one special friend in particular.

"Morning, Anderson," called Medibe, the sculptor. He called himself a mechanic, but he turned twisted metal into works of art. "How's the hand working?"

"Smooth and oiled," Anderson replied. He flexed his right hand, which he hardly thought of as a prosthetic any longer. "Thanks for fixing it up last week. It needed some work."

"Next time don't try to beat up a fungus larger than you are with it!" Medibe called, and Anderson chuckled and waved. He'd told the sculptor the story while he fixed up the hand. One of the patrols last week had found a section of growth in a cavern under Epsilon that must have been there since the original burn. Some of the structures were bigger around than his chest, and he'd narrowly missed getting a fungal spear to the leg by breaking off the mushroom's woody stem with his prosthetic. At maximum strength, it had more gripping power than two regular hands.

Other artists waved and greeted him as he passed. He slowed as he passed the booth where the elderly art seller used to display their wife's paintings. Both had passed on several years back, but Anderson still had her painting of the view over the biomass hung on the center wall of his living room. There would be more and more artifacts from Generationals who had passed on. Their numbers were thinning. The colony had stabilized around twenty-five thousand over the past several years, but now there were as many Grounders as Generationals, if not more.

Anderson stopped when he got to Gore's traditional place. The writer wasn't there, nor were any of his books. He'd printed lots of them physically in the last few years, using a thin resin sheet for the pages and a small printing press manufactured from spare ship parts and resinplast. It was a good approximation of books from Earth.

He wandered around the area, wondering if the man had moved places. He'd been sitting at that same table, every time Anderson came by, over the last almost fifteen years.

"Have you seen Gore lately?" He asked of the neighboring merchants, but she shook her head. No one else had seen him for three days. Anderson widened his search, the rush of adrenaline from Cora making his hands shake, then steady. She was a comforting presence after all this time, and he knew to trust her.

No one had seen Sona V. Gore. The man had been maybe fifty when they landed, which would put him near seventy now. He wasn't young, but he wasn't that old, either. He'd looked hale when Anderson saw him last—his cheeks rosy, his hair gray, but plentiful. He'd talked about the new romance he was writing, where Stacy and Farin *finally* got together after two books. Sona V. Gore wouldn't just not show up to the market. Something had happened.

And Anderson couldn't do anything about it. That wasn't the man's real name. Anderson didn't know where he lived; if he did anything else in the colony besides write. He'd thought about following Gore home many times—by stealth if need be—but always decided against it. The mystery had been part of the magic of their relationship. Something his implant couldn't solve for him. Something that captured his attention time and time again.

But romance wasn't the only thing Gore wrote. He was an author, pushing boundaries everywhere he could. Most of his stories were fluff, pure emotion that dragged the reader into an escape for a day or two. Other writings were more thoughtful, and not often complimentary of how the colony was run. Anderson wasn't stupid. He'd heard the whispers passed from Vagal to Vagal. How certain elite members went on night missions. How troublesome Generationals decided to "give it all up" and walk into the biomass. Some actually did get tired of the constant struggle. Others, he suspected, needed more convincing.

He looked down at the pad he held. He'd been coming to show Gore his latest book—the one he'd been working on for over a year now. Gore had given him excellent feedback, pointing out where the characters needed to show more of their feelings to each other, give them a reason to drive each other away before they got back together in the end. He wanted Gore's feedback on the later sections.

He nearly jumped as a person walked behind him, reaching for the 'thrower he wasn't wearing.

266 William C. Tracy

"Everything alright?" asked one of Gore's neighbors, a small pudgy woman who knitted things out of alpaca wool.

"I'm fine," he muttered, but he wasn't. He wiped sweat from his forehead. Why was he so jittery? Cora was sending chemicals through his system as if he was about to get eaten by a carnivorous mushroom, not as if he was standing in one of the safest places in all the arcopolis.

Then he shivered, and his head cleared. Focused vision, like he got when commanding an engagement that was going south. Cora knew what he needed, when he needed it. He'd already made the decision, and this was her way of forcing him to act.

Gore had been complimenting his work for years now, telling him to finish something so he could sell it in the market. Telling him the table had an opening for more books.

Anderson couldn't know for sure whether Sona V. Gore, or whatever his name was, had suffered a stroke, or been in an accident, or if his writings had finally been noticed by Admin. But he did know what to do next.

He moved behind Gore's table, reaching for the hidden drawer where the man kept loose items, bits and pieces, and objects to inspire himself. The extra stylus was still in there. As was a note.

Anderson,

I've always thought of you as my student, from the day you first found my books. I always knew you'd be a great writer. I've seen what happens when you put your mind—and Cora—to the task of solving a problem.

So, here's another. This colony needs minds to question authority. Autocracy by eight individuals is not healthy, no matter how long they live. But Generationals will only be here so long, and we are the only ones who remember the freedom of the fleet.

In fact, I fear some questionable actions I participated in just before we met may have finally caught up to me. I thought them long buried.

If I don't hand you this note in person, don't look for me. I'm an old man, and it's not worth it. You're not too much younger, but you'll be with this colony for many years to come.

Use that time wisely. Learn. Observe. Write. Grow. There must always be new ideas to challenge people.

If I don't see you again, then let me give you one last critique. Stop thinking about that last act. Put your book out there for others to read. You'll learn much quicker than I can teach you.

Your friend,
Sona V. Gore

Cora had quieted as he read, as she did when a situation was resolved. Anderson put the note in his pocket, settled himself behind the table, laid his pad out, and began to write. This table needed books to be sold, and his was waiting to be finished.

* * *

18 years 6 months after landing

"Christiaan! There's a Generational on the schedule today," Jane said. "You know my policy on seeing Generationals."

"Yes ma'am," Christiaan said. They still called her ma'am, though she hadn't insisted on that for years. Especially not after Yana and Ivan, their twins, came along. Christiaan had been the one to suggest starting two at one time. Get through all the teething troubles—so to speak—at the same time. They poked their head into her office from the next room where they were doing...whatever Christiaan did to keep everything flowing smoothly. "You may want to attend this one."

Jane rubbed her hands together, realized she was doing it, and made herself stop. She put them flat on her desk. It had been twelve and a half years since the Admins agreed on her directive—with a little encouragement—to limit the number of non-gene modded people who had access to the central complex in Alpha. Since then, things had started to run smoother, at least from what she saw.

The differences were only just starting to appear back then. Now, eighteen and a half years on the planet, the people they landed on Lida with looked old. The ones who were still alive. It was disturbing to her, and to them. The more years passed, the more Alessandro, and Dmitri, and the others praised her forward-thinking. Even Maria finally admitted it had been the right choice at the time, though it took her eight years to do it.

And this was only the beginning. Jane would live to see the Generationals' grandchildren's grandchildren. Well, the least she could do was see one of the transitory inhabitants, while they were still around. The most troublesome ones were long-gone, in any case. It was the one thing the biomass was useful for.

"Fine. Keep them on the schedule."

"Yes ma'am." Christiaan didn't bother to poke their head in this time.

A few hours later, she found Ahman and Rajani in one of the meeting rooms.

"They pulled you into this as well?" she asked. Her assistant was nothing if not thorough.

"It sounds as if it's an intriguing proposal," Rajani said.

"But you didn't read the brief, did you?" Ahman directed their clear gaze toward her. Jane frowned at them. Admitting it would only make her appear less informed. The eight Admins knew each other well enough that they hardly needed to speak some of the time. They'd been working with each other for a long time, and Jane knew when not to take the offered bait.

A woman entered the room, perhaps close to forty. She must have been one of the younger ones when they landed. Jane herself looked hardly older and she had been in her mid-sixties before she left Earth. Metal bands clinked in the woman's many braids as she took in the three Admins. She was slightly darker in coloring than Ahman, but less so than Rajani.

"We hear you have an intriguing proposal," Jane said. Ahman gave her side-eye, which she ignored.

"Good afternoon, Admin Brighton," she started, looking at Jane. "Yes, I do. I'm Doctor Elizabeth Harley. Thank you for seeing me today."

"It's our pleasure," Ahman said. "Your name was well known on the Khonsu even before we landed."

"Thank you, Admin Ragab," the woman said with a tiny nod.

"You say you have a way to fight back against the biomass?" Rajani asked, leaning forward. "I'm most eager to hear about it."

That caught Jane's attention. Perhaps she should have read the brief, but the quarterly population update had come in this morning, which had led to a long discussion with Dmitri on the power requirements for the new schools.

"I do, Admin Kumarisurajinder," Doctor Harley said. She flicked at something in her HUD and a display of a molecular compound showed above the meeting table, rotating slowly. Rajani and Ahman sat forward, while Jane slumped back. It was going to be *that* sort of meeting.

"So, this...mycophage, as you call it, will eat through the biomass in a matter of seconds?" Rajani summed up as Doctor Harley brought her presentation to a finish.

"That's the plan. It does need more development, but the rest of the bioorganics department thought the idea was complete enough to present to you," the doctor said. "It completely avoids the issue of fighting against the viral communication methods between the cells."

"Well, this is excellent," Jane added. She'd understood enough of the presentation to know the woman had created something precious. "With a little development, we can mass produce it, strap it to a drone and simply dust the biomass as far as the eye can see. We'll start with Epsilon Radian and then clear out the last three radians to get them ready for construction."

The doctor opened her mouth, then closed it again.

"Something amiss, Doctor Harley?" Ahman asked.

"As I mentioned, it does need more development," Doctor Harley began. "In addition, I would caution against using this over large areas of the biomass."

"Will it be neutralized too quickly?" Rajani asked, and the doctor nodded.

"What's this?" Jane asked.

"The biomass' adaptability is the issue," Rajani told her. "It covers the entire planet, save for our little pie wedge radians, so if we were to loose something to exterminate the biomass on a large scale, it would do damage, but the mycelial networks would adapt before long, especially with so many examples to adapt to."

"And the biomass would likely be even more resistant to the next version of the mycophage," Doctor Harley added, "much like the issues we've had in developing new resinplast recipes."

Jane frowned. "So, does it work or not? What do we use it on?"

"She did say it needs more development," Ahman said.

"Ah." Doctor Harley had one finger raised. Jane was reminded why she didn't have meetings with Generationals anymore. Too many dead-end paths. They didn't have the long-term thinking of the Admins. "Speaking of what to use it on, there is one more caution I would raise."

Ahman and Rajani joined her in frowning at the doctor, whose eyes widened a bit at the attention.

"We need to be careful in application with respect to the resinplast," Doctor Harley said. Rajani gasped and Jane jerked her head to the other Admin.

"What does that mean?"

"The resinplast has no adaptability," Rajani said.

"Will someone tell me what this means?" Jane attempted to control the frustration in her voice.

Rajani waved a hand at the Generational to continue. She looked pale.

"The resinplast recipe is processed biomass," the doctor said. "It is literally the same molecular compounds as the biomass, but stripped, processed, with genetic viral inhibitors to remove any further influence and reproduction from the mycelial networks."

Now Ahman looked pale. "It would have no resistance to this mycophage."

Jane stared around the meeting room. The central complex was mostly nanotanium, as were many buildings in Alpha, but the furnishings... The table, the chairs, window coverings, some pad replacements, new HUD parts, everything but what was woven from animal fibers was made of resinplast. It was their miracle material. They had no metals left, no wood, no plastics. Any sufficiently complex technology that couldn't be crafted from alpaca wool, or corn or bamboo husks, was made with resinplast components. Most of Gamma and Delta's buildings were made from it. The entirety of the last three radians would use resinplast. Their steelcrete reserves were depleted, the nanotanium long gone.

She looked back to Doctor Harley. "Are you telling me a single drop of this substance could start a chain reaction that would destroy the entire arcopolis save for what is made of metal?"

"I repeat, the compound still requires further research, but I am confident—"

"Confident you could destroy all we've worked for over eighteen years!" Jane broke in. She looked to Ahman and Rajani. "Do I have this right? You two are the technical experts."

"It...appears that way," Rajani said with an apologetic look toward the Generational.

"I agree with Rajani," Ahman said. They looked put-out, and given their placid nature, it took a lot to make Ahman look peeved.

"Not just that, but what are you using to create this compound?" Jane asked. She didn't let the woman answer. "One slip, and you could destroy the city just by spilling a bit on the ground! How have you gotten to this point without Administration's knowledge?" She shook her head at the woman's open mouth. "No, don't answer that. This meeting is over. If you have an actual working solution, contact one of our assistants to set up another time to meet."

She stood, along with Rajani and Ahman. Doctor Harley's mouth worked, but nothing came out. She looked between the three of them, blinked, then nodded, and swiped her presentation from the display on the table. She turned, shoulders high, and walked out of the meeting room.

"Christiaan!" Jane called, and her assistant poked their head in from the next room. "I want that woman to take a walk. Her ideas are too dangerous."

Taking a walk was the euphemism that had grown up over the years when a Generational got too close to upsetting the colony's growth. Jane may have started the trend, but by now, every other Admin had used it—even Maria. It kept their course clear of unnecessary distractions from people who would be gone soon enough anyway.

"Jane, that woman is one of our most brilliant scientists," Ahman cautioned.

"Too brilliant," Jane said, but Rajani was shaking her head as well.

"No—her idea has merit, even if it's far too dangerous. We need her. Maybe in another twenty or thirty years, we'll have the means to make her solution work. Getting rid of her might disrupt the arcopolis' completion."

"We have her research," Jane said. "We don't need the woman any longer."

"No. I have to disagree in this case," Rajani insisted. "We need minds that think the way hers does. She has no designs on us. Aside from in this one case, she's harmless."

"This one case could destroy the entire city," Jane said. She stared at the other two Admins. Christiaan waited expectantly in the doorway.

"Then keep her away from ways to do that," Ahman said.

Jane's fingernails scraped the table. She didn't like to be contradicted, but it was rare that both Ahman and Rajani would push back so forcefully.

"Fine," she spat. "Christiaan, wherever that woman is working, I want her out of there. Move her to a hospital on the edge of the arcopolis, a farm, a construction crew. I don't care. I don't want her jeopardizing the city."

"Yes, ma'am," Christiaan said. She could tell from their inflection they agreed with the others. She'd take it up with them at home tonight. If she overreached, it was only because it was her job to see this arcopolis finished. She had to stick to the long term. Generationals, by nature, could only think short term.

Another forty years on the edge of the city, and Jane wouldn't have to worry about Doctor Elizabeth Harley ever again. By then, Grounders would be taking over all the jobs, raised on Lida with no direct knowledge of how the Generationals ran the fleet. The sooner Jane could erase that knowledge, the safer the arcopolis would be for future inhabitants. She was almost there.

The only way this colony would be built was by her leadership.

* * *

20 years after landing

The children were a fascinating experiment, as they slowly integrated with the local structures and nodes. They were the most exciting obstacle encountered in recent memory. Their differences, already being subsumed, were invigorating.

Some of the recent experiments were growing toward fruition. It was inevitable, as had the experiments with every other species subsumed, cataloged, and put to efficient use. But there was so much more potential here.

The children who had eaten their parents had evolved once again, and more of the children were being created, though with significant differences between them. Perhaps because the original children had eaten of their immense parents, which had given them some strength. This new evolution of children used local nutrients and materials to build. Easier to see. Easier to blend with and communicate with.

Noises on a tight band of wavelengths emanated from a singular child of the second evolution, who had wandered too far from others. Only samples of the first children had been welcomed so far. This one, once separated from minders, was transported to the collection of first evolution children, no longer mobile, though still a vast repository of information. While many more of the original children volunteered themselves for that attempt at communication, the evolved one was much easier to understand.

Translations had been attempted of the wavelengths of noises the children emitted, and some meaning had been ascribed to them.

This one made more sounds as attempts at communication increased, some translated as calls for aid, others as expressions of rage. All were accordingly noted and catalogued.

Finally! Was contact possible?

An attempt was made toward motion. One of the evolved child's limbs twitched. Yes. Communication could be possible. There was resistance, but it could be broken.

A different limb twitched. Interpretations of the ambulatory motions of the children were copied. Two limbs twitched in tandem, lifting the child, moving it around this node. Balance was inferior with this design and the child's top limb smacked into the ground as communication was resisted and corrupted.

More noises emanated from it, but with the elevated connection, they were easier to decipher.

"...can't control! ...make do...against...will!"

Some of the noises were slurred from damage to the child's auditory orifice.

On the tenth try, the limbs were made to operate in tandem for an elongated period of time. The connection between filaments in the child's mass was deepened.

"No! ...feed...control..."

Many subtleties of the child's communication methods were primitive and thus lost.

On the 122nd try, it was discovered how all four limbs would operate in different directions at once, with the control limb, at the top, engaging in movement as well. The balance was ungainly, but the ends of the limbs were dexterous, though they did leak interior fluid.

On the 1,548th attempt, deterioration was noticed in the child. Some limbs were no longer as accessible. There was a comparison made between mass and dimensions of the child through the attempts. Several metrics continued to decrease, as the child leaked various fluids and solids. Attempts were made to repair damage, but some were not deemed acceptable.

On the 3,088th attempt, it was recorded that the evolved child had become non-mobile, much as the original children.

No matter. Much data had been recorded and was even now being processed by various higher-functioning nodes.

Communication had been made. From the very first attempt, soon after the children ate their parents, to this last one, much improvement was made. Subsummation was possible, and though the process was long, it was certain to deliver fascinating results. Several optical nodes lifted to record data outside the atmosphere. The parents had come from the stars, and in all likelihood, more opportunities existed there.

It was time to communicate with the entire collection of children who had eaten their parents. It was time to welcome them home.

End of the Biomass Conflux, Part I

You can read of Agetha's further adventures in the short story *Down Among the Mushrooms* in the Distant Gardens Anthology.

ACKNOWLEDGEMENTS

This book has been rattling around in my brain for over ten years. It started as a writing exercise with a market drop, passing important information (which will not actually occur until the second book), and a conversation on the beach about how mushrooms could really mess you up. They're an entirely different kingdom than plants and animals, and many of their reactions are hard to pin down, and sometimes stay in the body for months or years. I put this together with my love of generational starships and came up with the concept.

Naturally, I had to name it "Of Mycelium and Men," even though many of the key players aren't men, and that's not a great way to refer to the human species in the first place. As Terry Pratchett was fond of pointing out, Narrativium is one of the most common elements. It's powerful stuff.

As always, I must thank my wonderful wife Heather first. Especially this year, we've gone through a lot of trials, not to mention starting a small press, and she's been there with me every step of the way.

Second, thanks go to Reading Excuses and especially the READ group. Seri, Robin, Sara, Natalie, Katie, and Kelly: my books wouldn't be the same without you.

Finally, thank you to everyone who backed the Space Wizard Science Fantasy Year 1 Kickstarter! It was an amazing success and it means I can produce quality queer SFF for another year without worrying too much about production costs. Year 2 is already in the works!

ABOUT THE AUTHOR

William C. Tracy writes and publishes queer science fiction and fantasy through his indie press Space Wizard Science Fantasy, which is open to submissions (spacewizardsciencefantasy.com).

His largest work is the Dissolutionverse: a space opera with music-based magic, including ten books and an RPG. He also has a standalone epic fantasy with seasonal fruit-based magic through a LGBTQ+ small press.

William is a North Carolina native and a lifelong fan of science fiction and fantasy. He has a master's in mechanical engineering and has both designed and operated heavy construction machinery. He has also trained in Wado-Ryu karate since 2003 and runs his own dojo in Raleigh NC. He is an avid video and board gamer, a beekeeper, a reader, and of course, a writer.

You can get a free Dissolutionverse novelette by signing up for William's mailing list at http://williamctracy.com

Follow him on Twitter at https://twitter.com/wctracy for writing updates, cat and bee pictures, and thoughts on martial arts.

Please take a moment to review this book at your favorite retailer's website, Goodreads, or simply tell your friends!

Made in the USA
Middletown, DE
19 March 2023

26991186R00170